PASSENGER

PASSENGER

ANDREW SMITH

FEIWEL AND FRIENDS

NEW YORK

A Feiwel and Friends Book
An Imprint of Macmillan

PASSENGER. Copyright © 2012 by Andrew Smith. All rights reserved.
Printed in the United States of America by R. R. Donnelley & Sons Company,
Harrisonburg, Virginia. For information, address Feiwel and Friends,
175 Fifth Avenue, New York, N.Y. 10010.

Library of Congress Cataloging-in-Publication Data Available

ISBN: 978-1-250-00487-1

Feiwel and Friends logo designed by Filomena Tuosto

First Edition: 2012

10 9 8 7 6 5 4 3 2 1

macteenbooks.com

For Jean Feiwel

CONTENTS

part one

THE

ODDS

This is it.

Of course it wasn't over.

Things like this never end.

It has been two and a half months since Freddie Horvath kidnapped some dumb fucking kid who was too drunk to find his way home.

You can't possibly believe things just end, dry up, go away, can you?

Sometimes, when I look at myself, I see the likeness of Wynn, my grandfather, in my face. And I wonder if I'll still be carrying all of this around when I'm his age.

It's not like a sack of garbage you can just drop off at the side of the road and then keep going, pretending you had nothing to do with it in the first place.

Sometimes, it makes me very tired.

———

All this time I thought it wasn't me, it wasn't me.

But it was.

I need to tell you a story.

The garage steams with the smell of cat piss and something dead. The reek hangs in the still press of late-August heat.

Every one of us is sick and scared.

I tell them, "We said we'd do it, and we're going to do it, okay?"

My best friend, Conner, shrugs. "We got no choice."

I would die for Conner Kirk. Sometimes, I think I have died for him dozens of times, over and over again.

Conner looks at the other boys, as if his words are spoken to convince himself more than the rest of us. "Jack and me are leaving for St. Atticus next week. When the four of us split up, you're going to go crazy if you don't have the lens, and we can't just leave it here."

Among all of us, Griffin looks the most scared.

"It's okay, Griff," Ben says. "As long as we're together in this."

I watch a bead of sweat as it arcs up and over Griffin's collarbone, then streaks down his bony chest. And he says, "Well, what are you looking at me for? You were the one who said it was a good idea."

I wonder why I did this to them—Ben and Griffin—and I answer, *They asked me to, they asked me to.*

"The only idea," Conner says.

I squeeze my hand tight. "I don't have nothing better. It's getting late."

We're all soaked, but we're afraid to open the doors. We even put a canvas painter's tarp over the only window. Conner pulls his shirt off and wipes his face and armpits with it.

I can hear him swallow. He closes his eyes and inhales deeply.

"Keep your eyes up," he says. And then he looks at me. "Jack? You know."

He grabs my wrist.

I say, "I know, Con."

"If we get lost or something," he begins, but he knows I don't want him to say any more. Not now.

A ball-peen hammer rests on the table next to the vice. There is a lidless Mason jar with some cloudy paint thinner; the stained handle of a brush tilts against the lip of the inner rim. The things belong to Griffin Goodrich's dad—Ben Miller's stepfather.

No one else is home, just the four of us—standing around that workbench, sweating like junkies inside the boys' unlighted garage.

It is suddenly so loud when Ben cranks the vice open.

One turn.

He lets the knob-ended metal bar drop through its catch hole, and the steely clang makes Griffin twitch like he's been shocked.

Half an inch.

The Marbury lens is in my hand.

I know what I'm doing, don't have to see anything.

When I open my hand, it's like we all gasp for the same shortened mouthful of air—and it's not enough.

The familiar dull purple glow, like an aquarium filled with smoke and creatures swimming just below the surface of our blurry vision; writhing shadows like pendulous scythes that sweep across the stalks of our legs, asking us to fold before their blades, wanting us to go down into that swirling light.

Conner's eyes are locked on mine.

"Don't look," I say, and my voice sounds ridiculous.

Fingers feel the toothy edge of the vicemaw.

Griffin is shaking, his eyes shut tight. I don't know if it's tears or sweat I see on his face.

No. Griffin never cries.

Like Jack.

"Don't look," I say again, more to myself than anyone else.

I tighten the vice, let go of the lens.

The swimming shadows boil below us, urgent, pleading.

Just a peek.

Blindly, I reach for the hammer, line it up with my thumb.

I swing.

The lens cleaves. The upper fragment, freed, spins jaggedly through the air and I see flashes like I'm thumb-flipping through a book of unrelated photographs taken by strange hands at different times and places. I feel the broken piece as it lands with the weight of a dead bird on top of my foot.

Screams. Sounds like a slaughterhouse running at full tilt, a jangling of machinery: agonized, pained cries coming from somewhere, everywhere; and I'm thinking, *It's not me, it's not the kids, it isn't Conner*; and I can't see the garage anymore.

Nothing.

No Conner. Nobody.

I fall backwards through the slithering monochrome shapes that writhe up from the floor. I thrash my arms, try to grab hold of anyone, try to shout the names of my friends—I forget how to make the words leave my mouth.

My hand slides over something slick. It is Griffin's arm and I squeeze a grip on the boy and together we fall and fall through the forever of passing images. Endlessly slow and silent, like we are descending; downward through lukewarm pudding.

And I feel my fingers passing through Griffin's arm, like the boy has turned into steam, and all I can feel is a moment of moisture before my hand is empty.

Then I hit.

And I know only two things.

My eyes are closed.

And I am alone.

In time, I gave up worrying about whether I'd lost my mind. It didn't matter. Because my best friend, Conner Kirk, had been dragged beside me into hell. Ben and Griffin, too.

Now they were gone.

It's time to take things apart.

Monsters make monsters make monsters.

Ten weeks before, a man named Freddie Horvath kidnapped me. He was a monster, and I was something like a little bird that nobody gave a shit about.

I fell out of my nest.

Poor Jack.

Since then, all of the horrors that stacked and stacked, layer after layer—the killing on Nacimiento Road, being pursued by Henry Hewitt when I was lost and sick in London, stumbling and falling into the nightmare of a place called Marbury that made me feel more at home than I'd ever felt at any other time in my regrettable life—it all turned me into a monster, too.

I could not stop myself from having Ben and Griffin fall with us

7

into Marbury. It was what they told me they wanted, and I believed every sound I'd ever heard in Marbury. So after Conner and I returned from England and found them playing basketball in the park, we could not help ourselves.

Nobody could.

The four of us became willingly trapped.

Now we straddle the gap of nowhere, between this world and the not-world called Marbury. And Marbury is what we need more than anything.

I can't explain it; that's just how things are.

Freddie Horvath made me into a monster.

I made monsters of my friends: Conner Kirk, Ben Miller, and Griffin Goodrich.

And before Conner and I could leave Glenbrook, California, for the coming school year in England, the four of us monsters must divide our pathetic kingdom.

Here, in this piss-reeked garage.

one

I was in the garage.

But it wasn't the garage.

I rolled over onto my side and watched the gray light coming through the window, now uncovered, an asterisk of jagged fractures in the lower right pane centered in the quadrant of rusting muntin strips like someone had started a game of tic-tac-toe there with a hammer and then gave up.

X.

It all looked so familiar.

But it wasn't.

I don't know how long I lay there like that. There was the loose jumble of disjointed things I knew: I was in Mr. Goodrich's garage—I was certain of it—and it felt like I was about to puke, but I had to hold it back, think about something else, because it was my friends' house, after all, and I just didn't want to move yet.

But something was wrong.

I became suddenly aware that I had been drooling. Warm spit ran down my cheek and onto the oilstained concrete floor, and something black scuttled toward my feet.

Griffin's cat, I thought.

And where was Griffin?

Where were Conner and Ben?

I pushed myself up to a sitting position, my legs spread out like arrows, clockhands on the floor.

"Hey," I called. "Where'd you guys go?"

My clothes were different. The knees on the dusty jeans I wore had been torn through, and I was filthy. Somehow, I remembered it. The shirt hung open, unbuttoned, striped.

I don't have any striped shirts.

One sleeve was rolled to my elbow; the other hung limply, unraveled over my arm, like something dead. A number had been stitched across the left shoulder, above a spot where the pocket had been torn away.

373

It didn't mean anything to me, but I felt that tickle in my head.

I was supposed to remember something.

And I had work boots on.

I wasn't wearing boots. I never wear things like this.

One of them was untied, half hanging off my foot.

Movement again.

The bugs.

I could hear them eating, chewing, burrowing their way into a pile of stained rags crumpled across the bottom of the wide roll-up garage door. But I knew it wasn't rags.

Who was it?

"Hey. Con?"

I gasped, pushed myself onto my feet and immediately fell backward, dizzy. I slammed my hip against the workbench where we'd clamped the lens down in Mr. Goodrich's vice. My foot kicked the hammer; it spun a half circle and pointed to me.

Spin the hammer.

You really fucked up this time.

My eyes darted from the rags, the bugs, to the vice. I saw the lens, broken, dull, like it had been drained of something, and when I grabbed for it, I cut a deep gash across the palm of my hand and watched dumbly as my blood dropped thick and hot onto the floor, splattering the tops of my boots and the smooth wooden handle on the hammer.

The sting felt good.

Get a grip.

I closed my hand, sticky with my own blood, pushed the broken lens down inside my pocket.

Don't look at it.

No. These were not my clothes.

"Griff?"

I took three slow steps—counted them—toward the heap lying

against the door. It jerked, electric, as the bugs tore into their task beneath the canvas clothing that covered what once was a person.

Cleaning.

Always cleaning away everything dead.

One of the harvesters followed the dots of blood I'd left on the concrete. I heard scraping sounds from its jaws as it tried eating the little bits of me I'd scattered there. I pushed my foot down inside the untied boot and then stomped my heel square across the harvester's shell. It was nearly as big as a cat and it burbled a hiss when it broke in two, spastic legs twitching in slick goo, protesting while cousins came eagerly to pick it apart.

The thing beside the door had been a soldier. His uniform looked the same as those we'd once found on a train, and I couldn't remember when that had ever happened. Trying to figure out where that image belonged in Jack's head was impossible.

The soldier had been dead for some time, too. The bugs kept grinding away at the side of his skull, and I saw a jagged piece of what looked like a collarbone being pulled under a lawnmower, five feet away.

I couldn't see the name on his shirt. It was too stained.

I looked back at the door that led into the house—to the kitchen. I had been here plenty of times, took stock of the things in the garage that I knew would always be there. And I looked out the broken window again, could see the ashen sky.

I was in the garage.

And the garage was in Glenbrook, at Ben and Griffin's house.

But this was Marbury.

———

11

I thought if I pressed my palms hard enough into my eyes, maybe it would all go away. But the sound of the bugs kept me there, the sting in my hand, and I realized I had smeared my face with my own blood.

A door opened.

The door to the house.

I jerked.

Ben Miller stood in the dark of the hallway holding a rusted spike of rebar and pointing it out past the threshold, aiming the spear at the center of my chest.

"Ben?"

Ben twitched like the sound of his name punched him square in the face.

He didn't answer. He looked different: thinner maybe. His eyes were sunken and dark and his hair hung down on one side to the edge of his narrowed mouth. It was Ben, but it wasn't Ben.

And he was terrified. Of me.

"Ben Miller?"

I didn't move.

"We don't have any food, kid. I don't know what the fuck you want here. Go back to where you came from, Odd."

I felt dizzy again; drunk. Ben Miller was standing in the doorway, shaking, right in front of me. And I could see he had no idea who I was.

"Don't you know who I am?" I held out my hands. I looked down at myself, at the bloodstained gash across my right palm. I must have looked like a lunatic to him, blood smeared across the side of my face.

I argued like a lawyer in court, "You know me, don't you?" I needed to hear my voice. I didn't want to think it could be possible that I was here, that this was Glenbrook, that we were back in Marbury. But things were different.

Griffin hid behind Ben; I could see his eyes glint when they peeked out around the older boy's tensed arm. He whispered something. Griffin's hair reached his shoulders. He was shirtless, like always, if always had anything to do with where we were. And both of the boys were covered in smears of dirt.

Somehow, I knew we'd all gone back.

But it wasn't the same.

I knew it then, standing in that garage while harvesters picked away at the remains of a dead man; and while Ben Miller, this scared kid who didn't know who I was, held me back with a weapon I was sure he wouldn't hesitate to use; while Griffin stood in the dark, studying me, defiant and snot nosed, unwavering in his determination to keep me away from their home.

Griffin pulled Ben's shoulder and whispered to him again. Then he pointed at me, and Ben said, "I know. I saw it, too."

"Griffin Goodrich," I said. "Your brother. Well, your half brother's name is Ben Miller. Don't you know who I am?"

This time, I heard what Griffin said to his brother: "How does that prisoner know our names?"

Odd. Prisoner. It didn't make any sense.

"We know who you are," Ben said. "But we never seen you before in our life."

I couldn't tell what he meant. His face was stiff, determined, and when I took a step toward the doorway, Ben tipped his spear up like he was warning me back.

"Look," I said. "Are you going to let me in, or what?"

"You can leave the same way you came," Griffin said.

I don't know how I got here.

I put my hands down, looked back at the heap of rags by the main garage door.

"There's a dead soldier back there," I said.

Ben let the tip of his spear clink down on the concrete floor between his feet.

A warning.

"He's there 'cause that's the spot where I killed him two days ago."

Two days. What was two days ago?

"He didn't have any gun or nothing, if that's what you're looking for," Griffin said.

"And we don't have any food," Ben added. He scraped an arc across the floor with the point of his spear, and I could see how it was stained with what looked like dried blood.

Griffin pulled Ben's shoulder down toward his face again. "It's going to rain pretty soon."

"That's not our problem, Griff."

I looked down at the hammer. I looked at Ben.

Come on, Ben. You have to remember me.

He kept his eyes pinned on me, too.

"That door. There. You can go now and we won't tell anyone we saw you. You take one more step toward my house and I'll have to kill you."

Ben Miller wasn't joking.

I glanced at Griffin, then at Ben. The tip of the spear angled toward the side door. Outside was Forest Trail Lane, but there were never any forests in Glenbrook.

And this wasn't Glenbrook.

When I pulled the door open and looked out, I could feel Ben's eyes on me, the same way you'd watch a dangerous animal until it decided to change direction.

I said, "Try to remember me, Griffin. Ben. I'm your friend."

Then I went outside.

Everything is scarier, more brilliant and unsteady, when you're alone. After that door swung shut behind me, and I could hear Ben and Griffin on the other side, pushing things around, building a barrier between me and them, I felt like I was walking out into my death.

I looked back along the boys' house, where I remembered a flagstone trail led through a wrought-iron arbor to a backyard pool. It was the same house, but sections of the roof were missing. The curved red pottery tiles had spilled down in scattered shards and exposed the tarred and buckling plywood and flapping strips of black felt.

There was wind.

Every one of the windows had been broken, and in places, the concrete stucco of the house's siding had been pounded in as though pummeled by stones or shrapnel. There was no arbor, no flagstones, and when I walked around the corner I saw that the pool had been drained, now filled with broken debris: a realtor's FOR SALE sign; part of a wire-mesh picnic bench like the ones they had in Steckel Park; a life-sized fiberglass horse—the kind that you'd see on top of a feed store—but this one was headless; and an overturned station wagon that was missing three of its wheels.

And there was no fence, no sidewalks, no street I could see.

Forest Trail Lane.

I could tell where the street was supposed to be. A tilted fire hydrant, the skeletons of things marked a familiar path that was now covered beneath the gray salty ash that was everywhere in Marbury. I thought about my truck, how we'd all squeezed into the cab, sand sticking to our skin, when the four of us drove back to the boys' house from the beach.

Before I broke the lens.

I couldn't help myself, and I immediately felt stupid for doing it. I spun around and yelled, "Conner!"

Nothing.

"Conner!"

Wind.

Ash.

I whispered, hoping for anything that might connect here to anywhere I knew, "Seth?"

Seth had always been there before. He was the ghost, a part of me, who linked me between the gaps, Marbury, home, wherever this place was or was not.

But it was empty. Seth wasn't here, either.

I sat down in front of the house. I knew Ben and Griffin were watching through one of the cracks in their house, ready to fight, to defend themselves.

Against me.

The neighbors' homes were there—some of them. Most had been broken down to the foundations. The others were empty—I could tell—and not just because I could see right through them. There's a silent message you get from an abandoned house that lets you know exactly how things are.

A refrigerator lay on its side in the middle of what would have been the street. Its door had fallen open. There was a man's head inside. I felt the need to go there, make sure it wasn't someone I knew—someone else Jack dragged along with him into this pit.

They had their own aesthetic sensibilities, I thought. The

harvesters, the Hunters. They didn't eat everything. They didn't wipe everything clean. They decorated.

I didn't recognize the face. The eyes were squinted shut like they had been stung with vinegar, and the man had puffy cheeks that stretched his mouth into a narrow smile and showed a row of bloodied teeth that all looked ridiculously small.

Welcome back.

It's the same old Marbury.

Jack's hometown.

I started walking.

And I knew where I would go: Conner's house was closer, and then to see if I could find Wynn and Stella's.

All the way down Forest Trail Lane it was the same. Houses were burned or abandoned, things were strewn everywhere in chaotic order, and nothing moved except the small things that vibrated on the wind.

My foot struck against something in the ash. I nearly fell, but caught myself with my hand. The salt burned in my cut. It was bad. It should have stitches. I thought about how Griffin had never been afraid to do things like that—stitch us up when we got cut.

Whenever that was.

It was a book. I brushed it off and lifted it from the dust. A dictionary.

The cover warped like a dried orange rind; the pages inside pasted together as though the book had been dragged up from the bottom of a sea.

There was a flash of light and something exploded overhead, louder than any sound I'd ever heard.

I jerked, curled myself down against the ground.

I need to get out of here.

Out of breath, I watched the sky.

It came again. Lightning. But it was bigger, thicker than any lightning I'd ever seen, and the boom of the thunderclap felt like hammers pounding my brain.

Another hammer, I thought. *Maybe it will break me in half, too.*

And I'd never seen lightning in Marbury before. Not ever.

The burning light was so thick, so bright, it looked almost crystallized, as though, if I had the right timing, I could swing that hammer and shatter razor-sharp icicles of pure energy from the bolts. And every time they flashed, I felt the electric charge stiffen and prickle the hair on the back of my neck.

At the end of Forest Trail Lane, the old highway ran north and south. It was the main road through Glenbrook before they'd constructed the 101.

This isn't Glenbrook.

On the corner stood the lower half of a two-story. The only thing I could see on the exposed upper floor was a toilet and an overturned bathtub. It still had a ring of dirt around the bottom.

"Prime location for Glenbrook real estate," I said.

My voice sounded strange, tighter. But I knew I'd need to get under something until the lightning stopped, and the bottom level of the shattered house was the closest thing that looked capable of hiding me, so I carried the dictionary under one arm and ran for the doorway.

Another flash of lightning exploded. It hit the street back where I'd come from, sending up a glowing mushroom cloud of ash that seemed to set the air around it on fire.

This was like no lightning I'd ever seen anywhere.

Where the curb would be, I found a rusted yellow Tonka dump

truck and one boy's tennis shoe with a picture of a ninja on the side. The ninja had red eyes. The boy who wore that shoe at one time couldn't have been more than five.

Another flash.

I ran.

When I moved, the explosion of thunder was so loud it felt like it lifted me, pushed me toward the broken door at the front of the house. And, dumbly, I stood there for just a moment and nearly raised my hand to knock.

The door had a slot window in the center of it, but the swirled yellow glass had long since been broken, making a lamprey's mouth of needle teeth around the edges of the frame. I saw where the knob, the hardware, was vacant, leaving just a hole through the core. The door pushed easily inward and sucked a breath of air over me as if the house were tasting my scent.

I hesitated.

Another flash spit my shadow across the floor, and before the next blast of thunder came I scrambled inside, pressing the door shut with the heel of my boot.

Then the rain came. It smelled like burning aluminum and fell so thick and heavy that I couldn't even hear the cusswords I yelled.

"Is there anybody in here?"

Flash.

A snapshot image of the house's interior burned into my eyes.

To my left, a staircase rose into the darkness of the ceiling. Somebody had covered the opening to the upper floor, which was now the roof, with corrugated tin that roared and vibrated under the constant downpour. Water trickled in from the sides, spattering down on the house's rotten carpeting. I held my hand under the stream; washed my face. It made me smell like a foundry. There had to be something wrong with that water.

Thinking it almost made me laugh. What could possibly be wrong with anything here in Marbury?

The entryway at the foot of the stairs opened onto what was once a living room and kitchen. I put the dictionary down on a jagged pier of bar top that extended out from one wall. There was something about the book, I thought, that was important.

Something.

Even though the windows had been knocked out long ago, there was hardly enough light coming in for me to clearly see what was around me.

I called out, "Is anybody in here?"

Nothing.

Rain.

"Anyone? I'm alone. I'm lost."

Flash.

It was like a bomb going off.

One of the walls appeared to buckle inward then snap back, like the house was rubber. My eyes scanned across the floor. Junk was everywhere. Pieces of soggy drywall, a hair dryer with its cord tied into a noose, the gutted frame of a television, clothing, the door from a shower stall. I saw a belt, and thought about picking it up, but there was an entire human pelvis, picked perfectly clean, yellow-white, lying among other bones beneath it.

People had been here recently, too. I could smell them. The place reeked like an underground pisser in summertime, and the stink made me want to pee, too, so I did it, right there against the wall under the staircase.

Fuck this place.

Flash.

I watched the conical stain of my piss slick downward over the wall. It somehow made me feel good, like I was real, alive.

Another explosion.

I looked at my feet, and that's when I found the knife. Perfect and beautiful, like it had just been purchased at a sporting goods store, and I could almost smell the freshness of its leather sheath. Someone had taken care of it. Someone who didn't need it anymore. I turned it over in my hands, felt the sharpness of its edge, then unbuckled my belt and threaded the sheath onto my side.

Something crashed into the wall in the kitchen. It sounded like the door on a cupboard. It slammed three more times before I rounded a brick hearth where water splashed down from the shattered chimney somewhere above me on the naked second floor.

A man stood there, kicking his foot against the wood paneling beneath the place where a sink should have been. He was completely naked, deathly pale, but covered with brilliant tattoos all the way from his belly down to the soles of his bony feet; and nothing at all above his waist, just white, hairless skin. He looked like a centaur or something.

He turned and glared at me, his jaw working up and down like he was chewing something, trying to get words out, and my hand fell down onto the handle of the knife before I realized it was only a ghost.

Then he vanished.

"Wait! Wait! Please, let me talk to you."

He was gone.

"Come back!"

I went over to the place where he'd been standing and kicked the wall as hard as I could. I felt the wood cracking beneath my foot,

21

and when I looked down inside the empty black crib where the sink had been, I saw him again—the man—curled on his side, rotting in death.

Rain came straight down from the vacant square where a window had looked out—on what?—from over the sink, and it made his skin slick, snakes and fish, twisted cables of wire and swords, saints and skeletons that vibrated like cartoons inked on his rotting hide. Something black crawled up inside his nostril. I turned away and threw up beside a twisted heap of metal window blinds that was left crumpled on the kitchen floor.

Flash.

The lightning came less frequently, but the rain was constant, howling against the tin sheeting and bare floor above me. I kicked the metal blinds, turning them over. There were maybe a dozen harvesters that scattered out from underneath the heap.

And I saw the body of a little boy there, too.

He had only one shoe on. Nothing else.

I covered him again.

"Fuck!" I staggered out of the kitchen, around the fireplace, the smell of aluminum; the smell of aluminum and vomit.

I shut my eyes, and leaned my folded arms on the broken piece of countertop where I'd left the dictionary.

Flash.

I have got to get the fuck out of here.

Get a grip, Jack. You're not going anywhere.

Think.

I had to think.

The dictionary.

I peeled through the pages. Some of them tore. Some would not separate at all.

The rain kept pounding.

Pounding relentlessly against the anvil of this wrecked house.

The hammer.

The water came splattering down on the stairway. The stench was nauseating.

I couldn't hear the bugs. That was good.

I looked up *California*.

There was no such word in the dictionary.

There were no entries for *Washington, America,* or *England*.

Okay, asshole. Maybe this dictionary doesn't list the names of places.

So I looked up *earth*. Earth had to be in there, right? It wasn't just a name.

And it wasn't in the book, either.

Bet you don't have the balls to look up Marbury, *do you Jack?*

I looked up *Marbury*.

I found it.

Of course I found it.

Fuck you, Jack.

two

Flash.

So I threw the book against the wall, and it splattered like a crushed wasp and fell, fluttering dying paper wings onto the heap of the other dead things cluttered on the floor.

23

And when it slammed against the wall, I noticed the writing there.

At the top, near the ceiling:

373

The number had been written four times at different places on the wall.

373

Maybe the person writing it wanted to be sure someone would see it.

Maybe he knew I was coming.

373

Painted with two fingers; I could see how they pressed together, tracking the strokes of the numbers, smearing the curves and lines—a first and middle finger—dip and stroke, dip and stroke, with something dark, some foul concoction, because Marbury wouldn't easily give up anything pure.

373

Outside, the rain raged.

I moved closer.

My shirt still hung open, unbuttoned. I flattened the left side with my palm and looked down at the number stitched there.

373

Maybe everything had the same number here.

Fuck that.

Inmate.

I tore the shirt off. After I knotted it into a ball, I lifted the broken shower door with the toe of one boot and put the shirt on the floor beneath it. Somehow, water had begun pooling in the carpeting there, and I saw something that looked like a long black slug wriggling through the fibers. I could feel the sides of my mouth turning down in disgust and I pressed the door flat beneath my foot.

Now I was nobody.

Welcome back, Jack.

The lightning moved off into the distance but the rain never slackened at all. The sky shifted to the boiled paleness of the Marbury dusk. When I moved closer to the wall, I could make out what had been left as a message.

And there, just below the highest scrawl of the number—my number—my eyes fell upon a drawing of circles inside other circles.

At the midpoint of them all, the word **HOME**.

The center of the universe.

An arrow from the exact middle. It crossed the shape's perimeter, pierced the concentric interior of a second, larger circle.

In this one, **MARBURY**.

I am going to build something big for you.

From there, an arrow shoots into a third.

Trapped inside that circle are the words:

**I DON'T KNOW THE NAME OF THIS ONE.
I SAW THE PREACHER THERE.**

**IT'S ALL MARBURY, BUT IT'S ALL DIFFERENT.
THIS WAS THE HARDEST TO GET OUT OF.**

And then, the smears of letters that said:

YOU AND SETH HAVE THE KEYS.

The hardest to get out of.
A third arrow, another world.
The circle encloses the first three.
The final circle, an outer ring that surrounds them all.
I recognize the hand. Of course I recognize the hand.

**I DON'T KNOW HOW MANY MORE THERE ARE. IT
IS PROBABLY UNCOUNTABLE.**

And near the edge of the wall, just at the level of my own heart, floating out there, somewhere—who knows—in Jack's universe, in deliberate and dark lines, I trace my own fingers around the strokes that had been left behind.

Maybe it's blood, I thought, the tip of my finger following around a precise drawing of a hammer.

I know.
It is in Conner's hand.

Henry Hewitt had come to Marbury before I did. It was Henry who'd pawned the glasses off on me when I was alone in London. I couldn't count the number of times I considered getting even with Henry for trapping me, and now I'd done the same thing to my best friends.

It was clear we had all somehow fallen apart, fallen together.

Conner had gotten there before me.

Faintly, somehow, I began to remember. An argument about something, about the next steps. Conner yelling at me about how I fucked it up, saying, *Henry said you would bring things here. He didn't mean the lens. We weren't supposed to bring the lens here. We fucked up, Jack. We fucked up.* And first Conner, then Ben and Griffin, disappearing in the garage; falling, all of us.

That's why he drew that mark.

Conner got here first.

And one second might be a month through the Marbury lens.

Maybe forever.

I knew that.

We all did.

At the far edge of the wall, opposite Conner's drawing of my universe—our universe—I saw more writing:

MIND THE GAP.

FENT IS LOOKING FOR YOU.

THE BUGS ARE EVERYWHERE.

STAY OUT OF THE RAINWATER.

And, finally:

JACK—I WILL FIND YOU AGAIN I PROMISE.

WE WILL PUT THINGS BACK.

CONNER KIRK

I couldn't stay there. There were dead people in the room. And the rain poured down endlessly.

There was an inch of standing water on the floor. I kept wondering about the warning to stay out of the rain, and who—or what—Fent was.

A hallway led off to the right of the entryway, but it was so dark I couldn't see to the end of it. I stayed out of it as long as I could, but it was dry, so I eventually gave up being scared of what I couldn't see there.

At the end of the hall, there were two doors. One of them opened onto a small bathroom. The toilet was missing; there was a black hole in the tile floor where it had been. A slot window above the bathtub let in a steady sheet of rain, but it ran down the wall and into the drain. Here was where the shower door came from.

The other door led to a bedroom. It was dry, but very dark. The window had been boarded over with the broken slate top from a pool table, and the floor was covered with jumbles of dusty cloth: towels, sheets, clothing, drapes, blankets. I could see where people had been sleeping. There was a wide closet set back into one of the walls, but the doors were missing. When I got closer to it, I could tell it was the spot someone had used as a toilet.

There was nothing else I could do.

I shut myself into the room.

I pulled the knife I'd found out of its sheath and held on to it.

I took off my boots and socks and sat down on the matting to wait out the storm.

When I stretched out, I realized I'd laid my head down on a pair of green surgical scrub pants. Dotted with blood on one of the legs.

28

They were mine, from somewhere else.

Fuck you, Jack.

Henry said you would bring things here. He didn't mean the lens. We weren't supposed to bring the lens here.

And in the dark, I took the injured lens from my pocket and held it between my fingers.

Nothing.

Only rain.

I even pressed the lens up to my eyes; one, then the other, pleading with it.

The words from the dictionary swirled, a dizzying cloud in my head.

Marbury: (noun) Third planet in order from the sun. No natural satellites. This planet, as the only in the Solar System which is inhabited by humans.

Fuck this place.

Just before morning, the Hunters came.

I couldn't sleep. I lay on my side, curled on top of the blankets, so hungry and thirsty it felt as if I were dissolving, caving in on myself. The rain did not slacken at all; it became this constant white noise, like flying on an airplane that was never going to land.

I got up and walked the hallway, irrationally hoping that maybe it wouldn't be raining anymore once I got back to the front door. And I thought, *It's only rain; it's not like you haven't been in rain before; you need to get the fuck out of here, Jack.*

Everything smelled like warm metal. The air was so thick it felt like I was breathing in fibrous stuffing from torn seat cushions, just the way I'd remembered that unsatisfying Marbury air.

It's all Marbury, but it's all different.

I decided I was going to leave. I had to find some food, something better than this place, and I believed Conner was nearby, and that when we found each other, we'd be able to somehow fix things and put everything back where it belonged. Being around Conner always seemed to make things somehow *right*. I knew we'd messed things up here in Marbury. Maybe back home, too.

Maybe everywhere.

In the blank, pale light before the dawn, I saw them in front of the house. I looked out through that jagged slot window on the door, and there were two of them, wading in knee-deep black water. It was like a sea, and what was left standing of the other houses looked like moored ships, crewless and dead.

I saw the marks first—fiery sashes. On one of them, it stretched across his waist and curled around his thigh. The second Hunter was marked by only a small upturned arc below his left collarbone, a red smile. I ducked back, peering through the slot with one eye, watching them as they strained their way through the water. They stopped every few steps, smelling, looking around.

Maybe they knew I was here.

The bigger of the two, the one with the mark that cut downward to his thigh, carried a steel jack handle. At one end, in the usual style, was a sharpened human femur that had been lashed, somehow, to the bar. And they were both old, mature, covered in spikes and purple splotches. The smaller one had horns growing out of his nipples, curving upward, and he kept licking at them, nipping, showing his black teeth.

He carried what looked like the head of a three-tined garden cultivator, and was completely naked. Maybe the scalp loincloth fashion I'd seen previously in Marbury hadn't caught on here. Or maybe he was hunting for his first kill. The larger one had a pair of dried and purple human hands, fingers twisted together, overlapped and woven, cupped around his balls, braided onto a belt made from a Christmas tree light cord that had been strung on either side of his crotch through the dangling headless torsos of Barbie dolls.

It was Marbury, but it was different, too.

It was Marbury magnified, intensified.

We didn't mean for this to happen.

The Hunters sniffed the air, widening their nostrils. They moved steadily through the dark sea that covered this new world.

But the sheets of rain fell so constantly I was certain they couldn't possibly see me, as I watched them through the jagged mouth of the door's shattered window. And still, they kept coming toward the house, sloshing, swinging their heads from side to side, huffing and hissing to sniff for meat.

And I was standing there, barefoot.

I needed to get my shoes on.

I took a deep breath, slipped away from my doorpost back down the hallway toward the bedroom.

And I left a wet trail of blood with each footstep. I saw how it tracked my path behind me, so I opened the door onto the bathroom to let more light into the hallway.

Something was wrong with me.

One of those black slugs I'd seen had attached itself to the top of my foot. Sickened, I watched as it pulsed like an external heart, sucking my blood. Slender and slick with oily skin, uncoiled, it may have been two feet long. Then it detached and began worming its way higher, pulsing its head up the bend in my ankle.

I'd seen leeches before, but this was something else. It moved fast. It made a mess of me.

I slipped the edge of my knife beneath it and pried it away.

It made a squeak, like a crushed bird, and I flicked the thing onto the floor and sliced it in half. It popped like an overripe blueberry, spraying blood—my blood—exploding outward in an awful red chrysanthemum. The thing wriggled and fought before finally relaxing in death.

If I'd had anything at all inside me, I would have vomited. My stomach twisted and crawled upward toward my throat. I pulled my pant legs up and looked for more of the things.

Maybe I got lucky. Maybe not.

I'd have to watch that rainwater, I thought.

I went inside the bedroom, sat down, and started to put my shoes on. Before I did, I pulled the legs of my jeans up past my knees again, just to make sure that was the only one of those leech things I had to deal with.

The safest place to wait, I reasoned, would be in the hallway. I didn't think the Hunters could get inside the house behind me, and in the other rooms I might be visible from the outside through any one of the broken-out windows.

I squeezed the handle of the knife so tightly my hand began bleeding again. I waited in the middle of the hallway, leaning against one wall to make myself less visible. I felt like I was going to faint from the adrenaline rush, my heart pounding as loud as the rain.

Maybe this would be it, I thought.

Maybe Jack's universe would just end here in this broken-down house.

Maybe dying would be just like another trip through a lens, anyway.

Fuck this place.

Of course they knew where I was.

I saw the widening gray swath of light as the front door pushed carefully open. The rain got louder. Then there was nothing, but I could visualize what they were doing: sniffing, smelling me, listening, waiting.

When a shadow darkened the entryway, I leapt out from my hiding spot in the hall, hoping to surprise whichever one came through the door first. It was the big one. And when he caught his first glimpse of me coming from the darkness of the hall, he cocked the pickax back in both hands like he was getting ready to swing a baseball bat. But before he could hit me, I buried the knife up to my fist, straight into his armpit.

He wailed, swung.

I saw a flash of movement behind him, the other one, hesitating, pushing his way into the house.

The weapon arced over my head. It buried its point up to the jack handle in the damp wallboard of the hallway. The knife slipped in my grip as I tried to pull it free, twisting and turning, the gristle and bone tearing at its edge. There was so much blood, but I managed to keep hold on the knife as the big Hunter fell back, clawing at his side, releasing his weapon. I pushed him on top of his partner, and felt him twitch and gurgle when he fell onto the gig in the other one's clawed hand. The big Hunter collapsed between us, dying, wheezing, splashing in the rainwater and gore.

The smaller one ran out of the doorway.

I went after him.

As soon as I stepped past the open door, I was ankle deep in water. My mind flashed on the image of those black leeches, but I forced myself to keep my eyes up.

The Hunter was nowhere in sight.

I slogged around to the corner of the house, waited, breathed, before cautiously stepping around the side.

This had to be a trick or something, I thought. There was no way he could move that fast.

And just when I turned back toward the door, he was on me, leaping down from the edge of the upper floor. Before I could manage to move, I was completely underwater.

I thought I would drown. I was sure of it, and it struck me how I didn't care. But I watched in a sick kind of fascination, interested in how I could see the wavy image of the Hunter pinning me down above the surface.

Next thing I knew, everything was red, and his grip slackened.

For a second I almost believed I had gone through the lens— ended up somewhere else again. I half expected to hear the ghost, Seth, making his calling taps to me. But then I realized I was still underwater and clutching my knife. I pushed myself up, gagging and spitting, and got to my feet.

The thing that had pinned me down was choking, coughing blood from his nostrils, madly pulling at a slender steel spike that speared cleanly through his neck. But there was a barbed point on the spear's tip, and the more the Hunter tried pulling the projectile out of his throat, the worse his injury became. And I could see the frantic spray of blood with each beat of his heart, until he finally gave up and sat down and put his face down into the black lake I was standing in.

I looked up into the eyes of a freckle-faced redhead boy who was standing in the middle of a green fiberglass canoe, holding on to something that looked like an oversized red plastic squirt gun. He was smiling, shaking his head at me, cursing, "Good God damn, you're all kinds of stupid, Odd. You better get the hell out of the water before one of them suckers gets up inside your rig."

That was the first time I ever saw the kid.

three

I looked at the kid for a second, holding my knife point angled toward him while the rain came in relentless blurring waves between us. And he stood there with that relaxed expression on his face, one foot up on the gunwale of his stupid boat, just rocking, watching to see what I'd do.

I put the knife away. Then I pulled the dead one out through the doorway by his feet.

"Shit on a sidewalk," the kid said. "Did you kill that one all by yourself?"

I went inside.

I wanted to hit something.

I think I wanted to hit that kid.

"Fuck!"

I went down the hallway and threw myself onto the floor when I got inside the room, crazily tearing at my bootlaces and socks. Watery blood ran through the little hairs on my shin. One of the black things was snaking its way up my pant leg, so I grabbed the tail, but it slimed free of my grasp and kept going. I squeezed both hands around my knee, making a kind of tourniquet to block its path, and I tried pushing it back down. But the thing wouldn't move.

That's when the kid came in, holding the dripping spear in one hand while slinging his ridiculous red pistol over one shoulder. He seemed to be amused by what was going on, all gangly and gaunt, twisted up in a sodden tornado of clothes that were far too big for him.

"You are not going to win that one, Odd." The kid put his spear down against the wall. "If I was you, I'd get out of them pants quick as shit. There's probably one up the other leg, anyhow. Or two."

I really wanted to hit him.

"Fuck!"

I clawed at my belt. My hand throbbed with pain. The pants were glued to me. I kicked and flailed, pale and wet, until I finally got all my clothes flung down. And the goddamned kid was right. One of the things was all the way up inside my thigh, right next to my balls. I pried the creatures off with my knife blade and cussed a dozen times while I hacked them to pieces on the floor.

"They're pretty much dead, I'd guess, Odd," the kid smirked.

"Fuck that. Stop calling me that."

I looked like that tattooed dead guy in the sink, smeared and streaked all over from my crotch down with rainwater and blood. I grabbed a blanket from the floor and wiped myself clean, glaring at the kid the whole time I was doing it.

I picked up my pants, turned away from the kid. I shook my jeans as hard as I could and turned them inside out twice, then shook them again for good measure before slipping myself back into them, buttoning up. And I knew that kid was watching me the whole time, entertained. That made me even madder.

I could feel the heat and redness in my face like I was cooking from the inside.

"Fuck this place," I said.

Then I sat down and put my head between my knees.

"You killed the shit out of that big one, Odd. You must be one hell of a fighter for being so scrawny."

And I wanted to tell him to fuck off, that he was a good thirty pounds lighter than I was, even counting all the wet shit he was wearing, but I decided not to talk for a while.

Try to relax, Jack.

"What were you doing out in the water like that, anyway? Going for a swim? How dumb can you be, anyhow?"

I kept my head down. I wanted to punch myself, now, for thinking that all I wanted was to go home.

Awww . . . poor Little Jack wants to go home.

"But that other one never saw this shit coming at all. He probably pissed on you when that spear hit him in the throat. Ha-ha! I bet he did, too! Never seen shit like that. You ever seen shit like that, Odd? I damn near missed him altogether. That would have been a bad ending for you, Odd. A bad, wet ending. With suckers in it. In you! Ha-ha! I don't think he'd have given me the chance to try again. You ever seen shit like this?"

The redhead proudly waved his red gun around in front of me, but I didn't want to look at him. I realized I had the dead Hunter's blood in my hair, inside my clothes.

"It's a speargun, is what it is. Yep. When the Rangers came around taking all the guns from everyone at the beginning, I knew where my daddy had this one hid away. If Fent's crew caught me with it, well, shit, I don't need to tell you what they do to Odds with guns, do I? I bet I don't. I lay that you seen it for yourself, what Fent does, ain't that so, Odd?"

Fent is looking for you.

"Where's the old man, anyway? You seen him? You know that old man with tattoos on his nuts and everything? Damn, I told him, I bet getting your rig inked hurts worse than dying. You seen that old man, Odd?"

"He's in the kitchen."

That's all I said to him. I was relieved when he left, could hear him moving down the hallway, slogging over the junk in the living room. I kept my eyes on my feet. They were so pale, and I felt like I was never going to dry out.

The kid came back a minute later.

"You didn't kill him, did you? No. I know you wouldn't. I could tell just by looking at an Odd like you that you wouldn't kill that old man. You can just tell those things about people sometimes, don't you think?"

"There's a little boy in there. Dead, too."

"Dead? Shit, pretty soon there's going to be none of us Odds left. Rangers, too. Even if they have guns, they can't stop this shit. Every time you turn around, there's fewer and fewer of them. Us, too. I think Fent's and a few other squads is the last of the Rangers, but I don't know. I never been anywhere else, just heard about all the other elses. That's why it's better to just be nobody. Like us. We're the smart ones. That's why that Hunter never seen shit like that speargun of mine. Well, I guess he did one time. And that was enough. Ha-ha!"

I really wanted the kid to shut up. I shook my socks, squeezed them out, and started slipping them onto my feet, trying to ignore him. I could feel him coming closer to me.

"How old are you, anyway, Odd? What's your name?"

"You talk too much, kid."

"My name's Quinn Cahill and I'm fifteen years old, and I've lived right here for my entire life."

The kid wiped his palm off on his pants and stuck it out to me.

"I don't care about any of that, kid. I'm in the wrong place and I just keep fucking things up. I need to get out of here."

I shook out my boots, felt all the way down to the toes with cautious fingers, and began tying them up again. The kid dropped his hand, but I still didn't want to look at his face.

"Don't you have anyone else looking out for things with you?"

I said, "Don't you?"

"You ain't got a shirt, then? What happened to it? I bet I got a shirt at my place you could have."

"Don't worry about it."

I stood up, wavered a little bit. I wondered how much blood those things took out of me.

"Are you hungry? I bet you haven't eaten in a bit. Looks like it, anyway. I got some food, Odd. Anyhow, I suspect you had a shirt at some time, especially if you're the one that Fent's been hunting for these past seven days now."

"I don't know what you're talking about."

Seven days.

"Maybe you don't."

So I looked at Quinn Cahill.

I knew he was lying about being fifteen. He looked like a little kid, but there was still something in his eyes that showed me this boy was not at all uncomfortable with killing things, even if it was Hunters. And I also couldn't help but think he was playing me for something, and he knew exactly what he was doing.

39

"Hungry, Odd?"

I didn't answer him.

"Listen," Quinn said. "Hear that? It stopped."

I hadn't noticed how quiet it was. Maybe my breathing had become louder than the rain.

"I need to get the boat back before the water goes away. I got to leave, Odd. You coming?"

I didn't want to go with the kid.

But there was nothing else I could do, and I guess he saw the resignation on my face.

"Well, come on, Odd. You can help me get my boat back and then I'll fix you up with some food and maybe a nice shirt you can keep. You don't mind, do you? You ain't got any other plans, do you? Ha-ha-ha! Come on, Odd."

And Quinn Cahill stood to the side of the doorway, sweeping his arm like he was saying "after you," and he even patted my shoulder as I walked past him.

"We're going to be friends, Odd. We're going to be real good friends."

"What the fuck were those things?"

It seemed like my voice actually startled the kid who nothing else seemed to bother.

"What things?"

"Those fucking black worm things."

"What? Did you fall out of the sky or something?"

I didn't answer.

"Suckers, Odd. Suckers. They carry the bug, too."

"Oh. The bug."

Quinn Cahill looked at me like I was stupid or something. He pointed at his eyes. "Black eye. White eye. The bug. That's the only way of getting it if you're immune like us Odds. But it don't matter, anyway. They crawl up inside your rig and you're a goner in a week, anyhow. You grow spikes. You run around naked and start eating folks. That's what the suckers do to Odds like us. Nice."

I sat there in the canoe while the redheaded kid pushed us across this borderless black lake using what looked like a bridge cue for playing pool. And I felt myself clenching my knees together.

"Ha-ha! That one on you almost hit pay dirt, didn't it, Odd? Ha-ha-ha!"

And he held up two fingers, showing a gap of about an inch and a half, to signify how close that thing was to my "rig."

Quinn Cahill was unbearably annoying.

"Stop calling me that."

"Well, if you're not going to tell me your name, what else am I going to do? I think I'll just call you Billy."

"Don't."

"Why?"

"It's not my name."

"Well, it suits you. Kind of. Like Billy the Kid. Except I don't think you're a murderer, even if Fent's after you to settle it up for that one Ranger."

"Nobody's after me."

Quinn scooped his pool cue up from the muck on the bottom and held it out for me. "Here. You push for a while, Billy."

"I don't know where we're going."

Quinn slapped his thigh. It made me jump. "Ha-ha-ha! Neither do I. I was just making all that shit up about having food and a shirt for you, Billy!"

He was fucking with me.

I wanted to punch him again. I looked him in the eye. *Thirteen, maybe*, I thought. Quinn Cahill was probably only thirteen years old. Pale, white, orange-headed, and freckled, with white baby peach fuzz on his lip and cheeks, and eyes that I just could not figure out. And he was really entertaining himself with me, too.

I put out my hand to him.

"Jack," I said. "My name's Jack Whitmore. I'm sixteen. And I'm not lying."

Then Quinn smiled like it was Christmas morning, spit in his palm, and grabbed my hand, saying, "My brother. My brother Jack the knife boy! See? That wasn't hard, now, was it, Jack? Oh yeah. We're going to be real good friends, my man. Now let's go get you that food and a nice new shirt to put on. Well . . . kind of new. Ha-ha!"

And Quinn bent back to his task of pushing his boat home.

Canoes are fucking heavy.

The water disappeared—just vanished—in less than an hour, leaving a pasty white salt, ash, and me and Quinn at opposite ends of his fucking canoe. In the constant desiccated heat of Marbury, our clothes had completely dried even before the water was gone. Quinn led us in the direction of the Highlands, an area that would have been west of the freeway in Glenbrook.

But it wasn't Glenbrook.

It's funny how naked everything looked. There wasn't a single tree standing anywhere. It was like pictures I'd seen of the dusty gray erasures of places and things randomly dissolved in a nuclear explosion.

There would be mountains, the rolling foothills in between here and the ocean. But in Marbury, everything in the distance vanished in a colorless steaming fog like we were constantly at the end of the world.

Quinn had pushed us down the entire length of the business district, right past Steckel Park—and I only recognized it because three of the light stanchions over the Little League field were still there, bent like vandalized car antennas. When Conner and I were twelve, we climbed up one of them and painted the letters J and C in white—and nobody in Glenbrook ever complained because most of the people thought it was some kind of Christian sentiment about our town's values, so they liked it. And our initials were still there, somehow.

But this was not home.

Java and Jazz, the coffee place where Conner and I would sometimes hang out, was just the bombed-out brick husk of what it used to be. No roof, no windows, only the last two Zs on the sign above the door, like it was saying, *Don't bother me, I'm sleeping.*

I grunted. "How would you have gotten this thing back without me?"

"I wouldn't have come alone in the first place. I told you I was following you, Billy."

"You're full of shit."

"You cuss a lot."

"So do you."

Quinn laughed. "Shit."

I tried to, but couldn't think of a single quality about Quinn Cahill that didn't annoy me. *Probably food,* I thought. I was starving. I could put up with the kid for food.

"What happens to those things when the water goes away?" I said.

43

"The suckers? You really did fall out of the sky, didn't you, Odd?" Quinn wiped his nose. "They only live one day. Unless they get up inside you. Ha-ha-ha!"

And we walked right across the 101 freeway lugging that canoe. My arm and shoulder ached like death, but Quinn Cahill kept his end up like he was used to the effort. He was a lot stronger than I estimated.

We passed by what was left of a school building.

I didn't want to look. Quinn was in front of me, carrying himself like he was walking home from the toy store. On the playground, there was a tall rocket ship made of steel jungle-gym pipes with a ladder inside that twisted up through the middle of three separate floors.

There were bodies hanging from each of the floors—arms, legs, torsos that looked like the pieces of plastic dolls lashed to the outside of the ship. The feeding harvesters, the rat-sized bugs, cleaners of death, that were everywhere in Marbury, sounded like static electricity.

This was Marbury. One of the corpses hung by its ankle. It had been a man, and it dangled from the outside of the uppermost deck on the spaceship, tied to the pipes by his own inside-out Levis that trapped his foot there. His body had been opened from crotch to chin, and the open maw of his rib cage shuddered with black insects the size of my feet.

This was Marbury.

"Aren't you scared the Hunters are around?" I said.

"They only come out in town when it's raining, or at night. Usually. They've been getting more aggressive, though. Cocky." Quinn sighed. The first time I ever thought he might be getting frustrated at how stupid I seemed.

"Maybe I did."

44

"What?"

"Fall out of the sky."

"Shit, Odd. I told you that. Ha-ha! Well, something did, anyhow. Exactly seven days ago, too. Maybe probably was you."

"Shit."

"You'll see."

West of the school, we walked between piles of rubble: bricks, doors, the jumbled and splintered beams and joists of what used to be houses and strip malls. I was sweating and tired. I didn't think I'd be able to keep up with the kid much longer.

"Can I ask you something?" I said.

"You have permission to ask me something, Odd."

"What's the name of this town?"

Quinn stopped walking. It tripped me up for a moment, and I nearly dropped my end of the canoe. He ran his fingers through his hair and wiped the sweat on his butt. "Where are you from, Odd?"

"I don't know."

Quinn scratched his crotch. "Glenbrook. It's called Glenbrook."

"You ever hear of a place called New Mexico?"

"Shit. What's that?"

"New Mexico?"

"Never."

"Billy the Kid came from New Mexico."

"You're making that up, Odd."

Quinn started walking again, tugging me forward.

"Fuck this place, Quinn."

Fuck you, Jack.

Maybe I should just take the kid's red speargun and end it right here. Maybe, afterwards, Jack will wake up and he'll be in that piss-foul garage, sweating like a junkie, back in a different Glenbrook.

45

The same Glenbrook.

And Ben and Griffin, Conner, will still be here.

You are a coward and a failure, and you deserve this for what you've done to them.

I know this is not real. None of this has been real since the night of Conner's party at the end of school. Jack is just fucked up, is all. It's his brain. He has to wake up sooner or later.

Nickie.

God, Nickie.

"We can put the boat down right up there, see? See that old firehouse, Odd? That's where we live."

I knew the place.

"We?"

"You and me, Odd. You and me."

"I told you my name."

"That you did. But I believe you didn't want to do it, and you never did tell me where you come from."

"If you've been following me, then I shouldn't need to."

"Ha-ha-ha! You're a careful one, Odd. That's okay. I figure you've got some good ones to tell. All I need to do is get them out of you."

"I'm sure you've got some, too, Quinn."

Quinn turned back and glanced at me.

It looked like he was smiling.

It always looked like that kid was smiling.

four

Quinn Cahill was a survivor; I had to hand him that.

I imagined he pictured himself as some kind of king, ruling what he could from his palace in that dead old firehouse. And I was amazed at what that kid was capable of doing there, too.

Somehow, he'd managed to save the solar panels on the fire-house and hook them into a wiring system that ran through the old cinderblock building. It was mostly dark in Marbury, he explained, so the panels didn't do much more than power some flashlight-dim bulbs he'd installed. But Quinn had salvaged two science-lab steam engines from the schoolhouse, and these he'd hooked into a full-scale electric generator and an actual still he'd constructed from some old metal container drums that were left in the fire station. And Quinn used the still to make drinking water by recycling his own piss and the toxic rainwater he'd collect from the roof.

He'd even strung up one of those campsite portable shower sys-tems over the rusty tiled shower stall at the end of the firemen's bathroom.

Quinn Cahill's annoyance factor was equally matched by his in-credible talent for staying alive.

And he had food. Lots of it.

I must have drank a gallon of water, without stopping, from a yellowed plastic milk jug. I didn't even think twice about how Quinn produced that water; I was too busy thinking that it was the best water I'd ever tasted in my life.

"Don't drink that whole thing, Odd. You'll puke." Quinn put

his palm on the top of the milk jug to slow me down. "Come on, let me show you what I got here."

Quinn lived in the upstairs half of the firehouse. A slide pole descended through a hole in the floor, down to the garage. Quinn showed me how to use it if we ever had to get out that way.

There was hardly enough space in the garage to walk between the mounds of piled-up junk, even though I got the feeling that Quinn had inventoried every last item that was down there, knew where everything was. In the center of it all slumped the picked-over ruins of an old ambulance. It sat on its wheel hubs. Just about the only thing left attached to it was the windshield; no doors, no seats, not even floorboards below it.

The garage itself was impenetrable. The old roll-up metal door had been bolted shut and piled high with the rotting husks of furniture from upstairs—rusting cot frames, file cabinets, metal desks—whatever couldn't be used as fuel for Quinn's steam engines.

The floor near the slope that cut down at the roll-up door was wet from the rain. I stepped on a dead sucker there and it popped. I felt the water in my belly come up a little when I did that.

"I don't like it down here, Billy," Quinn said. "But if we ever need to get out this way, here's where we go."

Inside the doorless rear of the ambulance, on an exposed area of concrete that showed through a vacant hole in the old vehicle's rear compartment, Quinn pointed out a corroded manhole cover.

"Where's that go?" I said.

"I'm not really sure," Quinn answered. "I been down there a couple times. Got too scared to look around. I call it my last-chance bomb shelter."

I wasn't entirely convinced that Quinn got scared down there, or anywhere, but I wasn't going to push it.

"Here's where you pee," Quinn said. He'd taken me upstairs, to the old bathroom. Its useless white porcelain sinks and cracked mirrors hung from loose screws in the concrete block walls. Anchored to a side wall was a long, steel-trough urinal with a collector beneath it. That was for Quinn's still. He just looked at me with that dumb and eager look on his face like he was waiting for me to pee so he could show me how brilliant he was. And even though I kind of needed to piss, I ignored him.

The kid just gave me the creeps, like he was trying too hard.

"I know it's not the sweetest thing to think about, but you'll get over it. There's Odds out there who'll kill you for drinking water. I bet you seen that plenty, too."

"Uh. Yeah."

"And this is my shower." Quinn tapped my shoulder and nodded at his work.

Set back into the rear corner of the bathroom where the firemen used to take showers was a chest-high divider of painted yellow cinderblock. Hanging from the roof behind it Quinn pointed to a black plastic half-barrel that fed into a six-inch length of garden hose attached to a dangling spreader nozzle. I walked around the divider wall and looked. Naturally, in the bottom of the stall, the drain had been obviously rerouted back into Quinn's still.

"You want to wash that shit off, Odd?" Quinn pointed an index finger at his hair, and I could feel how mine had congealed, scabbed flat against my head.

I shook my head.

49

"Come on," he said. "There's more I want you to see. And I told you I'd get you a shirt, too, Billy."

I just wanted food.

Odd.

Billy.

I thought the kid was just trying to piss me off or something.

Fuck with me because he thinks I'm stupid.

I decided not to say anything about it, though.

There were two beds in there, like Quinn had been expecting me or something. They were cots—the kind you'd see in any barracks or jail—narrow and low, neatly made up with clean blankets, and white sheets and pillows.

Quinn pointed to each of the beds. "Yours. Mine. You hungry, Billy?"

I nodded.

"I could cook you something. Something good. I bet you never had food as good as what I can make."

He talked too much.

"Just let me show you a couple more things. So you don't do nothing dumb. So we can be safe here. You don't want to fuck things up, now, do you?"

You don't know me, kid.

I shook my head.

Quinn pulled me out into the main room.

He had a stove. He had everything. An entire room that had been filled with boxes and cans—more food than the kid could eat in five years.

"I'm good at finding food," Quinn said. "I'm the best. I know where to look where none of the Odds have looked. And mostly the

Rangers are dumb. They just wait for it to come to them. I guess that works, as long as you have guns."

Quinn poured some water into a pot. He placed it on the stove and then flipped a switch on the generator. It made a buzzing noise. Like insects.

"First thing: There is no generator at night," he said. "We can't make any noise. They'll hear us. This place has to look dead. Dark. You got that, Odd?"

"Okay."

"Second thing: blackout curtains."

There were no windows. Like so many of the buildings that had been left even partially standing, the windows in the firehouse had been boarded over with anything that could cover them. But Quinn had gone a step further. He'd brought in sets of those drapes they have in hotel rooms—the ones with heavy plastic backing—to cover any stray light that might seep out through an unnoticed crack.

"Last thing." Quinn opened a footlocker that was sitting beside the bolted doorway onto the staircase.

"Juicy death," he said. He slapped my bare back. It stung, and I wanted so bad to punch the kid. "Ha-ha-ha! These babies took the longest time to gather up and then get them to work right. Take a look, Odd. Here's how I turn them on, in case you ever have to do it."

Inside the trunk was a small brass-colored telegraph switch and eight automotive batteries—the big kind, like you'd see in a truck or an ambulance. They were all wired together, and then the wires fed into some kind of transformer box and more wires leading out from the bottom of the chest. It was an electric fence, Quinn said, that protected all the possible ways into the firehouse. He wasn't sure if it would kill someone; he was still waiting to find out, but he was certain his invention would buy enough time to get out of there if he ever really needed to.

"Why are you doing all this?" I said.

"Because I want to live," Quinn said. "It's winning, Odd. We all want to win, don't we?"

"I mean, why did you bother with me? You didn't have to save my life. You didn't have to bring me here."

For a second, Quinn looked flustered, like he couldn't answer, or he was embarrassed.

"I trust you, Billy. Don't you trust me?"

I hated being cornered like that. I've had that question aimed at me enough times in my life, and every time it had been someone trying to fuck with me.

Fuck you, Quinn.

So I said, "I really need to take a piss."

"Ha-ha!" Quinn laughed. "That's good for us, Billy. Good for the planet! Ha-ha-ha!"

And he slapped my shoulder again when I walked past him, saying, "I'll tell you what. You can take a shower if you want, so you can wash that Hunter shit off you and clean yourself up. You smell like death, Odd. Ha-ha! And I'll go find you some clothes and cook us some grub. Let's eat, Odd. I think we should have a special dinner in honor of us finding each other."

Finding me.

I couldn't help but wonder if he really had been following me, like he said.

But the clean water felt so good, and as I stood under the cooling flow, examining the small round marks those black things had left on my legs, I couldn't help but smell the food Quinn was cooking.

"We have to hurry up, Odd," Quinn called out from his post at the stove across the room. "The sun's going down soon."

I shut off the valve to the nozzle and stood there, dripping, leaning against the brick divider wall.

The kid even had towels. Quinn brought one out for me and slung it over the wall.

"Thanks."

"That's the first time you said that all day, Billy."

He was right, but it still pissed me off that he had to point it out to me.

"Is that all you're looking for? Okay, then. Thanks, Quinn. Thank you very much."

The kid shrugged.

I felt bad for what I said.

"Sorry." I looked down, pretended to dry my feet. "I'm an asshole. Sorry, kid."

I put the towel over my head, wiped my face.

"Don't sweat it, Billy. We all have bad days. More than not, I guess. But this is going to be our good night together. Right?"

My pants and socks were lying crumpled on the floor. Quinn nudged them with his toe, the way you'd prod something dead in the road. "You ain't going to put those things back on, are you?"

I wrapped the towel around my waist and stepped around the wall. "It's all I got."

"You know. I used to have a knife exactly like this one here," Quinn said.

I looked at him. "What happened to it?"

"I don't know," Quinn said.

Sure you don't, Quinn.

The kid bent over and picked up my pants, the belt with the knife I'd found attached to it. And I remembered the broken lens was still in the pocket. I didn't want Quinn to see it, but I could tell that his fingers had already felt it out.

"What's this you got?" Quinn said.

"Don't. Please."

I snatched my pants from Quinn's hand.

The kid looked at me. He was too smart, and I hated that. Because he didn't need to say one word for me to know that he was already thinking up a way that he'd find out what I was hiding in my pocket.

Quinn grabbed my wrist. Yeah, he was strong, and my hand was sore and swollen. "What happened there, Odd?"

He turned my palm over, lightly touched the cut that gapped my flesh open from the base of my thumb to the arc of Jack's lifeline.

"I cut myself."

"Come here. Sit down." And Quinn led me across the cool concrete floor while I dripped water and held on to my dirty pants and the towel I was wrapped in with one hand. He pulled me along by my wrist like he was helping a little kid at a street corner.

Quinn sat me in a chair at a small square table pushed up against the wall. He pulled my arm across the surface so he could look at the cut on my hand. His face was so close to me that I felt the tickle of the air he exhaled from his nostrils.

He didn't say a word, got up from the seat beside me, and returned with some bandages and antibiotic.

"Does it hurt?" Quinn smeared medicine into the cut with his index finger.

I thought about the messages that had been painted on the wall in that house.

"Yes," I said.

Then he wrapped my hand up with clean white gauze and medical tape.

"You gotta watch that, Billy. Things can get in you here. Don't you know that?" Quinn smiled and winked at me.

"I was too busy watching all the other stuff."

"Ha-ha-ha!" Quinn laughed. "It's been too long since I talked to any Odd with a sense of humor!"

I felt embarrassed. Quinn patted the underside of my forearm softly when he finished with the bandaging.

"Hang on, Odd. I'll get you something to wear."

So I rolled my pants tightly and wrapped my belt around them, making sure the lens was wadded up deep in the center.

Quinn came back from his closet and handed me a pair of green mesh gym shorts. G.H.S.X.C. was stenciled in gold on the right leg. Glenbrook High School Cross Country. They were the same ones Conner and I wore when we trained.

And I thought, *This is bullshit. The kid has to be fucking with me. This whole place is fucking with me.*

"These are good for sleeping in," Quinn said.

That's what was bothering me about Quinn: He was too hovering, like Stella had been, always watching me, standing a little too close, breathing on me, watching, always watching. It made me feel like a prisoner, like I was under glass. So I fumbled at getting those shorts pulled up without standing up or taking off my towel, because it bugged me how this kid was just sitting there taking in the Jack show like he'd been standing in line all his life just to bug the shit out of me from his front-row seat.

55

When I slipped them on, the shorts hung down past my knees, and I had to hold on to them with one hand just to keep them from sliding off my hips. At least they'd never actually been mine or Conner's.

Then he gave me a rust-colored T-shirt that was about two sizes too big.

"I guess the size doesn't matter," I said.

Because the kid himself looked like he'd been dressed in stuff that could be used as fumigation tents.

"You know," he said. "When the bug hit real bad, at the start of the war, there was just young people who didn't get it—us Odds and what was left of the Rangers. All the clothes is gone, Billy. Unless you want girl stuff. Heck, I don't even recall if I ever saw a girl since I was a kid."

Quinn kind of looked—sad, I guess, when he said that.

The kid pulled his shirttails out from his pants and began unbuttoning.

"There's really no girls?"

"Shit, Odd. What's wrong with you? The only ones that's left is with the Rangers. Ha-ha-ha! Or they're Hunters. You ever seen a girl, Odd?"

I didn't know what to say.

I missed Nickie so bad it hurt. I kept thinking that this time I'd never find a way out of this world and get back home.

Quinn slithered out of his shirt and hopped around while he pried away at his boots and socks. "After I clean up, we'll have some good food, Odd. You'll see. This is going to be a great night."

The redhead went around behind the divider wall and turned on his shower nozzle. "And we got lots to talk about, Billy. Lots and lots."

Quinn Cahill cooked macaroni and cheese from a cardboard box. He used canned milk and put some tuna and peas in it, too.

I felt bad for Ben and Griffin, thinking about how they were probably hungry, starving, and I decided, sitting there in those baggy PE clothes at Quinn's small dinner table, that I was going to have to do something about that. And I felt a little bit guilty, too, for acting like such an asshole to the kid all day long. He saved my life. Quinn took care of me, even if I didn't really care about where Jack would have ended up if the kid never showed in the first place.

I cleared my throat. "This is the best food I've ever had in my life, Quinn."

He looked at me, and I was certain he could tell I was serious. So I stuck my bandaged hand out across the table of food and said, "Thank you. And I apologize. And please don't spit in your hand before we shake."

Quinn beamed. He chewed with his mouth open, too. But he took my hand.

"You don't need to apologize, Odd. No big deal."

We ate in silence until everything Quinn made had been wiped clean. He washed the dishes in a plastic tub he kept inside the sink, and then he strained the dishwater through a wire screen and poured it back into his still.

I sat there watching. I could tell he didn't want me to help, like he was trying to teach me some kind of routine or something, show me how he was in control of everything—and it was all perfect. I realized that all day long Quinn and I had been locked in some kind of contest to decide who was really in charge, and though it may not have been determined yet, I was convinced that redhead kid didn't know anything else but winning, like he'd told me.

So I knew he was plotting out his cross-examination of me while he quietly packed away his kitchen.

When it got dark inside the firehouse, Quinn took out two oil lamps and double-checked his blackout blinds.

"Well, for someone who said we have lots to talk about, you haven't said a thing, Quinn. So I may as well start by telling you that everything I said to you today is the truth. I really don't know where I came from."

"What about that shirt you took off?" he said. "What about that stuff written on the wall at the old man's house? Do you think I'm stupid, Billy?"

I gulped. Had to think.

The kid really did know things about me.

And he'd found the shirt. He must have known every detail about the stuff inside that house.

Then Quinn added, "Number three-seven-three?"

I felt the blood rushing out of my head. I looked down at Quinn's spotless table and shook my head slowly from side to side.

"I'm telling the truth, Quinn. I figured I'm in some kind of trouble. I remember waking up inside a garage yesterday. But I don't know how I got there, and I don't know why I had that shirt on. But I guessed it had something to do with this Fent person. And I didn't know anything about the old man's house. That stuff on the wall was written by a friend of mine, but I don't know where he is, either. So I was scared and I thought I could just ditch the shirt and be nobody."

"Your friend's named Conner Kirk?"

I studied Quinn's eyes. They were still smiling, but he had a look like a cat that was about to pounce on something, too.

58

"Do you know anything about Conner?"

Quinn looked away. "Not much. They're looking for him, too."

"What about Fent?"

Quinn laughed. "Heh. Bad magic. Anamore Fent wants to kill you, Odd. Don't you know that?"

I cleared my throat. "Why?"

"When someone tells me, I'll let you know. How's that sound?"

"Am I safe here?"

"Do you trust me?"

Fuck you, Jack.

Quinn stood up, and waved for me to follow him. "Here. I want to show you something, Odd."

In the back corner of the firehouse, opposite the shower stall, a narrow black metal ladder rose up to a square hatch in the roof. Quinn climbed up and pushed the square door open. After he crawled out into the dimming evening, he stuck his face down inside and whispered, "Come on up here. Just be quiet. They're going to be out soon."

five

It was awkward climbing up that ladder.

The rungs hurt my bare feet and I could only work with one hand. My bandaged palm stayed hitched on the waistband of those goddamned shorts Quinn gave me. They ended up tangled around my ankles on top of the first step, and that redheaded bastard poked his face in the hatch and hissed a whispered laugh at me.

Balancing with my knees propped against one rung, I flipped him off, and Quinn laughed again.

"Come take a look at this, Odd. Tell me if you never seen it before."

The roof of the firehouse was a flat deck of some sort, surrounded by a waist-high cinderblock wall that extended up from the perimeter of the station. At one time, I could imagine firemen enjoying a pleasant day up here. Maybe when the world was different.

I sat at the edge of the open hatch, and then brought my feet up onto the roof before trying to stand. The sky was just going to nighttime dark in Marbury, a milky gray, the color of a rotten tooth. Quinn stood back, and faced away from me with his chin tilted upward.

"See that?" he said.

I looked up.

And, in what dark the Marbury night made for us, standing there beside Quinn Cahill on the roof of an abandoned firehouse that had become his sanctuary in hell, I saw the hole in the sky.

Overhead in the east, above the business district where the kid had pushed us in a canoe past Java and Jazz, there was a gash—a knife wound through the gray. The thing bled vacant light that seemed to spill downward like a waterfall and blind out the foggy haze around it; a liquid constellation, some kind of fire that rained down from nowhere and everywhere.

"What do you think that is?" Quinn asked.

I just shook my head.

"Well, I'll tell you, Odd. Like I said, when it happened things got worse. The Rangers been coming through trying to get anything they can take. Some of them's even headed out now, just leaving here altogether. Seems like, to be honest, there's more suckers, more Hunters, harvesters, and more of us dying. And I believe Fent's crew is getting ready to go too, and leave us all—what's left of us—to the Hunters. But those next few days after it happened, the Rangers rode through, roughing up all the Odds that were too young to conscript, and you know what some of them do to us who are older, don't you? They were looking for you. Jack Whitmore. See? I knew your name before you even said it, Billy. And they were trying to find your friend, too. They said you did something to him. Why do you suppose that is? You weren't just a prisoner, were you?"

When Quinn made his case, something started to connect in my head, but I couldn't feel it coming together. It was like those times when I'd look back through images—photographs that Nickie had taken of me—riding on a river cruise, touring London, doing things with her while I was in Marbury, while I was here—but I couldn't quite get the memory to surface.

I leaned my arms on the edge of the block wall and watched as the thing pulsed overhead in the sky. The kid knew things about me and Conner, and he was playing a game, they way you'd play with a hooked fish on a line.

Quinn knew more about Marbury than I ever did.

I had fallen into another pit inside my nightmare, a deeper layer, and nothing was finished yet. We all fell—me, Conner, Ben, and Griffin.

"You have to believe me, Quinn. I just can't remember what happened."

"All right, Odd."

I heard music playing.

Crazy Jack dreams up all kinds of shit.

And sometimes it's accompanied by music.

I held my breath.

I had to be out of my mind.

It sounded so far away, floating: a jangling, grinding, metallic sound, the wheezing strains of a high-pitched organ.

"Do you hear that?" Quinn said.

"I don't know what it is," I whispered. "It sounds like a circus."

Musical monsters.

"It's Fent."

Quinn nudged my shoulder and then went back toward the place where the hatch lay open. "Time for us to settle in, Billy."

We sat on our beds, across from each other, and listened to the music as it got louder at times, and then drifted away like a wind.

I'd been scared plenty of times—in Marbury, and in other places—but there was something about that music and the thought of it being connected to someone who was looking for me and Conner that was more unnerving than anything else I could remember.

"Why do they do it?" I said.

"The music? Fent just wants us Odds to know they're coming. Hunters, too. I guess it saves the Rangers on ammunition. Everyone runs from them."

"Do they know about this place?"

"Of course they do, Odd."

The music was clearer now. It sounded, ridiculously enough, like a single small accordion; the kind they call a concertina.

"It doesn't scare you they know about you?"

"You really don't know nothing, do you?" Quinn sighed. "Join or die, Billy. Join or die. They don't fuck with the Odds till we turn sixteen. Well, except for the depraved ones, they don't. Or till we look like we're sixteen."

Quinn shifted on his bed, leaning toward me, leering. "How old are you, anyway? Heh-heh."

That explained some of it, I guess.

"How old do I look?"

"You? You look like you've been around for a really long time, Odd."

He was fucking with me again.

I wanted to get out of there. If I didn't get away from Quinn, as good as things might be at his firehouse, I was certain he was going to push me into doing something bad.

I lay down and stretched my legs across the cot. I was completely exhausted.

"What do you want me to do if they show up?"

Quinn got up from bed and lowered the mantle on the oil lamp.

It was as black as if I'd shut my eyes, but they were wide open. I could hear his bare feet padding across the floor, the squeak of his bedsprings as he sat down again on his cot.

"Don't be scared, Odd. I'll take care of you. I can handle Fent and the Rangers. If they show up tonight, you just get up on the roof. You'll be safe there till I come get you. Okay?"

I gritted my teeth, forced the words from my constricted throat. "Thanks, Quinn."

"Don't worry about them."

"Okay."

I remembered something.

And I told him.

"There's a settlement across a desert. They call it Bass-Hove. You ever hear of such a place? There are people in it. Real people who don't call themselves Odds. There's girls, too. They still have some power there. Trains. Locomotives that take people out, to another city. A fortress behind big walls, named Grove. Did you ever know anything about those places? That's where the Rangers are going."

I had seen it all before. I had been to those places, could still feel the gritty, windless heat of the air at the Bass-Hove Settlement, could picture the sheer walls of the fortified city at Grove, where Conner and I took the other boys after we'd crossed the mountains.

"You're making that shit up, Billy."

I heard him roll over onto his side and exhale a tired breath of air.

And I was certain he knew exactly what I was talking about.

The Rangers came that night.

I was hard asleep, and at first I felt Quinn's hot breath against my ear when he whispered, "Billy. Billy, wake up."

He shook my chest gently, and I thought it had to be a weird dream.

I dreamed of being on the water again.

"Psst! Billy!"

Then I heard the music, louder now, the squeal of the concertina wheezing in and out, in and out.

It sounded as if it were right outside the firehouse door.

"Huh?" I shot up in my bed, disoriented, everything swirling and smearing like a watercolor painting that had been left out in a summer storm—Glenbrook, here, there, Marbury, my friends, the Odds, Quinn Cahill.

"Shhhhh . . . Quiet now, Odd."

Quinn's mouth was so close to my ear I could feel his lips moving. "Remember what I said. Get up the ladder now. Come on, get humping, Odd. They probably just want some water. I got to go down and talk to them."

I stood, shaky and weak.

Quinn lit a lamp. The kid lifted the lid on the footlocker. I heard him flip the switch inside it—his electric fence. Then he nodded at the ladder and went out the door and downstairs to the entryway.

This was it, I thought.

I started toward the ladder, holding my shorts up as I walked. Then, I'm not sure why I did it, but I looked back at the room. And I thought, *If they come up here and see two beds have been slept in, they'll know somebody else is here. Quinn can't be that stupid.*

He's fucking with you, Jack.

So I went back and pulled the blanket and sheet from my bed.

The music outside stopped.

I tossed my pillow across to Quinn's cot and I grabbed my pants and boots from the floor where I'd hidden them under my bed. I even slipped my hand inside to make sure the broken lens was still tucked into my pocket.

Same old Jack, no matter where he is.

And as I bundled my things in the bedsheet, I got the idea that I should leave. I glanced at the door, strained to hear anything, but it was all so quiet. I jumped across to Quinn's closet and slipped inside. I didn't bother to look, I grabbed as much as I thought I could carry—cans, mostly—and one plastic water jug.

My hand ached, but I got everything up that ladder and onto the roof.

Then I shut the hatch behind me.

I stripped out of the shorts and got back into my pants. I hooked up my belt, could feel the weight of that knife, as it slapped against my thigh when I laced up the boots.

65

Sure you used to have a knife like this one, Quinn. That's because you left it at that old man's house, didn't you?

I put the shorts he'd given me, and everything I stole from him, inside the blanket. Then I tied the corners into a tight bundle that I slipped over one arm. I knotted my sheets together and thought about how stupid I was, because this stuff never worked in real life, did it?

Yeah. This is real life.

I secured one end of my sheet-rope to the bar on the outside of the hatch and then threw the end that was probably going to break my leg in the best case, or kill me in the worst, over the side of the firehouse.

And even if I made it to the very end, I estimated I'd still have to drop ten feet—and that would be from a full-out stretch. So I clenched and re-clenched my injured right hand, wondering if I could hold my own weight; wondering what kind of shit was down there for Jack to land on.

But before I'd go over the edge, I had to see what was going on.

Just a peek.

You're an idiot, Jack.

I went to the front of the deck and looked down.

I could see Quinn, standing awkward and scrawny, naked except for a pair of baggy gym shorts, so he looked like he was maybe twelve years old. And he was talking to a group of soldiers—six or seven of them at least—who were mounted on horses that nervously twitched and shifted, rolling their eyes and throwing their heads back like they knew if they stood still too long the Hunters would come. I couldn't hear what they were saying, but Quinn was holding out his white arms, palms up, like he was imploring the riders to believe him. I wondered which one was Fent.

I found myself looking again, mesmerized by the pulsing slash of light where Quinn theorized something had fallen out of the sky. And something about that mark in the sky looked familiar to me— like I was supposed to remember it.

He said it happened seven days ago.

Maybe Conner came through first. Maybe he knew what was going on, only Marbury Jack hadn't tuned in yet, like Ben and Griffin hadn't.

Maybe they were still falling through, and that was why they didn't know who I was when they found me in their garage.

Shit, maybe the boys were still at home in Glenbrook—the real Glenbrook—watching while stupid Jack takes a swing at the only glue holding the entire universe together.

Jack did it again.

I had tried to make things right, to help my friends by splitting the lens. And just like most of Jack's other fixes, things only ended up broken worse than ever.

Seven days, seven years, it could all be an eyeblink here, a sneeze. So Conner left those messages for me at the old man's house, knowing I was coming. Sooner or later.

And out in the blank tract of nothing between here and the dust-covered highway, I saw a blazing line of red coming west toward the Rangers and Quinn's firehouse.

I saw the Hunters coming.

And that was enough for Jack.

I crossed the roof.

I do not pray. I have never prayed for anything. But when I grabbed on to the cord of sheeting and lifted my right leg over the edge, I shut my eyes tightly and silently repeated one name in my head: Nickie.

Then I went over the side.

And with each grasping hold, as I struggled to lower myself a foot at a time, pinching the sheets so desperately between my crossed ankles, I thought: Conner, Ben, Griffin, Seth.

I have to get back. I have to make things real again.

I tore open my hand when I climbed down from the firehouse roof.

The bandages and tape Quinn had so carefully wrapped around the cut soaked through with blood and pus that separated like light in a prism as the fluids migrated through the gauze and formed layers of colors—the broken-down spectrum of the stuff inside of Jack.

It hurt so bad that my nose ran with clear snot and my eyes watered. But I didn't break my leg. I made it down.

The bundle of food and water I'd slung over my shoulder was awkward and painful to carry, but I could do nothing about it. I dreamed of stumbling across some little kid's wagon to put it in; I fantasized about finding my truck, still full of gas, sliding in, my skin resting in the cool cradle of leather seats, turning on the stereo, tapping the wheel as I drove somewhere that wasn't here.

I kept moving. And I remember how my shoulders tensed, hunched up toward my neck on either side when I heard all the shooting start, off behind me somewhere in the direction of Quinn's palace.

So I justified in my mind that either the Rangers or the Hunters would have ended up with a trophy of Jack if I'd stayed behind. I was convinced that Quinn Cahill, the survivor like no other, would be fine and would slip back into his routine—maybe "following me," maybe just lying about it, but always winning his game.

And after I'd made it past the schoolhouse and crossed the dead darkness of what had at one time been a highway, I thought, *Please, do not start raining on me now.*

Two ghosts ran out in front of me, a boy and a girl, holding hands, barefoot, trailing wisps of luminescent fog like the unexplainable thing in the sky. They vanished in three short steps, and I kept thinking about how bothered Ben used to get over the ghosts in Marbury; how much he hated them.

Jack was going home.

I saw no other living thing that night as I passed through the ruins of the town, making my way toward the vacant miles of bare land that would have been vineyards at some other time.

This was the right place—I knew it—but there were no roads, no markers. Here, it was just drifts of soft ash that had taken over the undulating hills where Wynn and Stella grew grapes.

Occasionally, I'd see "things"—souvenirs of a past here: the lid from a galvanized-steel trash can, a mail delivery truck burned and tipped onto its side, half buried, twists of mangled wrought iron, and the strangest objects—bricks. There were bricks and cinderblocks scattered everywhere, randomly, patternless, as though anything that had been made of them just separated and flew in different directions.

They could have fallen from the sky, too.

But I wondered if maybe they were the remains of the walls that had surrounded Wynn's property.

And, just when the morning broke, pale and ulcerous, I saw the house.

It wasn't the house I noticed at first, but the huge oak tree in front of it—the one I used to park my truck under. But it wasn't a tree anymore. It was nothing more than a hollow, black log that stuck straight up through the white ash, barely taller than I was and wide enough across that I could have laid down inside it.

There was the house.

It was my house, wasn't it?

I think I stood against the husk of that oak tree for ten minutes just looking at it, trying to decide whether or not Jack had the balls to go inside.

It was coated in dust, the fine, sticky, annoying kind like you get from the inside of a vacuum cleaner bag. At one time Wynn and Stella's house had been a kind of peach color—all the houses in Glenbrook seemed to be painted that color—but now it had turned the same dull, rotten-meat shade of nothing that covered everything, everywhere.

The windows had all been broken. None of them were boarded. I already had learned enough here to know it meant nobody was alive. Not ever, probably. Sections of the roof had sloughed away.

But it was the same house where Jack was born on the floor in his grandparents' perfect kitchen.

You can't shoot an arrow anywhere and not aim at the center of the universe.

The boards were gone from the steps to the porch. I had to launch myself over the frame of the staircase from the bottom. I nearly dropped the satchel of food I was carrying, and I could hear the crotch ripping out of the jeans I wore.

Just great, I thought. I don't have any clothes and now my only pair of pants is coming apart, too.

The house was closed up.

Like the old man's house, all the hardware had been removed from the doors, and the leaded windows were broken out. When I pushed in against the front doors, the milky plumes of dust that rose up from the floor made it look like films you'd see of divers entering a stateroom in some long-sunken liner at the bottom of a cold ocean.

Welcome home, Jack.

I know it was stupid, but I almost choked when I stopped myself from calling my grandparents' names.

"Hey!"

Maybe there was a breeze raking over the jagged fangs of glass that jabbed out from the window frames upstairs, but I could hear a faint, hushed sigh—like someone was sleeping—breathing, whispering through the house.

"Is anybody in here?"

Down the hallway on the left side of the stairway—that was Wynn's room, where he would sit and watch television—I could see trails in the dust on the floor.

Things had been dragged.

"Hello?"

A curled brass light fixture, like a finger, a meat hook, dangled against the wall from its wires; the oak wainscoting had been pried away, the ragged splinters piled into a forbidding *X* where they crossed in front of the open doorway.

Shhhhhh . . .

Something was upstairs.

Maybe I was crazy.

Maybe I just needed sleep, but my heart shot up into my throat and I felt like I couldn't breathe, like I didn't want to, because I was afraid I'd make too much noise. And I cursed myself for having shouted my entry calls in the first place.

I was hot and cold at the same time, felt that feverish sickness of sweat on the back of my neck.

Quietly, I placed the bundled things I'd stolen from Quinn down on the floor, next to my feet.

I pushed the front doors shut behind me.

Shhhhhh . . .

I put my foot on the first stair.

How nice. Jack wants to go back to his old room.

Maybe he'll find something there to play with.

The stairs compressed under my feet, moaning. I walked along the wall. I was afraid they'd collapse in a rotten heap below me.

I was afraid.

This is stupid, I thought. *There's nothing here.*

It was my house.

But it wasn't my house.

At the top of the stairs, I glanced down the hallway. There was the bathroom, two guest rooms. One of them we called "Conner's room," because he was the only guest who ever slept in it. The light came in through the open doors from gaping window frames that spilled grayness across the floor of dust around me.

More signs that things—someone, maybe—had been dragged in the hallway, leaving nervous train tracks cleared through the dust on the floor.

At the opposite end of the hall, behind me, is Jack's room.

The door is shut.

A dim line, a crack of light.

I wait, listen.

A creak in the floor; I feel the vibration in the soles of my feet like I'm standing on an anthill. There is someone in my room; I am certain of it.

I think about the lens.

Jack always thinks about the lens.

I take it from my pocket and hold it just so it catches the little thing that squirms beneath the door.

Jack's door.

And for a moment, there is something in the lens, and it is gone again.

We have come to the right place.

Aching, I wrestle the knife from its sheath, pass it over to my left hand.

Nobody's allowed in my room when I'm not here.

It isn't my room.

And here I am.

I push the door open and stand back.

Welcome home, Jack.

Tap.

Tap.

Tap.

"Seth?" I whispered.

Nothing.

I was afraid to step foot inside my own room.

It's not your room.

The wind made a *hoosh* through the window.

I put one foot inside.

The door slammed open by itself. It crashed into the wall and made an angry dent in the boards. I didn't touch it. I could hear the screws in the hinges ripping at the wood.

Hoosh.

I held the fragment of the Marbury lens in front of me, like it was some kind of shield, and I swung it across my path, trying to see if it would pick up anything there in my room.

"Seth?" My voice was barely a breath.

I went inside.

"Can you help me?"

The door slammed shut.

Outside, rain began to fall.

As ridiculous as it all was, my room was still my room.

There was my bed. The sheets were missing, and one of the legs from the frame had collapsed, so the corner sagged down into the inch-thick dust on the floor. And there was dried blood at the foot end of the mattress.

Jack's blood.

From your ankle.

Remember that, Jack? How Freddie Horvath pinned your ankle to the bed frame using those sharp nylon bands?

The mirror had been shattered. There was one triangular piece jutting up from the bottom, and I could see my hand in it.

My hand was bleeding again, shaking, holding the lens.

Rain.

Sweat.

Lightning, and an explosion of thunder that nearly knocked me backwards.

I sat on the bed—my bed—and looked into the piece of mirror.

I put the lens back into my pocket; slid the knife into its sheath.

I watched the sheets of rain outside that waved their slate fibers like torn theatre scrims.

This is real.

In the mirror, I can only see my hands and knees. The gap between my legs. There would be something there, at least in Jack's world. Between the mattress and foundation of the bed, right in that corner.

It is the spot where Jack hid the lenses. I know where they are.

The last time we'd seen Seth, as he vanished, blue lenses fell on the spot beneath his faint image. Conner knows about them, even if I've been hiding them from him and the others.

I watch the mirror. I can see my unbandaged hand slip into the crack.

Something drags on the floor, cutting through the dust.

A finger, maybe.

It makes a drawing of an arrow that points to me, points away in the mirror.

I find it, Jack's stupid old sock, and, inside, there is something and it feels alive.

I can tell you, at that moment, when my hand found that wound-up sock hidden in my bed, I felt jangly and giddy—like the first time I touched Nickie's bare skin—I didn't know whether I was going to laugh or throw up, or whether my heart was going to explode.

I couldn't catch my breath. I unwound the sock and slipped my fingers inside.

I felt something, but it was not the same lenses Jack had left there. For a moment, my mind flashed on the image of a harvester twisted up inside the sock, waiting for a meal, or maybe one of those black slugs.

Crash.

The lightning came again.

I pulled my hand out.

There were eyeglasses. But these things were like nothing I'd ever seen before. They were beautiful and terrifying to look at; kind of like Henry's glasses were the first time I'd touched them when I sat alone at a table in The Prince of Wales, so long ago.

And these were different.

They were like goggles: loose, with a leather strap rather than stiff metal arms, and the eyepieces were cupped and vented. And each one of the lenses had been inlaid with dark blue glass the color of lapis, with round metal stems coming out from the top and bottom, like they were cooling tubes or pipes that carried some element into and out of the eyepiece.

They were made from the same pieces of glass, the lenses Seth had left for us in Marbury or, at least, they looked the same.

I guess we would never know for certain.

Attached to the left lens was a second, smaller, green monocle that was screwed into a double-action hinge system, so it could swivel up and down or pivot outward like a door.

I can't lie about it. It was exciting, and I didn't care if it killed me. I needed it.

Maybe it was a way home.

My hands shook and my belly knotted.

And when I held the lenses up, there was nothing remarkable I saw through either side.

Nothing.

Just blue glass.

So I put them on. Then I flipped the outer lens into place and opened my eyes.

And Jack was gone.

I could tell you that I knew it was going to happen, and I would be lying.

But you would believe me.

part two

BAD
MAGIC

SIX

How many crows are there?

They croak their crow-words and I can picture ink-black heads bobbing.

Cocking.

When it is hot and still, and you're covered with the damp stickiness of insomnia, crows make a sound, a twisting grappling hook in your gut.

I am on the floor.

I feel every individual fiber-end of the rough carpet that comes halfway out from beneath my bed, pricking into the skin on my back. Acrylic nettles. And somehow, my feet, my legs, are resting above me on the mattress.

Sometimes, in summers, when I can't sleep—this is how Jack doesn't sleep: faceup, feet on the bed, irritated by things like crows and his bare skin on carpeting.

"Fuck."

I swipe a palm across my swollen eyes, and I see that there is no cut, no bandage.

No Quinn Cahill.

No Marbury.

This is my room.

This is my room.

And then, for a moment, I am suddenly pissed off at Wynn and Stella because our house isn't like Conner's. I don't have *my* bathroom attached to *my* bedroom. Why should I have to get up and stumble down the hall?

Because I need to puke again.

What time is it?

The thought almost makes me laugh as my stomach clenches in rhythm with the cawing of the crows.

What fucking day is it?

I flush the toilet.

I go back down the hall, staying close enough to the wall so it can brace me up if my knees give out.

"Jack? Are you up?" Stella calls from somewhere downstairs. At first, she sounds like a blackbird.

Her feet make soft thuds like balls of warm dough dropping onto the staircase.

I open the door and lie down on the floor.

"No."

I listen to the crows.

I put my feet up on the bed and stare at the fan dangling from the ceiling above me.

Round and round.

This is my room.

Stella always knocked before she'd open the door to my bedroom. Usually, she would stand there patiently, and then I'd hear her going back downstairs if I didn't answer. This time, she waited only a few seconds and then my door cracked open.

"Jack?"

I looked at the spinning blades on the fan. I could feel her watching me.

"Huh?"

"Are you sick, honey? I heard you throwing up again."

"I'm okay, Stella."

"You don't look good, Jack."

How good could I look? I was lying there on the floor, pale and sweating, wearing nothing but a pair of damp boxer briefs that felt like I'd had them on for three endlessly hot days.

"I'm okay."

"I'm worried about you. You haven't gotten any better since you came back from London. Is Conner sick, too? Maybe you boys caught something there."

Something like that, Stella.

Conner.

"What time is it?"

I felt more than heard my grandmother take a couple steps inside my room.

"You came home late from your friends' house last night."

"What day is it?"

Stella sat on the edge of my bed. She put one hand on my foot. It felt cool, nice.

Worried.

I knew she loved me. So did Wynn. That didn't change anything. It never made me better.

"Jack, are you drinking? You're not drinking, are you?"

She didn't sound angry. It wasn't an accusation, either. Her voice sounded exactly the way her hand felt on my skin. But I still didn't care.

And I didn't answer her.

Stella said, "It's Saturday, baby. Almost two o'clock."

One day.

Not even one day since I was in the garage with Conner, Ben, and Griffin. Since we broke the lens.

I swallowed. I thought. I thought for a good long time about how I'd ended up here on the floor of my room like this. It was almost as though I could still smell the rain in Marbury, could hear the sound of cutting those black suckers to pieces with the knife I'd found. And I could swear I still tasted the dinner that Quinn Cahill had cooked for me.

Macaroni and cheese.

I felt the need to throw up again.

"I don't drink, Stella. I don't do anything like that."

I knew that would be enough. I couldn't ever lie to her. Not really.

And I said, "I mean, I have drank beer and stuff with Conner. A few times. But I don't drink. I haven't been drinking or doing anything else. Nothing."

Fuck you, Jack.

Stella rubbed the front of my leg.

"I called Dr. Enbody. He wants to come take a look at you."

I tensed.

The good doctor.

When I was a little kid, I used to call him Dr. Nobody.

That made people laugh.

I groaned.

"I don't want to see a doctor."

I sounded pathetic.

Stella squeezed my leg.

"We need to see if there's something wrong, baby."

I know exactly what's wrong, Stella.

You want me to tell you?

You want me to tell you exactly how fucked up Jack is?

Didn't think so, Stella.

My grandmother got up.

Outside, the crows argued.

"Can I get you anything, Jack?"

I wanted to scream.

Somewhere near the head of the bed, my phone began buzzing.

"No, thanks. I'm okay."

I propped myself up. And I could see those glasses just lying there on the floor beneath my bed.

The phone buzzed.

Stella quietly shut my door and I could hear her doughy footfalls going back downstairs.

I got up and grabbed my phone.

I didn't have to look at the screen to know who was calling. Saturday at two in the afternoon meant Nickie calling from England. Any call at two pretty much meant Nickie. Nobody ever does anything at two in the afternoon in California.

I cleared my throat.

"Hey, Nickie."

"Jack. Did I wake you? You sound out of breath."

"I was just laying here. Being lazy. Sorry it took a while to find my phone."

"That sounds like you." She laughed.

"I miss you, Nickie."

I wished things could be normal. I wished this world would stop coming and going. I realized my window was open, that I was absentmindedly counting the crows in the big oak tree outside, and I pictured the way it looked when I saw it in Marbury—burned, hollow, dead.

"Six more days."

I could picture the smile on her face when she said that.

And she said, "What's the first thing you'd like to do when you come back?"

When I come back.

I nervously cleared my throat again. "I'll think of something."

She laughed. "Jack."

Then I heard it.

And Nickie said, "Do you remember this?"

Roll.

Tap.

Tap.

Tap.

The horse. It was a little wooden toy that Seth Mansfield had carved as a gift for Hannah—the girl he loved—more than a hundred years ago. The horse just appeared one night in Nickie's bedroom, and she'd assumed I left it for her.

Because I loved her, too.

That's how shit happened in between here—or wherever I was—and Marbury: Things just came and went, popped in, popped out. No questions, no explanations. Just like the little wooden toy horse that meant Seth was around somewhere.

Nickie must have been playing with it. But when I heard the sound, I saw a flash—Seth standing just inside my window. I blinked and he was gone. I got up from my bed and looked outside.

Just crows.

"It's the horse," I said.

"I can't wait to see you again, Jack. I think I've become even more fond of you since you've been away."

"I love you, Nickie."

And as I looked out my window, I saw a black BMW pull up and park right behind my truck. Dr. Enbody.

I guess he had nothing to do at two in the afternoon.

Shit.

"Ander's here. Can you hear him telling you hello? We were watching some terribly long German movie and he played translator for me. He's quite good at German, although I think he made bits up."

Ander was Nickie's younger brother.

She laughed.

"Tell him I still have the shirt he loaned me. I'll bring it with me when I come back next week."

"I can't wait. I love you, Jack."

"Nickie? Remember what we talked about? I'm seeing a doctor today."

It was another lie. I wasn't seeing a doctor. He was seeing me. And I wasn't seeing the kind of doctor Nickie wanted me to see, one who could straighten out the bends in my brain. Dr. Nobody

85

had no idea just how fucked up this kid patient of his really was. He had no clue where to even begin looking.

Nickie didn't say anything. I could hear her breathing, could sense that she was trying to think of what, exactly, would be the right thing to say to me.

"You're brave, Jack."

"He's here right now."

"Oh."

"Nickie? Let me hear it again. The horse, I mean."

"You're funny."

Roll.

Tap. Tap. Tap.

The crows went silent.

Seth stood in the shade beneath the oak.

Then he was gone.

Something was wrong.

Footsteps outside.

"I better go. The doctor's coming."

"Call me after. If you want to tell me about it."

I don't want to tell anybody about anything.

"Okay."

"I love you, Jack."

Dr. Enbody tried to be nice.

He told me how long he'd known me, and how much I'd grown, but he asked if I'd been eating enough, too, and said that I should probably start going to a regular doctor, now that I was sixteen.

He made me lie down and he pressed his fingers into my belly and thumped on my rib cage. He peered up my nose and into my ears. He looked me straight in the eyes and asked about "bowel movements" and what color my urine was; if I had any concerns or trouble with my penis and testicles.

I shook my head.

Then he asked if I'd been "sexually active with girls or with other boys," and I almost choked. But I told him yes, that I had a girlfriend. And that pissed me off, too, but I wasn't sure exactly why.

I was so embarrassed, I guess. So Dr. Enbody told me that I'd better be using condoms, and I lied and said I always used condoms because I just wanted him to shut the fuck up and go away. I'd never even touched a rubber, and I couldn't imagine having balls enough to go into a 7-11 and buy a box of them.

It was the stupidest thing I ever had to talk about in my life.

When I closed my eyes, I saw Freddie Horvath, so I just kept watching Dr. Enbody until my eyes started watering.

He took my blood pressure and listened to my heart. He pressed an icy stethoscope onto my back and asked me to cough; then took my temperature. He tried to joke about how he used to do it when I was a baby, and I asked him if he ever mixed up thermometers, which made him smile.

Then he started doing the sneaky thing that normal doctors do when they can't find what seems to be the trouble: He began asking me questions about what I did in England, and how was the jet lag, and had I gotten back to regular sleeping patterns. Did I like English food? Did I try the beer there? I knew exactly where he was going, but it didn't piss me off. He wasn't trying to fuck with me— not like that other doctor. Dr. Enbody was just doing what Wynn and Stella paid him to do, so I answered his questions without volunteering anything else.

How was I getting along with my friends? Was there anything

that bothered me about myself? Was I having bad dreams? Getting enough sleep? Did I think I was too fat?

I joked. Yeah, I'm on the cross-country team. I'm a planet.

Welcome to Jack's universe.

Dr. Enbody laughed. It sounded like he really understood me.

For a minute, I tried to think what it might be like to actually *talk* to him—to tell him what happened to me. Not the Marbury stuff, the Glenbrook shit. I tried imagining what it would be like if I could let the words come out of my mouth. And I almost started to say it, but I couldn't.

He poked me and felt the alignment of my spine, bent my knees, and rotated my shoulders.

I answered his questions.

Then he went downstairs.

As soon as he was far enough away, I slipped out my door after him. Quiet, barefoot, nearly naked, I felt like something wild. Like a murderer.

Of course I knew exactly where to sit on the staircase so I could hear what was going on downstairs.

I knew Wynn wouldn't be there. He never wanted to have anything to do with stuff like doctors and problems and fixing things. Those were Stella's specialties.

So I heard Dr. Enbody telling her that he wanted to have her bring me in to his office this week so he could take a blood and urine sample from me.

Great.

Stella wanted to know if he thought I was on drugs or something, but the doctor told her no, he just wanted to see if anything was going on with me. He said my blood pressure was a little high, like I was stressed about something. And he got this condescending and calm tone in his voice when he said that teenage boys often have anxiety issues and get sulky when they're my age, so Stella shouldn't worry too much about it—it was all routine kind of stuff. Then he started asking her things about if she noticed I was getting depressed, not sleeping, maybe sleeping too much, or if I talked about dying or suicide.

That's when I wanted to punch the wall.

I didn't want to hear anything else.

Fuck this place.

I got up and went back into my room.

I lay on my bed, listening to the crows, waiting to hear Dr. Enbody's car drive away.

Conner.

I grabbed my phone and dialed.

"What's up?"

"Hey, Con."

"Dude. I thought you were coming over."

"Yeah. Stella made me see a doctor."

Conner laughed. "Did he need to do surgery to get your head out of your ass?"

That was Conner.

This was real.

"Nice mouth."

"Shit. What did he do?"

"Nothing, I guess."

I sat up in bed. Outside, I could hear the doctor's car start up. "Hey, Con, did something weird happen yesterday?"

Conner said, "Uh-oh. Are you tripping out about that shit again?"

Freddie.

"No. I mean, yesterday, after we broke that lens. Did something weird happen to you?"

I waited for Conner to answer.

"Um. What lens, Jack?"

I chuckled. I thought it sounded stupid. Like Quinn Cahill. "Don't fuck with me, Conner."

"Okay. So, we broke some lens? And then what?"

"You know. Marbury."

"Did Stella's doctor give you any meds, Jack? It sure sounds like you're on dope to me. And can you bring the whole bottle over? I want to try some of that shit."

I knew Conner. He sucked at acting dumb for more than a line or two.

He really didn't know what I was talking about.

Fuck you, Jack.

"Yeah. Well. Maybe he did give me something."

And it fucked up your brain, Jack.

"Can you operate a motor vehicle or heavy machinery?" Conner laughed.

"Do you remember when we were over at Ben and Griffin's house?"

"Who?"

"Ben and Griffin."

"Jack. What the fuck are you talking about? Is this something about that shit with that Freddie guy? Are you still fucked up about that? Dude."

It was Conner. He was frustrated.

"You're really not fucking with me, are you, Con?"

"Maybe you're just stressed about going back to England or something. Did you just wake up? 'Cause you sound fucked up, Jack."

"You don't know anyone named Ben and Griffin?"

"Am I supposed to?"

"I'm coming over."

"Let's go grab some food or something."

Or something.

I slipped into a pair of shorts and threw a T-shirt over my shoulder.

When I sat on the edge of the bed so I could get my socks and shoes, I thought about the glasses on the floor.

Maybe he was just fucking with me.

That was something Conner would do.

But not about this.

Never about this.

I switched my phone back on, flipped through my contacts list.

No Ben Miller.

No Griffin Goodrich.

Fuck you, Jack.

I reached under my bed and picked up the glasses. The third lens was swung out from the bigger eyepiece. There wasn't anything there; nothing living inside the lenses. I put my fingers on the outer monocle. I wanted to flip it into place, just for a second, just so I could prove to myself that I wasn't insane—that somehow I'd really fucked everything up. Everywhere.

Welcome to Jack's universe.

I had to put things back where they belonged.

I slid the glasses into my pocket, and their weight almost dragged my shorts down. Maybe Dr. Nobody was right; that I wasn't eating enough.

Who cared about that, anyway?

I fucked up.

I went into the hallway and slipped out of the house without Stella even noticing I was ever there at all.

seven

I guess it was Jack's day for black cars.

When I walked across the lawn toward the blot of shade at the curb where I park my truck, a big Cadillac SUV with blacked-out windows and no license plates pulled up and stopped right in front of me.

At first, I figured, with a car like that it was probably someone coming to talk to Wynn and Stella about insurance policies or their investment portfolio, or the kind of stuff that never meant anything at all to me.

But I was wrong.

The guy who got out of the driver's side stood in the street and watched me as I took out my keys and hit the remote.

I tried ignoring him.

I was so sick of people I didn't know watching, staring at me. It was like I could feel his eyes pressing into my skin.

And with just one glance, I thought I had him sized up pretty good. He stood there, sucking in his stomach with his hands on his hips. He was one of those edgy grown-ups who'd played football in high school and bragged to his friends about how he goes to the gym every morning, and he probably did part-time coaching for a youth program just so he could yell at kids and tell them what pieces of shit they were.

You see guys like that everywhere in California.

I kept my head down.

The walk seemed to take forever.

How far away did I park my goddamned truck?

But I knew he was going to say something to me.

"How's it going?"

I stopped.

Shit.

My hand was just touching the door of my truck. I calculated three seconds—if I had left my room just three goddamned seconds sooner, none of this would be happening and I'd be on my way to Conner's house.

I pretended like I didn't know the guy was talking to me.

I opened the door and started to get in.

He turned up his football-coach volume just a notch. Edgy. I could tell he thought I was another piece of shit.

"Hey. John? You're John Wynn Whitmore, right?"

What could I do?

Nobody ever calls me John.

I was wedged inside my open door, one elbow resting on top of the cab. I looked over at the guy, who'd come around and stood in the street between our cars. His face was blank, but as soon as he saw me look at him, he cracked a smile.

"Yeah. My grandparents are in there."

I nodded my head toward the house, trying to see if maybe the guy really was there to fill out beneficiary forms or some shit like that.

Nice try, Jack.

"I was hoping I'd catch you."

Catch me.

He closed the space between us, his eyes fixed directly on mine, unblinking, smiling that fake football-coach smile that made me feel like a piece of shit.

Then he put out his hand.

I thought of Quinn Cahill.

And he said, "My name is Sergeant Scott. Avery Scott. I'm a detective with the San Luis Obispo County Sheriff's?"

He said it like a question, like he expected me to say, *Okay, you can play that part in this game.*

When I didn't take his hand, he smoothly reached into his back pocket and pulled out a folding wallet with a gold badge and ID card.

"It's pretty fucking hot today, wouldn't you say?"

He kept the smile on. He was testing me. He wanted to see if my reaction would show him I thought he was cool for being an old guy who comfortably says words like *fuck* to a sixteen-year-old kid.

"I didn't watch the Weather Channel today."

Avery Scott laughed. He reinstalled his nice wallet into his pocket.

"I came out today. Well. I'm looking into a case we've got and I was hoping to ask you a couple questions. It has nothing to do with you."

Sure.

Nothing.

"Am I in some kind of trouble or something?"

"No, no, no!" Scott was a little too exaggerated. "It's just. Uh. Some background stuff. Do you mind?"

"Shouldn't my grandparents be around? I mean, if you're a cop and all, and want to talk to a kid?"

"Seriously, John. You didn't do anything wrong, son. But if you'd like to go inside, we could talk to your grandparents, too. It's about this thing you may have heard of. A doctor named Manfred Horvath. People called him Freddie. He was found dead. Not a nice guy." Scott shook his head. "A fucking sicko. You ever watch the news?"

At that moment, I felt my balls twist their way up, crawling like snails inside my stomach.

Then I was suddenly aware of the sweat dripping down my temples, running from my armpits, playing xylophone on my ribs.

"Sometimes."

Scott put his hand on the top of my car door. He had curly brown hairs on his fingers and wore a ridiculous class ring with a big green gem in its center.

"This is a sweet truck. You know the thing that's fucked up about parking under these big oaks? The crow shit."

Detective Scott pointed a finger at the grapefruit-sized splotch in the center of my truck's roof, reaching across so he was pinning me in the small triangular space of my open door.

"I guess."

"So, you want to go inside and we can talk with your folks?"

"Not really."

"I just want to find a couple things out. Just checking up on stuff. You know, put this thing to rest." He looked around. He cocked his head. Like a crow. "Hey. I know. Why don't we sit in my car so I can turn on the air? You look like you're burning up, John."

I looked back at the house.

The crows were totally silent.

I felt my knees shaking.

I was so tired.

"Okay," I said.

Avery Scott wasn't sweating at all.

He probably bragged about stuff like that to his friends, too.

And I didn't want to move once I sat down, because I was certain I'd left puddles of wet on his nice black leather seats.

Scott turned the air on high. I didn't look at him. I watched the little indicator that displayed the outside temperature.

103°

When he pulled his seat belt on, I instantly thought this was it. I was trapped in a car again with some asshole who wants to fuck with me and I didn't care anymore.

I was tired, and I believed I wanted to die.

"What do you say we get something cold to drink?" Scott laughed a fake football-coach laugh. "I mean, not a cop drink. You don't drink, do you, John? Well, you don't look like a kid who'd drink. A Coke or a shake or something. You want that?"

Hell no, I don't want that. I want to be in my truck, heading to Conner's house. I want to drive by Ben and Griffin's so I can see if any of this is real. I want you to leave me the fuck alone. I want none of this to be happening.

I want to go back, but I don't know where that is anymore.

I sighed.

"Do we have to?"

"Just a drink," he said. "I'll have you back in—" He rolled his wrist over. That was stupid. There was a clock the size of a goddamned brick glowing green in the dashboard right in front of his face. "Fifteen minutes. You got somewhere you need to be?"

No, coach. Whatever you say. I'm a piece of shit.

I shook my head and looked at my hands, pressing the legs of my shorts down against my thighs.

"Great! Buckle up, son. I'm buying!"

While we drove through Glenbrook, the cop went on and on and I hardly listened to him at all. He talked about my school—the football team, naturally—and asked if I did any sports. When I told him I ran cross-country, I could tell by the way he inhaled slowly that he was waiting for me to say something else, a different sport—something where boys hurt each other—because guys like Avery Scott don't consider running to be a "sport."

I didn't look out the window when we drove down Main Street past Steckel Park, the lightpost where Conner and I tagged our initials, Java and Jazz.

I knew he was trying to observe what I paid attention to, so I kept my face forward, watching the swirls in the wood paneling on the dashboard. I wondered if it was wood or plastic.

I just thought about the swirls. Strings. Stella's Russian nesting dolls. And I reasoned that there were all these strings, layers, stacking and stacking in every unimaginable direction; that they were all going through me—*the center of the universe*—and somehow I kept jumping from thread to thread.

I was a needle on a scratched black record.

The glasses, the broken lens, just skipping from channel to fucked-up channel.

And, what Conner wrote on a wall in that other Glenbrook:

THIS WAS THE HARDEST TO GET OUT OF.

97

And this is where I am, sitting in a Cadillac with a cop who wants to ask me things about a man I killed.

This is home.

THIS WAS THE HARDEST TO GET OUT OF.

"Are you okay, John?"

"Huh?"

"I asked if the DQ was okay with you."

"Oh. DQ. Yeah. But nobody calls me John."

Scott cranked the steering wheel and pulled inside the curbs to the Dairy Queen's drive-thru. A phone began ringing. I instinctively reached for my pocket, felt the glasses there.

It was the cop's phone.

He flipped it out from his belt and looked at it.

That was the first time I'd noticed he was wearing a gun.

Why didn't I notice that before?

He looked at his phone screen.

Fake smile. "Don't do this when you drive."

He sounded like Dr. Nobody telling me to use condoms.

He pressed the END button. "Fuck 'em."

Yeah, you're cool, Detective Scott.

"So, what do they call you, then?"

"Jack. My name is Jack."

We'd already been gone past Scott's promised fifteen minutes. And I never looked at his face one time. I kept the straw in my mouth and sucked. I couldn't even taste the milk shake I ordered. It may just as well have been a cup of my own sweat.

I still hadn't cooled off.

98

Scott didn't buy anything to drink for himself. He just kept driving around. I thought he was trying to get me to relax, or he was going to try to spring something on me and shock me into saying whatever it was he was looking for.

I hated cops.

They always knew the answers to everything they were going to ask, anyway.

So out of the corner of my eye, I could see him visibly flinch like he'd been splashed with cold water when I said, "Okay, this is a nice car and everything, but I didn't think I was going to be driven around Glenbrook all fucking day."

And I just kept looking at the swirls.

Scott cleared his throat. He probably had to stop himself from calling me a piece of shit.

"Would you feel more comfortable if there was a female detective present, or maybe a doctor?"

I started to crumple the wax cup in my grip, had to stop myself.

Fuck you, Avery Scott.

"Comfortable? Why does how I feel matter?"

"Okay," he said. "Okay, Jack. So, do you want to start?"

"I don't know what the fuck you want from me."

"Tell me about that guy. Freddie Horvath. When was the first time you saw him?"

I felt myself sinking, getting smaller, needing air.

"You mean did I ever see him on the news? I never watch the news."

The car turned.

I looked up as we passed beneath the archway sign reading DOS

VIENTOS ESTATES. The new development where Freddie used to live. I started to panic.

The detective said, "No. That wasn't what I meant."

"Well, I don't know what you're talking about. I thought you said I wasn't in trouble."

I felt myself going whiter than the wax inside my empty cup.

"I promise you're not in any trouble, Jack."

"How can you promise shit like that?"

Scott didn't say anything.

And then we were there.

Freddie's house.

I'd never seen the outside of Freddie Horvath's house in the daylight, but this was it. Avery Scott pulled his Cadillac right between the brick pillars at the end of the driveway and I looked up at the window where I'd climbed out onto the tile roof before I jumped.

And now it felt like only fifteen minutes had passed since I did that, barefoot, wearing those loose drawstring pants, bleeding, dizzy from the shit Freddie drugged me with.

It was like a dream.

Before the car even stopped rolling, I was out the door, on my hands and knees, puking my guts out, warm, sour vanilla shake, steaming all over the driveway.

I wished I'd thrown up inside that asshole's Caddy.

I spit between my hands. "Take me home."

The cop hurried around the front of his car. I could tell he was looking to see if I'd gotten any puke on his shiny wheels.

"Take me the fuck home right now."

I closed my eyes and put my hands in my hair. It was so wet; it felt like I'd just stepped out from the shower. I thought about taking the glasses out of my pocket, flipping that third lens down, so

Jack could just disappear, skip over to another thread somewhere, try to find a new and improved John Wynn Whitmore IV.

I want to go home.

Avery Scott sucked in his gut and leaned against the fender of his Cadillac. He wore slip-on shoes that had tassels, and no socks. I kept my head down and spit again. I waited for him to say something. When I looked at him, he was holding a brown can of Copenhagen tobacco, pinching some of it down inside his lower lip.

Football coach.

He spit.

And I knew exactly what he was thinking; what he was waiting for me to say.

"I should have told you I get car sick when it's really hot."

"Is that it?"

I looked at him.

"Yes."

He put his tobacco in his pocket and checked the display on his cell phone.

I wished I could force myself to stand up. The sun was already burning on my neck and it hurt my knees to be down there on the concrete of Freddie's driveway. The smell of my puke was nauseating. But I wanted to stay small, keep myself away from anything out there, so I leaned over my hands and watched the foamy white vomit find its way downhill.

Scott spit again.

"You going to be okay?"

I shook my head.

"I got bottled water in the back."

I thought about the last time I'd been given a bottle of water in this driveway.

"Come on." Then I felt Scott's hand cup under my sweating armpit and he pulled me up to my feet. "You don't look good."

"I told you."

I wiped my hand across my mouth, my face. Little bits of sand gritted into my skin. I could see a yellow paper that had been posted, taped, on the front door of Freddie's house. Some kind of notice. A warning. And Scott watched my eyes when I looked at the door.

"You ever been here before?"

"No."

The cop spit again.

"Strange," he said.

"Will you take me home now?"

"I told you, you're not in any trouble, Jack. It's not about you."

He tried to sound nice, compassionate. I wanted to punch him.

"I don't know anything about this place."

"Okay. Get in. I'll take you home."

That was it.

He didn't say anything else to me the entire way back to Wynn and Stella's.

I felt empty and sick, cornered.

When Scott parked his Cadillac in the stretching shade behind my truck, he put a business card from the San Luis Obispo County Sheriff's Department on top of my left leg.

I covered it with my hand, slipped it into my pocket and grabbed for my keys.

"I just want to know one thing, Jack. Why were you the only one he let go?"

I didn't get away from anything.

I opened the door, got out of the car, and took a deep breath.

It felt like I was going to fall down; I willed myself not to.

And as I slammed his door shut behind me, Avery Scott said, "Call me."

eight

How did he know about me?

I wanted to call him just to ask that question.

I wanted to throw his goddamned business card out the window.

And I wanted to go back to Marbury.

"Dude. You look sick, and I'm fucking starving. What took you so long?"

Conner was sitting on the edge of his bed, shoeless, leaning his chin toward the video game on the television in front of him, when I came into his room.

He looked the same, sounded the same. And I felt so relieved seeing him, like he'd been missing for years. I could have hugged him, but I knew what he would have said if I did.

This is real, isn't it?

I pushed the door shut behind me, and Conner turned off his game. It was one of those ones where you kill an enemy army. Nice.

"I got stopped by a cop."

Conner laughed. "Shit. Did you get a ticket?"

"No. I talked him out of it."

Keep it up, Jack.

And I could feel that business card in one pocket, the glasses in the other. And here was Conner, sitting all loose and comfortable in front of me, with one of his knees bent sideways on the mattress, propping an elbow on it. All of it, pulling me in different directions, tearing me apart.

No matter what, Conner Kirk never lost his composure. He was a kid who'd only break a sweat if he wanted to. And it would look cool when he did it.

I sat down on the desk chair, swiveled, and stretched my feet out on top of his bed.

The breath I exhaled made me slump down, deflate, relax. I was safe here.

It felt better just being in his room, smelling that Conner Kirk smell that made me know this was real. This was home.

Right?

"You okay?" Conner turned around on the bed and faced me. And I found myself staring at him, looking to see if there was some indication that things really weren't okay. I couldn't shake the idea that something was different about Conner.

"Uh. Yeah. Sorry about the weird phone call, dude."

"You were, like, on another planet."

"Yeah." I could tell he really didn't know anything about it— Marbury, Griffin, Ben. "Let's go get something to eat, Con."

"Dude. Jack." Conner got one of those wide grins. "You reek. How long since you saw some deodorant?"

I don't know, Con. Gee . . . Last time I took a shower was at Quinn Cahill's firehouse. For all I know, that could have been a year ago.

"Sorry."

"Jeez." Conner let out a sigh and launched himself up from his bed. "I seriously don't know how you'd ever make it through a day without me looking out for you. Here."

Conner began pulling out clean clothes for me to wear. His stuff was always nicer, more expensive than mine. Not that I couldn't have whatever I wanted. I guess I just never cared about price tags and labels.

He threw his clothes into my lap and pointed at the ice-block wall separating his room from his own personal bathroom. "Get in there. Rinse off. Wake up. Snap the fuck out of it, Jack. You have three minutes and then I'm going to come in and drag you naked into the street if you don't get your shit together. Now. Come on."

I'd kept those glasses and the cop's card twisted up inside my dirty clothes. Conner was right. He was always right. I smelled like a locker room. Worse. I threw my clothes behind the seat in my truck, but stood there, looking at them for just a moment.

Wondering.

Conner and I had identical trucks. Things were like that with us. We'd known each other and been best friends since we were babies, and nothing would ever change those things. Or, at least, that's what I hoped.

But ever since I broke that lens in Ben and Griffin's garage, things had been changed, moved around, and that was scarier than anything I had ever seen since my whole fucked-up journey started, back on the night of Conner's end-of-school party.

He drove.

I sat.

And I couldn't help but look back, one time, to see if maybe there was a black Cadillac following us, or maybe if we had Freddie Horvath's body tied up in the bed of Conner's truck.

I hadn't gotten away from anything.

We didn't have to say the first word about where we were going. We always ate at the same places: Chinese food if we went to the mall, or Uncle Herb's, a twenty-four-hour pancake diner, if we didn't. And we weren't going to the mall.

"Dude. Turn right up here," I said.

Conner glanced at me, shrugged. "Why?"

"I want to go by this place where some kids I know live."

"You don't know anyone that I don't know. And this is the crack-head part of town." He laughed.

But Conner turned at the corner. We drove around the park. I looked up at the Little League light stanchion, saw our initials. "You remember when we climbed up there, Con?"

"Huh? Oh. Yeah." Then he sounded a little perturbed, but it was just Conner. "You *are* tripping out on some shit today, aren't you Jack? That doctor really did pop you some pills, didn't he?"

I tried to laugh.

"Okay. Where am I going now?" he said.

"Here. This street. Forest Trail."

Forest Trail Lane was a cul-de-sac of older homes that had been built twenty years ago. This was the only neighborhood in Glenbrook that had apartment buildings, too, and every kid in town knew that if you wanted weed or meth, you could find it here.

"Go slow."

"Dude. What the fuck?"

Conner looked at me like he thought I was trying to score a rock or something. I lowered the window and put my arm out.

"Please, Con. Just go slow."

Ben and Griffin's house was at the end of the cul-de-sac; nice, tile roof, a gate on the side leading around to an old *L*-shaped swimming pool. I swam in it with them. So did Conner.

Just the way it was supposed to be.

Their station wagon was parked in the driveway. The back door on the driver's side stood open and Griffin's mom bent inside it, looping plastic Walmart bags onto her fingers.

"Stop here."

Conner put on the brake. We sat in the middle of the turn and I watched Mrs. Goodrich as she closed the door on her car.

"You never been here before?" I said.

"You're scaring me, Jack."

I waved my arm. "Excuse me! Mrs. G?"

And Mrs. Goodrich turned and looked right at me.

Let me tell you something. You know how sometimes you'll run into a person—at the mall, waiting in line for movie tickets, stuff like that—and you *know* you recognize the person? But then, when you make eye contact, you can plainly see that you're a complete stranger to them. That's exactly how Mrs. Goodrich looked at me. And there was no reason for it. Of course she knew who I was. She had to. I'd been over to that house plenty of times. I could tell you every detail about what was inside it.

She almost seemed angered, frightened, like she thought Conner and I were just a couple of punks who were screwing with her, or maybe we were going to rob her. She pushed the car door shut with a knee and turned toward her house, swinging her bags, ignoring me.

"Whoa." Conner laughed. "Ladies' man. What the fuck was that all about?"

I slumped down into the seat, put the window up.

I sighed. "I don't know. Nothing."

———

This is real.

I am sitting here in the front seat of my best friend's car in the town I grew up in.

This is all real.

And nobody knows anything about me.

We hardly say another word on the way to the diner. Conner asks what that was all about again and I lie to him and say it was only a bad joke. I say the names again.

Ben.

Griffin.

My friend thinks I'm insane.

I want to ask him about the lens, the garage. I want to tell him about the glasses I left in my clothes, but I am afraid.

I am afraid of what Conner will think of me.

This is real.

Welcome home, Jack.

"You're staring at me."

"Huh?"

"You keep staring at me, Jack. It's creeping me out."

Conner never ate syrup on his pancakes. He liked to roll them up and eat them with his hands. There were things I could always count on, always wanted to count on. But sometimes things slipped away and then came back as something else, too.

I felt myself turning red, getting ready for another one of Conner's Dude-you-are-so-gay jokes.

"Sorry."

"Well, quit it."

But I couldn't. I saw something in his eyes. Something that wasn't the same as before. So he kicked my foot under the table.

"There are these things that have been happening to me, Con. It's real. I thought I had it figured out, I mean, how it happens. So you have to believe me. I can prove it."

I drew circles with my fork in the syrup on my plate. Circles inside of circles; a line cutting through all of them.

Conner shifted in the booth across from me. "This is like a fucking horror movie."

I took a deep breath.

He looked around, guiltily, like he wanted to be certain nobody was listening to him and his crazy friend. The kids who killed someone. "Okay. So tell me."

"That woman getting out of the car on Forest Trail. Her name is Ellen Goodrich. She has two sons named Ben and Griffin. You could probably check in a phone book or something. I know who they are."

"And she knows you, right?"

I didn't say anything.

Of course she didn't know who I was.

Nobody did.

"So let me tell you what I think," Conner began. I eyed him over my cup of black coffee. How anyone could drink Coke with pancakes and eggs was beyond me, even if it was evening in Glenbrook.

If this was Glenbrook.

"Okay. I want to know what you think, Con."

He watched me lift a forkful of pancakes into my mouth.

"I have a feeling you were thinking about talking to that doctor.

Weren't you? Really talking to him, about that Freddie guy and what we did to him. Then you couldn't do it. You couldn't talk about it. That's what I think."

I swallowed. Picked up my coffee. "So?"

"So, then you started tripping out on all this other stuff. This nonsense about things we never did and people you don't even know. A lens thing, these kids, whoever. That lady you scared over in Cracktown. Just to get in the way of what you need to do."

"What do I need to do, Con?"

He always made everything so simple. That was Conner.

He crossed his fork and knife on top of his empty plate. "I figure you only have two options: You either forget about it and move on, we take off for England in a few days and it's done; or we go tell someone, Jack. But you got to get it over with, once and for all."

"That's it?"

"Yeah." Conner smiled and kicked my shin under the table. "Was I right?"

Conner's always right.

This isn't Conner.

I left him in Marbury, and he's trying to find me.

I was scared.

I looked my best friend straight in the eyes. "This isn't you, Conner."

Conner looked shocked, tried to laugh. "What the fuck is wrong with you, Jack?"

I pulled out my wallet, left a twenty on the table, stuck inside the ring of sweat made by Conner's Coke glass.

The center of the universe.

"You remember Blackpool?"

110

Conner shrugged. "What about it?"

"You remember having a fight?"

"Did I kick your ass?" He laughed.

"I'm not joking, Conner. Do you remember when we got into a fight on the beach?"

Conner shook his head. "Over what?"

"Nothing. Never mind. You're right, Conner. You're right. Let's forget about it."

I stood up and started to make my way out of the diner.

Conner followed. "What're you doing? Will you cool it?"

I didn't want to look at him. I pushed for the door, almost knocked down one of those cheap wooden stands with free Glenbrook real estate magazines in it. And Conner stayed right on my heels all the way out into the parking lot.

The sky was gray.

It looked like Marbury, but the sun had just finally dropped below the mountains to the west and a white-hot sliver of moon hung in the thick furnace of evening.

Marbury: (noun) Third planet in order from the sun. No natural satellites. This planet, as the only in the Solar System which is inhabited by humans.

I think, standing there at the front of Conner's identical-to-mine truck, facing away from him, at that moment I realized that I was totally alone.

There's nobody home, Jack.

It was like being dead, or standing in the center of an endless cemetery.

THIS WAS THE HARDEST TO GET OUT OF.

I was done.

So I made a list in my head—first, second, third—the things Jack would do; the last things Jack would ever do.

Fuck this place.

I needed to get out.

"I'm sorry, Con," I said. "I think I better go home. Maybe I need to sleep or something."

Conner opened his door and started the truck.

"I don't want you to do anything weird, Jack. Maybe you should just spend the night at my place."

I got in.

"Oh. I'd never do anything weird."

That made Conner laugh.

That was good.

I had to get away.

nine

It wasn't completely dark yet when I left Conner's house.

I promised I'd bring his clothes back in the morning, and he joked that I didn't need to bother returning them—because seeing them on me, he realized how gay they looked.

Before I drove away, I shook my head and rubbed my eyes. I felt like everything I ever knew was gone. I was just so tired.

I believed it was the last time I'd ever see my best friend.

But it wasn't Conner.

———

I left my truck in the lot at Steckel Park and then I found the bench—the same one where I'd passed out the night Freddie Horvath took me and drugged me. I thought it was the same bench, but I couldn't be absolutely certain.

I couldn't be sure anything was the same anymore.

I knew what I was going to do. I had that cop's business card in my hand. I was just trying to will myself to hit the SEND button on my phone. I'd already punched in the numbers, after I'd double-checked to be sure there was no contact listing for Ben or Griffin— like I'd almost convinced myself that I was just fucked up, that my friends would appear again out of nowhere, and everything would simply go back to being the way it was all supposed to be.

I'd talk to him and then I'd leave. I just needed to know one thing, and then Jack could pop out of this Glenbrook and not come back. And I didn't care where I ended up.

The glasses were wrapped up in my stinking clothes, sitting under the seat in my truck.

And I thought, *Maybe I just need to go find a dictionary, so I can see what words have been wiped out of this universe.*

I swallowed, gritted my teeth.

SEND

"Avery Scott."

"It's Jack Whitmore."

There was a pause. Maybe five seconds. And I heard him switch the phone in his hands, like he was putting it down so he could write something. Maybe he had to switch off the remote from the football game or the porn he was watching.

"Don't put me on a speakerphone," I said.

Another pause.

Things being moved again.

"Okay. You're not. You want to talk? I can come to you. Where are you?"

"What's wrong with doing it like this?" I said.

"If that's what you want."

"Okay." I snapped my face to the side. The lights overhead in the park flickered on and a moth nearly flew into my mouth. "I just want to ask you how you know about me."

"Look, Jack. I really think we should talk. Why don't I come there, wherever you are?"

And I wondered if maybe he had some way of pinpointing where I was calling from.

"I don't want to do that."

"Nobody's going to know anything about you. Is that what you're scared of? The newspapers, the TV, they'll never know your name or see your face. I just want to find out if you're okay, kid. I need to know more about that guy. For the other kids. You know, their families. That's all. I promise."

It was the second promise Avery Scott made to me that day.

"What can you tell me?"

"I can show you what I got, Jack. What I got about you."

He was lying.

There was nothing.

He couldn't have anything about me.

My heart was pounding so hard I could feel it in my throat.

"Jack?"

"What?"

"Where are you?"

I don't know where this is.

"The park."

"Five minutes."

END

Avery Scott sits beside me and hands a flat yellow envelope to me.

I can tell the envelope has never been opened; the edges are sharp and it smells like an office supply store.

He asks if I'd like to grab some coffee.

Or something.

The closest place is Java and Jazz, and I can hear the music.

Or maybe I only think I do, but I tell him no.

I'm not going to let him take me on any more fifteen-minute rides.

I flip the envelope in my hands, open the shining flap. My fingertip tacks across the adhesive. I can smell the glue, and it seems to say, *Put me in your mouth.*

Inside, there are papers. Stacked. Some are wrinkled.

"He had this remote file server," Scott says. "Do you know what that is?"

He thinks I am stupid.

Fuck you.

"It took a while to track it down. He was very organized. Different folders for every one of . . . you kids. All kinds of information. Medical stuff—weight, blood type, blood pressure, temperature."

The cop watches me. My face.

The top sheet is a color scan of my driver's license.

Jack is smiling. His hair is down in one eye. A sixteen-year-old kid who nothing ever happened to.

The next two are color photos of me.

Jack is lying on that bed.

115

The top picture shows the kid from the chest up. No shirt.

The eyes are closed, but you can see glistening slits where they aren't completely shut. His mouth is open. He looks like a dead kid.

The picture on the next page is taken from the foot of the bed. The kid is lying there on his back, one arm flopped out, dangling over the sides of the mattress, the other hand resting on his belly. And one of Jack's feet is bent up inside his opposite knee, making a figure 4. Passed out. This was before Freddie put that cable around the kid's ankle. There is nothing tying Jack down. He just looks dead.

It looks like a cheap amateur porn shot, maybe taken with a cell phone or a twenty-dollar webcam. Jack's lying there naked.

I look at the cop, wonder if he's getting some kind of kick watching me.

In that moment, everything is there. I can smell the inside of that room, the cigarettes Freddie smoked. I can feel the precise points on my skin where he pressed the stun gun, the cutting of the wire around my ankle, where his hands touched me, where the needle went into my thigh on that last night. And I remember how the shit he injected me with made my mouth dry and left a taste like nail polish.

It's funny how you remember stuff sometimes.

The last page has two pictures on it. They are small, cropped, and blurry.

Two more dead-looking kids.

One of them is Ben Miller. The other is Griffin Goodrich.

I turn the page over. I can't look at it.

This can't be real.

This isn't Glenbrook.

It isn't them.

My mouth is dry; I try to swallow and I slide the papers back inside the envelope.

Bye, Jack.

"You know those kids?"

"Fuck you. Fuck this shit. It isn't happening."

I started hyperventilating. It felt like the entire Cadillac was inside some kind of trash compactor, closing in, pressing down on me. I tried grabbing for the handle of the door. I missed, closed my hand on empty air, like when I felt Griffin's arm vanish in my grip.

I don't know how long we sat there. It was so quiet, and I found myself staring at the glint of light reflected on the dashboard. Fake wood. This wasn't real. That's all there was to it.

I needed to get out of here, before it sucked me in forever.

I realized he smelled like booze. When I called him, he must have been drinking.

"I think I know those kids."

"They were from here," the cop said. "Did he show you pictures of them or something? Films?"

"I don't know. I know them. Ben and Griffin."

"Okay."

"Where are they?"

Scott shrugged, like I shouldn't have to ask these things. And he delivered his answer like a tired fry cook handing over some change and a greasy sack of fast food.

"They were found inside a barrel in Freddie Horvath's garage. Their bodies were there for maybe four months."

That's a lie.

This can't be real.

"You want to come with me, to my office?"

"Not tonight."

"Okay."

"That's it? You're a cop and you're just going to say 'okay'? Okay, Jack. Everything's fine with me. Okay, Jack, these kids you know are inside a fucking can. Okay, Jack, see you tomorrow. Fuck you, Jack."

Jack doesn't cry.

I could tell he was waiting, listening to my breathing so he'd know when the piece of shit kid was calmed down.

"What am I going to do? Arrest you?"

"Maybe."

"For what?"

"How many other kids?"

"You were number eight, as far as we can tell. You three from Glenbrook. The others were back in Kansas City."

"Okay."

"How'd he get you?"

"I fucked up. My mistake."

I started to open the door. The interior lights came on. Outside the Cadillac, everything was black.

Scott said, "Two things, Jack."

I sat there with one foot dangling out the door. I wasn't sure if I'd be able to stand, anyway.

He said, "The date on the files, your pictures, was June twelfth. Not too long ago. They found the guy's body on Nacimiento Road, I don't know, three, four days after that."

I swallowed.

"How'd you get away? Or did he let you go?"

I stood up, leaned against his door. *I could make it,* I thought.

I could get away. I was not going to let him trap me inside that Cadillac again. But he wasn't making any effort to stop me.

"Let me go home. I'll call you tomorrow," I said.

"All right. Do that. Why didn't anyone call when you were missing, Jack?"

"You said you were only going to ask me two things."

"I did. That was number two."

He shifted in his seat. I could hear him leaning across, getting closer to where I stood. And he said, "Look at that. I guess they're doing a missile launch or something at Vandenberg."

I glanced back at him, then to the spot he was pointing at in the sky.

"You ever seen shit like that, Jack?"

"No."

This isn't happening.

There was a hole in the sky; the same green-gray slash I saw from the roof of Quinn Cahill's fortress, raining glowing dust, a waterfall of dead light.

"That's something," he said. "I never saw it go off like that."

My phone started buzzing in my pocket.

Or maybe it wasn't buzzing, I thought.

I couldn't take my eyes off the hole in the sky.

"Aren't you going to answer that?" Avery Scott was staring at me.

"Fuck 'em," I said.

I shut the door and walked away.

This is not real.

This is not real.

When I opened the door to my truck, the phone in my pocket began buzzing again, crawling around against my skin.

I have to get out of here.

I got in, slammed the door, locked it.

Conner was calling.

"Con."

"Where are you?"

He sounded sick.

"In my truck. What's up?"

"I'm here. I think I'm in my room. I'm fucking sick again."

I waited.

"What do you mean?"

Then Conner said, "Marbury."

"We fucked up."

"Big time."

I could hear him coughing, like he held the phone away from his face. Conner was throwing up.

"Did you see the sky?"

"Huh?"

"Go look at the sky."

On the other end, I could hear movement, the sound of Conner getting to his feet, a door opening, taking steps, then another door. And Conner said, "That's the same shit that was in the sky in Marbury."

"I saw it."

"I don't think we're going to get out, Jack."

"I know."

Neither did I.

ten

He was waiting for me in the dark, in front of his house.

I knew it was Conner as soon as I saw his eyes.

We hugged, and he slapped the back of my head, and I swear I thought I could almost feel him starting to cry. Maybe he was laughing. Conner would never cry over . . . what? Being lost?

He'd been in Marbury for more than a week, he said, but the rest of us weren't "there" yet, and he'd popped back here once, too, but this wasn't Glenbrook.

And it was so hard to get out.

It's what I figured.

I wondered if Ben and Griffin could be safe, wherever they were.

They're in a fucking garbage can.

Time to fill things in, replay the pictures I never thought had been taken.

Conner and I sat in my truck. Through the windshield, we watched the little light show in the sky, a pulsing ghost of a stab wound that tore through our universe.

So I went first.

I told him everything I could remember since swinging that hammer at our lens—about waking up in the garage and Ben throwing me out, the rainstorm, finding the dead people in the house where Conner had written messages for me on the wall. I told him about the black slugs, too, and all the while he nodded his head. Finally,

I told him about Quinn Cahill and how I'd stolen food from him and escaped at night when the Rangers showed up—that I was intending to bring it to Ben and Griffin, but I went home first, and next thing I knew, I was here, in another Glenbrook that wasn't Glenbrook.

But I couldn't bring myself to tell about Ben and Griffin, what Freddie had done to them.

We were not going to stay here. Not in this world. I'd already made my mind up about that, and I was pretty sure Conner had been thinking the same thing, too.

He didn't need to know about the cop.

"But I just don't get how I can wake up in that garage and you were already there for like a week or something. And Ben and Griffin haven't landed yet. Or, if they did, they're not in Marbury with us," I said. "And they aren't here, either."

"I never figured out any of this shit. One day, one second, one month." Then he said, "So, how'd you get *here?*"

I pulled the glasses out from under my seat, and Conner stared at them, his mouth hanging open.

"Damn. Those look like the same lenses from Seth."

"This little green one is what does it. When you flip it over the bigger one there, that's what brought me here." Then I thought of something. I looked at my friend. "How did *you* get here?"

Conner pressed his lips into something that wasn't a smile. I could see how he was biting the inside of his cheek. "You remember how Seth left those other lenses? Two blue . . ." He pointed at the eyepieces on the glasses in my hand.

"Yeah?"

He shifted in his seat and looked away from me. "I didn't tell you. I took one of them from your room. A long time ago."

At first, I felt myself getting mad at him. He wasn't supposed to *take* one. That wasn't how we did things.

And, as if he understood what I was thinking, Conner said, "I'm sorry. I didn't want you to get messed up again, Jack. I had it in my pocket, the day we were in the guys' garage. It must have disappeared or something when I went through. But I had that one broken piece. That's what did it. But it never worked right, and everything's been getting crazy fucked up. Maybe that's why Seth brought you to these glasses."

The light in the sky faded, then pulsed bright green again.

"It's like you can see stuff falling through that hole," I said.

"I don't know what that is," Conner said. "But I'm pretty sure we had something to do with it."

And I kept replaying in my head all those times Quinn Cahill tried telling me I'd fallen out of the sky.

"Everything's different. Before . . . when we went to Marbury, the lenses never came through. It was only us. Did you think about that, Con? Now, the broken lens is in that other Marbury, and these other lenses are here, coming through with me."

Conner shrugged and shook his head.

I said, "It makes me wonder. Maybe we're trapped. Maybe wherever the lenses are is the real world now."

Conner looked ahead. His fingers nervously tapped the armrest beside him. "I think it's all Marbury. I think *this* is Marbury, too."

"We have to get the kids out, Con. We have to get out of the hole."

He didn't say anything.

"Okay, Con. Then you tell me. What's going on there, and what do I need to do when we go back?"

123

"What if we can't get back?"

"I'm not going to think about that. But we're not staying here. We can't."

"I know."

So, maybe he did know what was going on with me, the cop, Ben and Griffin. Maybe he found his own fucked-up little rearrangements, too, and he didn't have the balls to tell me about it. And maybe my friend just didn't want to say the words, that we just might have been trapped for good this time.

Conner's Story [1]

I woke up sitting on a horse in the middle of a rainstorm.

It was the craziest shit I've ever seen.

Can you imagine? Blink. You shut your eyes inside a garage, and when you open them, you're dressed in some kind of uniform on top of a stinking horse, totally drenched, holding on to a shotgun, riding along with a group of guys no older than kids, all of us looking for something to screw, eat, or kill.

And I'm just wondering where the fuck I am, and where the fuck are you and the others?

That's what it was like.

Eventually I learned if you're going to pop into Marbury, you're better off popping in as a Ranger, rather than an Odd or something worse.

But I don't know how to tell time—what's the point of minutes and hours in Marbury? So I think I just followed along with the rest of the team—there were six of us—for a pretty long time, just shutting my mouth and trying to remember who I was.

When the rain started building up, and our horses had to walk

124

through streets that almost became rivers, the others all began taking off their boots and stripping out of their pants without getting down—riding bare assed. And I thought, *Okay, fine, I guess we're all going skinny-dipping or something,* so I followed along.

What would you do?

Crazy shit.

In Marbury, you just have to kind of wing it so you don't stick out and look like a total dickhead, or an Odd, which was worse, because who wants to pop in as some orphan kid with a target on his ass?

My strategy was to just keep my mouth shut and learn by doing. So, off with the pants and on with the new experience of my bare nutsack getting crushed into a very unpadded, old saddle that I couldn't stand up in because my legs were now an inch shorter without the boots on my feet.

Fucking Marbury.

But I found out later the reason we stripped was so we could keep a watch on each other's legs for those things that crawl up inside you from the water. Black worms as long as your lower arm. They called them *suckers.*

Those things were bad news, but they weren't interested in the horses, and apparently they didn't have a taste for Hunters, either. They only wanted human meat. Just like the Hunters.

We were always potentially on some asshole's dinner menu in Marbury.

Charlie Teague caught one on Jay Pittman.

They rode just in front of me and I about gagged when I saw the black oily thing squirming its way up Pittman's calf. But Charlie casually swung over and pinched the thing's head between the nails of his thumb and index finger, and it wriggled and spit blood in his grasp before Charlie flung it over his shoulder like he was flicking a cigarette butt out the window of a passing car.

Don't ask me how I knew the names of the Rangers on our fireteam. If I just looked at them and thought about it, the names instantly popped into my brain, like I'd known these guys all my life. Well, they weren't all guys, obviously enough now that we were waist-down naked, but that wasn't something I immediately remembered, either—who had a dick or not—especially because I was feeling so sick and scared and freaked out about what the fuck was going on.

Then I got one of the things on me. I couldn't even feel it or anything, and so I was lucky the Rangers had this kind of rhythm about switching off so that every so often a different rider would take the last position. Except for the one up front. That was our captain, Anamore Fent. A woman.

But the rider behind me swooped up and pulled the thing right off the outside of my thigh. That's when I leaned away and I really did throw up. Blood kept streaming down my leg in the rain. I guess those things had some kind of anti-clotting shit in their bites, because they could pretty much suck you inside out before climbing into your dickhole and turning you into a bug. Screw anyone who tries telling me how beautiful nature is. Come to Marbury, Nature Boys.

So I wiped my face off and said, "Thanks, brother," to the dude who saved me from turning into one of those Hunters, because the Rangers, the guys, had this way of calling ourselves *brother* all the time, and that's when I saw he was Brian Fields, from our cross-country team in Glenbrook.

I was almost stupid enough to say something, like, "Dude. Brian. What the fuck are you doing here?" But I caught myself. I knew Brian wasn't popping in and out of Marbury with us, and I'd been

126

back and forth enough times to know that's what happens—sometimes, you'll run into people you know.

Sometimes, they'll be monsters.

Sometimes, they'll even be dead.

Fucking Marbury. What can I say?

But the fifth guy in our team was an old man who kept his gun slung on his back and played a little accordion while we rode. I would say it was weird, but words like *weird* don't make any sense in a place like this. His music was constant and almost hypnotic. I didn't mind it at all, because it sounded real, like home, like where I wanted to be if I could just find my way back—and find you, and Griffin and Ben, too. He played to let everyone and everything know we were coming, and like I said, us showing up meant if you were alive you only had three possible uses as far as the Rangers were concerned.

Except for the Odds.

Rangers don't screw Odds—well, the decent ones don't—and we definitely don't eat them, and usually there wasn't any reason for killing them.

But anything else, if it moved, well . . . it was a simple multiple-choice problem and all the answers were correct.

Everyone called him Preacher, but that wasn't his name. I honestly don't think I knew his name until he said that one certain thing that kind of rang in my head—*All things have been accomplished*—and then it all began to click about the guy with the accordion and who he was, because I definitely knew his face, so it wasn't until I paid close enough attention to the name that was stenciled on his shirt that I began to put it together about him. He was the same guy, the preacher, Seth killed in Pope Valley maybe a hundred and fifty years ago.

Fucking Marbury.

So we followed Fent through what was left of Glenbrook. I knew we were going to the old train station. We passed the drive-in theatre that used to sit beside the 101. The white covering had all been peeled away from the giant screen, so it looked like a big patchwork of girders and crossbars. The Hunters had come through the night before and caught some of the Odds. I think there were about fifteen boys' bodies up on those beams. Most of them were tied there, stripped, upside down. None of them had a head. Most of them were missing arms or legs, had been gutted and castrated.

Hunters liked to eat those parts: livers, kidneys, balls.

I couldn't believe there were any Odds left at all. And the framing of the big screen vibrated and buzzed with feeding insects— harvesters so thick you'd think their combined weight could bring the entire structure down in pieces.

Jay Pittman was the first on our team to start taking trophies. He considered it psychological warfare, but he was just a sick asshole. Hunters didn't have any soul you could fuck with. Pittman tried arguing that it was magic, too. Who could say for sure? We never lost a single member of our team, even during the really bad times. Fent didn't like what he did, but Jay's collection of dried penises he cut from the Hunters unlucky enough to run into him wasn't one of the things she'd choose to fight over. So he kept them on a cord that hung from his saddle horn. Thirty-five of them, he bragged, counting the two he'd added that morning.

Charlie Teague liked the horns. They were harder than shit to break off, but he had enough of them on his string that, times it wasn't raining, they'd make a musical sound like wind chimes when we rode.

The army had broken up, at least, as far as we could tell. All that was left of it were these independent fireteams of Rangers, competing, sometimes cooperating, just so we'd stay the most important humans still standing.

That's how it was in Marbury. We had the guns.

But we were losing anyway. Every day there were fewer and fewer people, and the Odds were as good as invisible. It was a rare day when any of us would even see one of them. They didn't trust us, besides, and the ones who were still alive were pretty good at hiding and scrounging for their survival. Except for that one crazy redhead kid who kept to himself in the firehouse. I believe there were Rangers who were afraid of that kid. I didn't fuck with him, but I know that Fent made deals with him from time to time.

There were only five teams of Rangers left in this entire area, and we organized and made agreements or trades between the teams every day or so when we'd gather in the train station.

Politics.

Also, after the weather started changing, with the rains and the suckers, the main hall of the station stayed dry, elevated as it was, and it was big enough for all the fireteams to have sleeping space, and room for the other stuff we did.

Four of the fireteams were organized around women, girls really, because not one of us was past twenty years old, except for Preacher. The fifth team, their captain was taken a week earlier by the Hunters. Unlucky guys in that crew. No sex. Well, not with any girl, at least. So now there were four females left, maybe in the entire world. It didn't matter anyway. Whenever one of the captains got pregnant, she'd just bleed out.

Nothing took hold in Marbury, except for the Hunters and the bugs.

And the captains, Preacher was mostly responsible, were fooling themselves if they thought we'd be able to last much longer. Every

129

day, more and more of us were taken, eaten, or got sick from the bugs.

That's why all the Rangers were getting ready to leave, give up this region and drop back to somewhere we'd only heard rumors of. But they were nice stories, I guess.

I'll get to that.

Anamore Fent didn't say anything to me until we reached the steps at the front of the station. There was another team coming in at the same time. With the rain how it was, the place looked almost like pictures of Venice, the way the water came right up to the landing.

Maybe Venice during the plague.

I think she noticed how I watched her while we were getting dressed. I didn't care. I wasn't embarrassed, and here was this half-naked young girl standing just inches away from me. But when she did have all her clothes on, she looked almost like a boy because her hair was cut so short.

Except I remembered she was pregnant, and her belly did show that.

Nobody expected that to go much longer.

A lot of the females died that way. The rest got taken by Hunters.

She told me to get one of the privates from the other team—that was the one that was only men—to take our horses around to the platform. She told me to get this little kid named Strange to do it, and I thought that was the same name Ben and Griffin had on the shirts they wore when I first met them in Marbury, so I was hoping it was one of the guys. But it turned out he wasn't. I didn't know the kid. He had a twin brother, though, and they looked like they were maybe fourteen years old, a bit young, even for Rangers.

130

So while we got dressed on the landing, I actually looked at what I was wearing. There were three stripes on each of my sleeves, and my last name, KIRK, was stenciled on my left chest.

And when I buckled up my pants, that's when I could tell that I was holding half the broken lens in my right front pocket. The Marbury lens, from the kids' garage in Glenbrook. Crazy shit.

I wasn't about to take it out and screw around with it in front of this crew.

Who knew what kind of shit might happen?

That's when everything started to sink in, too, and I started to get more than just a little scared, wondering where everyone else ended up.

Because I figured that something big had changed. It never rained and thundered like this in Marbury before, *So maybe*, I thought, *this wasn't Marbury at all*. And maybe my friends had all ended up somewhere else, too.

So part of me wanted to bust that lens out of my pocket and see if I could find anything in it, but I was also afraid of all these other people, and just how bad we might have fucked everything up beyond our ever getting back.

"Okay, I'll take care of the horses," I said.

"Then eyes out for Preacher and Pittman inside. They're getting the food tonight," Fent said.

"Okay."

I turned to leave and she grabbed my arm and pulled me around.

"Is something wrong with you?"

"Uh. No," I said.

Anamore Fent studied my eyes, like she could see something inside there. It scared me a little.

She said, "You don't look right."

"Nothing's wrong, sweets."

I could never get away with calling her that if any of the team was around. She'd have kicked me in the balls so hard, I'd sprout a nut-sack from my throat. And she was a lot of things, but definitely not sweet, even if she did have an occasional preference for me over her other options. What can I say?

This wasn't Glenbrook, Jack.

She let go of my arm, and that was that.

Duties rotated among the groups for guard posting, but the fire-teams remained segregated during meals and sleeping.

Some of us were much better off than others; and that's just how it was. Social classes are always going to exist, as long as you have at least two people on the same fucked-up planet.

Competition.

Afterwards, Rangers would mix in the big churchlike main hall of the station, playing games, gambling, sometimes for food or equipment, guns, they'd even play for sex.

It's just how things were, and unless I was really drunk and brave, or stupid, I kept my distance from the game players. We, none of us, had had any alcohol for . . . how long? It doesn't matter, anyway. Some guys knew ways to get high by snorting a kind of black salt they could find after the rains. It wasn't actually salt, though, and I'd never put shit like that up my nose. It was actually a kind of mold, I think. I'd see guys fry their brains on that shit.

That first night was difficult, because all these memories started filling in like scrambled pictures and random snippets of sound.

I didn't say anything, I just hovered around the team, keeping a slight distance, and when the hall finally started to quiet down a little, and most of the game debts were being paid, we took our boots and shirts off and stretched out with our guns on the pew benches we'd walled into our own small areas—like five states—so we could listen to Preacher play his little accordion.

Sometimes, I thought I'd catch a glimpse of her and some of the others whispering about me. She knew I was different, but how could she tell? What could she possibly know about us? That she's just a fragment of something that might not even be real, that happens to be stuck on a wire we impaled ourselves on, like fish on a gill string?

That is, unless I am totally alone.

But I didn't even want to think about that.

eleven

Conner's Story [2]

Preacher played. It sounded sweet.

The old man was high. He snorted that shit all the time, and it made him tell the craziest stories. I don't know if the crew believed him or not, but they usually did shut up and listen to the fucker.

Brian Fields was out somewhere in the darkness of the hall settling a debt, and Fent put Charlie on watch. Even when it wasn't our turn on duty, she usually kept one of us guarding. We all preferred it that way. In the past, especially after the breakup of the army, Rangers suffered more attacks from our own than from the monsters.

Now that there were fewer than forty Rangers left, disputes over ownership weren't so likely to flare up, but with just four females to all these guys, we all watched one another with suspicion.

Jay Pittman lay on a pew across from me, and Fent took the one bridging our gap. I tried to keep my eyes away from hers and pretend I was falling asleep to Preacher's music, but she was too smart to be fooled. That's why she was still alive.

When he'd stop playing, he told his stories, ones he'd either memorized from his Bible or just made up on the spot. Nobody knew how to read. I'd maybe only seen a few books, trash, in my entire memory with the team.

Preacher coughed. He was just trying to see if we were still awake. When he unhooked the accordion from his hands, it made a dying sigh on its own as it folded down onto the floor.

He said, "God breathed demons out from his own mouth. He did this to entertain himself while the Jumping Man was up in the sky."

Pittman carried his chain of bug pricks around everywhere he went, like it was a kind of warning to the other Rangers, or some type of statement about his own masculinity, even though he was the only one of our team besides Preacher who'd never had sex even one time with the captain, at least as far as any of us knew.

"How do you remember this shit, brother? You just make it up as you go, don't you, Preacher?" Pittman said.

Preacher eyed him without answering. The bottom of his nose was black with salt and he didn't seem to care about the clear strand of snot that stretched to his upper lip. Younger guys would fight over words like that, especially if they were jealous, or hadn't screwed anything in a long time. The captain and I both knew it was just Pittman letting off steam, testing things, maybe trying to let her know he was man enough, and why didn't she ever show any interest in him?

I could have answered that.

The guy carried a string of penises around with him.

Case closed. He was a complete dipshit.

Preacher said, "It entertained our God to watch the demons pursue the Jumping Man. Everything else had been accomplished."

Somehow, that meant something to me.

I rolled over and looked at Preacher, and that's when I saw the name that was stenciled on his shirt: MARKOE.

Preacher. Uncle Teddy.

Now I remembered the name that went with the face—from everything we'd seen through Seth's eyes—his entire story about growing up in Pope Valley, and how he accidentally killed the Preacher when he caught Seth and Hannah making love.

Fucking Marbury.

What can you do about this shit?

I straightened up, so I could sit with my knees pulled in to my chest, and watched Preacher as he kept his eyes locked on Jay Pittman. Then Fent snubbed him even deeper when she got up and sat beside me on my bench.

She wasn't fooling around, either.

She cupped her hand right up between my legs and squeezed. It actually hurt, but I didn't pull away. I grunted, and she nodded her chin at a darker corner of the hall near the front entryways, where there used to be a small shop with a roll-down metal door. At one time, maybe they sold newspapers or tobacco there, but was now just a little hole Rangers used when they wanted to go have sex.

She said, "Let's go over there."

That's just how things worked.

The baby she carried was either mine or Charlie's. Preacher was the preacher, and Pittman, who joined the Rangers when he was fourteen and still looked like a little kid, carried around a string of dicks. And Brian Fields, well, he preferred guys anyway, which explained why he was off with the gamers.

Marbury. This is how things were.

No jealousy. No love. Who could care about anything that wasn't trapped right there in that very second? But you know that.

To be honest, I was curious to see if it would feel different—you know, the sex—in Marbury.

So I said, "Okay," and put my bare feet down in the dust on the cool floor. And just when I was about to stand up, a scuffle broke out behind us on one of the platforms.

Then a single gunshot blasted. It echoed so loud between the stone floor and domed ceiling of the big hall. I crouched down and grabbed my shotgun. You never know what could happen at times like this, so I kept my head below the level of the bench backs.

It could have just been two guys fighting over some game debt, but then the shouting started.

Someone screamed, "It's Charlie. He killed Charlie!"

Fent stayed back on my bench, and I thought, *Well, maybe next time.* Pittman and I ran toward the tunnel that fed off onto the old platforms.

Crazy shit like this always meant you were more likely to get shot in the head by one of your own guys. I doubted most of those were accidents, too, which is one of the reasons I didn't give Pittman shit about how he never got laid and how he was the biggest dried-up dick in Marbury.

Because he was just the kind of guy who would shoot someone on his own crew if he weren't so concerned about shit like "bad magic."

But if it was true that Charlie got killed, then that would be our fireteam's first hit, and Pittman would take it as a really bad sign for all of us.

It was like I could count on the little prick *making* something bad happen.

When I got out onto the platform where the horses were kept, a dozen or so Rangers blocked the way in front of me. It looked like four of them were holding down a thrashing and wild Odd boy while two or three others punched and kicked him.

One of them said, "Charlie caught him stealing horses. This little cocksucker shot Charlie!"

And all I could make out from the angry mass of pumping arms and kicks was some scrawny kid in the middle of it, moaning and trying to cover up his face and head under the steady rain of *whack! whack! whack!*

Charlie was lying on his side near where the horses had been tied down. The fingers of one of his hands were twisted around the barrel of his rifle, which had somehow been turned with its muzzle pressed against his face. There was a curled river of blood running outward from his forehead and a big spray of what looked like pink peanut butter spouting from the back of his head. His eyes were fixed open, dead.

Pittman carried an automatic with a collapsible stock. He looked down at Charlie Teague's body and said, "Fuck that shit," and then he swung his rifle around and pushed toward the guys who were beating on the kid.

Personally, I didn't care what Jay Pittman or anyone else wanted to do to the kid, but it was going to be Captain Fent's call, and I knew it would piss her off if she was somewhere back on the platform watching me stand there doing nothing while the rest of these kids made decisions for themselves.

"Hang on, brother."

I put my hand on Jay Pittman's chest, not pushing him, just steadying him so he'd calm down and stand back.

He did.

"Stop it!" I yelled.

The guys who were pinning down the kid didn't ease up. The others kept punching and kicking him.

He was probably dead now anyway, I thought. But I did let off one shotgun blast straight up into the sky. And that's when a few of the craziest things happened right in front of my eyes, all in the span of a few seconds.

But what's a second on Marbury, anyway?

The platform went instantly quiet. Rangers didn't fuck with me. Everyone out there was a private or two-stripe, anyway, so they knew better than to push it. But when I looked up in the direction of my gunblast, that was the first time I saw that thing—it looked like a tear right through the pale night sky, like it was bleeding dust and light down on us.

And, you know how when one guy's looking up at the sky, all dumbfaced with his mouth open, everyone else is going to look up there too? Well, the other Rangers loosened up, they saw the hole in the sky, and it pretty much shut up every thought that could have been in those dickheads' dime-sized brains.

They let go of the kid.

He wasn't moving, anyway.

But I saw he wasn't an Odd at all. He was wearing the striped shirt of a military prisoner. He had been one of us at one time, probably left out to die during the confusion of the battalion's breakup. Good chance he had the bug, the disease that turns you into one of those horned Hunters, anyway, like most prisoners.

But no matter what, he had to have done some pretty serious shit for him to end up in prison at his age, because he couldn't have been any older than sixteen or so.

I pushed through the guys so I could see whether or not the prisoner was still alive. He was facedown with his arms wrapped around his head on either side. I don't know if that strategy did him any good, though, because there was a gash in his scalp and a puddle of blood oozing out into the dust beneath his face.

So I rolled him over.

And I stood over him, looking face-to-bloody-face with my best friend, Jack Whitmore.

You.

Fucking Marbury.

What could I say?

"Fuck. It's . . . just a kid," I stuttered, because I really didn't know what I could possibly say to make anything better for you.

Who *wasn't* just a kid, anyway?

We were all just kids.

So you opened your eyes, but I didn't think you could see me. A bubble of bloody snot popped beneath one of your nostrils.

To be honest, I wanted to shake you and hug you. It was Jack. I finally found Jack. I felt like I should pick you up and carry you out of there. After all, it was you, right?

Jack.

And I wasn't alone anymore.

I put one hand on the side of your face and shook your shoulder with the other. I saw the inmate number that was stitched into your shirt: 373.

Nobody kept prisoners anymore. They had all been executed during the chaos. Some escaped. But, dude, you looked so skinny and starved, and felt so bony under my hands that I figured maybe you just now got out of wherever they'd been keeping you locked up.

I leaned closer to your face. "Hey."

Then I caught glimpse of Jay Pittman's rifle barrel pointing down at your forehead.

And Pittman said, "You getting all queer on the kid, Kirk?"

I bit my lip.

Pittman was testing me in front of other guys, and there was no way I could back down. So I grabbed the barrel of Jay's rifle, and as I stood, I pushed the butt of it into his midsection, hard, driving him backwards to the edge of the platform. He struggled against me, but backwards was no strategy against forwards, and in two lunging steps I pushed Jay Pittman over the edge; and he went out flat, flapping his arms as he splashed down into the deep rainwater that had pooled over the useless train tracks in the storm.

"Son of a bitch!" he yelped, gasping and thrashing around for his dropped rifle, frantically trying to launch himself back onto the safety of the platform. A couple of the guys who'd been previously occupied beating the shit out of my friend helped him up, and Pittman began crazily stripping out of his clothes with all the passion of a man who'd been set on fire.

He must have had about ten of those black suckers on him, all over his body. He looked like he was growing snakes or something. Pittman slapped and swatted at them, cursing.

He should have known better than to fuck with me. I didn't have to say another word about it. Pittman whimpered and shook, covered in stripes of his own watery blood, as the others helped pick the parasites from his bleach-white skin.

And that's how I found Jack Whitmore in Marbury.

You.

Only it wasn't really you.

Fucking Marbury.

We liked to think that our crew was a cut above the others.

We were good fighters, still knew where food could be found, and in spite of Jay Pittman's testosterone-fueled idiocy, we were the smartest, too. Fent believed that when all the other teams had gone, been run off or killed, we'd still be survivors. And maybe it was Preacher's nonsense that bled into our skulls about things working out in the world, these being what he called the glory days and all, but every one of us bought into that empty optimism, too.

Even in Marbury, you have to believe in something, I guess.

Charlie being dead was a bad thing, though. And standing where I was, and seeing how Charlie had fallen, I couldn't believe that you, scrawny Jack Whitmore, had anything to do with it at all.

Wrong place, wrong time.

If they ever made coins in Marbury, those words would be etched where you'd expect the "In God We Trust," or whatever.

Wrong place, wrong time.

Some of the guys were obviously mad at me, not just for what I did to Jay Pittman, but because I didn't point my shotgun at you. I could never point a gun at you, no matter what you were, no matter where we were. I saw the dirty looks they gave me when I put your arm around my shoulders and helped you stand.

I grumbled to the Rangers, "Get out of the way. I'm taking him to Fent."

And as they parted a pathway along the platform toward the main hall, I whispered, "Jack. Jack Whitmore. Don't you know who I am?"

But you didn't say a thing. You just kind of hung there like dead weight, bleeding on my bare skin and feet. I'd never had the chance to put on a shirt or my boots once the shooting happened.

When I got far enough away, Jay Pittman began shouting about how fucked up I was. That was okay. He was probably right, and guys are going to blow off steam when they need to. He had no way of knowing who you were to me, anyway, so I pretended like it didn't matter. Otherwise, he'd have gone for another swim. A longer one.

"Hey. It's me, Conner Kirk," I whispered.

You kept your head down, dripping little dots of blood from your broken nose.

But just when we stumbled past what was left of some kind of ticket booth at the end of the platform, you looked up. At first I thought you were going to say something to me, like, *Hey Con, thanks for saving my ass.*

But you still wouldn't talk.

The weirdest thing was that when you did lift your face up, one of the guys from another fireteam—a guy named Walpole—looked at you, straight on. And for a second, I swear I saw something reflected in the other Ranger's eyes. Something that looked just exactly like those first few times I caught a glimpse of all the shit swirling around inside the Marbury lens, back when you and I spent time together in the hotel in London.

It seemed so foggy, and so long ago.

And then the Ranger who was staring at you went completely white, just like all the blood had been sucked out of him. I'd seen enough corpses in that condition to know what that color looks like, and this was it.

———

The guy points a finger at you.

I say, "Back off, dipshit."

And Walpole says, "That's him. That's him. That's the Jumping Man."

And I'm thinking, this is crazier than shit.

The guy's got to be high, wacked-out on black salt.

"Shut your fucking mouth." I try to push past him and hope he's not going to start something and draw too much attention to us.

But this is Marbury, the land of *wrong place, wrong time.*

So this Walpole guy spins around and disappears behind the other Rangers that have all started coming over to see what the hell is going on.

And not three seconds later, there's another gunshot and everyone crouches, or starts running after the guy.

"We need to get the fuck out of here," I whisper.

But where could we go?

You didn't even seem to register what was going on. Your mouth hung open, dripping red, and your head lolled around like you were asleep on my shoulder.

I was pretty sure one of your teeth had gotten knocked out, too.

You were fucked up, Jack.

As I got away from the platforms and into the tunnel to the main hall, I caught sight of Pittman, hitching up his soaking pants, dragging everything else he'd been wearing behind him or slung over his shoulder, dripping and cussing, trying to catch up to us. There were still trails of watery blood streaking Pittman's skin.

To my right, a group of Rangers gathered around Private Walpole.

He was down on his back, staring blankly up at the stone archway of the tunnel's ceiling.

Walpole had shot himself clean through his own neck.

The front of his throat was an epaulet of meat hanging over his left shoulder.

I truly had never seen so much blood in my life. I had to practically jump over it, barefoot as I was, but you just drag-stepped your boots through it, leaving smeared footprints behind to mark our trail into the main hall.

"What was he screaming about?" someone said as we passed.

I ignored the Rangers. They were scared about what was going on.

And scared was dangerous.

Pittman caught up to us. "What the fuck, brother? What the fuck?"

"I don't know what that's about, Pittman. I really don't."

"A prisoner?"

Fent looked pissed when I got back to our little fort of pews tucked against the wall where a huge DEPARTURES AND ARRIVALS board kept a frozen record of the last trips through this one forgotten station in this fucked-up world.

Brian Fields had come back from his cruising. He looked tired and his clothes were half undone. I was sure Fent had already given him shit about that, but what was she going to do? This was Marbury, and guys were going to do whatever guys were going to do until it killed them.

Or maybe until they killed themselves.

"I guess he was a prisoner once," I said.

"Where's Pittman? And Teague?"

Jay Pittman sloshed his clothes and rifle over the back of the pew to answer her roll call.

Fent glanced at him, then back at me, and the corner of her mouth turned up just a bit.

She liked it when I beat the shit out of our penis collector.

No one had to explain anything.

Pittman sat down, fuming.

"Charlie Teague shot himself," I said. "Then another guy, Walpole, from Three, shot himself, too. I don't know what the fuck's going on."

I watched Preacher. He sat there on the floor, rocking in his glassy-eyed delirium and staring at you like he was ready for an attack or something.

I helped you onto a bench, then lifted your feet up so you could lie down. You were in bad shape.

"That's not how I saw it," Jay Pittman said.

Leave it to the dickhead to try and start shit with me again.

"They were screaming that this prisoner shot Charlie," Pittman explained. "They were all over the kid by the time we got there, and Kirk made them stop. Otherwise, he'd be dead by now, instead of here, taking up space where Charlie Teague should be resting."

Fent watched me while Pittman told his story. She was obviously trying to see whether I'd give any sign that Pittman might be lying. But I had to look away. She knew something was wrong, different. I could tell.

That's when you moaned and rolled onto your side.

Preacher studied you, like a bug under a magnifying glass.

Brian Fields was half asleep. He didn't care what was going on. I could tell he was worn out and stoned on black salt. Fucking idiot.

"You saw how Teague was holding his rifle. There's no way the kid could do that to him, brother. Charlie shot himself."

"Oh yeah?" Pittman said. He was still half naked, unfolding his gear over the back rest on his bench. There was no way it would be dry again by morning.

"The prisoner's bad magic. I'll tell you what, Walpole shot himself in the fucking throat after he looked the kid in the face. And I heard what he said before he did it, too."

"You're full of shit, Pittman."

Preacher sat up.

Fent took a step between us. She knew I was getting ready to hit Jay Pittman again.

"What did he say?" she asked.

"He called him 'Jumping Man.' Just exactly like Preacher was talking about. Jumping Man."

Then you opened your eyes and sat up. Preacher crawled across the floor and kneeled in front of you, staring into your glazed eyes.

And Captain Fent looked from me to Pittman to you.

"Bad magic," Pittman repeated.

I took a step toward him and Fent stopped me.

"He doesn't need to be talking crazy shit like that," I said. "That's the last thing we need right now."

Pittman stood up straight, like he scored some points with Preacher and the captain. "And there's something strange overhead in the sky all of a sudden, too."

Preacher pushed our prisoner's chin up with the edge of his finger, but you snapped your head away from the man.

It wasn't you; it wasn't Jack.

I could tell you weren't really here—in Marbury—yet.

146

Preacher said, "What's in the sky?"

"Looks like it's raining light," Pittman said. "Like a fucking hole or something."

Preacher got up from the floor, shaking his head. "I can't see nothing in that boy. Let's take a look at that thing in the sky."

"So I take it you don't feel like shooting yourself, Preacher?" I said.

I hardly ever said anything to Preacher, Markoe, Uncle Teddy, whoever the fuck he was.

Preacher didn't react. He had this blank, old-guy look on his face, the kind of look you get from math teachers who think you're laughing at them when their backs are turned.

What did I care? He was fucked up out of his mind, anyway.

Fent spun around and slapped the top of Brian Fields's head to wake him up.

Brian bolted, glaring. "Fuck!"

"I need you to keep watch on the prisoner," Fent said. "Stay awake. If he does anything, shoot him in the head."

Then she started off toward the front entrance. Pittman, Preacher, and I followed her. It was what we were supposed to do, and she didn't have to say it.

There was one less guy in our team now, and one less in Team 3, too.

And we were going to have to deal with this prisoner kid—you, Jack.

Or, at least, I'd have to.

I kept thinking about that as I followed Anamore outside to the front of the station.

I glanced back once to make sure that you were still there on the bench where I'd left you.

Most of the others were already assembled on the steps. They stayed huddled around their captains like drone bees on receptive queens. Except for the all-male squad; they were lost and hopeless. They tried to separate and mix in with the other fireteams so not to be noticed.

And people speculated, too, about what the thing in the sky was—if it had any significance. Pittman, shirtless, only shook his stupid head, muttering something about bad magic.

I wanted to hit him, but Fent would castrate me if I made our team look undisciplined in front of the others.

Even Preacher was reluctant to theorize on the hole in the sky. I was relieved for that, because I had the feeling that all these coincidences were going to pile up on me and you.

Preacher said, "I don't know what it is, to be sure. It's possible that it could be nothing. Just an anomaly."

"It's the breath of God," Pittman said. "Like you said, Preacher."

I clenched a fist. I wanted to punch that fucker so bad I shook.

Then Fent looked straight at me and said, "The water's gone down. When it's dry enough to walk, take the prisoner out and shoot him."

That was how she gave orders, especially when she was nervous about something. And I could tell she was getting close to being scared.

"Fine," I said. "One less human being in the fucked-up world."

I lifted my shotgun and chambered a round.

I started away from her and the others. "I'll fucking do it right now in the middle of the fucking station, so everyone can see how we take care of business."

Fent stepped in front of me. She had a look that said everything at once. She was pissed. I had gone as close to the edge as I could possibly go without falling off the planet.

She took in a long breath through her nose.

"That isn't what I told you to do." She was very calm, and her voice sounded sweet and thick. "Take him outside and shoot him. And you can do it now, Sergeant Kirk."

Her eyes locked on mine. I had to look away.

I lowered my gun and went back inside.

I hoped you had snapped out of it, that maybe you'd waken up from wherever we go when we aren't here. I was wishing you ran away from the drugged-out Fields, but you were still sitting there on the pew, exactly where I left you.

"Fuck this shit."

I slammed my gun down against the bench. Brian Fields jumped, startled from his empty-eyed staring at you.

"Your fucking fly's unbuttoned, asshole," I said.

Fields didn't move.

I picked up my shirt and put it on. I was so mad, shaking, I could barely steady my hands enough to tuck it in.

Of course Fent would want me in proper uniform when I took my best friend outside to blow his fucking head off.

Marbury.

The other three had just made it back to our team's little departures lounge when I finished buckling my gun belt. I picked up my shotgun. My brain raced. I knew I wasn't going to do what she ordered, and I was trying to calculate which of my options would keep my ass alive the longest.

149

It wasn't looking too good.

And it got worse when that dickface Pittman said, "I'd like to go with him, Captain."

Fuck that.

"I'd rather do it alone."

I didn't look at them. I checked the breech on my gun and made certain the clip was filled to capacity. I slung the gun over my right shoulder. If I was going to die for you, Jack, they'd remember us.

"Go with him, Pittman."

And Jay Pittman would be the first asshole to die.

I said, "Don't forget to bring your dicks."

I put my hand under your armpit and lifted you to your feet. You felt cold and small, Jack, and you wavered on your feet, but you were coming back around.

You knew what we were being sent outside to do. You had to know. Well, whoever you were, Jack, because you sure weren't Jack Whitmore from the cross-country team at Glenbrook High School.

So I pulled you along, not so much as glancing at Fent—and to think, maybe just an hour ago she wanted to take me away to some dirty fucking alcove and have a screw.

Fuck that.

I said, "Come on, kid."

And Pittman hurriedly attempted to get his wet uniform on correctly so he could tag along for the fun.

I had to think.

I was so mad I wanted to scream.

I practically dragged you over the stairs at the front of the station. Sorry, Jack. Halfway down, you stumbled, but I squeezed your armpit so hard you kept on your feet. You kind of yelped a little, too. It hurt. But you still didn't say a single word.

Pittman kept one step behind us.

"What did you do to end up here, Three-Seven-Three?" I said.

"Deserter," you said. "I deserted."

It was your voice.

Jack.

You lunged forward over the last two steps. Pittman gouged your lower back with the barrel of his rifle.

"Get off him, Pittman. I'll shove that gun down your fucking throat."

Pittman eased off.

I needed to get as far away from the station as possible, but the morning hadn't come yet. There would be Hunters out.

Pittman knew it; I thought he seemed a little bit scared. Maybe he was suspicious about me leading you both so far out.

Fuck him.

I kept a tight grip on your arm, but it wasn't like you were trying to get away. You just stumbled along, Jack, and we walked through the already-drying dust, kicking up chalky clouds with our feet.

I shook you, like I was mad at you. And I was. Why the fuck did you get me into this shit? Sorry, Jack. I just wanted you to snap out of it and show something on your face that meant you knew me, you remembered how close we were.

"Do you know who I am?"

You looked at me. You had a purple bruise under your left eye and a grape-sized bump on your cheekbone. Both of your nostrils were crusted around with dried black blood.

"Am I supposed to?"

"Mind the gap, Jack."

Your brows twitched. For just a second, you seemed to register something.

"Isn't this far enough?" Pittman said.

We stopped in front of an ancient strip of shops. Every one of them had been smashed open, with no glass at all remaining in the blackened storefronts. The roof had caved in.

I kicked one of those old swirled-glass Pepsi bottles. A vending machine lay on its side, with thick black power cables trailing like a bruised umbilical cord back toward one of the shattered storefronts.

The thing in the sky hadn't changed. It hovered overhead like a rip in a sail. It almost fluttered as the dripping flow of light dusted down from the gash through the sky.

You started breathing hard.

I thought you knew you were about to die.

It made me feel like shit, Jack, because you weren't going anywhere without me.

"Sit here," I said. I put you down on the side of the vending machine.

You were shaking pretty bad. I wanted to hug you and tell you it was going to be okay.

Pittman stood away, holding his rifle across his waist.

I glanced back at him. It was the only time I'd looked at that asshole since I led you out of the station. Seeing him with his string of penises around his neck made me feel better about my decision to kill him.

"Don't move," I told you. Then, keeping my back to Jay Pittman so he wouldn't see my mouth, I whispered, "Keep your eyes on me, Jack. Remember this: My name is Conner Kirk. If this doesn't work, there is an old man who lives in a house on Tamarind Street who helps Odds. Tamarind Street. Remember that. Look at me, Jack."

Then I backed away from you until I was standing just behind

Pittman. I imagined blowing a hole in his guts big enough to play basketball. I pictured Jay Pittman, covered with writhing, clicking harvesters. I could almost hear the sound they'd make chewing into his flesh. I dreamed he might be alive while it happened, so I could hear how he would wail and cry.

I put my hand down inside my pocket and found the Marbury lens.

There were only two plans I had in my head: First, I hoped that the lens might get you and me out of this. If it did, then I could only imagine that it wouldn't matter what Pittman did to us, because you and I would be somewhere else, and no place in the universe could possibly be worse than the spot we were in. If that didn't work, then Pittman was going to die, and the Rangers would have to hunt me down.

And I knew what they did to Rangers who killed our own.

But nothing worked out the way I thought it would. That's how it goes in Marbury, anyway.

Pittman said, "What the hell are you waiting for, Kirk?"

I kept my eyes on yours. "Look at me!"

I pulled the broken lens from my pocket and raised it between us.

The shit that happened next made everything else in Marbury seem like a birthday party with balloon animals.

I went blind. It seemed like as soon as I'd lifted the lens to the height of my chest, there was a flash of deep red light that burned a negative impression of everything around me into my eyes. Then my hand went higher, like some magnetic pull tugged the lens upward.

I could faintly hear Jay Pittman, as he stood in front of me.

He was saying, "What the fuck? What the fuck?"

But I could only make out his silhouette in the blaze of red; and his voice sounded so far away, like a freight train was passing between us.

And when my hand rose higher than my head, the broken edge of the lens lined up perfectly, matching like a puzzle piece with the gash in the sky.

Everything went black.

Jay Pittman began screaming. It was insane shit. He sounded like someone who'd been set on fire. His screaming went on and on, so loud and terrifying. I'd never heard anyone who sounded like that.

He began firing his rifle, and I felt certain he was going to shoot me. Round after round fired off. I could hear the bullets whizzing past me, inches from my face at times, and Pittman's cries began to weaken.

I closed my hand around the lens.

The sky went pale gray again.

I could see.

The hole in the sky closed up, and then opened again, like a mouth, as soon as I tucked the broken lens back inside my pants.

"Fuck that shit."

I rubbed my eyes, and tried to blink away the stain of red that made everything seem to blur and vanish.

It felt like all the air had been sucked from my lungs, and I gasped, struggling to clear my head and make sense of where I was.

You were gone.

Vanished.

The vending machine where you'd been sitting lay there in the dust.

The sky was getting lighter; morning was coming.

And, in front of my feet, Jay Pittman twitched and burbled small painful whimpers. He had shot himself through the side of his jaw. It looked like his head, from his nose down, was lying near the front of one of the strip-mall storefronts, ten feet away, and he had flung his rifle down behind us.

Jay Pittman was still breathing.

But he was black with the glossy shells of quivering harvesters.

They were eating him alive.

Just like I wished for.

Fucking Marbury.

twelve

I had the glasses in my lap. I didn't realize how long I'd been sitting there, listening to Conner's story. I was wet with sweat all over, and I never even once thought to put the windows down.

We had to find the others; had to fix things once and for all.

Fuck that cop.

Sitting with Conner in my truck, we stared at the rip in the sky.

The sun was coming up in the east; the night paled ahead of us.

"This isn't Glenbrook," I said.

Conner yawned and rubbed his face. "I don't think it is, either, dude."

"But that other place is a different Marbury."

"I don't think it's different," Conner said. "I think it's maybe a different *time*."

"What happened after I left?"

"To you? I have no idea. What you told me, about Ben kicking you out of his house, and you finding the old man's place on Tamarind."

"No," I said. "What happened to you, Con?"

"You must have been hiding out for a while," he said. "I didn't get to the old man's for a couple days, and he was alive then, when I wrote that shit on his wall."

"Did you see a little kid there?"

"The old man was always helping Odds, like I said. The Rangers didn't bother him. They thought he was crazy, running around naked, all tatted up like he was, from here down."

Conner held his hands flat, like he was showing the depth of a swimming pool, just below his rib cage. "But I didn't know what to do. I was too scared to go back to the station after what happened—what I did—to Jay Pittman, even if he was a dick. I kept thinking about what he said about 'bad magic,' and how that Preacher—Uncle Teddy, I swear it—had been talking about this Jumping Man crap, and he seemed especially freaked out about all the stuff that started happening as soon as you showed up."

"But you said it wasn't me."

"It *wasn't* you, Jack. I could tell. But I don't know. Somehow, the insane shit started tuning in when you and I showed up together. Things started getting all fucking crazy. So, after I sat there and watched Pittman die, I decided I wasn't going to go back."

"Where did you go?"

"You need to remember this, when we go back, Jack. It's what needs to happen so we can put things back together."

Conner was scaring me.

"Okay, Con. What do I need to do?"

"I know where you can get some horses. There's lots of them being kept by the Rangers at the ag school, and there's not enough of us to keep an eye on them. You'll have to get some horses. You need to take Ben and Griffin and get out of there. Go southeast. Go before everything runs out and falls apart. Everyone's going to die, Jack. There's too many Hunters now. You know where you're going. I don't need to tell you. The settlement. I'm going there, too. We will find each other. We can put things back the way they're supposed to be, and then maybe we'll be done with this shit and we won't fuck with it anymore."

Sure we won't, Conner.

"I think I know what you're saying, Con."

"I keep thinking how we need to put the pieces of the lens back together," he said.

We sat there for a few minutes, not talking, until it was light enough to see.

The thing in the sky had faded to just a ripple in the dusty blue of morning.

Conner cleared his throat and shifted. "It's really hot in here, Jack. Let's put down the windows."

I started the engine, lowered our windows, and turned on the air.

"We should go somewhere else to do this, Con. Let's not do it on the street here."

"I was thinking that, too."

We drove south on the 101.

We headed for the two-lane pass that led out to the ocean, toward Cambria. Along the way, the side of the highway was clogged in some spots with cars and motor homes filled with people who'd brought out their telescopes or cameras to wonder at the thing in the sky.

Most of them had pale and weary expressions of panic on their faces, like they were witnessing the end of the world, or maybe an alien invasion.

When I thought about it, I supposed they were right on both counts.

Conner and I were not from here, and this world was never going to be seen again.

We passed a rest area that was completely filled with motorists. Some of the cars there looked like they'd been packed up with household belongings.

"Look at that shit," Conner said. "What do you think they're doing?"

"I don't know, dude. Maybe they're scared."

"Of a fucking Christmas-tree light in the sky? I could show them some shit."

"Yeah. We both could."

I pull the truck off the highway and follow a lightning-bolt string of rusted barbed wire along a single-track path of wheel ruts cut into the drying summer grass.

The roof scrapes beneath the clawed fingers of low-hanging oak branches.

Another Jack would worry about scratching his paint.

At least there is shade here.

Conner doesn't say anything. He doesn't need to.

We've done all this before, and it always feels the same: We are standing on a cliff, looking down into deep black water, daring each other to jump first, watching.

Watching while your best friend falls and falls.

I get out of the truck, leave my door open, and a bell keeps ringing to say that I've left my key in the ignition.

Ding. Ding. Ding.

Conner gets out and we walk farther into the woods.

"I hope nobody ever finds us," I say.

"This place doesn't exist, anyway," Conner answers.

Ding. Ding.

I have the glasses in my right hand.

It feels like being at the front of the line, waiting to get onto the next roller coaster car that stops.

"It exists. But we don't belong here."

"We fucked up worlds, Jack."

I think about the thing in the sky, the jagged edge of the Marbury lens.

What can I say?

Conner grabs my shoulder and I stop. "How far do you plan on walking, dude?"

Ding. Ding. Ding.

"I don't know."

"Look. Let's try to remember what I said, okay?"

"Okay."

"I will find you, Jack."

"Okay."

"And, Jack? If something happens. I mean, if, let's say, we end up with one of us in hell and one of us in the Bahamas . . ."

Conner smiles.

I say, "Fuck that."
Then Conner hugs me and puts his face right up against my ear.
He backs off.
I raise the glasses.
Ding. Ding. Ding.
"Bye, Con."

part three

THE
UNDERWORLD

thirteen

How much time?

A second? A year?

There were neither clocks nor calendars in Marbury. They had gone away, disappeared along with certain words.

I lay on my side, curled up on the stained and bare mattress that tilted downward in the ruins of a bedroom that was mine in some other world.

It was mine here.

I watched the window. The rain stopped; there was no dampness beneath the sill, only dust. When I moved my hand, the glasses fell from my fingertips and onto the floor.

Clack.

This is real.

How much time?

I had things to do.

Get up, Jack.

I sat up, waited for the blood to stop swirling in my head, and took stock of what I was—this Jack.

The new and improved Jack Whitmore.

I turned my hand in front of my eyes, looked at my aching palm. Still bandaged, dry like parchment paper; the wound felt tight.

How long has it been?

I was dressed in the splitting dungarees, the prison uniform I'd had on when I woke up on Ben and Griffin's garage floor. My boots were the same fraying things that showed open windows onto my filthy socks, and I wore the loose, rusty T-shirt I'd taken from Quinn Cahill. On my belt, I had my knife—Quinn's knife.

It was stupid, but I suddenly felt so lonely and isolated. I almost wished the kid was there with me.

I shook my head, put my feet down onto the floor.

I nearly stepped on a finger-scrawled SETH written in the dust on the floor between me and my broken mirror.

"Seth?"

I listened. Nothing.

I bent down and picked up my glasses. The third lens—the smaller green one—was still flipped over the large blue eyepiece. Things moved and swirled in the glass. I had to shut my eyes and feel with my thumb until I could pivot the lens away, out of place, and jam the glasses back inside their sock.

"Con?"

Nothing.

I pictured him standing there in the shade of the oak forest, listening to another Jack's truck go *ding ding ding* because the key had been left in the ignition, on another world where people had been lining up on the edges of the highway to witness some unexplainable apocalypse.

"Con?"

I had to believe he made it here, too; that he had things to do, and that everything was going to be okay now.

I had to believe that.

When I stood, I noticed two things that had changed.

Things keep changing because you fucked everything up.

The door that had smashed open when I first came into my room was now closed. The upper hinge was completely disconnected, and half the brass screw plate stuck out like a busted lip.

And Seth Mansfield was standing in the corner, watching me.

I said, "Seth."

That was all. We just stared at each other. And of all the things slightly changed, moved just a bit, between there and here—the Glenbrooks that weren't Glenbrooks and Marbury, fucking Marbury—Seth looked exactly the same: pale and scrawny, barefoot, without a shirt, his torn pants held up by some kind of braided cord, his dirty yellow hair that hung down into his eyes.

I realized how much Seth looked like me, but I knew why that was, too.

Seth Mansfield was the great-grandfather of Wynn, my own grandfather. Seth was close enough in resemblance to me that we could pass for twin brothers.

I could almost smell him. I wished I could touch him, grab his hand, make him stay here with me because I was scared and alone.

I saw the wall through him. Seth was gray, like a bad television picture, and I could see the cracks in the drywall, how the corner of my room was separating like the house was coming apart right behind him.

He took a little step toward me.

"Look at your hand, Jack."

165

I turned my bandaged palm upward. "I know."

Seth faded, disappeared entirely, and instantly he was right there in front of me. He put his face down, barely an inch above the cut that had been wrapped up by Quinn Cahill. I could feel him.

"You have to put things back, Jack."

"I know."

Seth looked directly at me. "You can't bring everyone with you, Jack. You can't just build your world the way you want it to be all the time. Things don't work out like that, you know? It has to be only you, Jack."

I swallowed. I figured Seth was telling me something I didn't want to hear or think about, and it made me angry. Things never worked out the way I fucking wanted them to.

"Okay."

"Be careful."

Then Seth put his hands around mine and vanished. I could feel something like cool water flowing into the cut on my hand, and it made me not so scared. It felt good. I closed my hand tightly, then opened it.

I unwrapped the bandage and dropped it onto the floor.

The line on my palm matched the edge of the broken lens, the rent in the sky.

"Seth?" I called out. "Seth?"

I heard something rolling down the staircase, tapping every plank on the way to the bottom landing. That was how the kid did things. Seth was gone.

It was time for me to leave, too.

I fished the broken lens out from my pocket, and then dropped it down inside the sock with the other glasses. For just a moment, I wondered what might happen if I held the Marbury lens up to the sky, if I would see the red light that Conner had described.

Jack was afraid.

I wound the sock tightly and tucked it down inside the waist of my pants.

The food and water were still sitting, wrapped in the blanket on the floor near the front door. My hand felt better, stronger.

I slung my bundle over one shoulder and left the house.

I should have stolen that kid's speargun.

In Marbury, there was nowhere to hide for long, and now I had to watch out for two different sets of enemies: Rangers and Hunters. Maybe Quinn Cahill, too, if he was mad enough about Jack stealing things from him.

One time, as I walked down between ruined rows of buildings that marked where Main Street had been, I heard the sound of horses approaching, and so took cover beneath a flat sheet of roofing plywood that lay inside the burned-out shell of a hair salon. I stayed there and watched while a group of Rangers rode past, slow and nervous.

And they weren't separated out into teams the way that Conner said, but at the front of the pack there were two girls—only two. One of them was pregnant. She was dressed mostly in black and her hair was shorter than mine.

I knew it had to be Anamore Fent, from the way Conner had described her to me, and I knew they were looking for me, too. Me and Conner.

Just behind the two captains rode the old man with his accordion. He started to play just as they passed in front of the building where I hid, and the preacher snapped his head from side to side like he sensed I was nearby.

Maybe I was just fooling myself because he scared me.

I counted as they passed me.

Twenty-eight Rangers behind the two girls at the lead.

It must have been all that remained of the five teams.

It looked like they'd packed everything they owned on their horses. They were leaving, and I knew where they would go. I hoped Conner was far enough in front of them that he would never see them again.

Maybe they would give up looking for me, too.

After they disappeared, I waited nearly an hour before crawling out from under the collapsed roof. It was getting late; I had to keep moving.

I made it back to Forest Trail Lane without running into anyone or anything else after that. At times, I'd turn around quickly, thinking that I might catch a glimpse of a Hunter sniffing the air after me, or maybe see that crazy redhead kid slinking along, smiling, aiming his speargun, waiting for me to make a stupid mistake.

In Marbury, there was nowhere to hide. If someone wanted me bad enough, I was dead meat.

First came the lightning in the late afternoon, and then the thick blobs of metallic rain that hit so hard it stung. Rainwater puddled almost immediately. I had no choice; I had to get inside.

I pounded on the small door at the side of the garage, hammering with the edge of my fist until it began to go numb.

"Ben! Griff! Please, let me in!"

In less than a minute, it was as though I'd been standing fully clothed in a shower. The gray water pooled along the side of the house, flowing into a small river that ran back beneath the wrought-iron fence and toward the pool full of junk.

A black worm snaked over the concrete slab at my feet.

I rolled the edge of my boot sole over it, cut the thing in half, and kicked it away.

I pounded on the door again.

"Ben Miller! It's me, Jack!"

Then I heard something move on the other side of the door. Someone began clearing away the barricade they built when Ben and his brother kicked me out of the garage.

I looked down. The water came up to the edge of the slab. *If they didn't let me in soon,* I thought, *I'd have to try climbing up the outside of the house.* I didn't want to fuck with those black things again.

The door cracked open.

In the sash of blank light, I could see just one of Ben Miller's eyes and the tip of the sharpened steel spear held in his grip.

He looked different. His eye was sunken in, like he'd been starving to death. It was terrible to see.

Ben seemed to be trying to focus on my face, then he looked down the length of my body.

"Jack? Is it you?"

I was torn between wanting to shove my way through the narrow crack of doorway he braced with his foot, so I could hug my friend—it really was Ben Miller; he was here now, with me in this fucked-up place—and worrying about the black worms that began writhing up through the building water.

"It's me, Ben. I've been waiting for you. I have food."

Ben swallowed and turned his face back. I could see someone move in the dimness of the garage. It was Griffin.

But he kept his spear pointed toward me. "Is it really you?"

I said, "Mind the gap, Ben. Remember? Mind the gap."

He opened the door.

As miserable as Ben Miller and Griffin Goodrich looked when I first woke up here—lost, sharing the floor of their garage with a dead soldier—they looked that much worse, weaker and sick, now. They hadn't been eating; I could tell. They didn't have any water to drink.

That was bad.

And they backed away from me, scared, when I came inside.

Once I shut the door, it was almost too dark to see anything in the garage. I smelled the decaying rot of the dead soldier lying at the bottom of the main door, and I could sense by how they backed away from me that Ben and Griffin didn't know whether I was even real or not.

Dripping on the floor, I waited for them to do something.

I put the package of things I'd stolen from Quinn Cahill down next to my feet.

The rain roared against the outside of the house.

"Thanks for letting me in."

Ben's spear was still angled in my direction.

"Where you been, Jack?" he said.

"Fuck, Ben. Where do you think I've been?"

Griffin stood beside his older brother. "You're not sick, are you? You don't have—you know—don't have the bug?"

"I'm not sick, Griff."

"Show us," Ben said.

I didn't know what he was talking about.

"What?"

"Show us you don't have a mark," Griffin said. "There was an Odd came here yesterday, looking for help. He had it. We didn't let him go. We couldn't. So, you better prove it."

Ben and Griffin had to kill a kid.

"Take everything off, Jack," Ben said. "That's how it's got to be. Then we'll know it's you."

I sighed. "Fuck it, Ben. I brought you guys food and water."

"You want to go back outside?"

"Okay, Ben. Okay."

It made me feel like I was under arrest.

Marbury was a prison, anyway. So nothing mattered.

Fuck this place.

So I did what he said. I stood there, naked, with my arms raised, turned around.

Prison.

"There. Are you satisfied I'm not one of them, Ben?"

"Sorry, Jack."

And Griffin said, "Is it really you?"

"Fuck."

I picked up my pants. They dripped metal-smelling rainwater. I wrung them out and managed to squeeze back into them without tearing them too much more than they already were. I put the sock with my glasses inside the bundle of food, and left everything else I'd been wearing on the floor of their garage.

Then Griffin pushed past Ben and grabbed me around my chest.

"I'm sorry, too, Jack," he said. "This place is really fucked up."

"I got some stuff," I said. "You need to get something in you."

I followed the boys back inside their house.

It was dark; the windows had all been covered by anything that could obscure their frames: upended furniture, mattresses that coughed tufts of stuffing from gashes, even strips of flooring that had been ripped up from the back of the kitchen, where naked joists lay exposed above nothing but dirt and trash that looked like it had been piling up there for years. And all the wall sockets and light fixtures had scorched burns around them.

Ben said, "I know you're the prisoner the Rangers came tearing through here, looking for, three days ago. They said they were after you, and they said Conner's name, and another guy, too."

"Jay Pittman."

"Yeah. That's it."

I remembered the number on my shirt.

"When did you get here?" I asked.

"That same morning, before the Rangers came." Ben stopped right there in the hallway. "I was so scared. I didn't know what the fuck was going on, Jack. I thought we were home."

"I was here once before that. You threw me out, Ben."

He knew it, too.

"Right. I . . . I'm sorry, Jack. It's just, I didn't think me and Griff were going to make it. We never thought we'd find our way back without you." Ben turned down the hallway beneath the stairs.

"Well, it wasn't you, Ben. Or Griffin. Not really." I swallowed. "And I went back to Glenbrook. But everything there is different now, too. It's all fucked up."

"Like how?" Griffin said.

Like you're dead inside a fucking trash barrel, Griff.

"It's . . . It's not real," I said. "It's not really Glenbrook."

"Well, in that case, welcome home, Jack," Ben said.

Yeah.

The boys' house was laid out the same, just as I'd expected, but it looked like it had been through an earthquake. Worse.

At the end of the hall, where it teed into Ben's and Griffin's rooms, Ben pulled back a baseboard. There was a handle there, and he lifted a hatch door that had been perfectly invisible.

I could see the top of a ladder that dropped down into the blackness beneath the house. This was new.

Or something.

"We're going down in there," Ben said.

Griffin climbed down first, and I lowered my bundle of food to him after he'd gotten a weak flame burning on some sort of candle. I followed him, and finally, Ben sealed us inside with a four-by-four post that deadbolted the hatch.

"This is *the box*," Griffin said. "This is where we spend our nights. You know. That's when the Hunters come through."

"Here," I said, opening the blanket. "I have good water."

The box was something like a bomb shelter. Griffin's dad built it at the beginning of the war. The walls were concrete, but they seeped water along the upper corners. Nothing substantial, though. At least it was safe from the worms.

That was about all there was to it, and it was aptly named.

There were two narrow sets of bunk beds against one wall, a wooden bench, and a card table that held the boys' little candle. I figured they didn't burn it too often; that today was like a birthday party or something.

A stained plastic five-gallon pail sat in one corner. I didn't need to ask what that was for.

Both the boys looked like skeletons, like the gruesome images of prisoners you'd see from ancient wars.

Ben half squatted against the ladder and watched while I unscrewed the top to the old milk jug and passed it over to Griffin.

Ben watched Griffin drink. He rubbed his eyes. I thought he was crying.

He said, "It's good—lucky—you found us, Jack. I'm sorry about your clothes. After what we seen, I was scared it wasn't really you."

"Don't worry about it, dude. We're here now. It's okay."

Griffin handed the jug to me, but I passed it over to Ben without taking a sip.

"What happened to Conner?" Griffin asked.

"I know where he is, Griff. He's going to be okay."

I heard every swallow Ben took from the water in the plastic jug, how he exhaled a sigh when he tipped it down.

"Where'd you get this?"

"Another Odd. A kid named Quinn Cahill."

"Did you have to kill him?" Griffin asked.

I shook my head. "I stole it from him. He's going to be pissed about it, but he's got plenty. Here. You guys need some food."

I began placing the things I'd taken from Quinn out onto the table. I had a can of evaporated milk, some mandarin orange sections, beans, a small ham, and at least a dozen more cans that had no labels. I figured we'd save the ones without labels until we were really desperate. Desperate enough to maybe eat dog food.

"Well, whoever he is, thanks and Merry Christmas to Quinn Cahill," Ben said.

I smiled. "Yeah. Thanks and Merry Christmas to the wack job, wherever he is right now."

Then I took out my knife and asked Griffin, "What do we eat first?"

Things were different; I knew that.

And we were all tired.

I tried to explain to them, to piece together what had happened to me and Conner, about how all our paths had crossed before any of us really knew what was going on here, but it was a difficult map to draw out from memory.

And then Griffin said, "I'm tired of all this, Jack. I want to go home. I want my mom and dad."

What could I say?

And I've always wanted my mom and dad, goddamnit. It's not my fault.

But if it wasn't my fault, then whose was it? I fucked these kids up. I never should have brought them here in the first place, and now the lens was broken, and we were trapped.

You fucked things up good this time, Jack.

As far as I knew, none of us could ever go back home.

Ben took a deep breath. He just sat there, chewing, watching me, like he was waiting to see if I could fix everything on the spot.

And I almost choked when I said, "I'm sorry."

But I couldn't look Griffin in the eye.

Ben put the tip of his finger down on the table between us and traced out a jagged line. "That kid yesterday had a mark shaped like this right here."

He put his left hand on his ribs, just below his right arm.

"You know how they get those marks on them," he said. "So I killed him, Jack. Didn't have a choice. You know, he'd just come back for us. It's dumb, 'cause I know I've killed things before here. Lots of times. But this is *me*, Jack. Me. From Glenbrook. Me in tenth grade. I don't belong here."

I looked from Griffin to Ben. I couldn't eat any more.

"What do you want me to do?"

Griffin sniffed.

I was afraid he was crying, so I kept my eyes locked on Ben's.

And he said, "It took a long time for that kid to die. A real long time. It was harder than you'd think. You know, when someone doesn't want to die. I pushed him into the pool when I was done with it."

I reached down to the floor and picked up the sock where I'd stashed the broken lens, the glasses. "Here."

I placed the lens in the center of the table. I held out my hand so I could see how the pink scar on my palm matched up to the jagged edge.

"Can you see anything in it?" I said.

The boys leaned over. Each of them put their eyes directly above the lens.

Then they both sat back in their places. They didn't have to answer. For us, the Marbury lens was dead.

That door was locked.

"I think it can be fixed, but I'm going to need to find Conner."

"How did you get back to Glenbrook?" Griffin asked.

I pulled the glasses out and placed them beside the lens.

"These. But it isn't Glenbrook," I said.

Ben picked up the glasses, peered through the lenses from both sides. "Can I try?"

He looked at Griffin and bit his lip.

I thought about it. The small green lens was flipped out of

position. They just looked like old-fashioned airman's goggles to me. But I knew what they did, too.

Ben pushed the table, startling me. "Jack. I said, could I try them?"

"What if we lose you, Ben?"

"Then Griff follows me. And you can do whatever you decide."

I couldn't stop him. I'd done too much to them, anyway.

"I can't look," I said. "When you put them on, you flip this little one on top."

"Okay."

Ben held the glasses up to his face. "Don't look, Jack."

I lowered my eyes, studied one of the holes on the left leg of my pants. It looked like a sea anemone. I wondered if such words existed here. Then I heard the sound of Ben as he put the glasses back down on the table.

"Nothing," he said. "Black. I couldn't see anything, Jack."

"Let me try," Griffin said.

But Ben covered the boy's hand. "Not if I can't go."

That was done.

I have to admit I was relieved. The biggest part of me was terrified that Ben and Griffin would both end up somewhere and I'd never find them again; that maybe, eventually, all four of us would be trapped in separate universes, and they'd each be worse than the other.

I gathered up the glasses and the broken lens and hid them away.

Ben said, "You told me what it meant, Jack. If you looked through the lens and saw nothing."

"I don't know what anything means," I said. I wanted Ben to just drop it, change the subject. But what else are you going to talk about when you're buried alive, inside a cement coffin?

"You said it means I can't go back because I'm not alive there."

"It isn't Glenbrook," I argued.

Ben was scared. He slammed his palm down onto the table. Griffin jumped. "Then where the fuck is it, Jack? How the fuck do we get back?"

"I don't know."

fourteen

I dreamed of floating in the sky, being chased by demons.

Jack is putting on a big show.

I had no idea how they could tell it was morning. Being inside the box was like being trapped in a black hole.

I woke when the wooden post Ben used to bolt shut the hatch clattered down against the floor next to my bed.

He pushed the door open with the point of his spear, and I watched with groggy eyes while he and Griffin climbed out of the hole, black shadow puppets against the monochrome Marbury gray that came seeping in from the hallway above.

I followed them. I guess every morning went just about the same for Ben and Griffin. They half ran for the garage, to the side door, and then outside the house to pee in a spot where there used to be oleanders and a lawn. Now there were just broken things, dead things.

They were still angry about what was said the night before, I could tell. Everyone was.

None of us really blamed anyone for our situation, but that didn't make us any less pissed off about the truths we aired over the kids' broken-down dinner table. We all knew it would take awhile before we could talk to one another in a normal way.

That's just how things were.

Ben didn't look at me. He didn't need to. He knew I was right behind him while he pissed out onto the ashes, splattering noisily onto an open paint can lying sideways on top of the white dial face of an Edison meter.

"You want to see that dead kid?"

I looked at the pool. There were harvesters, making their little mad tracks over the edge of the coping, out into the ashes, back into the pool, the clicking, the buzzing, eating.

Breakfast time.

"Do you want me to go look at him, Ben?"

Ben turned around and buttoned his pants. "Not really. I was just asking."

But Griffin walked over to the pool's edge and reported back, "Not too much left of him anymore."

And that was all we said, the whole long morning.

We drank the last of my stolen water and ate some orange sections and beans for breakfast. I opened the cans with my knife. I think the boys knew what I was going to ask them, but I wasn't about to be the one to initiate the talking. If they wanted to be quiet, it was okay with me.

Finally, I went out to the garage and shook out my socks and T-shirt and put them on. The boys followed, watching me.

I sat down on the stained concrete floor and slipped on my ragged boots.

"Are you going to leave?" Griffin asked.

"You can have everything that's left of the food and stuff. Sorry I didn't bring more water."

Griffin nudged Ben, like he wanted the older boy to say something. "Where are you going?"

"I told you. I'm going to find Conner. He told me where I can get a horse to ride." I tied my boots and cussed when one of the rawhide laces broke. It had already been knotted together in two other places. This was number three. I stood. "I can't stay here. I have to find him."

Griffin said, "You didn't even ask us to come."

"If I ask you to come, and things go wrong, then what are we going to say to each other? I told you both I'm sorry."

Ben cleared his throat. "I'm sorry, too, Jack. None of this is on you."

"It's all on me, Ben."

"I promise not to say anything," Griffin said. "I promise not to ever say I want to go home again. Please just let us come with you, Jack."

"It's not up to me."

And Ben said, "Come on. Let's get that shit packed up and go."

There once was a supermarket between the park and Cracktown. The kids in another Glenbrook saw it as a kind of border checkpoint where sweaty punks who looked homeless would sit and smoke cheap generic-brand cigarettes along the concrete wheelstops that marked off slotted parking spaces.

During wars, supermarkets are the first territories conquered.

I could imagine what it was like: survivors, at first in large numbers, gathering around the oasis of the store, competing with one another, fattening themselves up, being hunted, and then the water hole turning to dust.

This was real.

180

We walked, Ben carrying his spear, Griffin, who wore his shirt tied up on his head like we were crossing the Sahara, and me, with one of the kids' school backpacks that held a few salvaged belongings from their home and the last of our food.

I think just the act of getting out of their house, out of the box, made us all feel a little better, like we had some purpose, something to do rather than just wait.

Maybe we weren't mad at one another anymore.

But walking past the husk of that old supermarket was scary. The front wall had been entirely destroyed, and most of the ceiling hung down on wires and aluminum framing, uneven and jagged like some abandoned mine. It looked like something where monsters would live, in horror films or nightmares.

Or here.

The entire floor was covered in broken glass and other discarded containers. There were bones scattered everywhere—skulls, pelvises—so many of them you couldn't tell the difference between the junk that used to be for sale and the junk that used to be a person.

I couldn't help it. I imagined what it would be like to round up every kid, teacher, custodian, and security guard at our school and bring them to the market and kill them all. That's what it looked like.

All along the roof's edge, skulls had been lined up like beads on a string. Every one of them was jawless, dried; some were pale yellow, and others were an amber so rich in tone they almost looked like withered oranges. I saw the heads of children and adults, indiscriminately integrated—all fair and equal access on the roof's edge. Some had hair on them, but most had been picked clean.

In the darkest depth of the building, a glint of red flame flickered and then dropped behind a pile of rubble the size of a bulldozer.

I stopped and watched, held up my hand so the boys wouldn't move.

"What do you see?" Ben whispered.

I kept my eyes pinned on the interior of the market. "One of them. He's back there."

Ben and Griffin crouched slightly and strained to catch a glimpse of what I'd seen.

Griffin nudged my shoulder. "Where is he?"

I pointed. "Over that way. Against the back wall, I think."

"Do you think there's more?" Ben asked.

Hunters never came out alone. He knew that.

I sniffed. Sometimes you could smell them. They smelled like old piss.

"There has to be more."

"We could maybe take two of them," Ben said. "Any more than that, we should get the fuck out of here now, Jack."

And go where? I had to think, calculate the distances to our options. The ag school was maybe two hours' hike. I hadn't planned on running into any Hunters out here during the day, but now an unexpected variable had been added to my math.

I sighed.

The firehouse was about fifteen minutes from here. At a dead run, we might make it in five or six. And what if Quinn wasn't there? What if he wouldn't let us in?

I pulled out my knife, held it low, next to my thigh. "If we wait here a couple more minutes, and they don't show themselves, then we know they think they can't take us. Look at us, we're just kids."

Odds.

Griffin moved up between me and Ben. "Do you think he saw us?"

"He knows we're here," I said.

Then Ben tapped my arm with the back of his fingers. "Holy shit, Jack."

He was facing toward the west end of the building, and until he'd said anything, I didn't even notice that there were ten or more of the things who'd come around in a line, watching us, drooling, licking their teeth.

This was a hunting party, out in the day, which meant they were winning; confidently taking over this other Glenbrook. They were all males, looking for food, for something to bring back to their mates, their offspring. Meat.

More of them started coming out, climbing over the hills of trash inside the supermarket, emerging one by one.

With nothing but a skinning knife and a steel rod, we had no chance against numbers like this.

But they were taking their time. They were going to enjoy doing whatever they wanted to do to us.

In the center of their ranks, the largest male stood at the point of their phalanx. He wore human scalps, molded into a codpiece that covered his nuts. One of the scalps trailed long white hair halfway to his knees, the other, black. The hair had been twisted together, not braided, but clotted with some unimaginable concoction of paste. He was covered in thick purple splotches, and his skin glistened like he'd just pissed on himself. Tusk horns curled around his jaw from the back of his skull, and completely hairless as he was, he looked like some kind of salamander. He was missing his fingers; both hands were twisted into long, hooking claws with talons that looked like they'd been carved from obsidian. In one of them, he held the stump of a club that had been spiked with glass and fragments of bone. Even at my distance, I could see a strand of saliva dripping from his chin, leaking onto the necklace of little pink fleshy souvenirs he wore. Jay Pittman in reverse. And, like all of them, he had one black eye, one white.

The other Hunters in his party stood in the open, uncovered, completely naked. Their scalp-taking had only just started, but some of the others had adorned themselves with decorations: strands of long-dead cell phones, teeth, dried tongues; one of them even had the entire head of a dog hanging in front of his belly, strung through its ear canals on a rope that was likely made from braided intestine. Another wore a pair of women's glasses on a pearl strand around his neck. It looked like something you'd see on a matronly librarian. And every one of them carried a weapon of some kind. The flankers at either end of the line held bows, pulled tight, arrows angled inward at the three of us.

There was no perceivable way out.

We were dead.

But they all stood still, waiting for the slobbering Hunter at the center of the line to direct their game.

Time for fun.

I didn't move. "Griff, listen to me. Unzip the backpack and take the sock out. The sock with the glasses in it."

"Don't leave us, Jack!" Griffin was beginning to panic.

I whispered, "I'm not. Just do what I said."

The Hunters began creeping toward us, completely unconcerned, certain they were going to have exactly what they wanted. I could hear their mouths working, licking, teeth clattering, nearly choking on the flowing saliva of their anticipation.

I felt Griffin opening the pack.

Ben faltered. He was breathing so hard. He jerked around, turned as if to run.

There was no way we'd outrun them. Trying to run would only make them more excited, horny for us. It was pointless.

I grabbed Ben's shirt and held him steady. "Don't."

Ben couldn't catch his breath to answer. I thought he was going to pass out.

I squeezed the knife in one hand, then I let go of Ben and put my other hand out for Griffin. "Give me the lens."

There was always a peculiar weight to the Marbury lens. It wasn't from gravity; it came from something else altogether. And even though the lens was dead to me now, I could still feel the heaviness it contained when Griffin placed the fragment onto my open palm. And as soon as he did, the boy whispered a hushed "What the fuck, Jack?"

Then the world went red, as if I were looking at it through a glass of wine.

Ben turned and stared at me. His mouth hung open, and when I lifted my hand in front of us, everything began to change, dissolve before our eyes; like being back in that garage on the day I smashed the lens.

Something pulled me up, by my hand, like it was on a string.

Ben and Griffin, the Hunters, the wreckage in front of us, the endless scorched nothingness of Marbury, all of it began smearing together in the red light, melting, liquefying.

I could hear Ben repeating *Holy shit! Holy shit!* but it was almost as though my eyes had been pulled out from my head and were floating in the stagnant air above, because I clearly remember that I was looking down on the three of us, seeing us as we stood there and watched the Hunters moving in, surrounding their kill.

From above I watched, and everything became so intensely bright and clear—Marbury, but in color, like a cartoon rendering of hell.

Then came the shrieking; the pained, hissing cries of the Hunters. Some of them began circling; just standing in place, but circling around as if they were completely surrounded by the worst things they could imagine. The one with the dog's head hanging on his chest began clubbing the Hunter next to him, wildly smashing his skull, pounding and pounding even after the Hunter was clearly dead, until there was nothing recognizable left from the shoulders up.

And the archers on the flanks turned toward their own, releasing a volley of arrows. More screams and wails. Reloading, and more arrows. I could hear the sound made by their whisking fletches, by the impact of each arrowhead popping through strained flesh like an overripe plum.

In the center of the mass, the big one, their leader, began wildly clawing into his own eyes. It looked like he was suddenly growing hair, and I noticed that all the standing Hunters started tearing at one another with their hooked hands. The dark hairs got thicker, squirming, wriggling, and I could see clearly how it was the worms, the suckers, bursting out from their skulls, erupting from the taut, naked hides, from every surface of their splotched skins, until each Hunter that was still alive became a writhing and frantic clot of black maggots.

The sound was sickening—like thousands of toothless babies suckling hungrily—until every one of the Hunters fell in wriggling heaps of gore.

I closed my hand.

Everything went dark.

I don't remember hitting the ground.

fifteen

"Jack?"

I am looking up.

The sky is infected, gray, rotting. It's always like that.

"Come on, bud."

Ben is floating in the air over me, his face so close to mine I can feel the tickling exhalations from his nostrils. His hand is on the side of my head, rubbing my hair, patting me.

"Are you here? Do you know where we are?"

I say, "Fuck."

"You stopped breathing." Ben tries to smile. He looks pale, scared.

"Was I dead or something?"

"I don't know."

My voice is a distant croak. "Did you see that shit, Ben?"

"Yeah."

It's like a camera, panning back. Now I see Griffin kneeling there beside my head. His face is wet. Griffin never cries about anything. He's been crying now.

I look at him. "Don't say you want to go home, Griff, or I'll get up right now and fuck you up."

I know the kid wants to go home.

He wipes a trail of snot along the back of his wrist. "What the fuck was that, Jack?"

I cough. "Fuck."

And Griffin says, "Well, unfuck it, Jack."

I honestly can't say what happened to me.

It was pure nothingness.

Ben and Griffin told me that I'd stopped breathing and they both exhausted themselves trying to resuscitate me. They were going to give up. More than an hour had passed between the time when Griffin placed the broken lens into my palm and my eyes opened to look up at Ben, floating in the gray sky above me.

If that was what dying was like, it wasn't as terrifying as I'd convinced myself it would be.

It was complete.

My entire body felt so rested, like every joint had separated, every fiber in me unraveled entirely.

"Help me up."

They each grabbed beneath my shoulders and I sat. I drew my knees in and looked across the dirty dust at the gaping grimace of the supermarket façade.

There was blood everywhere. Strands of innards snaked through the dust in the gobs of mucus excreted by the worms.

Ben took a long, deep breath. He swallowed. "We thought you were dead."

"I didn't think anything." I braced my hands on the ground beside my hips. "Let me see if I can stand up."

It was real, all of it.

I guessed there were maybe thirty Hunters who'd come after us. They were scattered everywhere between where I stood and the front of the market. And the sound of the eating harvesters that had already swarmed over the corpses, as they picked between the leathery and dying worms, tearing, pulling, grinding, was like the crackling of a bonfire.

The smell was horrendous.

I turned away, looked at the sky. It was already getting late.

Griffin wore the book bag. One look at him was enough to say everything. The shit we saw scared them. Bad.

"The lens?" I said.

Griffin patted the pack's shoulder strap with one hand. "It's in here."

"Okay."

And when I started walking again, past the supermarket, my knees buckled and I nearly fell face forward. But the boys must have known I wasn't all there, so they caught me before I went down.

"Take it easy, Jack," Ben said.

"We need to get out of here."

I'd never seen Griffin look so scared and lost. His face was streaked with the ashy Marbury filth that muddied his tears. He said, "Maybe we should go back to the box. So you can rest. We can try again in the morning."

"We're just going to keep getting trapped there, Griff."

Ben sighed, frustrated. "What do we do? Tell us what to do."

"We're going to get horses tomorrow. The ag school might be too far for me right now. I know where we can go."

"Where?"

"The fire station."

It's the water that kills you in Marbury.

Without it, you give up, go crazy, make stupid choices, become a meal.

And the rain is poison; it brings the worms.

Fuck this place.

189

The boys knew their way. I tried pushing them to get to the station as quickly as possible. I didn't want to have to deal with any more Hunters. I knew that if Jack stopped breathing again today nobody was going to be able to spit and slobber enough life down his fucking throat to bring him back.

Welcome home, Jack.

I fell down twice, tripping over broken cinder blocks. The knees of my jeans were torn through, dotted with stinging blood.

And each time I'd fallen, the boys would rush over to me, frightened, to help me back up. They knew I was in bad shape, too.

We never said a word.

We were so thirsty.

I don't know how we kept going; why we didn't simply sit down, give up, and rest.

When we passed the little schoolyard, I looked over at the playground, the rocket-ship jungle gym. There were more bodies there. Three little Odds. Fresh, stripped, gutted, headless, hanging upside down by their feet.

I saw Griffin looking at the display. Maybe he'd known one of them, played flag football against him in PE at another school in another Glenbrook where things like grass and drinking fountains were so commonplace they became invisible.

It was almost impossible to believe that there were any kids left alive here at all.

They came out searching for water.

"Don't look at that, Griff. We're almost there."

Then I fell down again, got a mouthful of ash. It started to choke me, and I would have thrown up, but my stomach was like hardened concrete.

I stayed there on all fours, trying to spit my mouth clean, but nothing would come. My mouth felt like tree bark in a desert.

"Here." Griffin sat down, Indian-style, in the dust beside me. He swung the pack around onto his lap and opened it. He pulled out a can of sliced beets.

Who eats those things, anyway? No wonder Quinn Cahill found them.

"Let me have your knife," Griffin said. "We can drink the water out of this."

I didn't care anymore.

I handed Griffin my knife and watched while he pried two triangular holes into the top of the can. Then he handed it to me and I drank. I felt the ash in my mouth clot like a scab, but I swallowed anyway. When I spit down onto the ground, it looked like I was spitting out my own guts.

"Fuck." I wiped my mouth with the back of my arm and passed the can to Griffin.

He grimaced when he swallowed. "This tastes like piss."

Ben finished the liquid from the can of beets. "You want to eat this shit?"

I shook my head.

Ben dropped the can onto the street and we kept walking.

The rain came again.

When we got to Quinn's firehouse, we were soaked, our pants plastered against our legs. We had taken off our shirts and wore them on our heads.

The water rose slowly here; the firehouse sat on a hill, so we were safe from the worms for the time being. It was the ash everywhere on the ground that prevented the water from soaking into anything, and as soon as the rain would stop, the Marbury heat sucked the temporary seas dry, back up into the ulcerous gray sky that delivered them.

Griffin kept watching his feet while he cupped one hand under his balls.

Ben said, "If he doesn't open the door, we're going to have to bust in."

I saw Quinn's canoe sitting on the side of the station beside a post office mailbox with its gut-door pried off. There was what looked like an arm bone inside. Nothing else.

"He's got the place booby-trapped. It's dangerous. We can figure something out." I pounded my fist against the door. "Quinn! Cahill! It's me, Jack!"

We waited.

It poured.

Ben kicked the door. It made a sound like explosions inside the cavernous firehouse. If Quinn was inside, he knew we were there.

Griffin pressed up against me when the first boom of thunder erupted over our heads. Here in Marbury, it came so loud, you could feel thunderclaps echoing in the center of your guts.

"We need to get out of the rain," Griffin said.

The water inched its way toward us, higher up the slope of the hill. I could see the worms slithering at its edge, like they could smell us standing there. And for a moment, I couldn't help but picture the image of all those millions of black worms sprouting like weeds through the skin of the anguished Hunters.

I pounded a second time. "Quinn Cahill! Please!"

Another explosion of thunder. I could feel both of them—Griffin and Ben—jump at the sound.

And then, from above: "Billy? Is that you?"

The three of us looked up at the same time to see a scrawny redhead kid smiling down at us from his rooftop deck.

Quinn Cahill.

"You been a bad friend, Billy. You took from me. That just ain't right. You should have did what I told you."

Why was it that I always found myself wanting to punch him? At least the adrenaline rush of Quinn Cahill's constant pissing me off had a weird rejuvenating effect on my sorry state.

And Ben whispered, "'Billy'? Who the fuck is Billy?"

"He just fucks with people," I said. "Constantly. He's a little fucking prick."

Then I raised my voice so he would hear me. "I apologize for that, Quinn. I was afraid of the Rangers, so I ran. Please help us. We're kind of in a jam."

Quinn's head disappeared and then popped back over the edge of the building. He swung his arms into sight and pointed the bright red speargun directly at us. "What do I want with some useless Odds, Billy? You can all get on back to wherever you came from. Well, them two can. I'll allow you to stay, Billy. Just you. I like you, Billy. But them other two need to get."

I looked down, whispered, "He's fucking insane."

Griffin pressed his body flat against the door. Quinn was just posturing. There was no way he could shoot one of us from where he stood. And I didn't think he was honestly crazy enough to actually kill another kid—an Odd—anyway, but I wasn't willing to test my theory about that either.

"I can't leave them," I said. "I've known them forever."

"Okay. Well, good-bye then, Odd."

And Quinn Cahill disappeared behind the wall of cinderblock above us.

I kicked the door. "Fucking sonofabitch."

"Is he joking?" Ben seemed unable to grasp Quinn's cut-and-dry outlook on things.

Griffin stomped his foot down. I looked. With the heel of his shoe, he'd cut one of the black worms in half. "We need to get out of here."

I raised my hand to pound again, but I gave up. It was no use. To Quinn, everything was about winning, and knowing that should have made me wonder why he was always so eager and willing to keep me around. What was the gain?

"I fucking hate that guy."

What could we do? The water was rising fast. We'd all be struggling against the worms in a minute. And that was a fight we'd end up losing. Our only chance was taking Quinn's canoe—stealing from him again.

I sighed. "Fuck." Then I bent over and began untying my bootlaces. Someone was going to have to wade out after the canoe, and I couldn't expect Ben or Griffin to do it; not after all the shit I'd already put them through.

By the time I'd gotten my socks pulled off and managed to roll my pantlegs up over my calves, I already had one of those black things worming across the top of my foot, slithering up from between my toes. I pinched it, flicked it away, and daubed at the bead of watery blood left behind by its circular bite.

"Anyone else want to come with me?"

Ben and Griffin just stared at me like I was a lunatic. "This is going to be fucking fun."

I took a deep breath, and was just about to step out into the water when the firehouse door opened and the redhead stuck his face out.

And he was still pointing that speargun of his, directly at the center of my back.

"I'll shoot anyone who touches my boat, Billy. That's just how it's going to be."

I spun around, my hand clenched in a fist, ready to unload on him. "What the fuck do you want me to do, Quinn? You want to fucking stand there and watch while we get eaten alive?"

Griffin and Ben moved away from me, as near as they could get to the edge of the water. I couldn't blame them for stepping back. It was a rock and a hard place, and I'd never expect them to take a shot that I deserved. After all, it was my idea to come to the fucker's house in the first place.

Everything was my idea.

Quinn waited in the doorway and stared at me for a while. He had a hurt look on his face, like a kid who nobody wanted to play with; who got picked last for a team.

"Okay, Billy. No need using foul words. I was just seeing how you'd stand. Who you'd stick up for in the game. You know . . . yourself or your partners there. You are partners, right?"

I wanted to howl, to kick him in the teeth.

"Yes. We're partners, Quinn. That's how it is."

Then Quinn pointed the spear tip down at my foot. "Uh. You want to watch that, Odd."

Two more of the worms were on my right ankle, coming up. A third was already disappearing inside the left leg of my pants. I pulled it out through the hole in my knee, ripped it apart between my fingers. Then the other two. Both of my legs and hands were covered in blood.

I held my palms out, open to Quinn.

"What the fuck, Quinn? Come on."

Quinn lowered the speargun and swung his door open. He stood back to let us inside. Even though he was giving in to me, Quinn Cahill made it clear that he was the winner.

"I was just measuring you up, Billy. You're okay. You two part-ners got a good friend there. A real good friend!"

And Quinn patted Ben and Griffin warmly on their wet backs as they went through the door to his firehouse. I bent down and picked up my socks and boots.

Quinn said, "Now don't be tracking in any of them suckers with you, Billy! Ha-ha-ha . . ."

But as I passed him in the doorway, he put his arm around my shoulders and whispered, "It would be better if it was just you and me, Odd. You'll see. We don't need them two, Billy. Okay?"

As he led me up the stairway to his living floor, Quinn kept squeezing me tight, like how you'd hold on to someone you'd been missing for years, patting me until I finally broke down and said what he wanted to hear.

"Thank you, Quinn. You're a good friend."

And I knew then that if I ever had to kill Quinn Cahill to protect the boys, or to make certain we'd be able to get home again, I'd give it about as much thought as plucking one of those fucking worms off my nuts.

Quinn slapped my shoulder.

"I told you we'd be friends, Billy. Told you."

First he had to give my "partners" a grand tour of his palace.

Quinn pointed out the two beds, explained how the one with no sheets was "Billy's," and told Ben and Griffin his story about the ungrateful Odd who made a rope with sheets and ran away when Anamore Fent's team came by, hunting for him.

"But you two Odds can sleep down on the floor. Don't worry, I got plenty more bedding, which I intend is not going to be put to use for anything other than you two fellas sleeping on."

Griffin glanced at me and shrugged, and I tried to give him a look that said to just go along with the idiot.

"And what's your names, anyhow?" Quinn said. "If you got any names, that is."

Some Odds didn't have names, or didn't need to remember them.

"Ben."

And before Griffin could say a word, Quinn snapped, "Ben's a easy name to remember. Okay. Good enough. Ben and not-Ben."

He smiled his toothy, freckled, redhead smile at Griffin, who was now going to have to endure Quinn's permanently calling him not-Ben.

"My name is Griffin Goodrich."

"That's fine, not-Ben. You just hang on to that memory. You never know when you might have to tell it to someone who cares."

Now, I was sure, at least two of us wanted to punch him.

Then, naturally, Quinn showed the boys where to pee, and how he had his big urinal trough hooked up to a collector so he could make drinking water from piss.

"Heh-heh . . . we're going to have plenty of new drinking water, ain't we?"

And Quinn rapped his knuckles against the lower lip of his steel urinal, so it made a ringing sound like a church bell.

"Turning our pee into water. You're just like Jesus in reverse," Griffin said.

Quinn's smile vanished. His face went blank. "Who?"

"Jesus," Griffin said.

"I don't know what that is. No one never showed me nothing about making water out of my pee. I figured it out on my own. From intellectual reasoning, not-Ben."

Griffin said, "Oh. Okay, Quinn."

I think it rained harder that night than any time I could remember here.

I slipped into the shorts Quinn had given me; everything else I owned was wet or falling apart. Quinn didn't offer any dry clothes to the "partner boys," but he did provide plenty to eat and lots of drinking water.

Ben and Griffin insisted that I drink first, and they watched my face to see if I'd show any sign that it tasted like anything other than what Quinn promised it to be. Griffin must have drank more than a gallon on his own. He said he was trying to make himself pee, because he wanted to see how Quinn's still worked.

Eventually, everything had to be turned off in the night with the exception of one dim oil lamp, so we lay there, all of us just staring up at the ceiling, listening to the incessant roar of the storm against the concrete of the firehouse.

When Quinn finally lowered the mantle on the lamp and everything went black, I could tell that none of us had fallen to sleep. You know how you can hear guys breathing, moving around, flipping over, so you know they're thinking; and the thinking is what kills sleep every time.

So I said, "Do you remember anything, Quinn?"

"What are you talking about, Billy? I remember saving your hide when you were two feet underwater with a big buck Hunter strad-dling you like he was going to make you his special boy, ha-ha!"

What a prick.

I sighed. "I meant, do you remember anything from before? From the beginning of the war."

"Don't you, Billy?"

"I'm not sure."

"Well, what about your partner boys?"

"None of us do," Ben said.

I heard Quinn roll over in his bed, could feel how he was looking straight across the room at me. I wondered if the little freak could maybe somehow see in the absolute dark of the firehouse.

"I remember being about half the size of not-Ben, without even the first strand of hair on my nutsack, and how we all were living in-side a basketball gymnasium with wood floors. That is, to be honest, the first thing in my life I remember. Nothing else. I don't remember having a mommy or daddy, or nothing about no brothers or sisters. Just us Odds."

"How long was it like that?" Griffin said.

"Shit." Quinn laughed. "Did you all three fall out of the sky?"

"Something like that," I said.

"Well, not-Ben, it's been like that forever. For-fucking-ever. But then there were a lot more of us Odds. Thousands, in places like that all over the city, too. Then, most of us started getting sick. We didn't know what it was at first, but it was the bug. The Rangers came, took the sick ones. You know, just got rid of them. Who needs more Hunters, anyway? They took all the girls, too. That was . . . Shit, that was so long ago."

"Yeah. Before you had hair on your nuts," Griffin said.

"You fucking with me, not-Ben?"

"Well, it was, wasn't it?"

I realized that Griffin Goodrich had a much more stylized way of fucking with people than Quinn Cahill did.

"I suppose it was," Quinn said. I could hear how he lay back down in his bed, and his voice sounded relaxed, like he just assumed that Griffin, not-Ben, was a stupid little kid.

"How did you end up here?" Ben said.

"Well," Quinn began. He sounded like he was an actor onstage, and he had waited all his life to have an audience for the incredible epic that was his story, even if his only listeners were stupid, lost kids. "Things got bad. They ran out of food, and the Rangers stopped bringing it around, since we were only boys left in the Orphan Detention Dormitories. Did you know that's where *Odd* come from? Just boys. Odds. So, one day, this old Ranger come and he tells us to all get out and go, or else they were going to come kill us all. I don't know if he was telling the truth or not, because he got killed not two days after that. And so four of us came here to the firehouse, and we fixed the place up like this."

"What happened to the others?" Griffin said.

"Shit."

I could tell it was probably the only time Quinn Cahill didn't have that annoying smirk on his face.

"How long have you been alone?" I said.

And Griffin blurted out, "Since he had hair on his balls. Oh, wait . . . he still doesn't. Never mind."

I heard Quinn's feet slap down onto the floor, the relaxing of his cot springs as he got out of his bed.

"You fucking with me, not-Ben? You want to fuck with me? Let's see who's got balls, little shit."

Something happened. I heard Griffin grunt.

"Get the fuck off me!"

Then Ben must have gotten up. From the sound of it, he threw himself onto Quinn, and in less than a second, both boys came sliding across the floor until Quinn's head ended up banging into my knee.

"Don't you fucking touch him!" Ben said.

I slid my arm down between the boys and pushed myself off the bed, taking Ben down onto the floor. Ben would have killed Quinn in a fight. No two ways about that.

"Hey!" I pushed my face right into Ben's ear and pinned him against the jumble of twisted sheets where he and Griffin were supposed to be sleeping. "Fucking cool it! And you back the fuck off, too, Quinn! The kid was just joking around. Back the fuck off, all of you!"

For a moment, there was nothing, only blackness and the sound of the three boys panting like they'd just run a footrace. I felt around on the floor until I found Griffin's bony bare knee and gave him a little swat.

"Apologize," I whispered.

Griffin didn't attempt to keep his voice down. "That fucking pervert had his hands on my fucking balls, Jack."

"Apologize, Griff."

"Screw it. I'm going to take a piss."

And Griffin slapped his feet across the floor toward the shower room. In no time there came the echoing sound like someone was emptying a garden hose into a tin drum.

He called back, "I'm sorry, Quinn. I didn't mean to hurt your feelings."

Which was just another way for Griffin Goodrich to fuck with the kid. But for all his ingenuity at game playing and survival, I didn't believe Quinn had any idea what was going on when it came to communicating with other boys.

Quinn didn't say a word, just stepped over me and Ben and went back to his bed.

"I made this place," he said.

Griffin came back. "I filled that shit up."

Then he lay down on the floor next to his brother, and I went back to my bed.

I said, "This is a fucking palace, Quinn."

Quinn rustled around in his bed. It sounded like he threw the covers off him. It was so hot and stuffy in the firehouse, made even worse by the heavy, damp smell of four boys who'd been wrestling with one another. And finally, Quinn said, "What about you, Billy? What's the farthest back thing you remember?"

I said, "Honest?"

Quinn said, "Honest."

"Waking up on the floor of Ben and Griffin's garage, wearing a prisoner uniform. What was that, four or five days ago?"

"And you don't remember nothing else?"

I cleared my throat and rolled onto my side. There was the dribbling, metallic sound again. Ben had gone off behind us, and was peeing noisily into Quinn's trough. And I realized that it stopped raining outside.

"Well, some things my friend Conner told me about what I'd done. And you remember that cut on my hand? How you fixed it up?"

Quinn said, "Oh, yeah. That was a nasty one, Billy. How's that thing doing?"

"It's gone."

"Nuh-uh. Let me see if it is."

And Quinn raised the light and got out of his bed again.

He kneeled at the side of my cot and grabbed me by my right wrist. I opened my hand, and Quinn put his face an inch or two away from my palm, staring at the pink and jagged scar that had been left behind when Seth healed me.

"Billy, this looks exactly like that—"

"I know."

The hole in the sky.

Ben stood over us, watching. "Like what?"

"That thing in the sky," Quinn said. "It's like a picture of it, stamped right there into Billy's hand."

"What thing in the sky?" Ben asked.

I pulled my hand away, closed it. "The boys haven't seen it."

Quinn's mouth just hung open, like he couldn't believe there was anybody—any Odd—who didn't know about the hole in the sky.

He looked from Ben to me, back to Ben again, and I could see he was trying to figure out what our story was, even if we didn't know enough about ourselves to tell it.

"Well, let's go look then." Quinn nudged Griffin's butt with his foot. Griffin tried to cover his face in the dingy sheet.

"You, not-Ben—stop tugging on your little pecker or it's going to fall off. Heh-heh-heh. Let's get up on the roof—there's something you boys need to see."

And as Quinn led the way back to where his metal ladder stretched through the ceiling and onto the roof deck, Griffin pulled my shoulder down toward his face and whispered, "I want you to give me permission to kick the living shit out of that fuckstick, Jack."

I just nodded and followed the redhead.

"One of these days, Griff. I promise."

sixteen

The rain was gone; the air, thick and hot.

It felt like we were bugs, competing for air, trapped beneath an overturned cup.

The four of us stood at the edge of the roof of Quinn's firehouse, barefoot and sweating, looking at the thing above us while the pale redhead pointed it out like he owned it or something.

Quinn stared at Ben, noticeably taller and more muscular. Maybe the kid was sizing Ben up, using his "intellectual reasoning" to conclude that if I hadn't gotten between them in their fight, Ben would have inflicted some serious damage.

"You never seen that before?"

Ben shook his head. "What is it?"

"I don't know," Quinn said. "Nobody does. It looks like the end of the world, doesn't it?"

"It looks like fireworks to me," Griffin said.

"I'll tell you what it looks like, not-Ben."

Then Quinn reached over and grabbed my wrist.

He pinned my arm against the edge of the block railing, and I was surprised by how strong the kid was. It hurt. I clenched my fist.

"Show them, Billy."

"That hurts. Let the fuck go, Quinn."

I kept my hand closed tight.

"What are you scared of? Just let them see it. Prove I ain't crazy."

You are fucking insane, asshole.

I pulled my arm back, but Quinn's grip was like a vice.

Remember the last time you used a vice, Jack?

"It's not funny. Let go!"

I tried pushing him off me with my left hand. The kid didn't budge. I glanced at Ben and Griffin. Somehow, I almost got the feeling that they were curious to see the scar now, too.

"Fuck this shit," I said.

I punched Quinn square in the center of his rib cage.

It wasn't intended to hurt; I was just trying to knock him away, make him let go. But he got this crazy grimace on his face, and he began twisting and prying at my fingers.

I guess he was fed up with us, with our intrusion into his perfect world. Quinn Cahill was always trying to prove something about being in charge. After all, he was the king here. He didn't like or want company. Just me, for some reason. And whatever that reason was, it bothered me from the first moment the kid started hovering over me.

Ben put his hand on Quinn's shoulder and pulled him around. "That's enough, kid. Leave Jack alone."

I could tell that Ben was trying to restrain himself.

But Quinn nearly broke two of my fingers, so I gave up, let him have his way, and I opened my hand.

The first time Quinn showed me that thing in the sky, I knew it had something to do with me. Or, more likely, that I had something to do with it.

I felt it.

It was like a wound, a stab, an incision that somehow cuts through all the layers, stack after stack after stack, piercing all the insides and outsides that collapse down and converge at the center of Jack's universe.

And here I am now, standing with my hand open in front of Quinn Cahill's face. I accept it.

I accept the fact that I fucked up—that all of this isn't happening *to me*—it's happening *because of me*.

I knew it all along.

I knew it when I was tied to a fucking bed at Freddie Horvath's house.

But I just didn't want to think about it.

I open my hand.

The light comes first. It is always the light, and then the sound.

Of course the mark is the same. Everyone can see that.

The scar in my hand.

The hole in the sky.

The center of the universe.

The boys are saying something. I can't hear them. We are standing inside a thousand jet engines, beneath a churning wall of water that endlessly crashes upon sawtoothed rocks.

And I am looking directly through my fucking hand.

I am looking directly through.

The boys are saying something.

Quinn is screaming.

He's afraid.

Fucking prick should have left me alone.

So I am looking.

In my bathroom, at Wynn and Stella's house, a house that is in a place called Glenbrook, the mirrored door of Jack's medicine cabinet opens in such a way that I could put my head between the door and the larger mirror above the sink, where Wynn taught me how to shave before I ever needed to. And there would be an infinity of layers there, accordioned together, blurring away into dark blue nothingness ahead of me, behind me, and I am the center.

That's what this looks like now.

Only there are no mirrors, and I can see step after step, endless ladders like train tracks, each of them framing a narrow glimpse of here, another Marbury, a Glenbrook, Marbury again, the inside of a Cadillac, Marbury, that fucking cop, inside a barrel, the fucking inside of a plastic barrel and I am there, cramped among the bones of the friends I love, a dirty fucking bed where I am tied down, bleeding, Freddie Horvath's hands on me, fuck this place, fuck this place, fuck this place.

And out of the infinity that expands before me, a throng of ghosts, faceless and bleak, run toward me, step after step, in the bed, in the barrel, Marbury, another Glenbrook, the barrel again. I am tied down on top of a bed, a naked photograph of Jack where I must be asleep, so don't wake me up. This all must be inside his head. The ghosts coming and coming, out from my hand, out from my mouth, and I finally see among them a boy's face.

Seth.

I cannot breathe. I am hanging by my neck, my hands tied behind me, kicking, kicking so hard my shoes come off, my pants begin to fall off as I twist in a circle, winding and winding, a spring, facing the sun, the tall trees around me, silent in the brilliant light of afternoon.

I can smell the hangmen.

And then I see Seth in Marbury, and he is a boy—a real boy— not a ghost at all, but it is a different Marbury, and I can remember it. It was like this.

Someone is screaming and screaming.

Quinn Cahill.

I look away from the image frames.

I force myself.

Shut my eyes.

Close my hand.

Make it stop.

The door slams shut.

I hear music.

An accordion.

I didn't wake up until the following night.

Later, Ben would explain how he alone carried me tied to his back down the ladder, using rope they found in Quinn's garage. He'd wrapped it beneath my armpits, across my chest. He shrugged apologetically and showed me how the nylon cord had cut marks into the flesh around his shoulders.

They refused to leave me up on the roof, even if they did believe, at first, that Jack was dead.

Everything hurt.

It felt like my ribs had been broken.

Maybe I was dead, I thought. Nothing made sense. The last thing I remembered was breaking up the fight between Ben and Quinn, and now here I was, lying on my side on a sweat-soaked cot, staring at what looked like someone's kneecaps right in front of my face. And I swear I could hear the faint sound of accordion music coming from somewhere.

"Ben! He opened his eye. Jack's waking up!"

Griffin's voice was a rasping, urgent whisper.

"Shhh!"

I couldn't see where Ben was standing. Only knees. They looked like clay faces where all the features had been pressed down into nothing. But they were staring at me.

I couldn't focus on anything but the little gold hairs on Griffin's bony kneecaps.

I tried to say something, but my mouth wouldn't move.

Why can't you understand me, Griffin?

I am talking to you, kid, listen to me.

But I wasn't talking.

He couldn't hear me.

I shut my eyes.

"Hey! Jack?" Griffin lowered himself to the edge of the cot. He shook my shoulder and I opened my eyes again. "Can you hear me? Do you know where you are?"

That was a trick question, right?

"Um. No. What happened?"

"You fucking did it again, Jack."

I closed my eyes. "I'm thirsty, Griff."

I heard him pop open a plastic jug that sat on the floor beside my cot. And then I could see Ben, leaning against the wall, pressing an ear up to the seam where one of the windows had been sealed over and covered by a blackout curtain.

He concentrated on listening, but he watched me as I drank.

There was music, so faint. And then it stopped.

"I heard it, too," I said. "It woke me up. It's the Rangers coming."

I couldn't sit up. I spilled more water onto my bed than I got into my mouth. Griffin kept one hand on the base of the jug to steady it.

Ben moved away from the window. He looked tense, ready for a fight.

"Next time, you're going to fucking kill yourself."

What could I say?

It wasn't my fault.

Wrong, Jack. Everything was my fault.

"You mad at me, Ben?"

He exhaled and got down on the floor next to Griffin.

"Are you okay?"

I nodded. "I'll be okay. What happened?"

And I noticed that the hand I'd been using to tilt the jug of water had been wrapped up in what looked like a sock. Medical tape wound tightly around my palm and knuckles.

"What's this?"

The boys looked at each other, like they were both trying to figure out which of them had the better explanation.

Griffin took a drink and recapped the jug. "You've been knocked out since last night. I don't even need to tell you, but we thought you were dead for good this time. You remember going up on the roof?"

I kind of did. Not really.

"There was shit coming out of your hand, Jack," Ben said.

"What kind of shit?"

Griffin shrugged, shaking his head, as though he didn't know what to say.

Then I thought of something, lifted my head. It made me dizzy.

"Where's Quinn?"

"Fuck," Ben said. "There were ghosts, Jack. Hundreds of them. You know how I feel about those fucking things. They were all coming out of you, like you were setting free a swarm of bees or something, like bats from a cave, going everywhere. It freaked the shit out of that kid."

I remembered.

"Did you see that boy? The kid named Seth?"

Ben shook his head, but Griffin said, "I saw him, Jack."

"I didn't watch them. I can't," Ben said. "That fucking Quinn started screaming. Like he was looking straight into the worst nightmare you could ever have. And, next thing, he tried to jump off the fucking roof. I pulled him back and then he tried to do it again. So I punched him. I'm sorry, Jack, but I had it with that fucking kid after he put his goddamned hands on Griff, and so I beat his fucking face."

I guess I saw that coming from the beginning.

Ben swallowed, like he was trying to gather his thoughts. "Then Quinn just jumps down the ladder. That was right when you collapsed, Jack, and the ghosts were scattering everywhere. The noise was insane. And then that fucker just ran away. I looked over the side of the roof for him. I saw him come out the door and go running down the street, carrying his speargun and yelping like a fucking dog."

I took a deep breath. I thought about asking the boys to help me up, but I didn't want them to think they'd be carrying me, watching out for me like I was going to be some kind of cripple. So I gathered every bit of will I had and pushed myself up into a sitting position. I put my feet down on the floor.

My head spun so bad I was sure that I was going to pass out. Ben and Griffin were still talking to me, telling me something, but I couldn't hear anything they said over the rushing tide in my ears.

Don't fall down. Don't fall down.

I stood up, holding on to the waist of my shorts and slurring my speech like a drunkard. "The lens. Glasses. He didn't take them, did he?"

"The pack's under your bed," Griffin said.

I aimed myself for the block divider in front of the shower and took wide steps until I could catch myself on it.

It was like walking across the deck of a boat in a storm.

I heard Ben, behind me. "Jack?"

But I ignored him. I didn't want any goddamned help.

I turned the shower on and got under it. It felt so cold.

Then I was suddenly looking at the backs of my hands, how they were holding me up on either side of Quinn's floor drain, a black metal grate the size of a baseball. It looked like a planet floating between my dirty, bandaged hand and outspread fingers.

Nice.

The fucking universe.

I heard the boys come up behind me.

"I'm okay. I'm okay. Just get away from me. I'm okay."

I don't know how long I stayed there like that, on my hands and knees with the water raining down on me. Probably too long. The shower stopped by itself. The upper tank had run dry.

I shook my head.

Better.

I got up and made it back around the wall without falling down. Dripping water everywhere, I sat on the edge of my cot and began putting on my clothes. My prison clothes.

"We need to get out of here. The Rangers are coming. It's a guy named Preacher, and a girl, the captain, named Anamore Fent. They're hunting for me."

"A girl?" Griffin said.

"Get dressed. We need to go."

Ben said, "We shouldn't go out at night, Jack."

"I think I know what to do. Get your boots on. Now."

We hurried. I ran down to make sure Ben had thought to bolt the main door shut, then I locked the second door at the top of the staircase.

I told the boys to drink as much water as they could hold, to gather together as much as they thought we could carry on our backs. We found an empty canvas pack hanging from a peg on the wall by Quinn's stove. I tossed it across the room to Ben. Fuck Quinn Cahill. He took off, left us here; so we were going to claim whatever we wanted.

In ten minutes, we were ready.

Griffin carried the extra pack. We took as much as we could from Quinn's store of rations, along with most of the contents from his first aid kit, and all this we stuffed inside the backpacks. And I made certain the lenses were safe.

Jack and his habits.

In ten minutes, we were ready.

But it was already too late.

They were here.

Quinn showed me what to do when he first brought me to his firehouse. So I opened the footlocker beside the doorway and flipped the switch gates to his electric fence—what he'd called "juicy death."

Now there would be only one way out.

Down.

Into the garage by the fire pole. Then down again, into Marbury's underworld.

As soon as I flipped the switches, we heard pounding and kicking at the lower door.

Griffin's eyes went wide. "What do we do?"

"It's okay. I know a way out."

"Well, what are we waiting for, then?" Ben was rightfully impatient.

Pounding again.

"Fuck them," I said. "They'll have a surprise if they come up the stairs."

Of course, I didn't have any idea how—or if—Quinn's trap would work. But I knew we'd have enough time to get down, and I was scared of the idea of getting out that way.

Once we did that, there would be no turning back, and I remembered how Quinn told me he was afraid of going down below.

"Billy! Billy, open the goddamned door! It's me, Quinn Cahill!"

I closed my eyes and exhaled.

It was like getting punched in the stomach.

Fuck this place.

"What are you going to do?" Ben said.

Griffin pulled on my arm, snapping me out of my confusion and disgust. "Fuck him, Jack. Don't let him in. What if he's fucking with us?"

It was Quinn. Of course he was going to fuck with us.

More urgent kicking on the door.

"Billy! Don't leave me out here, you fucking ingrate!"

Fuck you, Jack.

I shook my head. I wished someone would slap me.

I sighed. "I can't leave him outside. He didn't do it to us when he could have."

"Fuck him," Griffin repeated.

But I opened the trunk, turned off Quinn's electric fence, and unbolted the door to the stairway.

If I had turned the booby trap off three seconds sooner, the Rangers outside would have killed me, and I wouldn't have known anything about it. When I was halfway down the metal stairs, there came a blast of automatic gunfire. The outer door splintered into shards and swung crookedly open as if pushed by a ghost.

There was no smoke, no smell, just the tinny sound of shell casings raining down on the concrete pathway in front of the station house and the peppering of wood fragments dusting a cloud of debris across the lower stairs.

I started to turn back, and I saw Quinn push his way in past the shattered door. He carried his red speargun, and when he saw me standing on the stairway, he had to have figured out that the path up to the firehouse was safe.

He sold me out.

I knew it as soon as I saw him. He brought the Rangers here to hand me over to them. I looked at him as he hesitated at the base of the stairs below me. I could see the guilt in his stupid fucking eyes. He didn't need the Rangers to make it back home. He owned this place. Quinn Cahill was the king of the Odds, but the Rangers must have promised him something special for turning me in.

That's what was behind his act. Following me. Promising how we'd be such good friends. It was always, only, about winning the game for Quinn Cahill.

I wondered what they gave him.

Fuck you, Quinn.

I spun around. Ben was waiting at the upper door.

Below me, the man they called Preacher appeared in the door frame behind Quinn. He carried a small shotgun in one hand, and his hat was tilted back so I could clearly see his face.

I knew everything about him. In another world, at another time, he was the man Seth Mansfield killed in a hayloft.

Quinn said something like, "That's him there."

First there was a rainlike noise that sounded like insects—a swarm of locusts hurling themselves at the doorway, clicking their shelled bodies by the thousands against the walls of the firehouse. Arrows.

The Hunters had followed.

We were trapped, and trapped again.

By the time I'd made it back to the upper floor, Quinn was two steps behind me.

I glanced back over my shoulder and saw Preacher stagger backwards into the wall. He'd been shot in the face with an arrow. It entered below his cheekbone and came out through the ear on the same side. He grunted and snapped the shaft, pulling it out through the back of his head. His blood flecked the wall behind him, but the man seemed unfazed by his wound. He pointed his gun out the door and began firing wildly.

"Get up, Billy! It's an ambush!"

Quinn panted, so close to me I could feel the heat from his body.

I went through the door, and Quinn followed me, slamming it shut as the firefight in the street erupted into full warfare.

I didn't even acknowledge Ben and Griffin. They stood there, waiting to see what I'd tell them to do. We were fucked, and now we were trapped inside the firehouse with the sonofabitch who dealt me over to the Rangers.

I slapped the speargun from Quinn's grasp. He seemed to have no idea what was going on, and as soon as his gun hit the floor, I kicked it away. The gun scooted and spun along the concrete floor toward Ben. Then I grabbed the redhead by his T-shirt, ripping it in my grasp as I lifted him above my own head and slammed the kid over and over into the door.

"What the fuck, Quinn? What did you fucking do?"

I couldn't stop myself. I started punching him.

It felt good.

216

Ben didn't say anything. He just picked up Quinn's stupid speargun and watched.

I don't know if he was more stunned by what I was doing, or from all the noise coming up from the floor below. Griffin ran to the back of the room and scrambled up the ladder to take a look from the roof.

When I stopped punching Quinn, he fell to his knees.

He didn't swing back one time; didn't even try to defend himself against me, which made me feel even more disgusted by him. The fucker didn't even know how to act like a real boy. His nose trickled blood over his lips and down to his chin. The kid was crying, trying to cover his wet and blood-streaked face with quaking hands.

If I had the time, I probably could have felt bad for him, for what I did, but Quinn Cahill had been working up to this for a long time. He had it coming.

The wrapping on my right hand was spotted with his blood.

"What the fuck was that about?" Ben seemed perfectly calm. Maybe he was just trying to keep his voice down because he was afraid of setting me off. But hearing him ask it made me madder.

I looked at Quinn, then at Ben.

I slid my knife out from its sheath and held it.

I grabbed a fistful of Quinn's red hair in my left hand and lifted his head up, forcing the kid up on his toes so he'd stretch out his freckled ivory neck.

Quinn shut his eyes, sobbing, leaking snot and blood, unable to unchoke any words.

"Remember your fucking knife, Quinn? The one you left for me at the old man's house?"

Quinn tried to turn his face, so I shook his head.

"Look at me, sonofabitch!"

Quinn opened his eyes. "I didn't—"

Ben said, "Jack."

Griffin came flying down the ladder. "Holy fuck! Holy fuck! We gotta get out of here!"

I pulled the knife back.

Quinn squealed faintly.

I plunged it forward, and missed the kid's throat by a finger's width. I slammed it into the door. It sounded like a gunshot.

"I'll fucking kill you, Quinn! Next time, I'll fucking kill you!"

I let go of his hair, pulled the knife out of the door.

Quinn curled up over his knees, heaving, pressing his face down against the floor.

seventeen

"It's a fucking slaughterhouse out there."

Griffin was frantic.

I slid my knife back into its sheath and hefted the pack over one arm.

"Are you going to tell us what that was about, Jack?" Ben said.

Griffin grabbed Ben's arm and pulled him around. "Listen! There must be five thousand of them out there. Hunters. It's a fucking massacre. There's so many, the whole sky's red from their marks."

I looked at Griffin. It finally began sinking in; what was going on outside. For a moment, it was like the only thing that mattered in my entire universe was trying to make Quinn Cahill pay me back for what he did.

Quinn looked up from the floor. He was a mess.

For all the posing and strutting he'd done since I met him, what

I saw now was a pathetic little boy, sobbing like someone stole his birthday present from him and pissed on his cake.

Ben held Quinn's gun carefully, like he wasn't sure whether or not he was supposed to give it back. I shook my head at him, and he understood.

"We're going down the pole, to the garage," I said. "There's a way out."

Quinn snorted, inhaling a big blob of snot and blood. He coughed and spit a red, puck-shaped wad of jelly onto the floor. "You have to take me with you."

I started back toward the circle where the slide pole dropped down to the garage.

"Fuck you, Quinn," I said.

Griffin picked up the pack and his brother's rebar lance. Ben followed behind, holding Quinn's speargun like he knew how to use it.

"Billy!" Quinn pleaded.

I had one hand on the slide pole.

"You boys'll all die down there. Trust me on that. There's things down there. You need me."

I looked at the boys. We didn't have time to take a vote. But I could see in their faces they were shocked at how bad I'd beaten the kid up. Maybe it was the realization of what was going on outside the firehouse that scared them.

And maybe, I thought, *they felt sorry for the pathetic little bastard.*

"This is the last time you'll ever hear me say it, Quinn. Don't fuck with me again."

———

So there we were, down in the belly of Quinn's garage with nothing more than a roll-up aluminum door between us and the bloodbath taking place just feet from where we stood. The shooting died down to just occasional bursts. But we heard grunting, moaning, the sick sound of fresh, living meat being torn apart.

Hunters and harvesters were eating.

And we gathered like hospital visitors around the open tail end of a dilapidated ambulance, staring down at a manhole cover that appeared to be coated in rust and shit.

Quinn's last-chance bomb shelter.

When we spoke, it was only whispers.

Hunters hear.

They smell, too.

Quinn sounded as though he wasn't finished crying. His voice shook; his breath was spastic.

"I want my speargun back."

Ben didn't even look at the kid. "You're not getting it, Red."

That was good, I thought. Now Ben was fucking with the kid by making up a name for him, too. We'd see how Quinn liked playing our game now that we were in charge.

"Then fuck you guys. You can figure the way out on your own."

Ben eyed the kid squarely. Without a sign that he'd think twice, Ben pushed the point of the speargun snugly between Quinn's legs.

Quinn backed away until he was up on his tiptoes, pinned between Ben and the rusting body of the ambulance.

Ben said, "You just pull this trigger. Right?"

Quinn's eyes got as big as the drain on the floor of his shower.

He swallowed. "I have some flashlights in the ambulance. You just shake them if they start running low, and it charges them."

Ben pulled the gun away. "Okay. We're waiting. Red."

Quinn reached an arm down below one of the front seats and pulled out two torches. He kept one and handed the other to me. He nodded at the roll-up door. "Don't turn your light on till we're in the Under."

The Under.

The kid had a name for that, too.

Quinn, apologetic and hurt, looked at me as though he were waiting for me to say something.

Fuck him.

Griffin had already climbed inside the back of the ambulance and was squatting, froglike, hooking two fingers through the pry hole on the heavy lid.

He grunted and strained, but the cover wouldn't move.

"That's not how you do it," Quinn said. "Move out of the way."

And I thought, *The kid knows a lot more than he's letting on.*

Quinn got down onto his knees. He pointed at the rebar spear Griffin leaned against the fender. "Give me that, not-Ben."

Griffin looked at me and then Ben, trying to see if it was okay.

He handed the bar over to the redhead.

Ben kept his eyes locked on Quinn. We all knew how easily you could kill a kid with a weapon like Ben's spear. Ben had done it himself at least twice that I knew of.

And Griffin put his face next to my ear and whispered, "Thanks for beating the shit out of that pervert, Jack."

Quinn slipped the end of the bar into the hole on the cover and levered it against the ambulance's rear gate hinge.

In a few seconds, the way down was open.

I said, "Give back my friend's rebar, Quinn."

Quinn didn't hesitate. He handed the weapon over to Griffin.

All we could see was a black hole, about two feet in diameter.

The dark below it was so complete that it almost gave off a kind of glow in the lightless garage, like it was sucking in whatever faint light was there, inhaling whatever it could from the world above. At the lip of the mouth was a crusted-over handle, the first rung of something that led down into a deep and silent nowhere.

"How far down to the bottom?" I said.

Quinn shrugged. "Far. Don't slip, Odd. It'll kill you if you fall."

"I'll go first. Then Griffin, Quinn, and Ben's going last."

Quinn said, "We need to slide the cover shut once we get in. So nothing follows."

I looked at Ben; he nodded. "I can do it, Jack."

"Okay."

I held on to my flashlight and climbed—two feet feeling their way onto each downward rung—one hand at a time, slowly, watching while the gray circle above me diminished into nothing when Griffin came down the ladder after me.

I don't know why, but I half expected it to be wet down there, but when my feet finally planted on a solid base, I could smell the dry dust kicked up into the air by my weight.

"I'm down," I said. I turned the flashlight on and swung it around, casting distorted and rare shadows out across the Marbury underworld. I thought I saw movement in the tunnel ahead of me, a flash of yellow; something cat-like and fast. Then it was gone. It must have been just a distortion from the flashlight's beam.

I was definitely too tense.

I squeezed shut my eyes and opened them again. Maybe I imagined it.

I was dizzy, breathing too hard, and it stunk down here.

Get a grip, Jack.

Something dropped, clattering next to me, striking into my shoulder.

I jumped, fumbled with the flashlight, watching dumbly as it fell into the dirt.

"Sorry, Jack. You okay?"

Griffin dropped his spear.

"Fuck, Griff! You could have killed me."

One of us was going to die down here. I knew it.

Maybe all of us.

At least Ben was able to make it down and still manage to hold on to the speargun without any more accidents, and when we were all standing together at the base of the ladder, the lights Quinn and I pointed showed every one of us a new, undiscovered hell that lived inside Marbury.

The Under.

It was at least twenty degrees cooler than up in Marbury. Cool enough that you might actually feel *cold* here if you spent too much time. And the tunnel was massive. You could pave a freeway down the center of it and have room for houses on either side. The manhole we'd climbed through was invisible now, at least sixty feet above my head, and wherever I'd look, the beam of my flashlight faded to nothing in the lightless void of the tunnel.

At one time, in a normal world, this may have been some immense flood-control channel leading to a sea. Now, here, in Marbury, Quinn's Under was a world of its own.

It was like being swallowed by a whale. And one look at the corrugated steel walls surrounding us proved that we were not the first people to ever think to hide, or maybe to get trapped, down here.

A few yards to the side of the ladder, a rounded hook had been welded to the steel wall. It was the kind of thing that was intended to be used as a guide for cables or telephone fibers. A skull was impaled on the hook, so that the dull end of it came out through the hole of the nasal cavity. A patch of scalp and some short blond hair spiked out from the left side of the skull. A few large scattered bones littered the dirt below the hook.

I wondered if any of the others were thinking what I was: What kind of thing could possibly have been tall enough to hang a body from its head, more than ten feet off the ground?

The skull couldn't be reached from the ladder, and as far as I could tell, there was no other way to get up to that hook. It was like something you'd do to save food from scavengers. Maybe it was a sign.

Nice decoration.

I lowered the light beam away from it.

I turned to Quinn. "Which way now?"

Quinn shook his head. "I told you I didn't like it down here, Billy. I never been no farther than you could throw a marble. Your guess is as good as anyone's."

I shined the light on the kids' faces. "We vote. Which way, Ben?"

"Let me see your flashlight."

Ben aimed the light down the tunnel in the direction of our only two choices, then up at the kid's skull that hung from the metal hook. "I say that way." Ben pointed. "The side with the hair on it."

"The ag school would be in that direction. If there's a way out, that's the way to go," I said. "What do you think, Griff?"

"I'm with you guys."

I looked at Quinn, then again at the other boys. "You good with that way, Quinn?"

Ben sounded agitated. "You gonna let *him* vote, Jack?"

224

"If he's going to come with us, he's going to own what he does."

"Then one thing," Ben said. "I want to know what all that was about upstairs. When you nearly killed the fucker."

I shined the light straight at the center of Quinn's chest. I wanted to see his face, and I wanted to be sure that Ben and Griffin saw him, too. Quinn's T-shirt had a shark-mouth rip beneath one arm from when I'd grabbed it and thrown him against the firehouse door. His ghastly, alabaster skin looked unnatural, like it caught the light and glowed; his nipple was an orange moon hovering in a whiteout.

"He made a deal," I said. "Quinn traded me off to the Rangers. That's why they were there; what all the shooting was about. They came to kill us, Ben. Well, they came to kill *me*. I guess they weren't expecting a surprise."

Quinn's eyes darted back and forth, between each of our faces. "I'm sorry, Billy. I didn't know they wanted to do you harm. I swear it. All I knew was they were looking for you. I'm sorry I told them I knew you."

Quinn was lying. He had to be. He knew gamesmanship better than anyone. He wouldn't do anything unless there was some object to gain. That's why he'd been tracking prisoner 373, following me; why he'd left his knife behind so I'd find it at the dead man's house, and been so prepared for his new "good friend" at the firehouse when we first paddled his fucking canoe across town.

"What'd they trade?" I said.

Quinn's eyes kept flickering. I found it hard to believe the kid could possibly be embarrassed or even put on the spot, but his face turned visibly red when I pressed him about it.

He cleared his throat—stammered. "Well, Billy. They's only two things Rangers could give me that I wanted."

"What was it?" Griffin said.

225

Quinn looked pleadingly at me. "Don't be mad, Billy. I swear to you I didn't know they wanted to hurt you."

"Sure thing, Quinn."

But I kept staring at him, so he'd know that I wanted to hear the truth about what he sold me out to the Rangers for. He took a deep breath. "They offered me a gun. Or . . ."

"Or what?"

"If I took a gun, I was sure they'd end up shooting me, Billy. You know how they are about Odds with guns. So, one of the captains . . . she . . . you know . . ."

I couldn't imagine. Well, I didn't want to. I looked at Quinn's face, and the kid really wasn't lying this time.

"She let you have sex with her?" I said.

I could almost feel the embarrassed heat coming from Quinn's pale skin. He looked down and pulled nervously at his dick.

"Fucking pervert liar. Bull. Shit." Griffin laughed.

"I'm sorry, Billy. It's just. I haven't never—"

"Shut the fuck up." I didn't know whether to laugh at Quinn—at whatever captain allowed a horny kid who looked more like a cave salamander to slime his way onto her—or punch him again. "And stop fucking calling me Billy."

"Sometimes I can't help myself, Bill—I'm sorry. Truly I am." Quinn sounded like he was going to start crying again. "It's just . . . you know . . . an Odd's rig calls the shots when it gets . . . well . . . desperate, and mine's been thinking powerful thoughts on its own lately. So I figured if they were going to shoot me anyway, I may just as well allow my pecker to—"

"He said shut up, Red." Ben started walking off, into the dark. "Nobody wants to hear about it."

And when Ben had disappeared into the black, he yelled,

226

"Dumb. Fucking. Idiot!" so loud that it echoed and rippled its way in every direction along the ribbed steel guts of the Under.

But that was Quinn Cahill.

He was definitely no more than I expected him to be, and I can't honestly say I was ever surprised by anything he ever did anyway.

We walked through the dark, following Ben.

It was reasonable for him to be in the front, and not just because he was frustrated by our situation and pissed off at Quinn. He had the weapon. There was no way Quinn would be getting the spear-gun back, or even asking for it, anytime soon.

Griffin stayed close on my right. Even though he carried Ben's spear, I could tell the kid was scared. Who wasn't?

Quinn paced himself, walking like a prisoner halfway between Ben and us.

I never knew there was such darkness anywhere in Marbury. It seemed that every step we took, as we got farther away from the hole to the firehouse, distances distorted, became greater, and time—if it even existed here in the Under—slowed down.

At least on the surface, there was some bland recognition of the passing of a colorless day into a washed-out night, but here in the Under, there was only the cool black and absolute quiet.

I'd seen films of what it looks like in the deepest trenches beneath the ocean, but this was perhaps even lonelier, and scarier, too.

We walked.

Occasionally, we would kick things embedded in the dry dirt beneath our feet: bones; several shoes—I wondered why shoes seemed to last longer than anything else—corroded soft drink cans; and an entire television set, the kind with a glass picture tube—an antique in anyone's world. Griffin uncovered a blue vinyl pouch, the type you'd use to organize roadmaps kept under the driver's seat in a car.

None of us were paying attention to his discovery. I think we were all nearly blind by concentrating our eyesight on the narrow and dim beams cast forward from our flashlights.

"Fucking sick," he said.

I stopped, shined my light on him. "What?"

"There's a dried-up kid's hand inside this thing. Look." Griffin turned the pouch over and something that looked like a large gray spider fell out onto the ground at his feet.

My stomach turned.

"But I think this is a map, Jack." He carefully pulled out a yellowed clump of folded paper, pinching it between two fingers like it was poisonous.

"Let's see that."

Ben and Quinn stopped, maybe fifty feet down the tunnel ahead of us. When Quinn swung his light around in our direction, the thing that had fallen from the plastic pouch—the hand—took off, skittering across the top of Griffin's foot, away into the darkness. I tried keeping my light on it—whatever it was—but it was too fast.

Griffin screamed and kicked wildly at the air. "Fuck! Shit!"

He looked like he was dancing, and the paper he'd been holding fluttered away into the nothingness.

"I don't think that was a hand, Griff."

"What the fuck was that?"

I could see Ben's silhouette in the light cast by Quinn's torch. He was walking back toward me and Griffin. "You guys okay?" he called.

"Griff picked up something that was alive. It ran off."

"What was it?"

"Shit!" Griffin said, backing away from his spot. "It was fucking disgusting, Ben."

Ben looked at me. "Harvester?"

I shook my head. "We thought it was a kid's hand. It looked like a hand. I don't know what it was."

"Welcome to the fucking Nature Channel," Ben said. "Hope whatever it was doesn't eat boy meat."

He had to say it. I was certain at that moment we all were thinking about that kid's skull hanging on the hook we passed.

"But there was a map or something in there, too," I said. "Griff flung it over there. Help me look for it."

I began scanning the ground with my light.

Click. Click. Click. Click.

Quinn came back, shaking his flashlight to recharge it.

Click. Click. Click. Click. Click.

Ben eyed the kid. He had a button-pushing, fuck-with-you look on his face. I'd been through enough with Ben that I could see what was coming, and I dreaded it.

The last thing we needed down in the Under was for all of us to start getting on each other's backs.

And Ben said, "You shake that thing pretty good, Red. I bet you practice a lot, don't you?"

"Huh?" Quinn was reasonably clueless.

Griffin laughed and spit. "Fucking grab my balls, pervert."

Quinn took one wide step over to Griffin and shoved the smaller boy's shoulder, spinning him around. "You want to start fucking with me again, not-Ben?"

"Hey!" I spun around and aimed my light directly into Quinn's face.

He stopped cold. Done.

Click. Click. Click. Click.

"Oooh . . . Ahhh . . . Rrredddd . . . ," Ben moaned.

I felt myself getting hot. "Cool it, Ben. Please."

Quinn forced a laugh. "Heh-heh-heh . . . That's a good one, Ben. I get it! And damned if I'm not pretty good at it!"

Quinn angled the flashlight up, pointing out from his crotch.

Click. Click. Click. Click. Click. Click.

Griffin whispered, "What a fucking dork."

I ignored them. I scanned the ground behind Griffin. "There it is."

I bent down and picked up the folded paper. It could have been a hundred years old; it was so faded and clumped together. But it was a map. I glanced back to where Quinn was playing jerk-off with his flashlight, and my eyes followed his beam across the expanse of the tunnel.

Where the light hit the ridges of the steel wall, I saw writing.

"Holy shit." I dropped onto one knee and aimed my flashlight at the words.

Quinn was oblivious; his light epileptically darted all over the place, clicking and clicking.

Griffin caught on first.

"What the fuck is that, Jack?"

I could only shake my head and stare.

Quinn froze.

"Don't mind that, Billy. We sometimes used to come down here to play, is all."

"He's a fucking liar." Ben started across the dirt floor toward the smears of graffiti.

I said, "What's it mean, Quinn?"

The kid dropped the beam of his flashlight down onto his feet.

Quinn said, "Nothing. I told you we used to play down here, Billy. When I used to have other friends."

And on the wall, scrawled in thick rusty letters that advertised a kind of urgent warning:

I WILL KILL YOU IF I CATCH YOU DOWN HERE AGAIN, QUINN

Below it, in another hand, a response. Some of the letters were backwards, a jumble of lowercase and capitals:

I aM kiNG oF maЯBuRY BiLLY I WiLL puT YOuR hƎaD ON a hOOK FucʞER

We all saw it.

I shined my light directly at Quinn's pale and expressionless face.

"*That* was a game, Quinn?" I said.

"I told you it was," Quinn said. "We used to play like that down here."

"You and someone named Billy?"

Quinn's voice was low and unsteady. "I was just messin' with you. Uh. Jack."

Ben stormed toward us. Even in the starved light cast forward by the torches I could see the great clouds of dust he kicked up with his feet.

"He's a fucking liar, Jack."

"We shouldn't have brought him," Griffin said.

Quinn dropped his flashlight into the dirt and took off running, back in the direction of the ladder up to the firehouse. Maybe it was the darkness, but the kid seemed to almost fly.

Griffin grabbed the collar of Quinn's T-shirt, and the entire thing ripped from Quinn's bony and luminescent body as he struggled to get away. Ben launched himself at Quinn, wrapping both arms around his knees.

Quinn tried to kick free from Ben's tackle, and his pants split right up the middle. He lost a shoe before Ben finally took the kid down.

Then Ben was all over Quinn, punching, pulling his hair, slapping him with such force it sounded like a toy cap gun from another time when kids played games that didn't involve hanging their enemies' heads from spikes on the wall.

"You fuckin' kill that kid, you piece of shit, Red?" Ben panted and swung. "You fuckin' kill your friend?"

Ben brought his knee up, again and again into Quinn's balls.

"Get off him, Ben," I said.

I didn't care what Ben did to Quinn Cahill. I just didn't want Ben to hurt himself.

"Ben?" I said.

Ben Miller shoved himself away from Quinn.

His arms were streaked with Quinn's blood. Ben was a filthy, muddy mess. His eyes shone crazily like twin white stars in the dim light.

He said, "I think we should kill him, Jack. I'll fucking kill him if you think we should."

This is what Marbury does to boys like Ben.

I looked at Griffin. I was taking a vote, and Griff knew it.

Ben said, "We'd be better off if we just do it quick."

232

Griffin shook his head.

"I don't think we should kill him," Griffin said.

I stood over Quinn. His eyes were shut. There was a cut along the swollen ridge of his left cheekbone. Ben had knocked the kid out.

I nudged Quinn with my foot.

"Get up, Quinn," I said.

Ben walked out into the dark and threw up.

This is what Marbury does to boys like Ben.

I shined my light on Quinn.

The kid was a mess.

He lay on his side on the ground, curled up with both hands inside the rip in his jeans, holding his nuts.

"Get up," I repeated.

eighteen

We were tired.

If we were above, we'd have been asleep for hours by now, but we pushed ourselves beyond exhaustion.

We had no choice.

And now we had learned a little more about Quinn Cahill, the King of Marbury. I couldn't help but worry about the other wonders we'd find down here.

Like Ben said, welcome to the fucking Nature Channel.

Quinn struggled to keep up with us, but we pushed on as long as we could. None of us wanted to rest without some sign that we might get out of the darkness of the Under, but I knew the boys needed to find someplace where we could stop.

I think it may have been the longest stretch of time ever in which Quinn Cahill said absolutely nothing. He just limped along, two steps behind Ben, who now carried the other flashlight. I walked at the back of our line.

And I don't know exactly who was worse off: Quinn, who'd been beaten and deposed by three kids who didn't belong in his kingdom, or the three of us outcasts who'd likely never find our way out of this hole.

Maybe we walked three miles; maybe it was three hundred feet. Who knew? But it was going to happen sooner or later: We came to a branch in the tunnel network and had to make another decision about which way to go.

Ben and I stunk like corpses. Ultimately, the three of us ended up abandoning our shirts, having to use them for wipe rags to smear the burning dust away from our eyes.

I tried telling myself that if we'd gone the other way—the way without the little bit of hair on the boy's skull—that we'd already be dead. But that was a stupid thought.

Billy.

There was no escaping the idea that maybe if we were all dead, Ben, Griffin, and I would wake up back in their garage, or maybe stretched out on the deck beside their pool, lounging with Conner Kirk in the sunlight, talking shit to each other.

Maybe.

We stopped.

Ben punctuated his question by aiming his flashlight. "Right, left, or straight?"

The tunnel that intersected the one we'd been following was smaller; maybe only three-fourths the diameter, so it seemed darker, more cramped. It looked like something bugs would live in.

"How about we sit down right here and get a little food and water in us?" I said.

Griffin let out a big breath of air. "I'm fucking tired, Jack."

I watched him peel the pack off, drop it, and in less than a second, Griffin was down in the dirt, stretched out, using his backpack as a pillow.

I shined my light on Ben. We were all so filthy. We looked like pictures you'd see of trapped coal miners—all dirt, teeth, and wide, haunted eyes. Without saying anything, Quinn sat down on the ground beside Griffin, grunting a little, holding on to the crotch of his jeans to keep it from yawning open and letting anything out.

He put his head down on the pack right next to Griffin's, and then rolled onto his side like the kids were spooning or something. "I ain't trying nothing, not-Ben. I'm hurt and I need to lay down."

Griffin kept his eyes shut. "You touch me and I'll jab my thumbs so far into your fucking eyes you'll be looking out your asshole."

Ben and I sat down.

I took Griffin's map out of my pocket.

"Try to sleep if you want, Griff. Me and Ben will keep a watch out. But when I wake you up, you're going to get your butt in gear."

"Okay," Griffin mumbled.

"And no complaining," Ben said.

I dug into the pack and pulled out one of our water bottles. We passed it around. Griffin drank some.

We let Quinn have some, too.

I unfolded the map, and it fell apart. I had to lay the little parched rectangles together like a mosaic, flat on the dirt between my legs.

"You ever seen a map of this place before, Quinn?"

Quinn didn't move. He stayed on his side with one hand pressing the cut on his cheek and the other cupped beneath his crotch.

"I never seen one, Billy. I heard about 'em, though."

"Anything else you heard about that you're not telling?" Ben asked.

Quinn didn't answer.

Griffin breathed like a little boy when he slept, nasal and deep. The kid could sleep anywhere, through anything, like flipping a light switch.

I shined the light down on the puzzle of map lying in the dirt.

"Fuck this place," I whispered.

"What do you see?" Ben leaned over, but he kept his own light pointed away from us. He was always watching.

Here was a place called Glenbrook. The streets and highway interchanges were all laid out the same. I could have drawn the identical map from memory. But nothing else outside, away from Glenbrook, was the way it was supposed to be.

Not-Glenbrook.

Ben could see it, too.

"I found a book when I came here the first time. A dictionary. I looked shit up in it."

Ben just stared at me like I was stupid or something, like he was saying, *Why the fuck would you want to expand your vocabulary when you're in a fucking trap like this shithole?*

"They didn't have the word *earth* in it. No *California*, either."

"You're making shit up again, Billy," Quinn murmured, his eyes shut, still pressed up against Griffin.

But I could tell by the look on his face that certain things began registering with Ben.

"You know what the book said about Marbury? That it's the third planet from the sun, that this is where humans come from, and that it has no moon."

"Jack. You've seen the same shit we all have. Do you think this is home? Do you think it's supposed to be the way you expect in your head?"

"You guys are all fucking nuts," Quinn said. "If you think I'm going to believe you came from somewhere else, and you ain't Odds just like me, you're all full of black salt and shit."

And Ben said, "You ever hear of California, Red?"

Quinn pushed his face down lower into Griffin's shoulder. "Leave me alone. I'm going to sleep."

"If Jack wasn't here, I'd fucking kill you."

Ben looked up at the ceiling, then drew a circle around our spot in the dirt with his light. "Sorry, Jack."

"It's okay, Ben." I leaned closer to the map, and Ben looked, too. "I promise I'll get us home. I swear to God I will."

"I trust you, Jack."

There was an obvious coastline on the map. Lines that could have been highways—maybe before the war, maybe a long time ago when Marbury was some other place—connected the twisted veins of not-Glenbrook to a sea that had the word ENDLESS written in dark blue print that stretched toward the old edge of the map. Near the top of the paper, positioned on the coast, another knot of roadways clumped together at a place called Grove. It was the city where the four of us—Ben, Griffin, me, and Conner—found safety the first time I'd stumbled into Marbury.

I put my finger on it.

"You remember that place, Ben?"

"Things are different now."

I glanced over at Quinn. He seemed to be asleep, too.

I whispered, "This is how we got here. I'm pretty sure we've gone back in time, somehow. But we also moved things around."

"I don't think this is Marbury, dude."

"I saw it in the book."

"Fuck the book."

I sighed. "Look." My finger traced a path toward the lower right corner of the map. "Bass-Hove. Do you remember the battle there?"

"Honestly?"

I nodded.

"No. I don't remember anything anymore."

"Do you remember a guy named Henry Hewitt? He was the guy who took you and Griff across the desert, and everyone in our crew except us three got slaughtered there. Remember?"

Ben looked down at the fragments of map and shook his head.

I sighed, pointed again. "This is where Conner's going. Maybe he's already there, waiting for us."

"He knows we're coming?"

"I promised to meet him. It's the way we can fix the lens. I'm sure of it. We get things back—the way they were, the way they're supposed to work out—and we can go home."

Ben flashed his light around again. It felt colder now.

"What makes you so sure?"

I shook my head.

I didn't know.

"There are people there, Ben. Regular people. Not Odds and Rangers. I just know it."

"Okay, Jack. If you say so. All I care about right now is getting the fuck out of this goddamned cave."

I sat down and scattered the leaves of the map away from me.

"Me too."

———

Sitting, waiting, made me shiver from the cold.

Ben started to nod off, but I could tell he felt guilty about it, so fought the urge to lie down and sleep.

"I don't care if you sleep," I said.

"I don't care if you do."

"I smell too bad to sleep."

"I'd throw up in my dreams."

Ben smiled.

"We came far enough this way," I said. I looked at the options: the main tunnel stretching ahead of us, and the narrower one that bisected it, leading away on both sides. "I think it should be pretty light outside by now. At least, that's what I'd estimate. So, if there was a way out that wasn't too far from where we're sitting, maybe we'd see a little light down one of these tunnel branches."

"I was thinking that," Ben said.

"Let's get them up and stick our noses down there and see if there's anything that shows up."

"Like the fucking Nature Channel?"

"Fuck that shit, dude."

I pushed myself onto my feet and held out my hand to hoist up Ben.

He kicked his brother's feet. "Time to go, Griff. Red, get up."

"My name ain't Red."

"Shit if it's not," Ben said.

We thought to first explore the tunnel that branched off to our right. If it happened to lead to a way out, I calculated that this would be the right direction to put us somewhere closer to the horses at the ag school.

But calculations based on time and place in Marbury were as pointless as dogs solving arithmetic in dreams.

I think we were all prepared to potentially fall into a different world with every footstep we planted ahead of us; with the possible exception of Quinn. I was convinced he was still keeping secrets; that he knew far more than he'd let on, as though knowing what might lie ahead of us gave him some likely edge to victory, winning whatever game he believed he was still playing.

Even as scuffed and banged up as he was, Quinn was next to impossible to figure out. Or trust.

We had to step up a good three feet in order to get inside the narrower side tunnels. Quinn complained that he couldn't take the climb, that his balls hurt too bad, so Griffin gave him a boost by letting Quinn use the kid's knee as a foothold, and I pulled him in by his hand.

Ben and I decided we'd give it five hundred feet, just to get a feel for what may be down that way, before turning back and exploring the tunnel that led in the opposite direction.

The narrowness of the passage kept us packed in a tighter group. There was no dirt covering the floor, only the ribbed steel of the drainpipe construction that made it seem as though we'd been swallowed and were passing through an enormous intestine.

Occasionally, we'd step over bones: pelvises, arms, and legs, mostly. The smaller things like teeth or fingers went mostly unnoticed. I found a skull with a hole in the back of it big enough to poke three of my fingers through. And everywhere there were shoes and belts—things made from leather or plastic that never seemed to go away or wear down into dust.

I picked up a wallet and thumbed through its contents. There were bank cards, receipts, a corner of a sheet of notebook paper with a girl's name on it—Julie—and a phone number. No bills, but there were three undistinguishable coins that jingled inside a snap pouch. I took them out and put them into my pocket. I wanted to look at them more closely when—if—I got the time. And then I found an ID card from Glenbrook High School. There was some grime obscuring the lamination, and when I wiped it away with my thumb I could read *Glenbrook High School 2011–2012.*

Fuck this place.

The photo was of a leering sophomore boy named Chris Baker. I recognized him. He was the same kid who'd handed me a can of beer from his back pocket when we took a piss on the side of Conner's house at his end-of-school-year party. That would have been—what?—maybe nine weeks ago.

In another world.

Fuck you, Jack.

And I stood there, trying to decide if I should hang on to the kid's wallet or just leave it behind, entombed in the spot where Chris Baker was surely a meal for something once hungry in Marbury.

Ben kept walking. He was about twenty feet ahead of me, shining his light upward in front of us. "What's that shit?"

I tossed the kid's wallet away.

Sorry, Chris. Or not-Chris.

I looked over to where Ben pointed his flashlight. Up in the tunnel, great torn sheets of what looked like black rags hung down from the top of the pipe.

"Don't touch that," Quinn said.

We stood just behind Ben, who was close enough to the hanging drapes of black that he could reach out and grab them.

"What is it?" I asked.

"It's a kind of fungus. It gets you stoned, Billy. The Rangers call it black salt. It fucks you up good. You snort it up, or get it in your eyes or mouth, and you'll piss yourself."

"You do that shit?" Griffin said.

Quinn looked down, shaking his head. "Fuck. Why would I tell you, not-Ben?"

Ben shined his light through the forest of hanging moss, trying to see if there was any pathway through.

"But I never seen it growing so thick," Quinn said. "It's hard to imagine what some of them boys would trade you for just a handful of this."

"Maybe another blowjob for you, huh, Quinn?" Griffin said.

"If that's what I wanted, not-Ben, I could surely have it."

Ben squatted down, duckwalking beneath the strands of mold that dangled like inverted seaweed, holding the speargun out with one hand and his flashlight in the other.

"I wouldn't do that," Quinn said.

Ben paused, looked back at us.

I got nervous when Quinn warned Ben. The fucker knew things about the Under.

"Ben," I whispered. "Get out of there. Let's go back the other way."

"Yeah," he agreed. "It doesn't look like there's any chance of us getting through here."

And just as he started to pivot his body around, something small, the color of charcoal ash, slipped down from one of the black strands above him and fell onto Ben's back, hitting him with a soft thud right between his shoulders.

"Fuck!"

Ben jerked and thrashed, swatting at whatever it was that landed on him. When he spun again, I could see that it was some sort of spider, soft and fuzzy, as big as a hand. It was the same kind of creature that had been curled up inside the map pouch Griffin found.

But this one was biting Ben.

Ben wasn't wearing a shirt, and I could see the thing digging its fangs right into the flesh below his right shoulder blade.

"Don't move!" I dropped down and began crawling toward Ben beneath the drapes of fungus. But it was too late. Ben yelped and backhanded the spider with his knuckles. When the thing let go of him and scooted away, farther down into the tunnel, Ben jolted to his feet. He stood up directly into the fans of black mold.

The fungus crumbled, turned to crystalline grains that rained down on Ben, covering him in black glitter everywhere. He looked burned, like he had crawled out from the soot in the bottom of a potbelly stove.

Ben coughed twice, and after that, he just stood there, staring at me with his mouth locked open in a yawn as I made my way toward him.

"Don't get that shit in your mouth, Billy!" Quinn called. "Just let him come out of there on his own."

I stopped.

Ben didn't even blink. He could have been a statue carved from black glass, standing so still with the speargun pointed down at his feet and a flashlight held against his thigh.

"Ben?" I said. "Are you okay, man?"

His face was blank. I couldn't even tell if he was breathing.

"Ben!" Griffin yelled from somewhere behind me.

I heard sounds of a struggle. Quinn and Griffin started fighting.

When I turned around, I saw that Quinn had tackled Griffin and was straddling the smaller boy's chest, pinning him down.

"You can't go in there, not-Ben!" Quinn's voice was choked with the pain of having to wrestle the kid down despite his injuries.

I glanced back at Ben. Still not moving; just staring.

"Griff! Listen to me. Just stay there. I'm going to get Ben. Please."

Griffin barked, "Get off of me, you fucking pervert."

I turned my light away from them. I needed to get Ben out of there. Griffin and Quinn were still fighting. I could clearly hear punches landing.

It was going to happen sooner or later, anyway. I had to ignore them.

I whispered, "Just don't fucking kill each other."

I waited a moment for the smoky rain of black salt to settle down. Then I slid my way farther in, beneath the hanging strands of mold.

Ben gasped and started breathing again, fast and hard. It was almost as though he'd forgotten how to inhale and then suddenly woke up. But he wasn't awake. The muscles on his face and chest all seemed to clench, and he didn't move his eyes or even blink. He couldn't see me crawling my way along the floor of the drainpipe toward his feet.

"Ben! Ben! Look at me!"

One of the spider things dropped down on the floor of the pipe, between me and Ben. I could see it clearly in the flashlight's beam. Its body was gray and hairy, striped across with black, bigger than both my hands put together. And the sets of legs on either side were incredibly long. Folded in half, they were still more than a foot in length, which explained how fast the ones I'd seen had been able to run away from us. The spider had a long rope of a tail that curled and flicked at the end of its butt, but the most alarming thing about it were the two ivory white fangs that looked like curved swords, clicking together just a few inches from my face.

I held my breath. I laid the flashlight down so I could see the thing, and slid my hand down onto the hilt of my knife. When the thing came at me, I stabbed down, directly into its abdomen, but the knife made no mark at all on it. The spider just flattened out and thrashed its tapping legs. It was almost as though the thing were made of metal. The blade of the knife did nothing to the spider. It just kept biting at the air, clicking its legs and whipping its tail.

I scraped the knife forward until the point found its way into the segmented joint between the spider's head and body. A weak spot.

I breathed a gasp of relief. I didn't think spiders slept, and I would have been there pinning the thing down with my knife for a long time before one of us got tired. But its head came off under the edge of my knife, and the rest of it ran off somewhere on the other side of the tunnel where Ben was standing.

I swatted the head out of my way and crawled the rest of the distance to where Ben was.

Ben stared straight ahead, oblivious to everything: the dark; the boys, who were thrashing each other not ten yards from where we were; me, crouched around his feet, trying to get him to pay attention. I grabbed on to his shin and pulled on the leg of his trousers. They were completely soaked with his piss. And I realized I was sitting in a warm puddle of it.

Something else Quinn knew about.

Fuck this place.

Ben didn't react, so I pulled him harder. His hand jerked, and he dropped the speargun down into the urine.

"Fuck," I whispered. I picked up the weapon, grimaced in disgust, and slung the dripping strap on the gun's stock around my neck. Then I reached up and pried the flashlight from Ben's fingers. He was stiff. He stunk. He felt like a dead body, but his breathing was so fast and strained. The skin on his chest and belly dripped black tears of perspiration mixed with the fungus that coated him.

Finally, frustrated, I hooked my fingers into the waist of Ben's jeans and pulled so hard that he fell on top of me. I rolled over on my backpack and caught him, but his knee came up squarely beneath my balls, and I felt my guts twist and knot their way slowly through my chest, snailing their way toward my neck.

I couldn't do anything. I had to lie there like that for a minute with Ben on top of me. His mouth hung open, panting, and he drooled onto the side of my face. All sweaty and piss soaked, Ben's eyes were frozen open as if he were transfixed by the best show he'd ever seen, and so didn't want to sacrifice an eye blink.

I grunted and rolled onto my side. It was all I could do to avoid getting the granules of mold that had fallen on the floor around us into my mouth. I turned Ben faceup.

When my head cleared, I realized there was no way I could pull a kid as big as Ben out of there if I had to crawl away and keep us both down beneath the hanging mold. So I slid my hand into the backpack and felt around blindly until my fingers closed on the coil of nylon rope we'd taken from the firehouse.

As I moved Ben so I could wind the rope beneath his armpits, I saw the bite marks left in his back by that spider creature. They were angry and red, about two inches apart, and looked like small parallel slices into the flesh over Ben's ribs. Clear, glistening fluid, venom, oozed out from both wounds. I wiped it away with my thumb and squeezed the area around the bite, causing an eruption of poison from the holes in Ben's back.

Squeeze. Wipe. Again.

The fucking Nature Channel: Every unimaginable beast can be found here in the Under.

Once I'd gotten a loop knotted around Ben's chest and put him on his back, the boy seemed to start loosening up, but his breathing continued to pulse in gasping pants.

Then he spoke.

"What are you doing?"

It sounded like Ben was talking in his sleep, anesthetized, like he didn't really *care* what I was doing to him, he just wanted me to tell him about it.

"Getting you out of here."

"Why?"

"This isn't a good place. You'll be okay."

"It's a good place. I feel fine. Leave me alone."

I sighed. "Don't move."

I began crawling back toward Griffin and Quinn, holding one end of the rope in my hand, and Ben said, "I'm not going to move."

"Glad to hear it, dude."

I slid and squirmed along the bottom of the pipe. I realized I was just as black as Ben—coated in the granular dust of the mold growths, made even worse because I was soaked with Ben's piss. With each stretch forward, my mind raced all over the place—maybe I was falling under the effects of the drug, too.

Ben will be okay.

He has to be okay.

Fuck this place.

247

I'm going to fucking beat the shit out of Quinn if he hurts Griffin.

I am never going to feel clean again.

Ben has to be okay.

Keep crawling, Jack.

You fucked up everything.

Fuck you, Jack.

The fight between Griffin and Quinn was over by the time I bellied out from under the black jungle. Both boys were seated, faced in opposite directions, nursing their wounds.

At least they were both still alive.

Griffin held a bloodstained hand to his face, pinching his nostrils shut, and Quinn, worse for wear, slumped his head down over his bent knees. It looked like every wound on his body had opened up again and started bleeding.

Quinn was obviously crying.

He just had no clue about how to get along with other human beings.

Odds.

"You guys are stupid," I said. I stood up and pulled the rope tight, shining my light back at Ben, who was still lying on his back, staring up at nothing, watching the show. "I could use some fucking help."

I handed Griffin the flashlight I'd taken from his brother.

He was about to say something, too. And I knew what it was. I could tell. He was about to call Quinn a cocksucker or a faggot or whatever boys Griffin's age call other boys when they get into fights, but I didn't want to hear it.

I held up my hand. "Don't start any more shit, Griff. The fight's over. Let's get your brother out of there."

Griffin sniffed and wiped at his bloody nose. He looked like hell. I looked worse. Griffin said as much. "You look like you crawled through a shithole, Jack."

He grabbed the rope behind me and we pulled together, slowly. Griffin sniffed again. "And you smell like piss."

My stomach turned. "Fuck." I shook my head.

With each pull, I could hear Ben grunting, "Unh. Unh."

Then Quinn got hold of the rope behind Griffin, and we kept tugging until Ben was clear of the mold. I lifted up his shoulders.

The three of us dragged him all the way back to the junction just before the main tunnel.

Griffin leaned over his brother. He wiped his hand across Ben's face and hair while I poured water on him.

We tried to get him to drink, but Ben choked and gagged, spitting the water all over both of us.

"He's a fucking mess," Griffin said. He patted Ben's cheek. "Ben? Hey? Can you hear me?"

Quinn hadn't said a word since I came back out of the mold, he just hovered over us, watching, pouting, sniffling. And Ben stared at us while we tried washing him, but we could tell he wasn't actually seeing us. He'd just murmur things that didn't make any sense.

"Wow. It's okay. It's moving. It's opening up. I can see forever. Jack. It's you and Griffin. Jack. The hole in the sky is the way through for everyone. I know who you are. Jumping Man. I can see you. I love you, Griff."

Griffin chewed at his lip, and kept his hand in Ben's hair.

He was scared and I could see it.

"Ben never says shit like that."

"He got bit, Griff," I said. "One of those things got on his back and bit him. It was like the hand you found, only it was some kind of spider."

"Where'd he bite him?" Quinn's voice, cracked and strained from the fight with Griffin, from crying, surprised us.

"On his back," I said.

I turned Ben onto his side and Quinn cautiously stepped toward us to look. Ben's arm flopped limply across his chest; slick drool ran down the side of his cheek.

"Did it unfold its legs?" Quinn asked. "Did it have really long legs that were folded up, and then he was maybe bigger across than the kid?"

I looked at Quinn and nodded. "What is that thing?"

"A whip spider."

Just the way he said it—the tone in his voice—told me it was something bad, and Quinn knew what it was, too.

Griffin leaned in and put his face right up to the marks on Ben's back. They seemed bigger now, and there was a spreading red mass that seemed to be growing across Ben's skin. It looked like it was snaking in both directions along the boy's spine.

Griffin put his hands flat on either side of the bite. "It feels like he's on fire."

I shined my light on Quinn's face. His cheeks were streaked with mud. "How bad is this thing?"

Quinn didn't flinch. He frowned and shook his head.

I put my hand on the side of Ben's head and then looked at Griffin. He knew what Quinn meant.

I dropped the flashlight and stood up. I got right up against

Quinn, so our chests touched. He felt soft and small, afraid. "What the fuck, Quinn? What the fuck?"

Quinn started backing away. He was scared, and I'll admit a big part of me wanted to punch him again, but I felt sorry for him, too. And I was so tired of the kid at the same time. But I couldn't help thinking about Ben Miller's bones inside a fucking trash barrel with Griffin's, secreted away in Freddie Horvath's garage, and how that fucked-up version of the world couldn't be real; and now here we were and this redheaded fucker was telling us how Ben was going to lie down in a fucking sewer and die right in front of us while we watched him go.

And this couldn't be real, either.

But we couldn't escape.

I couldn't get Ben and Griffin home.

And it was my fault.

I put my hands on Quinn's shoulders, not hard, not threatening, just like I wanted to hold the kid down, to make things okay. It took all the will in the world to keep my voice restrained, to not claw my fingers into his pasty white flesh, to not shake the living shit out of him.

Deep breath, Jack.

"I'm not going to hit you, Quinn."

I could feel the kid begin to relax, loosen up, under my touch.

"What do you know about those spiders?"

He shook his head, tried to look away from me. "He ain't gonna make it, Billy."

nineteen

"What do you mean?" I said. I shook the kid angrily. "What the fuck do you mean?"

But I knew what he meant.

Quinn didn't have to say it.

I probably would have hit him if he did. He stood there sniffling, looking like he was getting ready to cry again.

"You're full of shit," Griffin said. "You've always been full of shit, you fucking prick. I should have said yes. I should have told Ben we needed to kill you."

Griffin poured water across Ben's chest, washing his brother, wiping his skin with a shaking hand.

The muscles in Ben's neck had tightened, so his head tilted back, and his mouth stretched open even wider now. Except for the movement of his ribs when he inhaled, he already looked dead.

"I don't know what to do, Griff." I sounded pathetic, like every fucked-up thing I'd ever done to them had all clotted in my mouth and was choking me.

Griffin wouldn't look at me. I knew what he was thinking.

He kept trying to clean Ben's skin.

I slipped the noose on the speargun away from my neck, let the weapon rest on the floor beside my wet and black-stained boots. I dropped the pack next to it.

Then I began unwrapping the bandage from around my hand. But even as I did it, I had an understanding that nothing would happen—I needed to be outside, under the hole in the sky. And if we were outside, what could I expect? To drive everyone to madness?

To send Quinn running off in terror, looking for a hook where he might hang himself? Or maybe I'd deliver Ben and Griffin back to the cramped prison of a plastic waste barrel inside a killer's garage in a Glenbrook that is not Glenbrook?

Bad magic.

Everything came through Jack.

I was the arrow through every fucked-up layer in this universe, and when I broke the lens, the shaft of the arrow splintered everything. That's what I did. Ben knew it, too. The hole in the sky was the fracture of the lens was the cut in my hand was the doorway to every not-world I never wanted to see.

Griffin put his face down on his brother's chest. I couldn't tell whether he was resting, giving up, or trying to hear if Ben was still alive.

I looked at my hand.

My skin was white and puffy with moisture. I stunk. The black salt had soaked through the bandage. Was there any spot on my body not covered in some kind of filth?

The mark was a deeper color of pink now, zigzagged in the identical pattern to the thing we'd all seen in the sky. If I laid the Marbury lens in my palm, it would match like a puzzle piece. If I had Conner's part of it, too, maybe we could put things back.

I shined my light on Griffin, and kneeled down on the opposite side of Ben's chest.

That was exactly the moment Ben Miller stopped breathing.

"Stop fucking around!" Griffin yelled at his brother. He pushed his hands down against Ben's unmoving sternum and pushed. "Don't fucking do this to me!"

Griffin put his mouth over his brother's and began blowing gasps of air into Ben's lungs. And when I put the flat of my palm over Ben's heart, I could immediately feel how cold and stiff the boy was.

I grabbed his hand, squeezed it.

His skin was like wax.

This can't be happening.

I felt sick, choked. I wanted to scream, but everything locked up in my throat.

"Ben? Ben?"

Then Griffin pulled his head away from his brother's and said, "Get the fuck away from us."

I pulled my hand away from Ben.

I deserved this. Griffin had every right to say it.

Then we heard noises at the opening to the main tunnel.

It sounded like metal clicking against metal. I couldn't see Quinn. He was gone again, and I thought maybe he'd taken the other flashlight, but it was here with us.

Tick. Tick. Tick.

Getting louder.

Tick. Tick. Tick. Tick.

Coming toward us.

I got up, scanned the floor for the speargun.

It was gone.

I flashed the light across the opening out to the main tunnel. Something moved in front of the circle of black.

I grabbed my knife and walked toward the noise.

Tick. Tick. Tick. Tick.

"Quinn? Are you there?"

Tick. Tick. Tick.

Ssshhhhh . . .

Another flash of movement, at the edge of the light's beam. Something gray.

When I shined the light on it, the form became unclear. I was looking directly through it, could see the wall of the pipe on the other side of it.

Seth Mansfield stood there, watching me from the edge of the drainpipe.

Seth.

Griffin wailed and coughed behind me.

His brother was dead.

It was the worst sound I think I'd ever heard in my life. Out of all the places I'd ever been, all the not-worlds, here was the darkest.

"Seth!" I said. "What can I do? What can you tell me to do? You came back, Seth!"

Seth looked tired and small. I could see his ribs straining the skin above his belly. He wiped his eyes and looked at me. "I never left you."

"Please. I need you to do something, Seth."

"I know. But he's afraid of me. That one named Ben is. He might fight it anyway, Jack."

"Will you try?"

Seth turned his hands up. "You need to put things back before too much more time goes by, Jack."

"I'm trying."

"You might not ever get out."

"I don't care about me. I need to get those boys home. Please help me do that."

Seth turned gray, flattening out into a snaking pale mist that flowed over the floor past my feet and scattered like ash on a wind in the direction of the boys.

Ben jerked.

His chin went down onto his chest and his eyes finally closed, then he threw his hands out in front of him and began coughing.

Griffin screamed. "Jack!"

Ben shook and gagged. He rolled onto his side, wracked in spasms. It hurt. I knew how much it hurt. Griffin tried to hold him still, but Ben was too big, too strong. He kicked and thrashed with his arms, catching Griffin in the mouth, splitting the smaller boy's lip open.

I stood back and watched, afraid of getting too close to them again.

That's when I heard Quinn running out of the tunnel, clattering noisily away from us.

The idiot didn't even have a light with him.

I ran.

I jumped down from the side tunnel, out into the expanse of the first underground channel we'd followed all the way from Quinn's firehouse. Fifty feet from where I landed, Quinn stood, square, with his legs slightly parted.

He held the speargun pointed directly at my chest.

"You don't play nice, Billy," Quinn said.

"Just go away and leave us alone, Quinn."

I slid my hand back along my thigh, shining the light at Quinn's face so he wouldn't see I was feeling for the knife.

"You stole from me, Billy."

Quinn swallowed.

"I'll give everything back," I said.

Quinn shook his head.

"I am King of Marbury," he said. "You know that, Billy?"

"I know that."

"I want you to show me where you boys really come from."

I looked back into the tunnel where I'd left Griffin.

"You're standing in the center of it," I said.

I dropped the flashlight, startling Quinn.

I dove to my right, and Quinn fired the speargun. I watched the arrow, ghostlike in the dusty dark of the Under, buzzing like a wasp through the haze of the flashlight's beam.

The arrow sailed over me and clattered invisibly against the steel wall of the channel, lost forever in the hungry darkness that swallowed everything here.

Quinn threw the empty gun down into the dirt and bolted off, farther into the Under, his milk white skin fading like a sick glow down in the depths of the tunnel.

This was how Quinn used to play with his friends down here.

Fun game, Quinn.

I picked up the flashlight and went back for Griffin and Ben.

Griffin heard me coming. He never looked away from Ben as I approached.

"He started breathing." Griffin wiped a hand across the bottom of his nose, then glanced up at me. "You look like hell, Jack."

I didn't say anything. I picked up my pack and slung my arms through the straps. Then I stepped over to Ben's side so I could take a look at him. He blinked. I could see that he recognized me.

I kneeled down beside him and put my hand over his heart. It amazed me how the last time I'd touched him, I knew I was touching the skin of a dead kid, and now Ben was warm and I could feel the life in him.

257

"You and I both need to stop dropping out on our own." I patted his chest.

Ben swallowed. I watched his Adam's apple bounce up and down. "What happened?"

I shook my head. "I don't know. Let me see your back."

I lifted Ben's shoulder. He winced and rolled onto his side. The marks where the whip spider had bitten into him were gone, completely healed. And Griffin had managed to bathe away most of the black salt from Ben's skin.

Ben closed his eyes. The kid was wiped out. He wouldn't be going anywhere soon.

I told Griffin, "Keep your eyes open and wait for me."

"What are you doing?" Griffin said.

"Hang on to your spear."

I stood and turned away from the boys.

"What are you doing, Jack?" Griffin's voice was angry, sharp.

I shined my light out into the main tunnel.

"I'm going to look for a way out."

"You can't fucking go by yourself."

I answered him by jumping down into the larger channel. Griffin yelled and cursed, but I knew he wouldn't leave Ben alone.

Griffin didn't need or want me around right now, anyway. Maybe never.

I could do this.

I had to.

Fuck you, Jack.

I'd gone a few hundred yards before Griffin finally quit cussing and screaming for me to come back. I moved fast, in part because it scared

258

me to imagine the kinds of monsters that might catch me if I didn't, and also because I was so exhausted that I believed I might drop off to sleep while still on my feet.

And I knew Quinn was out there, watching me, waiting for something.

I tripped over a rotting car battery, landed hard on my chest, spitting and choking on a mouthful of dirt. I fought the urge to stay down, to sleep.

I walked.

An hour later, I found Quinn Cahill in the Under.

At first, I thought the kid was sleeping, or dead. My light fell across the paleness of Quinn's body as he curled on his side in the dirt twenty feet in front of me.

He was hurt.

"Quinn?"

He saw the light, but he did not lift his head or look back at me.

"Go away, Billy. Go away. I give up. You won."

I took a slow step forward, my knife held point outward. It was Quinn, after all. It had to be another trick.

"What happened?"

I stood back, ready to drop the light if I had to, muscles tensed, so I could spring on him if he did anything. I wanted him to do something.

"I busted my foot up."

When I shined my light on Quinn, I saw that he had run himself out of one of his boots. His bare foot had a bloody gash along its outer edge. He must have stepped on a jagged piece of metal, maybe glass or bone.

The kid was crusted in filth and blood.

I could only imagine how messed up I must have looked, too.

Quinn had nothing on but one black-stained boot, and hardly more than a rag for trousers. Small trickles of blood ran down his chest from beneath the cut on his face.

It was no trick. The kid was giving up. It was not a good place to lie down and quit.

"Can you get up?" I said.

"Leave me alone, Billy."

"Fair enough," I said.

I shined the light farther ahead.

Nothing.

Quinn said, "Okay, Billy. I know there's a river down that way. And it's good water. We . . . I used to have to come down here to get drinking water. Before I made the still."

I stood over him. I shined the light onto the kid's face. His orange hair was dark with filth, plastered down to his scalp with the mud of dust and sweat and blood.

"Is it a way out?"

"That's all I know," he said. "I ain't never been no further than the river. And I stopped coming down here once I was left on my own."

"Left?" I said. "You knew that other boy. The one up on the hook."

Quinn said nothing.

I nudged him with my foot. "Well? You did that to the kid, didn't you, Quinn? Hung his head on that hook?"

"Fair enough, Billy. Fair enough," Quinn said. "I'll tell the truth. I stuck that little faggot with my knife. Yep, Billy, you were right all along. That *is* my knife you picked up at the dead man's house. The same one I used on that little kid up there."

Okay, I thought, *so everything I ever guessed about this fucker turned out to be true.* So how come it still felt like he'd just kicked me in the balls?

I swallowed. "I appreciate you finally being straight with me."

And Quinn got a mean, hard look on his face that seemed to age him right before my eyes. "The river ain't too far, Billy. Good luck gettin' out."

It was going to be like this now. No more games between me and Quinn. The first time I ever saw the kid, as I flailed around, drowning in the rainwater, when I took off my clothes and pulled those fucking black worms away from my nutsack, Quinn looked so clean and innocent, like he was maybe thirteen years old and belonged in the soprano section of an all-boys church choir.

Now I realized I was wrong about so many things.

"Get up," I said. "You're coming, too."

"Leave me here."

"If I leave you here, Quinn, it's only going to be after I stick this knife down your fucking throat. Get up. I'm tired of your bullshit."

We walked.

Quinn whimpered with every step, but we said nothing as we kept a steady pace farther into the belly of Marbury's Under.

In the quiet now, no running, no panting breaths, I could hear the low roar of rushing water.

At first, I jumped when the flashlight's beam ricocheted off the surface of the river. It almost looked like a glistening snake out there, sliding toward us. I stopped and watched, hoping Quinn would say something, maybe tell me what to expect, but the kid stayed quiet and waited beside me.

"Please tell me there aren't any monsters in that water."

"If there are, I don't know about 'em, Billy."

"No worms?"

Quinn shook his head and pointed a finger above us, into the darkness. "They only live up there."

It was a hundred feet wide, deep and fast.

The river cut across the main channel of the Under, roiling in frothy, churning currents through an enormous grated opening to my right, and spilling down the opposite side in a torrent of falls over the concrete spillway lip to a gaping and lightless abyss.

It had to flow out somewhere, I thought, *maybe into the Endless, but there was no way of following it down the impossible cascade.*

I could smell the water, feel the dampness rising in warm humid billows through the fetid air of the Under. And I realized how parched I was, how desperately I wanted to tear myself out of my pants and boots and plunge my filthy body into it.

But I was afraid.

I flashed the light on Quinn's chest. "You say it's okay to drink?"

"It's good, Billy. Trust me."

Yeah. Right.

"Get in."

Quinn's white skin drained to an even paler hue. He shook his head. "I'll drink it, Billy. But I ain't getting in it. I can't swim."

"Strip down and get in the water. Or I'll fucking throw you in."

Quinn closed his mouth, straight, tight. The muscles in his jaw clenched, and he stared at me for several unblinking seconds. Then he reached down and slipped off his one boot and unbuckled his pants.

"Don't look at me," he said.

"What?"

"Don't look at me, Billy. I don't like it. It's embarrassing."

I rolled my eyes. Like Quinn would ever be embarrassed about anything.

Quinn slipped his bony legs out of his pants and tiptoed to the edge of the river. Of course I watched him do it. I'd never trust that kid, and he had to know it.

His naked body glowed luminescent white in the darkness of the Under. He gave me a dirty look, limping bad while keeping his hands fanned in front of his dick and what few pubic hairs he had.

"Don't look." Quinn had a rare edge of agitation in his voice.

The grown-up, self-conscious, angry Quinn Cahill.

"Fuck you, Quinn. Just get in the water."

He turned away from me and awkwardly dropped into the river.

The edge plunged straight down. The river flowed through a square-walled concrete channel, so there was no telling how deep it was. But it was obvious that the volume and weight of the rushing water were massive.

Quinn's head vanished beneath the churning river, and when his pale, ghostly hands thrashed above the surface, the current had already pulled him fifteen feet down the bank, toward the falls. He grasped the edge and held tight, spitting and wheezing.

"There. You happy now, Billy?"

I nodded. "I guess I am."

I dropped the flashlight and backpack. As quickly as I could, I stripped out of my boots and pants, and holding on to my knife, I jumped into the river after him. For a moment, I didn't care what kind of horrid monsters might be swimming around below the surface, because I believed that I'd never felt anything as good in my entire life as that rushing, powerful flow against my exhausted body.

I drank, I swam, scrubbed the flakes of filth and blood from everywhere on me, out of my hair; and I was finally clean, reborn. But the current was so strong that it was a struggle for me to swim back to the safety of the edge. I understood how someone like Quinn,

263

unable to swim, would be so fearful of the river. But the water was incredible. It was as warm as a heated swimming pool, and as much as I'd try, I couldn't get myself anywhere near to feeling anything at all on the bottom.

And with my eyes just above the surface of the river, I could see the dimmest trace of a gray line—light—far away, down the tunnel on the opposite side.

There was a way out.

"Quinn!"

No answer.

I called him again. "Quinn! I see a way out of here!"

Nothing.

I realized that I'd drifted far from the spot where I left my flashlight and clothes lying at the edge of the river. I'd intended to wash out my piss-soaked pants and scrub the black mold from those filthy boots.

Out in the darkness, a good fifty yards from the fading glow of our dying flashlight, I pulled myself from the river and started back to where I'd discarded my things.

That's when I saw it.

A red slash floating in the blackness of the cave.

I rubbed my eyes. The red glow—I recognized it instantly—meant only one thing. Hunters. But it hovered above the exact spot where I'd dropped my clothes, a hooked slash of fire like a shepherd's crook, a thin, beckoning finger in the dark that dipped and jerked nervously.

I froze, waited.

It was on Quinn Cahill.

No wonder he didn't want me to see him naked, tried to cover his body in front of me. He wasn't embarrassed; he was sick.

He had the bug.

And he was turning into one of them.

That's how it happens—how it starts. With the little mark.

And he had no idea I'd been standing there watching him in the dark while he panicked and pulled his pants on so quickly to cover himself; fumbling past the injury on his foot while he thought I was bathing.

I closed my eyes as tight as I could, and opened them again.

The little red mark was gone.

Maybe I was hallucinating. Maybe it was from the water, or from the black salt I'd crawled through. Maybe it was just a stain on my eye from having looked away from the flashlight.

I was being paranoid.

Most of me didn't believe it. The kid didn't seem sick.

I stayed there, hidden, dripping onto the dirt, thinking.

When Quinn picked up the flashlight and began shaking it, looking around, I called out to him again.

"Hey! I'm over here! I found a way out!"

The light hit me, and I raised my hand to shield my eyes. I didn't want him to see my face. I was sure he'd be able to tell from my expression that something was up; that I had something new to be afraid of.

There's always something new to be afraid of.

I lowered the knife, so he wouldn't see it.

I thought about things. It disgusted me. I thought about where I should stab Quinn Cahill in order to kill him quickly. I remembered Ben telling me how hard it was to kill a kid who didn't want to die.

"That river swept me down pretty far."

I pretended to rake the water from my hair with my fingers, not looking at Quinn. "But I saw some light on the other side. There's a way out."

"Yep." Quinn sounded like he knew it all along. And he kept the light fixed on me as I came nearer to where he was standing.

"We can use the rope. We'll get you across the river," I said.

"I'm not scared, Billy."

I bent over, began gathering up my things.

"I'm going to wash out my clothes."

"That's a good idea, Billy."

Quinn pointed the light at me the whole time, so I couldn't really see anything other than his silhouette.

"You should wash your pants and boots, too, Quinn. Get that blood and shit out of them."

"No way I'm getting back in there," he said. "But now you believe me?"

I had to think about that.

"About the water?" I said. "Yes. No more games."

"No more games, Billy."

Sure as shit, Quinn.

I tied the laces on the boots together through the belt hoops on my jeans, so I wouldn't lose anything in the water. I was so careful. The knife was always ready. Quinn knew it. There was nothing he could do.

Quinn watched me. I thought about giving him shit for staring at me, but I was unsure about talking to him, trying to sound normal—whatever the fuck that meant here, of all places—like he might figure out that I was hiding something from him.

This is just how Quinn Cahill used to play with his friends down here.

I was going to kill this kid, and there was nothing he could do about it.

And I thought, *It's bullshit. He's the one hiding stuff. He's sick. It's been nothing but lies since the first time Quinn Cahill opened his goddamned mouth after the storm. He's going down. White eye. Black eye. He's a fucking goner. Then what are you going to do, Jack? What are you going to do when he tries going after one of the boys?*

He will try to kill the youngest kid first. Then he will eat him. It's what they do to Odds.

I shook my head, tried to clear my brain.

The Rangers used to take the sick Odds out and shoot them in the fucking street.

Leave them for the harvesters.

What was I going to do?

I rolled my pants and boots into a ball and tucked them under my arm. I stood up and shrugged. "You done eyeballing me yet, Quinn?"

"Heh-heh, Billy. See how you like it?"

"I don't really care." I stood and watched him.

It was a stare-down, and neither one of us was budging.

This was Jack's game.

I was the King of Marbury.

I turned around, got right up to the edge of the river. "Your clothes stink, Quinn. You should seriously wash that shit out of your pants."

My turn to fuck with the kid.

"I'm okay, Billy."

"Sure you are."

I jumped into the water.

Staying close to the edge, I scraped the uppers of my boots and

267

washboarded my jeans against the concrete wall of the river, but all the time as I worked at cleaning my stuff, keeping afloat, pulling myself back toward the shadows cast by the flashlight Quinn held on me, watching him watching me, I thought about what had been done, and what still needed doing.

I was going to kill this kid, and there was nothing he could do about it.

And it hit me, how the black worms never once got after Quinn—they stayed away from Hunters, or Odds who were already infected—and why he tried to jump from the roof of the firehouse after he forced open my hand so he could show Ben and Griffin the thing. The mark. The hole in the sky. The doorway into and out of every not-place in the fucked-up universe. How fucked up Jack was. Just like the Hunters at the market, it scared him bad enough that he wanted to kill himself; and even Quinn couldn't understand what had happened.

Because he was one of them.

And now I was going to kill this kid.

I put my head under the water and screamed.

I sloshed my wet things over the edge and onto the dirt at the bank.

I suddenly felt so worn, like I didn't have nearly the strength to pull myself out from the water. I twisted the hilt of the knife around in my grip. I was nervous and excited, trying to force myself to just get it over with, but I didn't want to watch myself do it.

Quinn stood there on the bank, beaming the light and his stupid expression down at me.

Watching.

Fuck you, Quinn.

"Need some help, Billy?"

He offered his open hand for me, stooping at the edge of the river.

I stayed there for a moment, considering what might happen if I yanked him out into the water, let the current take the kid down, over the falls. That would solve a small problem.

I had to do it.

And I thought, *Maybe I should try to find Seth again, to beg him to do something for this kid who I didn't particularly like, and certainly didn't trust.*

If I could find Seth.

But I wanted to ignore things, to convince myself that it wasn't Quinn whose diseased body I saw; that the kid wasn't sick, and he wasn't going to do what all Hunters end up doing once things went the only way they could go.

"Thanks, Quinn."

I grabbed his wrist.

He pulled me from the water.

I spent a few minutes squatting by the river, wringing and rewringing out my pants until they were reasonably damp enough to put on. All the while, I kept the knife pinned beneath my bare foot.

Quinn knew. He watched.

Quinn always watched.

Boys who survived in Marbury always watched.

I had no idea how long we'd been down in the Under.

It seemed like forever.

Click.

Click. Click. Click.

The sound startled me, and I jumped.

It was only Quinn, charging up the flashlight again.

He noticed, smiled. "Sorry, Billy."

I was too nervous, preoccupied in wondering how to deal with Quinn, what I would say to him if I had the guts to bring up the subject of having the disease, the bug.

It had to be something that happened to him recently, too, otherwise Quinn would already be coughing and getting nosebleeds. Once that started, there would be no skirting around the issue.

But I couldn't will myself to kill the kid. I thought about the horrifying sound of a knife plunging into Quinn's soft flesh. Would he scream? Would he cry?

What would it sound like?

How hard would he fight back, and how long would it take for him to die?

Zip.

Quinn was fucking with my pack.

"What's this thing you got in here, Billy?"

Fuck.

The lenses.

I whirled back to see what he'd done, but it was too late. Quinn held my wadded-up sock in his damp white hand while he awkwardly pried into the opening, trying to steady the flashlight he pinned under his armpit.

I grabbed for his hands. "Leave that alone!"

Quinn turned away. "Looky here!"

And speaking to no one in particular, like he was making a judgment call for this lightless and fucked-up universe, Quinn said, "We agreed no more games, Billy. I ain't hiding nothing from you."

"You're a fucking liar, Quinn."

I slashed at him with the knife.

Quinn ducked away from the blade.

As my arm swiped past him, Quinn closed in and grabbed my wrist.

The fucker bit my arm, and I heard the *chink* of the broken lens when it hit the ground in front of Quinn's feet.

The next thing I knew, the entire cavern lit up with a fierce blue light.

Quinn had somehow flipped the smaller lens down on the glasses.

He spun around and around, waving the glasses out through the dark, where we could both clearly see them.

part four

THE
PASSENGER

twenty

Welcome to another not-world, Jack.

I hear Quinn screaming, but that is all. I can't see him, can't see anything here.

Open your eyes.

Open your eyes, Jack.

Just screams.

And dark.

I fall.

The water is cold and salty. It stings my eyes and I am held under by white pillows of foam. I hit the bottom, feel my fingers digging into the familiar grit of sand, coil my legs, and push up toward the light.

When my head breaks the surface, I have one thought: blue.

The sky is blue.

This is it.

My surfboard's leash had come unfastened.

Conner picked on me about it. It happened all the time. I needed to get a new leash.

I kicked, took in a deep breath of misty air, and looked back at the face of the wave rising behind me. Conner was at the top, paddling just at the lipped edge of the swell's peak. He got it. I watched him.

Conner was beautiful and perfect.

There is just this moment when your surfboard bites into the wave.

Conner pulled his arms in and pressed his shoulders up, arching his back like a seal sunning itself, like some carved decorative god on the bow of a warship, and *flip!* his feet snapped right into place beneath his hips as he pressed the board on a clean and brilliant carve, down and up and down again on the curling hand of the Pacific Ocean.

The Cayucos Pier was our favorite place to surf.

The break here wasn't that good, but no place needed to be better than this when Conner and I came surfing together.

This was the most beautiful and perfect thing I have ever seen.

This is it.

I want this to be it forever.

I heard my friend whoop and howl as the wall of whitewash came toppling over me and pressed me down again.

I flattened out and kicked toward the shore, stumbling in the shallows to retrieve my board, which had come to rest on a tangle of rust-colored kelp in the shadow of the pier.

Conner watched me.

I imagined his playful irritation at Jack for always fucking up and losing his board. He came out of the water two hundred feet down the beach from me and headed up to the warmth of the sand where we'd left our things.

It was always like this.

It all seemed perfect.

Our clothes and backpacks rested atop the same towels we always used: Conner's was an old flag he'd stolen right off the pole from a Holiday Inn motel in Las Vegas, and mine was a giant terry cloth Twister game.

This is it.

My clothes.

Conner's clothes.

Everything was right.

Perfect.

I had no idea how we'd gotten to Cayucos, and I didn't care.

I was not going to say anything to fuck things up again. I was not going to check my cell phone, or ask Conner what happened after I shattered the lens.

Clack clack, clack clack.

Above us on the beach, two boys were playing with lacrosse sticks, just fucking around, testing each other.

Clack clack, clack clack.

I glanced at them, thought I knew them, but I didn't want to see. I looked away.

I didn't care about anything except being here with Conner.

This is it.

Conner was lying on his back, shivering. His hands and feet looked so pale, like pink marble, where they emerged from his black and sand-peppered wetsuit. This was surfing in California.

I dropped my board and sat down next to him.

"I am so happy to be here," I said.

Clack clack, clack clack.

Conner sniffled. He kept his eyes closed.

"Dude. One of these days you are going to fucking die out there losing your board."

"Shit."

Conner wiped his nose with the back of his hand then reached down and adjusted his balls.

"Did you see that last one I caught?"

He looked perfect. This had to be it.

"Sweet ride, Con."

"Shit yeah."

I was not going to say anything to fuck things up. Being here was too good.

Conner opened his eyes and propped himself up on his elbows. He was happy. I could see that. There was nothing better than this.

He looked down along the length of the beach. I could tell Conner was thinking about going back in the water.

Clack clack, clack clack.

And Conner leaned against me with his shoulder.

"Dude. Numbnuts. Right hand red."

"Huh?"

Conner grabbed my wrist. "You're bleeding."

I hadn't felt it at all. Where my hand pressed down into my towel, there was a pool of blood seeping out between my fingers.

Conner turned my hand over in his grasp. Always careful of me, always Conner.

"Shit. You must have got skegged or something."

I felt sick, drained.

Clack clack, clack clack.

Drip.

Drip.

"You need to get stitches, dude. It's fucking bad."

Conner tucked his legs in and pushed himself up to his knees.

I did not want to leave.

Clack clack, clack clack.

My blood was all over Conner's hands. Of course I knew what it was, but I didn't want to say it.

Drip.

Conner was scared. "Jack. Lay down. You're bleeding bad."

I was being emptied out onto a goddamned Twister game towel. This had to be it.

I said, "Con, this is home, right?"

Conner twisted the edge of my towel tightly across my palm.

"Dude. Just hold that shut. I'm going to put the shit in your truck, then I'll drive you."

He started to gather up the boards and our packs.

Zip.

Conner opened my backpack, looking for the keys to my truck.

Clack clack, clack clack.

"Why can't we stay here?"

"Dude. You are fucked up."

I turned my head to look back at Conner. I wanted to cry, to scream. I wanted to grab on to him and beg him to stay there and make this real.

I did not want to look at the kids playing lacrosse on the beach behind us.

Conner said, "What the fuck? What the fuck?"

He pulled the glasses from my pack.

Time to go, Jack.

Open your eyes.

There is a tired dampness between my legs, and I am pressed up against a wall.

Cool wood. It shines like the dashboard insets in that fucking cop's car.

But this is not here.

The world rocks gently; I hear a *clack clack, clack clack* of train wheels below me.

I am lying naked under a single sheet, heavy with warmth, sweat, gasped exhalations, and I feel the tickling, the bristle of the girl's pubic hairs against the skin of my butt as she presses her body into mine. I smell her, play with her sleeping fingers in front of me, in the dim space between my chest and the shuddering wall that flashes light-gray-light-gray-light-gray; the shadows of things that pass outside the window.

I unfold her perfect hand to put the tips of her first two fingers just inside my lips and lick.

I taste her.

There is no screaming here, no words, only the sound of the train wheels, the rocking, the sallow pulse of light, me, and Nickie.

This is the world.

This is not the world.

Marbury.

This is the train to Grove.

Nickie puts her mouth on a place between my neck and shoulder. I hear it when she inhales; she is smelling me, and I feel the warmth of her breath on my skin.

"Would you like to have breakfast, Jack?" she says.

"I'm having it right now," I answer.

I gave up wondering where I came from. Nothing else can ever matter when the center of the universe is the blood-splattered floor of a kitchen. I wanted this to be Jack's world—a forever that can't be measured in heartbeats, seconds, the meshing of a cog's gears, the equatorial rotation of some planetary object—gazing, my eyes locked on Nickie's, across the table from me sipping ice water with a thin slice of lemon that I could smell, that surrendered small bits of itself against the cold crystal of her glass while she brushed a strand of black hair across one eye with a single finger I'd tasted in a moment that floated like that lemon slice inside some other trapped forever.

She was so beautiful and perfect that I couldn't swallow.

I want this to be the whole world.

What are you doing here, Jack?

You have things to put away. Time to tidy up. Time to fix it.

What's in your pocket?

What's that in your pocket, Jack?

I closed my eyes tightly. Maybe everything would be gone when I opened them.

"What are you thinking about?"

I hadn't touched the food on my plate.

"You know what I noticed? I think you turned just a little bit red when you said that, Nickie. I want to go back to bed with you, that's what I'm thinking."

She laughed softly. "You are going to wear yourself out, Jack."

Her foot brushed mine beneath the table.

"That's exactly what I'm trying to do."

"Eat your breakfast."

"Are you scolding me?"

She turned even redder.

I tried anything to keep myself from thinking.

This is not Nickie.

I had some vague memory of getting on the train, how we'd locked ourselves inside our sleeper as soon as we departed, tearing at our clothing, tangling ourselves on the floor, then, with Nickie seated on the edge of the table, her naked back pressed against the cool window, and, finally, straining, crawling up into our bed.

She ate a strawberry.

I rearranged the triangles of toast on my plate.

I remembered being in the Under; I could still almost hear Quinn screaming when the light came over us and washed me away. I felt cheated by the transient flash of Conner on the beach where we surfed, and I wanted so desperately to be able to hold on to the people I loved, to find an anchor somewhere. And I knew I'd left Ben and Griffin alone back there, but this was Marbury, too, and I wanted this to be my world now.

I wanted it so bad that I refused to remember anything else.

There was no Glenbrook, or not-Glenbrook, the thousand other not-worlds; I pushed those things away. I wouldn't let myself remember them. No Freddie Horvath. I was here in this forever where Jack was never tied down and drugged, brutalized. Raped by a fucking murderer. Ben and Griffin aren't dead. They don't exist. No fucking plastic barrel of bones, no goddamned fucking cop. There is no Conner, no Henry Hewitt.

No hanging boy in the trees.

And no boy with the glasses.

Just this.

My Marbury.

Welcome home, Jack.

One thing: Check in your pocket, kid.

I'm not going to say I didn't know what I was doing. That would be a lie. And there's no reason for me to try to make myself sound good or pure or selfless.

This was it.

This could be forever.

Fuck everything else.

Right?

"Please?" I sounded like a little boy begging for another helping of ice cream. Nickie knew it. She smiled again, blushed.

"I want you to eat your breakfast, Jack."

I put some egg on the corner of my toast and bit it.

"There."

"Good boy," she said.

"Where are we going?"

Nickie had this amused expression, like she thought I was teasing, playing a game.

She was only partially right.

I looked out the window. Flat. Endless fields of something green that was planted in perfect rows, tall enough to reach the windows on the train. It looked like corn, but it wasn't.

Marbury: (noun) Third planet in order from the sun. No natural satellites. This planet, as the only in the Solar System which is inhabited by humans.

"We have four hours to Grove, I think," she said.

I grinned, calculating. "That's a lot of time."

"I have a feeling the woman in the compartment beside ours has been listening to us through the wall. She's likely complaining to the steward right now about our noise."

Nickie smiled and nodded slightly.

I turned around. Our neighbor was sitting alone, two tables away from us. An old woman with an unhappy expression on her face, staring at me while one of the white-suited dining car servants poured a quaking stream of black coffee into her cup.

Clack clack, clack clack.

We were the only passengers in the car.

I nodded a good morning and turned back.

"It was probably a bit too . . . um, stimulating for her," I said.

I held Nickie's hand across the tabletop. The server loomed over us, offering coffee from a silver-handled decanter that was swaddled in a perfectly folded, spotless white napkin.

Somehow, I knew I'd seen them all before.

He poured.

Steam rose.

The train rocked and shuddered.

Clack clack, clack clack.

This was Marbury.

Nickie sipped her coffee. "Perhaps she's spying on us. For your mother."

My mother. Amy. In another world, Amy left me on the floor of a kitchen where I'd been born. In another world, my mother abandoned me.

This is not the world, Jack.

Amy had seen us to the train. Back to school for Jack, with Nickie as chaperone. School was the only safe place for boys during wartime, and Amy was just looking out for her baby.

It hadn't gotten too bad yet.

This is the world.

Right?

Clack clack, clack clack.

I took another bite. When I swallowed, I thought it might fill me up, give Jack all the missing pieces, shut all the open doors, make this be forever.

A conductor, his uniform perfect, dark blue, unwrinkled, walked through the dining car. He smiled warmly at us and said hello. I stared at the glint of light reflected from the oval brass name badge he wore.

This is real.

I know that man.

I have seen him place after place after fucking place.

Quit it, Jack.

When he passed us, the door at the far end of the car opened. A family—a man in a freshly pressed striped shirt, a woman, and three small children—spilled in to take the only large table in the diner. The two little girls giggled and teased at their brother.

What's that in your pocket, Jack?

I swallowed. "I'm not hungry, Nickie."

She squeezed my fingers. Nickie turned my hand in hers and traced the crooked line of the pink scar that stretched across the center of my right palm. It tickled. She liked doing that to me. And Nickie said, "Shall we take a walk?"

It wasn't much of a walk.

The sleeper was two doors up from the dining car.

And we both smiled, an untold joke between us, when we heard the door to the next compartment slide shut. I was lying on top of her. It was hot, and we'd scattered the sheets of the bed down onto the floor and cracked the window open, so I could feel the cooling rush of wind streaming over my naked skin.

I started to say something, but Nickie could tell I was only going to screw with our interested neighbor, so she pressed her fingers onto my lips and whispered, "Behave yourself."

I nipped at her hand. "Behave? I didn't hear you saying 'behave yourself' when we were undressing each other."

Nickie pulled my face down onto hers. She slid her tongue past my lips.

I don't think we'd had clothes on for more than twenty minutes for that entire train ride.

I said, "Behave."

Then the train stopped.

There is an overwhelming quiet that smothers a train when it stops. Especially when it happens in the middle of nowhere, somewhere other than its destination.

I lifted my chest up from Nickie and looked at her. Our skin was soaked between us, and the air in our compartment, still and hushed.

"This can't be Grove," I said.

I glanced out the window, only to assure myself that the train was no longer moving. Farm fields and windmills. All perfectly still, brilliant green beneath the late summer sky.

I shrugged. I wasn't about to get up. "Maybe the train's ahead of schedule, and we have to stop at a switch for another train."

Nickie didn't look concerned. I licked the side of her throat. She whispered, "Now we'll have to be especially quiet."

Then came the voices, urgent, distressed. Something like an argument in the corridor outside, and the sound of people—many of them—moving recklessly through the car, banging open the doors on the sleeping compartments.

I stopped, pulled myself away from Nickie. Somewhere down in the mess of cast-off clothes had to be something I could wear. I kicked through the pile, handed the top sheet up to Nickie.

"I want to see what's going on."

I slid into my pants, hurried. It felt awkward and wet—no underwear, socks, or shirt. I may just as well have walked out naked.

And there was something in my pocket.

Of course I knew what it was.

But I was going to get rid of it.

This is real.

It has to be.

As soon as I leaned out of our compartment, I came face-to-face with a uniformed man holding a rifle. He had one hand grasping our door, and was trying to force it open.

The hallway was choked with Rangers.

There must have been fifty of them.

My first instinct was to duck back inside, but the soldier, a sergeant whose last name was Ramirez, stuck his hand under my arm, as though he would lift me by the armpit. He yanked me out into the hallway in front of him.

"What are you doing in here?" he said. "Go that way. Forward."

"I'm a student. I'm on my way to school. I have my student docs in there."

I tried to push past him, back to my compartment, to Nickie.

"It doesn't matter what you have," Ramirez said. "Move. That way. Now."

Then he goaded me toward the front of the train, jabbing my belly with the barrel of his rifle.

"Fuck this shit!" I pushed the gun away and tried to squeeze past him in the narrow hallway. That's when I saw another Ranger duck his head inside the open door to the sleeping berth.

"Nickie!"

Next thing I knew, I was facedown, sprawled on the floor at the Ranger's feet. My mouth was bleeding. The sonofabitch had punched me, and he pressed down on the back of my balls with the toe of his boot, trapping me there in agony.

I screamed, jerked. But I could feel how he'd butted the rifle barrel squarely into the base of my skull, pinning my face down into the floor.

"I'll fucking blow your head off, kid."

I blacked out.

It is not time.

There are strings—the most delicate imaginable strands—and they connect everything. I think they're something like the gaps between neurons—the trigger mechanisms in your brain—so that when someone asks you what your phone number is, or how to spell your middle name, you don't need a roadmap to find your way home, to the right answer, to the *real* world.

You just follow the string.

You mind the gap.

But what if every time you answered, every destination, gap, each connection on the map, was different, and they were all equally real, correct?

I am the worm, and I am the hole.

I am the King of Marbury.

You can't just have something like the Marbury lens drop into your hands one day and then not begin to wonder at it, to figure out what the fuck's been happening to you.

Wait.

It didn't happen *to* me.

None of it did. Not from the moment I splashed down on Wynn and Stella's goddamned floor, and all the stops along Jack's roadmap: my parents who'd left me on my own, what Freddie Horvath did to me, how Conner and I killed him, Henry Hewitt, Seth, Griffin, Ben, Nickie.

Nickie.

Marbury.

The not-worlds.

None of it happened *to* me.

Everything happened *because* of me.

I fucked up.

It's the strings. Like tuning a fucking television channel, and there's always that moment, a fraction of a second spent inside the gap, in between stations when who knows where you'll end up?

And I thought, in those moments on the train lying tangled up with Nickie, that I could simply decide to make the randomness end. That this would be Jack's world from now on. But something happened when I swung that hammer into the lens at the boys' house.

It was like swinging a baseball bat through a universe made entirely of spiderwebs.

The strings were broken, and Jack was trapped.

All of us were.

Bouncing around, endlessly.

Inside a gap.

So I was lying against a corner, my arm trapped beneath me, blood-less and numb, in the space where the floor met the wall.

Who knew how long I'd been there?

I had some memory that I'd been dragged down the hallway, tossed into this corner. When I fought them, something hit me in the head.

Two men talked over me. They sounded agitated, tense. My mouth and nose were full of blood. The taste gagged me, and it felt as though my guts had been yanked out with fishhooks and were stretched along the stinking carpet, trailing all the way back to the spot outside our door where that fuckhead stepped on my balls.

One of them laughed. "Caught the kid having sex with that girl in one of the compartments."

That girl.

Something about the way he said it, with a certain finality, like they knew the end of our story.

I felt the jabbing prod from the toe of a boot. It lifted my hip, turned me onto my side.

"Little fucker didn't even get his fly buttoned up. Who the fuck's kids are these nowadays?"

Funny. Someone laughed about it.

Open your eyes.

I slid my hand along the raspy carpeting, up toward my face.

Inhale.

The shapes blurred in front of me. The Ranger pulled his boot away from me, and I rolled back onto my stomach. I curled my knees in, tried to get up, moaning, spitting blood into the corner. There were pink roses printed on the wallpaper.

Nickie.

I managed to push up to my feet, steadying myself, leaning with my naked shoulder. They had me in some kind of storage car, one for baggage. There were very few seats inside; mostly open floor space with luggage racks that had already been stuffed with canvas duffel bags—the gear for the soldiers.

Six Rangers stood there, making a semicircle that pinned me against the wall. They all looked so dirty, hungry. Their eyes seemed to say they needed something. Maybe something from me. And every one of them was carrying at least one gun.

A bloodstain dried in a crusted line from my chin all the way down my belly to the button on my pants, and another handprint of mine was stamped in blood over a pattern of roses on the wall.

The train stood still, and I could hear people shouting, crying, through the open doorway that led to the other cars.

"Return to your seats," I heard someone announcing, a Ranger.

"Return to your seats immediately. The train has been commandeered."

My head began to clear.

Somewhere, a woman and a little kid were crying, terrified.

"There's an army of Hunters ahead. Return to your seats now, or you will be shot."

I needed to get to Nickie.

More Rangers begin filing into the baggage car.

Most of them seem disinterested in me. Half of them are my age, anyway. Maybe they remember being treated exactly like this on their conscription days, how they became *men* through abuse, the shit they had to go through before they got their issues—the uniforms they wore, the guns they carried.

Two of them are twin brothers. Just kids, maybe fourteen years old. They look like kids we'd take on in basketball at Steckel Park. The Rangers aren't picky. They take what they want, even if they have to dress them in clothes that are far too big for them.

The kids' last name is *Strange*.

This is real.

I remember who they are.

In another Marbury, Ben and Griffin wore those boys' clothes. Everything those kids have on. In another Marbury, we stripped their corpses.

In another world.

I can't look at them.

I push through the soldiers, toward the doorway. Barefoot, beaten, I'm walking like a drunk.

At the end of the car, there is a side door that is standing open. A Ranger balances outside on the rocky bed of the train tracks, pissing into the cornfield.

Maybe something happened to me.

What's that in your pocket, Jack?

This is Marbury.

It is all so brilliant—the color of the sky, the huge stalks of the green plants that aren't really corn, the diamondlike glint of light that shines through the arc of the soldier's piss stream.

Ramirez appears at the doorway to the next car and blocks my path into the hallway.

"Where are you going, recruit?"

Fuck this place.

"I'm not a recruit. I'm going to get my . . ."

"Your what? Girlfriend? Underwear? Shoes? What? Your room's emptied out, kid." Then he puffs up his chest and adds, "Recruit."

"Where's the girl?"

Ramirez swallows. He looks out the open door, smirking. Outside, the soldier is buttoning up his pants. He wipes a smear of piss from his hands onto his leg and squints in the sunlight.

"Fuck her. Last I saw, she was out there. In the field."

I feel the blood drain from my head. It is a sickening sensation, like being in a very fast elevator. My knees buckle, and I catch myself on the edge of the doorway.

"What?"

Ramirez pushes into me. He smells like sweat. He calls out to the men in the car, "Someone get this kid some clothes!"

I worm around the sergeant, squeeze into the hallway.

"Nickie!"

The sleeper is one car back. I stumble down the aisle between rows of seats. There are a few passengers in here. I don't look at their faces, and they aren't moving from their seats. I can tell they're trying not to look, not to see.

Ramirez spins around, comes after me.

"Stop!"

My foot catches one of the rows of seats. I trip, just as Ramirez fires his rifle. I hear the bullet whiz over my head, the *thunk* it makes when it cuts a perfect hole into the wall at the end of the car.

This is real.

Nickie's okay.

She has to be okay.

This is supposed to be my forever.

I squeeze between the seat rows, over to the side of the car. I can hear Ramirez stomping down the aisle toward me. There is another side door here. I pull the lever down and slide it open. I fall from the train, land hard on my back against the sharp and grimy rocks of the rail bed.

My head spins. It is so bright, and my eyes fill with water. I lie there for that brief second and gaze up into a blue I'd never seen before in Marbury. And I can clearly see the gaping, oozing maw of the hole in the sky.

This is not the world.

I know what they've done to her. I don't need to see it.

I sit up. I hurt everywhere. Ridiculously enough, it bothers me that my fly is open. There is rustling in the field, and a group of Rangers, some of them shirtless, sweating, come wading through the green and perfectly lined stalks. They move tiredly toward the train, carrying guns.

One of them is wearing the T-shirt I'd discarded on the floor beside our bed.

I feel Ramirez standing behind me. I know he is standing there, that he is pointing his gun at me. I can tell by the way the Rangers in front of me stop and stare, wide-eyed, ready for the show. And I am certain he is just trying to decide how to kill me. The quick way, or maybe the fun way.

For a moment, I imagine lying beside the pool at Ben and Griffin's house.

I look up at the sky.

I slip my hand inside my pocket.

I take out the lens.

twenty-one

At first, I believed Ramirez shot me in the head.

I thought, this is what it's like to die.

The pain was blinding, deafening, when the red light poured across the horizon and stretched in every imaginable direction. I tried to grab my head, to cover up, but I couldn't move my arms.

There must have been a wind.

But it wasn't wind.

I couldn't feel it.

And all the stalks in the field collapsed, blown toward me, to lie flattened against the perfect plain of the farmland. In the distance, the wire-frame structures of the windmills crumpled, too, disintegrating, sinking into nothing like ashes from the end of a cigarette.

"Holy shit!" The sergeant fell back inside the train. The door slammed shut behind him.

Then came the rain of arrows.

This is the center of the universe.

All arrows point to home.

All arrows point to Jack.

Beyond the outer edge of the fields, a massive black line had assembled: Hunters, tens of thousands of them. The ones at the back sat atop horses, and were covered with electrified, writhing coats of harvesters. I could hear their shells clicking, the buzzing of their wings. And then came a chorus, the tense snaps from the bowstrings, the whooshing flights of black-fletched arrows that flew in swarms as thick as locust plagues, collecting in a whirring and angry cloud against the sunlight.

Screams—the *shuk shuk shuk* of the arrows as they mowed down the Rangers in front of me, every one of them struck dozens of times. The stone arrowheads came down so hard, arcing so steeply, that several of the men's skulls split open, halved like melons before their thrashing bodies descended to the ground.

The Rangers had no chance against the onslaught.

And not one of the arrows so much as fanned air onto me. It was like I wasn't there at all. When the second wave came, pointless, the gruesome swarm of arrow shafts picketed the ground, reforesting the field in death, hacking apart the corpses of the Rangers who'd made their way in from the field where they'd discarded Nickie.

Some of the boys were half naked, some wore the cast-off clothes that had been mine. Those who weren't dead moaned and writhed, pinned into the ground, contributing their innards in great liquid waves to a collective pond of gore that stretched along the entire length of the rail bed as I sat and numbly watched it.

This is real.

Everything had gone red.

The color washed over the world like the spout of a fountain, erupting from the center of my hand.

A second wind came, the exhalation to the first. It blew out, away from me.

At first, the arrow shafts shook in the gust. Then the flattened cornstalks began to move, tumbling, lifting, carried back toward the army of the Hunters. The arrows themselves tore free from the ground, twisting in reverse, cracking through the tattered rib cages and splintered heads of the Rangers, blown back, assailing the ranks of archers who'd delivered them.

The wind continued to howl, smearing everything with blood. And all the fragmented parts of the soldiers' bodies reanimated, disjointed, separate; they began some ghastly migration—arms, limbless trunks, feet, heads, and hands—away from the train, away from the boy with the broken lens, until the ground was clean again.

But it didn't end there. The rocks of the rail bed thundered and clattered, pulverized in the red sky until everything was blanketed in gray dust, salt. I could taste it. The powder covered me, coated my hair, clumped in the sweat under my arms and on my chest, clotted in my nostrils. I closed my eyes.

I squeezed my hand shut around the broken lens.

And everything stopped.

It was so still, so quiet.

This is Marbury.

It was me.

I did this.

I sat there for the longest time, waiting for something, but I didn't know what.

Breathing, blinking, looking out at the desiccated blankness of Marbury. Everything was gone.

But Jack was used to losing things, being left alone.

In my mind, I tried to devise a way, calculate some mathematically precise method for finding my way back through the broken strings, inside those hours and minutes Nickie and I spent together on the train; looping them around, endlessly, forever.

I felt paste, salt mud, forming around my eyes.

I sat there crying.

This is what it's like to be dead.

Fuck you, Jack.

Finally, I stood up.

For a moment, I thought about brushing myself off, but that was as pointless as worrying about my unbuttoned fly.

I looked like a ghost.

Everything, every spot on my body, was covered in salt. It looked as though I wore some perfect suit, even though the only article of clothing I had on was a pair of pants.

That, and a broken piece of lens, were all I owned in this entire universe.

I licked my lips and spit.

Welcome home, Jack.

Now this looks like good old Marbury.

Everything is nothing.

Everything is everywhere.

Flat, colorless, and dry—as far as I could see.

The sky that had been blue and perfect was now shrouded in the washed-out gray of Marbury. Maybe the hole in the sky closed. Who knew? I couldn't see anything.

The Rangers were gone. Everything wiped away, or covered under salt and ash. No horizon. No fields. No Hunters.

No Nickie.

But when I turned around, the train was still there, sitting behind me, ominous, now buried above its wheels in fine dust that seemed to cough up small unsettled clouds where the last of it came to rest.

Maybe I was totally crazy, damaged, but it almost felt good to see Marbury again the way it was supposed to be, to stand there, completely alone and abandoned, just like I was the first time I fell into this place.

It smelled the same, tasted the way I remembered it.

I slipped the lens back inside my pocket.

Something moved in the train, inside the car where the Rangers had dumped me after dragging me down the hallway from the sleeper. I could hear it, but nothing showed through the windows. They were as obscured beneath dust as my own skin.

One of the side doors on the last car had been left open. I could clearly see the gap of the doorway, like the mouth of a cave facing out onto the storm that wiped everything away from the world.

Barefoot in the silt that covered the ground, I felt like I was walking on a perfectly clean beach as I made my way toward the open door.

I should have known not to go inside.

A second-class passenger car: just rows of seats, most of them point forward. Some are grouped together; they face each other over small tables.

There are fifteen people seated in this car.

I count.

Fifteen.

All of them are dead.

They look artificial, like clay models that have spent too long inside a kiln. But they are perfectly arranged, seated peacefully, frozen in the final eyeblink of the moment that swept them away.

I pass through each of the train's cars, moving toward the last one, where the Rangers have gathered, the place where they'd dumped me facedown in some corner on the floor. In every compartment, more of the same. The people are all dead, hollow mummies that look as though they've been sitting on this train for centuries.

Maybe it has been centuries.

The dining car is perfectly clean, arranged for the afternoon meals. The three servers, immaculate in white, statues of saints, lie huddled against the far doorway. I have to step over their bodies to make my way through to the next car, and, from there, into the sleeper.

Ramirez wasn't lying. I didn't think he was, anyway. The compartment where Nickie and I had slept together is completely empty. All of my things have been taken. The bedclothes are freshly replaced, changed with cleanly pressed linens, and the other fold-down beds on the opposite wall have been lowered, as though the new passengers, the soldiers, intend on using them for their own rest.

I don't think they'll be sleeping here now.

I slide the door shut.

The way into the baggage car is blocked off behind a windowless double door. I wait there, holding my breath, listening. There are Rangers inside the car. I can hear them talking, arguing. I can't make out the words, but I know they are scared.

Worse than scared, they sound terrified.

Panic.

I don't care about them at all. I wonder only about those two boys, the twins; what will happen to them? They're just little kids. I consider opening the doors, going inside, but—really—what will I say?

Hey, guys, want to go outside and play flashlight tag with Jack?

300

It's really fun.

Wait till you see what I can do with the thing I have in my pocket.

I turn around, start walking back down the narrow hallway through the sleeper car.

Then I hear the first gunshot from inside the baggage car.

Of course. This is what happens.

I freeze, turn back to watch the door.

A second shot.

Then a burst of them.

It is like listening to a bag of popcorn while it cooks inside a microwave.

The last two gunshots come so much later.

Maybe a full minute.

Then it is done.

I don't need to go inside the car. I know exactly what happens in there. I can draw a picture of the precise spot where some of those boys fall down after they shoot themselves in the head, where Sergeant Ramirez would be right now, at this precise moment. He is seated against the wall, sucking on the barrel of his rifle with its butt tucked down between his knees, his thumb jammed into the trigger guard, and his brains are painting the outline of a tornado up across the rose-patterned wallpaper, all the way onto the ceiling.

Jack has been here before.

Jack is here now.

And Jack never had any idea that the twenty-two kids inside that fucking baggage car blew their brains out because they were so scared of Jack and his little piece of broken glass.

Fun game.

This is Marbury.

I am King.

I take a two-liter bottle of water from the dining car.

That's all.

And I close up every door on the train when I leave.

twenty-two

The train didn't want to go away.

I walked for what felt like miles, hours, but every time I'd turn around I could still see it, as if the train were watching me, calling out, *Come on, Jack. Come back and play some more.*

Eventually, in the whiteout waste of Marbury, I found myself in the middle of a horizonless nothing. No more direction, no features to aim myself toward or away from, and just the slightest difference in shade between the colorless sky and the emptiness of the ground.

This was the center of the universe.

And I had three objects in my universe: a broken piece of glass, a warm bottle of water, and a pair of pants whose knees had ripped when I fell out of that train I'd been trying to get away from.

Nothing else.

I crossed the blasted salt flat of the Marbury desert barefoot, without a shirt.

Alone.

After a while, my eyes began to fail. I supposed it didn't matter anyway. I walked, counting steps, sometimes with my eyes shut tight. And when I'd open them again, nothing at all looked different.

I began to get tired.

Are you halfway there, Jack?

I thought, *If you keep going just halfway to your destination, then halfway again and halfway again, you will spend forever in an infinity of halfways.*

All the not-worlds.

I closed my eyes.

Fifty steps this time.

Open your eyes, Jack.

Through the blank ash of the fog, I saw the outline of something big, pale, with a perfect row of blackened circles like eyes that stared back at me. At first, thinking I had walked in a huge circle back to the train, or maybe I'd gone entirely around this world, I squatted down to my knees, keeping myself low, small, as though crouching would be sufficient to make Jack invisible to everything he was afraid of.

I thought the black eyes were moving.

You know how objects, when you stare at them long enough, begin to pulse with some kind of life? Because the thing had to be a sort of structure. It was just so hard to tell what it could be; everything was washed out by ash and fog, and my eyes ached.

I tried pouring water onto my face. It was a mistake. It made my eyes burn so bad I thought I'd go blind. When I was tired of waiting, listening, scoping the thing out, I finally stood up and started moving toward it.

It was a plane.

Not an entire plane; most of a jetliner. Maybe a hundred feet or so of the body. It stuck up at the end where the tail section had broken away, and the nose was either buried in the salt flat, or was perhaps sticking out, unmarked, on some other string, somewhere else entirely.

The way it was tilted, with the circular windows leaning toward me, it was possible that I had been standing—walking on top of— one of its wings.

It was an amazing thing.

I needed to touch it.

It was from the same airline that flew me to England, to St. Atticus Grammar School for Boys. It wasn't even a question in my mind—I was absolutely certain—this was the same plane. I mean, this was Marbury, after all.

What else could it be?

When I walked toward the buried nose of the plane, the windows dropped down close enough to the ground that I could see inside it. Of course I was drawn to it. I had to look.

Curious Jack.

So I wiped the salt from one of the portholes and cupped my hands around my eyes. I pressed my face against the glass.

At first, all I saw were the gray disks of light—the unobstructed portholes—on the other side of the plane. I waited for my eyes to adjust. As they did, the inside of the plane seemed to liquefy, pulsing like waves on a windblown pond.

Harvesters.

Millions upon millions of them, clustered in endless carpeting gobs over every surface in the plane, a nest of them. Waiting, sniffing, hoping to detect some great field of death out here in this desert.

I felt my stomach convulse. I pushed myself away from the window and walked around the front of the plane.

On the other side, the left wing angled out from the wreckage and rose above the ground. The jet engine was half buried, but the wing itself extended like a massive awning. It didn't cast any shadow.

There were no such things as shadows in Marbury.

I took a drink, wiped my mouth with the back of my forearm, and kept walking.

Halfway there.

Halfway there.

And in the white vacuum that swirled around me, enclosed me, that surrendered its boundary another few inches with every step I took, I heard music.

An accordion.

I walked toward it. What else could I do?

Halfway there.

When I saw him, it was like looking at the scene of a shipwreck.

I saw something big, dark, and low to the ground, that had been washed up on this endless beach of desert.

A dead whale, maybe.

I stepped closer, careful, and I could see the man playing music. He was seated in the salt, his legs stretched out in front of him, with his back propped against the carcass of a fallen horse.

I circled around.

He had no way of knowing I watched him. I moved silently, and his music was so loud.

The song he played sounded mournful and plodding; a dirge that repeated after the first bars, over and over, as though he had no intention of ever stopping the tune or breaking his rhythm.

Of course I knew who the man was. I didn't need to see his face, because I had seen him before, other times, in other places. But not in this Marbury, and not with this Jack's eyes.

Uncle Teddy.

Preacher.

Maybe he'd been left behind by the Rangers, the same ones who stopped the train. It didn't make sense that they'd abandon an old man like this, but I couldn't expect anything the Rangers did to be justly calculated when weighed against such counterbalances as right and wrong.

I could smell blood before I was close enough to see it.

Black-shafted arrows jutted like spiny quills from the horse's neck and side. They vibrated like tuning forks. The animal was still breathing, and I'm sure that if it wasn't for the wailing of the accordion, I would have heard the horse's gurgling death-gasps.

The old man had one arrow completely through his right shoulder. The point of it, pasted over with clotted blood, stuck out level, aiming directly at me, a stained and accusing finger.

I watched him play.

He couldn't last.

The harvesters would be here soon.

The music stopped, in mid-beat.

I thought he died, but the man said, "Are you here to kill me?"

"I'm not going to kill you."

"Then why are you standing in back of me, like that?"

"I came from this way."

"Where are you going?"

"I'm not sure."

He put his little accordion on his lap. It wheezed. Maybe it was the horse.

"You got a long walk." He tried to move. He looked as stiff as a statue. "Come around this way, so I can see what you look like, before you kill me."

I took one step, then stopped. "I told you I'm not here to kill you."

Preacher coughed. The arrow twitched like the needle on a lie detector.

306

"No matter which direction you came from, you walked straight through death. And now, here you are, unscathed. Don't tell me you're not here to kill me, boy. You are just a boy, right? You sound like one."

I walked around the horse's head. I could see its eye, crazed, rolling with a slender crescent of white as it followed me.

I stood in front of the man, my legs apart. The water bottle dangled from my hooked fingers.

He said, "It's you."

I held out the bottle. I didn't say anything.

Preacher raised his hand. I unscrewed the cap, helped him drink.

"I've seen you before," he said.

"A couple times."

The man swallowed. He grunted when he tried to hand the bottle back to me. "Thank you."

There were three red dots, like planets, on the bottle. Preacher's fingerprints in blood.

He kept a gun lying across his groin. It looked like a .45. I could see that the hammer had been pulled back; it was cocked.

"It's been a good show you put on, boy. Heaven must be amused."

I sat down with my legs folded. I made sure I was far enough away that he couldn't reach me. But I wasn't afraid of him trying to shoot me. Maybe I should have been.

"I'm not anyone you think."

"You're him," he said. "It's you. The Jumping Man."

"You're a crazy old man."

I turned my head, looked around us.

I don't know what I was expecting to see. Maybe a sign with an arrow, pointing *This way, Jack*. But I felt like there was something else, someone else, nearby.

307

Maybe I was supposed to follow the arrow sticking out of the old man's back.

Preacher lifted a finger, crusted with blood and ash, pointed up. "What's the sky look like now?"

"I don't know."

"Well," he said, "I'd think a boy would know what the sky looks like."

"It looks like nothing."

"And the ground?"

He was fucking with me.

"It looks like endless fields of grass and clover."

Preacher grimaced, a smile. His teeth were black, and he hadn't shaved in days. The white stubble of his beard looked like spines on a cactus.

"In another world, we could have a long talk, I think."

"Do you want me to help pull that arrow out or something?"

He shook his head. "The horse is dead now."

I looked at the horse's side. The arrows had stopped twitching.

"I keep coming back to this place. And every time it's different."

"This is how the world has always been. It will continue to be this way after we're gone." The old man's voice was a raspy croak. "But I do suspect a new broom sweeps clean."

"I don't know what you're talking about."

"Maybe."

"I was in Pope Valley, California, in 1888."

"You think I don't recognize you?"

"I knew who you were, old man, the first time I saw you."

The old man shut his mouth. He swallowed.

I said, "Do you know what this place is?"

308

"I only know what it isn't, boy."

"You could start with that, if you want."

"It isn't Pope Valley. It isn't the tree you and your father were hung from."

I spit down into the ash between my legs.

"You were with Anamore Fent's team, weren't you?" I said.

Preacher's chin dropped. I thought he was looking at his legs, or he was falling asleep. I counted my breaths—five of them—before the old man answered.

"Captain Fent is dead."

I didn't see any of the others on the train. I might have remembered who they were, if they were the ones from Fent's team. Probably.

Then Preacher said, "It's just you and me here, boy."

Brian Fields would be the only one left.

"There was one of them. A kid named Conner Kirk. Do you know what might have happened to him?"

I looked down. I drew a circle in the white salt. Another circle enclosing it.

Preacher said, "Kirk. I know him. The sergeant. Good-looking boy. He was quiet and mean. Always got what he wanted."

"Do you know anything about him?"

Preacher started to laugh, but it came out as a cough. He spit blood. His eyes squinted at me, like he was sizing me up, waiting for me to say something. He shook his head. "We went looking for him. Fent made us go after him. He was her boy, you know. Favored, at least. What did you do to him?"

"I didn't do nothing."

"After that morning he and Pittman took you out of the station.

Kirk took you out. He was going to shoot you. I imagine he failed at that, judging by our current engagement in this conversation. He never came back."

"He is a friend of mine."

"We did find Pittman, though. Well. Pieces of him."

I tracked the tip of my finger in a line through the ash. I drew an arrow that pierced the center of my circles.

The old man said, "Bad magic. That's what Pittman feared most. He brought it on himself. He was a dark man."

"You believe that? About bringing things on?"

"What's in the sky, boy?"

I put my hands flat on the ground, pushed myself up, and stood. My legs ached. If I didn't start moving, I'd die here, right alongside the old man and his horse. I felt like I could sleep, but I had things that still needed to be done.

"Is that it? Are you going to kill me now, son?"

"No."

"I believe I'd prefer it if you did."

Preacher's hand slid over his lap. He grasped the gun, but it seemed like it was too heavy for the old man to lift. He tried aiming it at me.

I felt something, a warm wind, like a breath, and with it came a sighing sound, a low whisper.

Shhhhhh . . .

As I turned away from the old man, I saw the ghost of a boy standing ten feet from me, floating up like steam from the burned ground.

Every time I'd seen Seth before, he looked small, frail, like a little kid. But here, this time, he was older. At first, he just stood there watching me with his arms flat to his body, palms pressed against his thighs as though posing for a portrait. He didn't say anything to me.

I could clearly see the deep marks that coiled around his neck.

The old man coughed, his voice creaking. "Devils."

When I looked at him, Preacher had the butt of the gun resting on his leg, and his trembling hand held the barrel pointed directly at me.

"I guess all things are not accomplished, old man."

In the wind, smoke clears behind the preacher.

But the sky is still white, empty.

He is shaking so bad I can see the point of the arrow behind him as it nods up and down, up and down; a seesaw.

That's how we play in Marbury.

There is a horizon now, formed by the rising light that establishes all the things in front of me: a crooked shell of a plane, a wing, a black centipede miles back that is a train filled with the dead.

This pathetic dying man, serving out his mission.

Against the wind, the gray shadow of Seth floats between us.

Me.

Seth.

The man with the gun.

There is a white explosion around the old man's hand. It burns my eyes, but I can clearly see it through Seth's back. A shell ejects, it tumbles in the air, a circle, an eye, opening, closing.

Forever.

The flash hangs around the muzzle of the gun, splashes outward, dances, curls.

Fireworks.

311

It is a clear yellow-white, brilliant, and I realize I have never seen a color this pure, this beautiful. Through Seth, the blast from Preacher's gun resembles swaying tentacles, an anemone fanned by the tide.

The light gets bigger.

Until all I can see is just the light.

Nothing else.

I am staring at a sun.

It must be the center of the universe.

twenty-three

A ball of yellow light.

That was all.

I thought the old man shot me.

When my eyes focused, I realized I was lying on my side.

My mouth was open and I could feel the clay grit, taste the dirt that gathered in pasty clumps on the inside of my lips and stuck to my tongue.

But I could see only a blob of yellow light.

The old man must have shot me.

I moved my arm. I ran my hand over my face, felt down along my neck, my chest. I rubbed across my belly, the waist of my pants, my legs. I could feel the straps of a backpack looped over my shoulders.

Think, Jack.

I was wet, cold.

Maybe I pissed myself or something when the old man shot me.

But there was no blood.

I closed my mouth. It was awful. And I could smell river water.

I was staring into a flashlight.

I lay on my belly, in the dirt at the edge of the river. I could hear the rush of the water.

The Under.

I fumbled for the light. My hand didn't work right. It took me a couple attempts before I could pick it up, pivot the beam away from my face.

I remembered.

My knife lay pressed to the ground beneath the back of my forearm.

Quinn Cahill.

Quinn found the glasses. I remembered how he was holding them in his hands. It was the last thing I saw.

Before Conner and Nickie.

I sat up in the dirt. I immediately vomited all over myself, down my chest, onto my lap. It was mostly just water. Hot, burning with bile. I remembered drinking the river water. I smelled like algae and puke.

I threw up again.

This was Marbury.

Jack's fun back-and-forth games.

A seesaw, an arrow.

I am King.

"Quinn?"

I spit.

How long had I been lying here? It couldn't have been long.

It could have been a lifetime.

I had to get up. I had to get back to Griffin and Ben.

"Hey! Quinn!"

My voice echoed in the black void of the Under.

I got to my feet. I was so dizzy, I had to concentrate on not falling.

313

In one hand I held the light; in the other, my knife. I put them carefully in front of myself, ready to break my fall if I collapsed.

I swept the light around me, everywhere.

Quinn was lying on his back with his face turned away from me. I had to kill the kid.

He was sick.

He was dangerous.

I was going to kill the kid.

Where do you stick the knife?

Where do you stick the knife so the kid will not fight and scream too much?

"Quinn?" I whispered his name.

The kid was not moving. I knew what it was like. Who knew what world or not-world he was in? Maybe he was whole. Maybe he was decent. Maybe he was lying at the side of a pool in another Glenbrook, talking shit with me and the boys.

I was going to kill the kid.

I moved.

I had to be sure.

"Quinn?"

Nothing.

My stomach twisted and retched. I unfastened Quinn's pants, pulled them down past his knees so I could see the burning red crook of the mark that snaked through the kid's pubic hair and curled across the top of his thigh.

He was a monster.

I was a monster, too.

He was not heavy. He did not struggle.

I was the king of all the monsters.

I dragged Quinn Cahill to the edge of the river, rolled him into the water, watched as the soft whiteness of his naked body fluttered toward consciousness and was sucked between the teeth of the churning spill gate.

I vomited again.

I pressed my face down into the dirt and cried.

At the edge of the river, I drank. It made me feel alive. I slid out of the backpack and lowered myself over the side. I had to get the smell of puke off my skin, out of my pants.

I had to wash my trespassing hands.

Better.

When I climbed out, sloshing, I picked up the pack and turned around, scanning the ground with the flashlight.

Quinn's solitary boot sat in the dirt, about fifteen feet from where I stood. I walked over to it. When I kicked it, I uncovered the glasses.

Instantly, the dark cavern filled with moving light.

Look away, Jack.

A flash of that cop, Avery Scott, fanning out photographs on a table in a small room with no windows.

Look away.

I shut my eyes, turned my chin back into my shoulder, the way you'd snap your face away from a burning fire. I groped around blindly in the dirt until I had the glasses twisted up inside the sock in my backpack. I felt the wad with my hand, made sure the outer lens was flipped out of place. Then I zipped the pack shut. Hidden again.

"Quinn?" I whispered.

I shined the light out onto the surface of the water, looked for something white, pale.

Nothing.

I picked up the pack and ran into the tunnel, back to where I'd left the boys.

When I had gone far enough that the pale haze from Griffin's flashlight glowed dimly at the mouth of the smaller side tunnel, I began to pick up my pace. And every few feet, I'd look back and sweep the beam of my light across the tunnel.

I was sick about what I'd done, what I'd had to do.

I thought about Ben and the boy he killed and then dumped in their swimming pool.

I imagined Quinn Cahill was following me, dripping water, smirking, blazing the red slash, the question-mark brand of disease.

Then I ran toward Griffin's light.

It scared the boys when I came clattering up into the rise of the tunnel.

I dropped my flashlight and it clanked against the metal, scattering a frenetic dance of light that looked like a soundless firefight in the dark.

Griffin and Ben looked good. My friends.

It felt like I'd been away for months.

"Jack!" Ben lowered the spear when he recognized me. I could see the energy in his eyes. He was back, healthy.

And Griffin said, "He's fucking clean."

I put my arms around the boys; squeezed into them with my face between theirs. I wanted to cry, but I wouldn't let it happen. I had to force myself to think about something else, not Nickie, not Quinn, not what happened on the train, or back at the river.

Think about getting out of here.

"How long was I gone?"

I let go of the boys, stood back, wiping my face.

Griffin shrugged. "Seemed like a couple hours. I wanted to go looking for you, but Ben wouldn't do it."

"I found a way out. We need to move."

"Jack." Ben's voice was low. I already knew what he was going to say. "What happened to the kid?"

I looked directly at each of them.

I didn't have to spell it out.

"It's done."

Griffin bent down, picked up the second pack. I heard him mutter, "Fucking bastard."

"We have to just get out of this shithole," I said.

I shook my head, trying to get the image of Quinn out of my mind.

Ben's eyes were locked on mine. I could tell he understood exactly what I was thinking.

He said, "Which way?"

And we kept Griffin between us as I led them out into the main tunnel.

It energized the boys to see the pale light on the other side of the river, even if it was still only Marbury up there. At least it showed a way out of here.

And anything was better than here.

I shined my light onto the rushing surface, down toward the falls.

"Right there is how I got myself clean, Griff."

"Is it good water?" he said.

"It's good."

Griffin seemed to be calculating the distance, the flow. He shined his light at the edge, where the river tumbled over the precipice and into a chasm so big and dark, it looked like a starless and growling universe.

That was where Quinn's body was now.

Ben knew his brother was worried.

He said, "You can make it, Griff."

Griffin shook his head and sighed. "Shit."

We sat down in the dirt and removed our boots. We stuffed them inside the packs that Ben and I would pull across the river, last, with Griffin.

I uncoiled the nylon rope and tied it to my waist as tightly as I could. Then I fed the opposite end through the straps on the backpacks and knotted it, finally, in a loop around Griffin's chest.

"Listen. Don't be scared. When I get to the other side, sit down, so we can anchor Ben. He can hold on to the rope and use it as a guide to pull himself across. Once he's over, I want you to put the flashlights inside one of the packs. Then Ben and me can pull you over."

Griffin nodded.

Ben said, "Let's do this. Let's get the fuck out of here, Jack."

So I dove into the river, as far out from the edge as I could jump.

The swim was much farther and more difficult than I thought it would be. Before I got to the other side, I felt my legs begin to drag below me. I was out of breath, and started drifting toward the falls.

If I had been doing it alone, I probably wouldn't have made it across. But I just couldn't stand the thought of letting Griffin and Ben down again.

When I finally did pull myself from the river, the flashlights on

318

the other side looked like tiny specks—fireflies—and my muscles burned so bad that I couldn't stand up.

I heard the boys shouting to me.

I blew long strands of snot from my nose and yelled back to them.

"Ben! Wait! I'm not ready yet!"

I wanted to get directly across from the flashlights, so I could make the rope shorter, tighter for him. When I was in place, I gave Ben the signal to come, and told Griffin to get down onto the ground.

I'd underestimated the force of the current on Ben. The rope tore into his palms, blistering his flesh, and the tighter I tried to pull it, the deeper down the water seemed to drag his light body.

Ben nearly drowned.

I couldn't believe how long that kid could hold his breath.

The pull of Ben's body in the water dragged Griffin through the dirt. I watched the glint of his flashlight as it scooted downstream and closer to the edge, but there was nothing any of us could do now.

When Ben finally got over to my side of the river, his pants were pulled completely off, inside out, twisted around his ankles so bad that he had to flop up onto the shore like a beached dolphin.

It took him several awkward minutes to free his feet from the tangle of his dungarees.

"Fuck that," Ben said. He spit and held his hands out like they'd been burned.

"Hang on, Griff! I'll tell you when!"

I took up all the slack in our rope. Ben pulled his pants up. I could tell how much his hands hurt, but Ben would never say anything about stuff like that. So I wrapped a double loop around his waist and said, "Don't grab it, dude. Your hands are fucked up. Let's pull him over with our legs, by walking that way."

I pointed back toward where the gray light seeped down into the Under.

Ben nodded. "Okay."

Then I yelled for Griffin to jump, and Ben and I nearly ran as we pulled the kid over to our side as fast as we could.

When he came up, Griffin gagged and coughed up big mouthfuls of river water. The weight of the packs had pulled him under. We had no way of knowing the kid was submerged for his entire trip across the river.

But at least the three of us made it over, alive.

So far.

But the fucking flashlights had been destroyed by the water.

So we had to guess at which boots belonged on whose feet. We were certain we'd all gotten it wrong, too, but we had to move quickly in the dark.

None of us wanted to spend another minute in the Under.

"At least we have something to aim for," I said.

So we ran toward the light.

twenty-four

None of us had any idea how long we'd been in the Under.

But when we made it to the source of the light, I saw that it was daytime on the outside; could smell that it had just finished raining.

Great.

Hunters, spiders, worms, and some lost boys from California who didn't belong here.

The food chain.

And it was impossible to tell exactly where we had arrived in Glenbrook, or not-Glenbrook.

Our way out was obstructed by a wall of junk: enormous broken boulders of concrete, an overturned fire engine, the remains of a crumpled mobile home, and what looked like about three-fourths of the tar-papered and shingled roof from a gas station. The gaps we found in the barrier weren't big enough for Ben and me to squeeze through. When we tried to, we ended up scraping gashes on our bellies and backs, so we abandoned attempts to get out in several places before Griffin finally managed to wriggle through an opening that was just wide enough for us to follow him.

Once we crawled out, the three of us sat there on a chunk of cement, dazed, raked with scrapes that looked like claw marks across our chests. We stared down at a concrete flood basin that widened out and dipped away from the piles of wreckage blocking the way back into the Under.

"I'd rather fucking die than go back down there," Ben said.

"I have a feeling whoever piled all this shit up here was thinking the same thing," I said. "Or they just wanted to keep what's in there from ever getting out."

"Any idea where we are?" Griffin said.

I looked around.

Nothing.

I shook my head.

So we sat there and waited while the rainwater receded. None of us was too eager to get to his feet and commit to a new direction.

I opened the backpack and took out one of our water bottles. I felt for the glasses.

A habit.

I always felt for the glasses.

We had one can of stewed tomatoes and a can of something called hominy, which I'd never heard of before in my life. Still, it was food, and after I opened the cans, we passed them around and dipped our fingers into them, scooping out what we could.

And when the cans were empty, I wedged them down into a crack between the chunks of concrete.

Griffin nodded his head. "That was good. Thanks."

"Yeah," I said.

The water eventually disappeared. The ground dried. For some reason it was incapable of absorbing anything; so it returned to its usual ash and dust. To get out, we needed to climb the walls of the channel. It was the only way for us to get some idea of where we were, to see if there was anything I could use as a landmark to direct us toward the old ag school, where we might find horses.

The sides of the ditch were slanted concrete. They were steeper and higher than they looked from where we'd been sitting. Our boots couldn't grip at such an angle, and we ended up having to pull ourselves to the top by crawling on our raw bellies.

When we got up, and could finally see beyond the concrete walls of the channel, all I could guess was that we had somehow ended up far outside of what used to be Glenbrook.

There was nothing at all that looked familiar to me here.

I could see the lost expressions on the other boys' faces, too.

On the opposite side of the canal, there was what looked like an auto salvage yard. Of course I knew it wasn't actually a salvage place. Maybe it had been a commuter parking lot at one time. It was filled with cars, trucks, even a few school and transit buses. Maybe half of the vehicles had been turned completely over, or were resting on their sides.

Ben nodded his chin at one of the buses. "Skulls."

Even as far across the wide channel as we were, we knew they were skulls. Skulls had a certain shape; a color that you never saw on anything else.

Everyone in Marbury knew what skulls looked like.

And we knew what they smelled like, too.

A row of them—one above each broken window—adorned the rusting roof of a school bus that sat crookedly on its axles next to the bent supporting galvanized poles that at one time held a chain-link fence in place.

Hunters liked to decorate with their castoffs.

We saw a few harvesters crawling around on the outside of the bus, too. Their presence meant that some of the dead in the yard were recent kills.

I looked back over the vacant terrain on our side. There was nothing to see except for the dead skeleton of an old oak tree and the remains of two homes: a crumbling chimney column that marked one of them, and an empty frame for a garage door on the other.

That was it.

"We've got to get as far away as we can. I don't think there's any of us left at all around here."

And Griffin said, "Fucking Odds."

So we set off in a direction I could only assume was east.

Once we'd passed beyond the wreckage of the homes, the ground rose in gentle undulations.

There had been a housing tract outside of Glenbrook called The Knolls, and I felt like this could be it—if I imagined that subdivision being wiped out in a nuclear flame.

I'd used my knife to cut out the lining of one of my pockets, and this I fashioned into a sort of fingerless glove that I kept tied tightly on my right hand. The boys knew why. They'd seen what happened to me on the roof at Quinn's firehouse, and ever since we'd stumbled out from the Under I worried about keeping the scar on my palm covered.

We walked through fields that had been littered with bones and the small things that could offer quiet testimony to a different world: empty eyeglass frames, a microwave oven, a television remote control, the front door of a dishwasher. And with every step we would kick up and uncover from the ash smaller clues of a different past—the shining curve of a compact disc, acid-encrusted batteries, and the constant scattering of bricks.

Griffin stopped suddenly. "I smell horses."

I kept my eyes on the kid, watched how his nostrils flared, chin pivoted, and his stare focused, so alert, scanning for what he knew had to be out there.

Maybe it was the power of suggestion, but as soon as he'd said it, I could smell them, too.

A sudden rush of adrenaline electrified me. Tense, muscles twitching, I spun around. But there was no place we could hide. There was nothing here; only trash and bones.

It was habit, survival. The three of us faced outward with our backs forming a triangle so tight we were practically leaning into one another. Ben had his spear ready, and I held the knife.

Griffin didn't have anything.

I saw them first.

They appeared like smoky black phantoms through the ashen fog kicked up by the flat and shoeless hooves of the animals; coming slowly into focus through the scrim and swirl of the constant Marbury haze.

They were neither Hunters nor Rangers; I could tell that right away, but it didn't lessen the tension at all.

I pointed. "Over there."

The boys turned, watched the riders, who seemed to hesitate, clump together.

I slid my pack from my arms without taking my eyes from the horses. I let it drop into the ash behind me.

I needed to get the lens, I thought.

The lens fucks with everyone here.

Except for us. The people who don't belong in Marbury.

Because if they were Rangers or Hunters, we were certainly going to be killed. But here, in Marbury, those riders could have been something even worse.

I opened the pack.

Ben whispered, "What are you doing?"

And Griffin said, "They're kids." He tapped my shoulder. "Jack, they're Odds."

I looked up. I already held the broken lens, covered in my hand. I slipped it inside my pocket.

The group was clearer now, maybe a hundred yards away, riding down the gradual slope of the knoll like it was covered in soft November snow. There were seventeen of them, all boys, with several riderless horses, packed and tethered in a line.

Odds.

It was difficult to say whether or not they noticed us standing there. In the fog, the three of us, skinny, wearing nothing more than ash-coated rags for pants, may have looked like just another random chunk of garbage, unworthy of any careful attention.

But the group continued slowly, deliberately toward us.

And riding at the point was a man who wore a loose duster coat

325

and a dirty cloth hat that didn't fully contain his sand-colored locks of hair. He was not just another Odd. I could tell by how he carried himself, adult-like, even though he looked like he was hardly out of his teens by much, and that was evidenced by the scant and uneven blond beard that curled in gapped wisps under his jaw and nowhere else on his face.

His gray eyes were pinned on me like he was waiting for me to step forward and say something to him.

I wondered if he recognized me.

Because I knew who he was.

I was looking right at Henry Hewitt, the man with the glasses. The guy who opened the door into the prison of Marbury for me the first time.

Henry was the reason I was here.

I stepped toward him as he rode closer.

Ben put his hand on my shoulder, like a warning, trying to pull me back.

But I slid my knife into its sheath and said, "I know that guy, Ben. I've known him a long time."

I couldn't help but think about all the other times, the other places, I'd seen Henry Hewitt. Most of those times, I hated him intensely for what he did to me, or for his inability to answer my questions. But now I saw Henry as a kind of anchor, a lifeline back to the world where we belonged. Now, maybe, he could finally help me.

I put my hand up as he rode to meet me.

The other Odds stayed back, watching, the horses uninterested in anything that was happening in front of them.

"Hello, Henry," I said. "I can't say it's a funny thing, running into you here. Welcome home."

Henry froze. Then he leaned forward, squinting and straining as though he were trying to read something—anything—on my face.

"You know me?" he said.

I looked back at the boys, then at the other young Odds who watched our meeting from a distance. But it was clear to me that Henry didn't know who I was. Or he didn't remember.

"It's me. Jack."

He shook his head. "I knew a kid named Jack. I lived by him in Bass-Hove. That was years ago. *That* Jack? His parents were named Mike and Amy."

Of course it was me. It was meant to be. I remembered the time Henry told me about it. We sat in a pub, in London, and he explained how he knew me when I was a little kid, that he knew my mother and father. Here. In Marbury.

But I didn't tell him.

I thought about being on the train.

Nickie.

I shook my head.

"Not from here. I know you from another place." I whispered, uncertain whether or not I should even say it, "London."

The word seemed to punch Henry in the guts. He pursed his lips shut, and shook his head. Then he got down from the horse and stood directly in front of me, so close I could practically feel the damp of his sweat.

And here I was, doing exactly the same thing to Henry Hewitt that he'd done to me, so long ago in a bar called The Prince of Wales, where he'd told me how he knew me from this place called Marbury.

"You're from there, too?" he whispered, and his voice was urgent and impatient. And the way he said *there* left no question he was talking about a different world. It was the way you'd talk about heaven, or maybe hell, when you weren't allowed to actually utter such names.

"I . . . I met you there, Henry. A few times. We've had beer together. I've been to your flat."

He looked lost, scared.

"You don't remember me, Henry? You gave me the glasses. The Marbury lens. It's me. Jack."

Henry grabbed my shoulder, squeezed. I could feel the tips of his fingers like they were biting into my skin.

"Can you tell me how to get back?" he said.

And those desperate words seemed to punch me in the stomach.

Was he stuck here, too?

How could he not know the way back?

How could he not know who I was?

I said, "I thought you'd tell me the answer to that question."

Henry looked nervous, glanced at the boys in back of him, and then at Ben and Griffin, who started walking toward us.

"How long have you been here?"

"You mean this time?" I asked. "I keep popping in and out, but I can't get anywhere that isn't here. Marbury."

"I want you to show me how," he said.

Ben and Griffin had come right up behind me. The Odds riding with Henry looked a little apprehensive. Maybe they were worried the three of us were going to do something to the man.

"And you don't remember Ben and Griffin?"

Henry shook his head. "Are they from there, too?"

Ben planted the end of the spear down beside my foot. It crunched into the dried crust of ash. "Who is this guy, Jack?"

Griffin said, "They have horses. We should go with them."

Henry eyed Ben and Griffin up and down, like he was trying to gauge their abilities.

I asked him, "How long have you been here?"

Henry looked at each of us, thinking. "I started keeping track of the days. I tried to, at first. I was sixteen years old."

His voice was a whispered rasp. "I was sixteen years old when I got the glasses. Sixteen! It's been ten years in this hell. I can't be certain."

He grabbed me again, shook me. "Tell me how I can get out of here."

twenty-five

They knew it was long past time to leave.

What remained of the city was completely overrun with Hunters. There were no more people here.

No more Odds.

No more Glenbrook.

Ben pleaded with Henry to take us along. In the end, he didn't really have a choice.

They gave us horses.

We rode with Henry and his Odds.

It was what we were supposed to do, and I knew it. It was the only way for me to find Conner. And Conner, the rest of the lens, was our only chance to get out of here.

Henry barely said anything else to me after our first meeting in the Knolls. Maybe he was waiting for me to do something, but I didn't know what it could be. I got the feeling he was saving something up, planning. I knew he was scared about telling the other Odds about where he came from; that they might somehow turn against him if they knew the truth about Henry and me, and the other two boys who didn't act quite like Odds.

It rained once more before the first evening came. We stayed on the horses, but in the foothills there was no flooding like we'd see drowning the old streets. That probably meant none of those black suckers, but I wasn't going to get down on the ground just so I could find out.

And it turned out to be the last rain we would ever see in Marbury, too.

When it stopped that night, the hole in the sky seemed bigger, more intense. It spread open directly above us, and showered cascades of what looked like burning-hot embers downward, shards of stars that disappeared and died in the Marbury sky. The hole began to resemble a gaping mouth, its upper lip a sneering mirror image to the wound on my hand: hungry, drooling, yawning open, wide enough to swallow the world.

It was coming.

By mid-morning on the third day, we had crossed into the desert, heading on a path toward the settlement called Bass-Hove. Our direction was decided for us by a plastic toy compass Henry kept in his pocket. It looked like something a kid might have dug out from a box of breakfast cereal at some other time, in some other world.

Nobody knew if the compass meant anything at all. Its needle seemed to be made from tinfoil, half of it painted blue, and every time Henry consulted it, he would have to carefully pile a loose hill of ash on the ground as a support to tilt the thing at a steady angle so the indicator could find a balance point and not stop up against its red plastic case.

Seventeen kids rode with Henry. We made twenty. And nearly all of them, from what I could tell, were fourteen or fifteen years old. It made sense. Younger kids had been easy prey. They got taken first. And older Odds were always conscripted into the army, or something worse.

It was natural and every other kind of selection.

So, next to Henry, I was the oldest in the group, which gave everyone enough reason to be suspicious of me.

It was almost as though that prisoner number—373—had been plainly tattooed across my chest, and they all could see it.

Some of the other Odds flatly refused to talk to me at all. To them, I seemed nothing more than a non-paying passenger. But for the most part they seemed to accept Ben and Griffin easily. They were younger, the right age to be part of the group.

I'd heard the riders talking about the boys—how some of them recalled stories about the two Odds on Forest Trail Lane who lived in a bunker beneath a house and killed a Ranger in their garage.

They gave us clothes that had been taken from the dead, so at least we were covered against the desiccating heat of the desert, even if our uniforms were hole pocked and bloodstained. The band of Odds carried water and food that they carefully rationed, stored in bundles of blankets and drapes that were lashed to the pack horses with anything that could bind—electric cords, networking cables, even a rotting garden hose.

In the group, there was a loose and unstated hierarchy. Everyone followed Henry. And a tall, black-haired Odd named Frankie, who was missing the little finger on his right hand and had a wispy tuft of fuzz sprouting beneath his chin, seemed to enforce rations and turn taking when it came time for jobs or sleep.

But they were all boys. Naturally, there were episodes of conflict and cussing, sometimes fighting, and even nastier stuff than that.

Boys.

I don't think any of them had the intent to stay within their association once our group made it to the settlement.

On the fourth day, Frankie showed the others how we could use two plastic tarps and a collector can to distill drinking water from our piss, so we wouldn't have to open the precious bottles we carried. He explained we'd have to save them until they meant the difference between living and dying. That day, we stayed camped in the middle of a formation of melted lava rocks—maybe they were giant meteorites—where we rested the animals.

The boys never gave us any weapons.

The other Odds were scarcely armed themselves. A few of the boys carried bows they'd taken from dead Hunters, with a supply of arrows that had been pulled from carcasses of their friends, of people they'd known.

There were some Odds with knives, and many of them carried spears made from all sorts of metal debris.

And then there were the rocks. Rocks for throwing—they were kept in whatever pockets were available—and every one of the boys had a favored rock for bashing, one that fit comfortably in his grip, some of which had been scabbed over with tarred blood. No one would carry the maces or cudgels of Hunters, though. Those were always made from sharpened human bones.

But out here, in the desert, there was no life.

Only ash and salt.

The days were monumentally boring, made worse by the fact that the Odds only stared at me; they never spoke.

Ben and Griffin felt guilty about the ease with which they fit in among the other boys, but I couldn't hold a grudge against them for it. I put us here, after all.

So I sat beneath a craggy overhang on one of the boulders, watching, absentmindedly flipping the broken lens between my fingers inside my pocket, carefully tracing the sharpness of the edge that had cut my hand so bad. And I stayed there, tucked into my little hiding place with my pack jammed into the crevice behind me.

We'd been taking turns on the watch, seven or eight at a time, posted on top of the jagged boulders around our perimeter where we could look out in every direction.

Of course the Hunters would be following us, tracking game.

It was Ben's and Griffin's turn up on the watchposts.

Frankie stood in the center of our encampment, carefully shaking out the top sheet of plastic, filling his can with the dewy distillate. That day, the entire place reeked with a thick fog of piss, and every hour or so, Frankie would remove his can and dole out a portion of drinking water to whichever Odd came up on the mental list he managed.

I was always last in line.

But I kept myself occupied by watching him, observing the other Odds in their bored frustrations.

One of the boys, a wiry and frail-looking skeleton of a fourteen-year-old named Ethan, had an English accent like Henry's. He rarely spoke. The boys teased him about how he'd peed himself when he slept every night the first week after they found him alone, hiding beneath the ruined grandstands at a soccer field.

A few of the other boys were relentless in picking on Ethan.

There are always small clusters of boys like that within larger groups. They congeal together like cold grease in water. The assholes. Three of them: a small, muscular tank with white hair named Alex, and his two followers—a slow-witted nose picker who everyone called Fee, and his brother, a towering pole of a kid named Rum, who never wore a shirt so he could show off the tattoo of a dragon that wrapped across his belly and around his back to the spindly knobs of his spine.

They were like pack animals, I thought, *and the English kid was chosen to die first.*

That's just how things worked for kids like Ethan.

He must have been strong, or fast, or something the others underestimated, for him to have survived for as long as he had. And I thought if anyone was going to talk to me, maybe Ethan would. But then I realized trying to do that might just get him picked on even worse.

I was lonely, and I wanted to go home.

It scared me to think that home might not even exist at all anymore.

When it was my turn to drink, Frankie glanced in my direction and raised his dingy can. Then he called for Henry and I watched while the boy asked him to bring a drink share over to his friend, "the Ranger."

I glared at him.

"Fuck you, kid."

Frankie puffed up his chest and grabbed his basher from his back pocket. He came storming over to where I was sitting in the rocks. Henry just stood there, holding the water can, quietly watching us.

I hated being forced into doing the "guy thing," but I couldn't let Frankie start off this new day by labeling me as some kind of enemy outsider in front of the other boys, either.

That's just how things were.

It meant there was going to be a fight, and neither one of us questioned or doubted the laws that dictated our nature.

So before he'd even taken three steps toward me, I launched myself up and ran straight for him. I wrapped my arms around his midsection and slammed him down into the ground.

Frankie managed to hit me one time on the back with his rock. It hurt. I could feel the point of the basher as it cut into the flesh above my shoulder blade. Then there was a general roar, and whatever kids weren't on posts immediately formed a tight circle around us.

I kept wondering why someone didn't do something. I was convinced that one of us was going to end up dead, but I wasn't going to look around and plead for intervention, either.

I pinned Frankie's hand beneath one of my knees. Hard. It felt like I was grinding dried chicken bones against a sidewalk, and I knew it had to hurt him. But Frankie refused to let go of his basher. I twisted my fingers into his greasy hair and pressed the back of his skull down into the gritty ash.

Frankie had his free hand up at my throat, clenching, trying to push me back, but he wasn't really doing much. He squeezed, and I could feel his dirty fingernails cutting into my skin, but I didn't even hit him or anything. And I knew I could have messed him up bad, but I just looked down at the kid and saw how his eyes started welling up with tears, and I realized right then how horribly foul Frankie smelled, so I was kind of disgusted. I loosened up on him.

I said, "Don't fuck with me, kid. We all want the same thing here."

And then I looked up at the circle of Odds who were watching us, right at the faces of the assholes—Alex, Fee, and Rum—and I let go of Frankie without so much as punching him even one time.

I stood up and wiped my hands on my legs.

That kid stunk like rotten meat.

Then Alex said, "You should have made him kiss your nutsack, kid," and his followers shoved each other's shoulders and laughed.

Frankie got up, stinging.

I wasn't sure if he was going to come back at me again, so I watched him. He was wet with sweat, and gray ash like bone dust coated the back of his head. He still gripped the basher.

I took the water can from Henry and swallowed just one gulp. Then I handed it over to Frankie.

"Here. Fighting against each other in this heat is a sorry waste of our energy."

Frankie tucked his rock back in his pocket and nodded. He looked at Henry, then at me, and he took the can from my out-stretched hand. He drank.

Frankie licked his lips. He was thirsty, and I didn't realize he'd been making everyone else drink first, even me.

"It may be some time before you get another sip of water."

Henry sat down next to the place where I was trying to sleep beneath the crag of the rock. I'd been using my backpack as a pillow. It was dumb, though. It was just as hot beneath the rock as if I'd been staked down like a martyr in the middle of the ash field.

"I'll last," I said.

"I came to ask you about things," Henry said.

"The last few days, I didn't think anyone was talking to me. Even my friends."

Henry shook his head and sighed. "I need to hear it. How did you get here?"

I scooted out from beneath the rock, attempted to brush the salt and ash away from my sweaty body, and sat next to Henry.

We leaned our backs against the rough surface of the boulder. From where we sat, I could see Ben and Griffin standing at the top of the ridge on the lookout post above the opposite side of the clearing the Odds had camped in.

"It was you," I said. "You sent me here."

So for more than an hour, Henry and I shared each other's stories. In some ways, it was like meeting for the first time. But in other ways, it was like we'd known each other for our entire lives, too.

Henry had been there for ten years; since he was a kid. He told me that he'd lived in the settlement, next to my house when I was only five or six years old.

Of course.

That was always meant to be.

Henry and I know each other everywhere, don't we?

All these strings keep connecting, over and over, knotted together—things inside of things inside of still bigger things—me, Henry, London, Glenbrook, Marbury.

Not-Marbury.

I am the worm and I am the hole.

It was why I'd run into the same people and places again and again; even if, now, everything was slightly off, altered. Tilting. The knots were all unwinding.

And all arrows point to the center.

Here and there blur into one.

And the gap is gone.

Henry told me he'd "been back home" a few times, and that he always swore to fight the urge to return to Marbury, but, in the end, it was entirely out of his control.

Just like Jack.

This last time, he said, he'd been here so long that he began to believe that there was no other world than this; that everything else had been a dream, or some kind of psychosis; maybe something all kids imagine when they pass through adolescence.

He believed it until Jack and his friends showed up five days ago, after we crawled out from the Under.

"You know what?" I pulled at the threads unraveling from the tear on my right knee.

He looked at me and I said, "I broke the lens."

Henry didn't say anything, didn't react at all.

"I shattered it with a hammer. Then we ended up here. But something's wrong. Everything's off. Every time I turn around, there's something that's changed, like it's broken, too. And every time I try to get out of here, I end up somewhere worse. It's always the same: It starts out looking like things are fixed, like it's going to be okay or, possibly, even better than before, and suddenly everything gets fucked."

I shifted uncomfortably.

My back ached where Frankie hit me with the rock. Across the clearing, where the string of horses had been tied, I could see the boy with the missing finger.

He was watching us.

Frankie had to know something was up, that Henry and I shared some connection that went beyond just trying to get across the desert, to escape the Hunters pursuing us. I could tell just by looking at the kid's eyes that Frankie was smarter than most.

My hands were sweating. I wiped my palms on my jeans and rested my arms across my bent knees. I slipped my hand out of the filthy and stinking pocket I'd been wearing as a glove for nearly a week and raised my right hand, like I was holding something for Henry to read, directly in front of him.

"The lens cut me," I said.

Henry stared at the mark in my flesh. Then he looked up at the sky. He didn't need to say anything. I knew he saw the connection.

More tangled strings.

"I want you to show me," Henry whispered, like we were keeping some desperate and poisonous secret from the other boys.

I thought about it.

Here I was in this complete reversal of roles, finally capable of fucking with Henry Hewitt the way he fucked with me when I was just a paranoid and unsuspecting kid wandering around London alone. It would be easy enough, I thought: Just open up the backpack, unroll the filthy sock, and

flip!

Good-bye, Henry.

Good-bye, Jack.

Fuck us both.

"I'm scared to do it. I messed shit up and now everything is coming apart. I have to believe things will fix themselves, Henry. I think we will see each other in London, just like we did, like we're supposed to. But I have to do one thing first."

Henry wasn't looking at me. I thought maybe he was mad, like I was holding back a present and he wanted it bad enough to do something desperate. Or maybe he was thinking of some way to take it from me.

After all, that's what Jack would do.

I didn't so much as glance at my pack. I didn't want to tip off Henry that there was anything inside it that might interest him.

But he had to know.

He was dying to find out.

And it was almost like I could hear those fucking glasses whispering my name, as though they had a heart and it was beating, pumping, and I knew it was going to make me open the pack.

Don't do it, Jack.

Do it.

Come home, Jack.

I tried to breathe, inhaled deeply.

"There's one more of us here," I said. "A boy named Conner Kirk. He's..."

And I thought, *He's what, Jack? The only person who cares about you? You love him? You love him and you know you fucked up his life forever? He's what, Jack?*

"I know he's heading for Bass-Hove, too. He has the other part of the lens. I think we need to put them back together."

"Is that what you think?" Henry said.

He wasn't even trying to disguise the sarcastic tone in his voice.

"Yes," I said. "That *is* what I think, Henry. What do *you* think?"

I heard him take a deep breath. He nodded his chin out toward the circle of clearing between the boulders. "Me? I think it doesn't

340

matter. This is always the world. Home. We may be the last people remaining, but this is what we do."

He shrugged. "We cross deserts looking for others who may be left behind, too."

Henry sounded just like he did when he tried to explain about Marbury to me; the night when I was so sick, after I'd lost the lens in Blackpool and we sat together at The Prince of Wales.

"You told me that you weren't sure whether this was the beginning of the world or the end of it."

He looked directly at me. "Let me see the lens, Jack."

My hands shook.

"Jack."

I began to sweat. I could feel droplets as they rolled down my skin, tickling, insects.

And I was so thirsty.

Across from us, there was movement along the top of the boulders where the Odds had been posted on lookout. They raised their arms and pointed off, across the desert in the direction Henry's little toy compass told us was the way out.

"Show me."

I couldn't stop myself.

My hand shook so bad. I dragged my fingers through the ash.

I tried telling myself that maybe this was the key.

Maybe being with Henry could make things right.

I didn't look.

My hand found the backpack and I dragged it out and placed it between my legs.

Don't do it, Jack.

"Not the lens," I said. "It kills things now. There's something else. Another way."

Henry grabbed for the backpack. He was acting like a drug addict, desperate to get his fix.

"Don't!" I grabbed his hand to stop him from opening the pack. "Listen to me. Wait."

Henry tried to wrestle the pack open.

I twisted his wrist.

The kids on the rim began shouting.

They saw something in the desert.

Henry was sweating, panting.

"Listen to me! It's something else. It doesn't even work for Ben and Griffin."

Because they're dead and inside a fucking trash barrel.

I said, "It might not be anything for you."

"Let me see it."

I can't stop myself.

On the rim, Alex, or maybe it is one of the other assholes, shouts Henry's name.

"Henry! Come look!"

It is always thrilling. My chest heaves. It's a nervous rush, like having sex.

I am excited and terrified at the same time, and I know Henry feels it, too.

Zip.

My fingers fumble through the folds in my sock.

Fuck you, Jack.

I keep my nervous hands working inside the pack. I have to hide what I am doing from the other Odds. I unravel the dirty sock. I flash on a thought, but it is gone before I know it: *Should I feel sorry for what happened to Quinn Cahill?*

I can see a glint of the blue glass, the small eye of the outer green lens that is flipped away.

"A rider!"

Someone calls from the lookout.

"Henry! There's a rider!"

Henry sits beside me, so close we lean against each other. I can feel his body quaking.

I say, "Look."

Then I flip the lens into place.

twenty-six

There is a thrashing noise.

It comes clattering in drumbeats, arrhythmic, like a fight. Someone is kicking something.

My shins ache.

I am lying on a dirty wood floor and I've been bashing my legs against a doorjamb.

It's not shaking. It's jerking, convulsing, like electric current is shooting through every muscle fiber in my body; killing me.

My legs do not belong to me.

Quit it.

I kick the wood frame again.

Nice.

Welcome home, Jack.

Now where the fuck are you?

343

I smell cigarettes.

They aren't burning now, but wherever I am someone smokes here.

It was always like this.

Every time.

I lay there in a doorway, half in, half out, staring at the little creases in the jamb's wooden frame, the finishing nails, a spot where the varnish didn't soak into the surface, the uneven texture of the plaster wall at the baseboard. Nobody cares about those parts of walls; they are always canvases of imperfection. I heard an electric hum and bubbling water. It struck me as funny that I was lost again, in a dimly lit room, and wherever it was, there was an aquarium in here with me.

And cigarettes.

I swallowed.

Good. My throat still worked.

My legs stopped thrashing on their own, but my shins ached like fire.

I moved my eyes, tracking along the surface of the floor and into the room where my head was. I saw something. It took a while—maybe ten seconds—for the words to come into my head, but that's how it always was.

A rusted radiator heater stood against the far wall.

I marveled at the perfectly slatted ribs, how they were coated in thick green paint—an entirely nauseating color—with small cuts of tarnished rust showing through. I counted the ribs. I don't know why. Maybe it was the only thing I was capable of doing at that moment.

Counting.

And watching.

Then I moved my hand.

It was a remarkable thing.

It was almost as though I had forgotten I had arms—or a body—at all.

This is my hand.

I had to think again—right or left?

I couldn't remember.

I spread open my fingers above my eyes, a bloom, a firework.

My palm was cut.

Bleeding again.

Drip.

I didn't even flinch when the blood dropped, warm and heavy, onto my lips.

It tasted good.

I squeezed my hand shut and ran the other one over my body, feeling—what I was wearing, if everything was still connected.

Jack always did that, too.

Inventory time: a T-shirt. My fingertip snared inside a hole over my belly. I could feel my skin. I felt smaller, empty. Jeans. I ran my hands over the thick metal buttons.

Where is this, Jack?

You've been here before.

Think.

Everything felt clean, not like it was after scrambling out from the Under and then surviving for days on horseback in the desert. And I became aware of my feet, that I was wearing shoes without any socks.

These were not Jack's clothes.

A phone began ringing.

Double rings.

I knew this sound.

I was in England again.

Somebody pick up that goddamned phone.

I moaned, tried to sit, but my head weighed as much as a fire truck.

Something crashed to the floor. The phone.

The noise was so loud it almost hurt, but at least the ringing stopped.

And somewhere, Henry said, "Fucking hell."

"Henry?"

"Where are you?"

I put my hands down on either side of my hips and pushed myself up, so I sat with my spine pressed into the doorjamb.

"On the fucking floor."

Every day is just like being born again.

I looked at the smear of blood I'd wiped across the floor beneath my palm. I was in Henry's apartment. In London.

Sitting in the doorway between the bedroom and the toilet.

And it was raining outside.

Maybe this was it, I thought.

Maybe this was really it, and Jack was home.

And maybe I'd step outside into a wriggling mass of those fucking worms.

The clothes I wore belonged to Ander, Nickie's younger brother. I remembered how I'd shown up at their house, soaked from the rain, and he'd given me his stuff—jeans, a T-shirt, tennis shoes, and a jacket—so I had to go barefoot inside his shoes, with no underwear, too, and Nickie took all my clothes from me, so she could launder them.

Ander's black T-shirt that said THE RAMONES on it. I stared at a small circle of pale skin where there was a finger-sized hole over my belly.

This had to be it.

I was home.

And that night, maybe it was tonight when I showed up drenched from the rain at Nickie's front door, I remembered that I had the lens in my pocket. Lost and found, after Conner and I got into a fight on the beach in Blackpool.

I could feel it there now.

This had to be it.

I was home.

Henry's feet moved, covered in sheets and blankets, twisted around on his bed.

"Are you okay?" I said.

His hand swung over and dropped onto the small stand where he'd knocked down the phone.

"Fuck. I need a cigarette."

Paper and cellophane rumpled in Henry's hand. For some reason, the sound turned my stomach. Then came the grating friction wheel of a lighter, and I could almost smell the metallic spark that preceded the flame, before the sucking sound, the burning of paper and tobacco. And all this over the sickening and constant percolation from a bubbling, lukewarm aquarium.

I had to throw up.

Welcome home, boys.

I leaned forward and dog-crawled to Henry's toilet, tracking a smeared palm print of blood along his floor.

When I got up, I washed my face. I wound a strip of toilet paper around my hand and squeezed it shut, but the bleeding didn't slow at all. Then I went back to the bedroom.

The place was a mess. I stumbled over the canvas jacket I'd been wearing—Ander's—and kicked it onto a pile of newspapers. There were clothes, food wrappers, trash, scattered everywhere around Henry's bed. The room looked like a place where junkies had spent the last few days cooking their brains out.

It was night, and through the rain-smeared panes of curtainless glass I could see rows of lighted windows from the apartments across the street, yellow rectangles blazing against the featureless silhouetted masonry of row housing.

I knew where this was.

The aquarium sat bubbling on a low dresser with three wide drawers. Its inner glass was so overgrown and blackened with algae that I couldn't tell if there was anything at all swimming inside it.

Henry sat on the bed with his feet on the floor. He faced away from the window, smoking.

I shook my head. "How can you do that right now?"

"What? This?" Henry held his cigarette out in front of his eyes. I could see how pleased he was smoking it. It must have felt like years since he'd had the last one, even if it may have only been half a minute.

"Cigarettes stop me from puking. You should try one."

He inhaled again.

I tripped over something, took two steps toward the bed, and sat down.

"Is this it? Are we done?"

Henry looked around, taking stock. I guess we all did that.

"This is it." Henry nodded. "Home. Thank you, Jack."

I ran my uninjured hand over my legs, pulling the denim away from my thighs. I didn't want Henry to notice the shape of the lens in my pocket. Maybe he couldn't go back now, anyway. Maybe neither one of us could.

And I didn't want to ruin it for him. Henry was relieved, happy as he sat there smoking his cigarette, but I knew something had to be wrong. I expected it. The lens was still broken. And my hand was bleeding.

And something else.

I was supposed to have my cell phone in my pocket.

I remembered it being in the pocket of these same jeans the night Nickie hung up on me. I knew exactly where I sat—on a greasy bench in the Green Park Station—when she told me to leave her alone. I felt my pocket, but I knew my phone wasn't in it.

Henry watched me. "What's wrong?"

"I thought I had my phone."

I looked at the jacket I'd kicked on the floor, calculating the distance, the number of footsteps. It was difficult to coordinate my arms and legs. I wanted to lie down.

Something was wrong.

Henry stood. He was a mess.

Henry was always a mess—unshaven, with the feeblest scrub of facial hair dotting his jaw, a dingy white T-shirt twisted uncomfortably around his emaciated frame, spider arms, burgundy corduroy pants that hung in draping columns over his knees and leg bones. "I believe I've got some beer in the fridge. Want one?"

"Huh? Oh. Yeah."

Henry padded out the doorway. A light came on in the living room. I could hear him moving things, the clinking of glass, cupboard doors opening—all nauseating sounds that hovered like some avant-garde orchestral score above the flat, droning accompaniment of the aquarium. I picked up Ander's jacket, knew by its weight that my phone had to be in a pocket somewhere.

Found it.

Henry came back, carrying two glasses. He pressed a light switch with an elbow.

I cupped my phone in my bandaged hand, took the beer in the other.

"What happened there?" Henry extended a finger from the side of his glass, pointed at the wrapping of tissue around my hand.

"Nothing," I said. "I got cut."

Henry's brow pinched together, like he was thinking about something, remembering. Then he said, "Cheers," and clinked his glass into mine.

I drank to the bottom of the glass without stopping. I don't think I'd ever tasted anything as good in my life. Then I thought about what that meant. My life. What life? This life now? This life was only about five minutes old. The water in the fucking aquarium would have tasted just as good.

Henry drained his glass, too.

A couple newborns.

He said, "I'll get more," and took the glass from my hand.

It all looked the same. Henry's apartment smelled the same. Sweat, cigarettes, and damp wool.

I followed Henry into the main room. I stood there in the doorway, watching him. I flipped open my phone.

Do you really want to do this, Jack?

This was Jack's phone.

In the center of the universe that Jack built.

I checked the recent calls.

There were two calls to Nickie.

There were no calls between me and Henry.

But there was a call to Ander.

I never had Ander's cell number.

I scrolled down and saw five calls in a row to Avery Scott.

The fucking cop.

And there were phone calls listed to the name Quinn Cahill.

No Conner.

No Ben or Griffin.

Another not-world.

Fuck you, Jack.

I had to sit down.

Drip.

I couldn't stop the bleeding from my hand.

Henry poured beers, a fresh cigarette dangling like a white slash from his lips. I moved over and slid one of the wobbly wooden chairs out from his small kitchen table. I dropped my phone onto the floor.

Everything sounded so horribly noisy.

He put the beer down on the table and I stared at a spot on the floor between my feet.

Drip.

I didn't bother picking up my cell phone.

Henry sat down, lifted his glass. "Cheers."

I just looked at him while he drank. I don't know why, but I wanted so bad to punch him at that moment. I was seething with anger and I needed to scream, to break something. Of course Henry could tell; how could he not notice something like that?

He took another long swallow. "Sorry about the place. Were you expecting something else? You've been here before, didn't you say?"

I clenched my wounded hand into a fist. It stung.

I don't know how I managed to sit there, to stop myself from leaping across the table and driving my fist into Henry's face.

He laid on his soothing, condescending tone. "You should be happy. We're finally home."

I took a deep breath, filled up my lungs with the smell of Henry and his cigarette, the stale aquarium fog, his Chelsea flat.

"This isn't the place. If it was the right place, you would know who I am."

Henry didn't react at all. I slapped the table. "Look at me! This is what I was wearing the last time I saw you! You don't have a fucking clue who I am, do you?"

I sighed, looked down at my feet again. "We don't belong here."

I heard him take a long swallow. "I belong here." Henry put down his glass and said, "What about you? Where do you belong, Jack?"

It was like he was telling me to get the fuck out of his house. He was done with me. I could leave.

I nodded. I drank the beer he'd poured for me. I stood.

I was horrendously drunk after two glasses of beer.

Stupid.

I almost felt like laughing.

"I'm going to get my shit and go," I said.

My mouth felt numb. If he'd offered me another beer, I'd drink it, but then I'd want to fight for sure.

I kicked my cell phone toward the doorway, satisfied I'd made a goal into the bedroom with it.

I was drunk; and it was 5:44 in the morning.

As the sky grayed outside, the windows across the way didn't appear so bright; the buildings paled to not-black.

Something was wrong.

"Where are you going to go?" Henry sat at the table in the kitchen.

I didn't know where I was going.

"I have a hotel room." I slurred the words. "Near Regent's Park. Or my girlfriend's house in Hampstead."

I couldn't know if any of that was true. I just said it.

I bent down, picked up the phone, and slid it into my back pocket. But when I tried scooping up Ander's jacket, I lost my balance and ended up on all fours.

Jack is a fucked-up drunk.

Henry heard me, came in from the kitchen. The room was lighter now, all washed in gray, and I had my face pressed down into Ander's jacket, trying to see if somehow it smelled like Nickie, like the house in Hampstead I remembered sleeping in.

There was a noise.

I knew it.

Roll.

Tap. Tap. Tap.

I took a quick breath. Maybe I was just drunk.

I turned my face so I could look at Henry. He'd heard the sound, too, but I could tell he had no idea what it meant.

"Seth," I whispered.

I pressed myself lower against the floor and peered beneath the bed.

I felt the vibrations of Henry's steps as he got nearer to me. "What are you doing?"

It was totally dark under the bed, just black corpses of trash and cast-off clothing.

"Looking for something," I said. "You're going to know this isn't it, Henry. You'll find out. I don't know how it's going to hit you, but it *will* happen."

Where are those fucking glasses?

I slid my hand under his bed, sweeping my fingers around through the debris, trying not to think about what I might be touching.

Then something tickled the hair in my armpit.

Whatever it was came out through my shirt and began crawling toward my hand.

I jerked my arm back from under the bed.

Stretching nearly the entire span from my elbow to wrist, a green-black harvester clung to my forearm, looking for the source of the blood it smelled, the cut on my hand.

Then the thing bit me, right over my middle knuckle, laying open a smiling, white-lipped gash in my skin. I was horrified and sick.

"Fuck!" I swatted my hand back at nothing, and the bug tumbled away, clicking its shell open and futilely buzzing the cellophane wings that could never support such weight. "It fucking bit me!"

Harvesters don't eat living things.

The thing sailed past Henry and he moved aside nonchalantly, like he was stepping from the path of an errant tennis ball during a summer match in the park.

I sat up against the bed, squeezing my hand, watching the blood from the bite wound pool and run in a thick scarlet streak that dripped down onto Ander's T-shirt and jeans, where it left button-sized stains on my crotch.

Henry looked amused, his cigarette dangling loosely. Barefoot, he stepped on the thing. I couldn't see it, but I could tell by how Henry's stomps encroached in succession toward the baseboard that it took several attempts for him to kill the harvester.

But by that time, two more had climbed up inside the back of my T-shirt and began eating me. I got up, pulling at my shirt, trying to swipe my arm behind myself and get the things off me. I could feel their jaws, slicing, biting, like tiny carving knives that cut into the skin on my back. I could hear them chewing.

"Henry!" I lifted my shirt and spun around, urgently assuming Henry would help. He hit me. I didn't care. I wanted those fucking things off my back.

As soon as Henry swatted the second harvester from me—and it was sickening that I could feel how it dug into my skin and didn't want to let go—a sea of bugs came spilling out from under the bed, washing toward our feet, like an oozing black flood of tar, like the entire apartment was sinking into a roiling ocean of the monsters, and someone had just pulled a drain plug from the floor.

Henry froze. I shoved him back into the living room and slammed the bedroom door shut. But the harvesters had already reached the doorway, and flattening themselves, the first ones began wriggling through the crack above the floor, frantically scratching with their clicking legs, jaws snapping, flexing, open, shut.

I crushed the first ones with the edge of my shoe as soon as they began to squeeze through. It sounded like I was stomping on light-bulbs, and a burbling mass of rust-colored snot erupted all over the floor, up the leg of my jeans, past my ankle, inside my shoes. Behind me, I heard things tipping over, breaking. Henry was pulling up a thick rug and upending the furniture.

Panting, his cigarette still pinched between his lips, Henry jammed the rug down into the crack beneath the door, and wedged it tightly with his fingers until the opening was sealed. But there were so many harvesters on the other side of the door that I could hear the rasping clatter of their shells and legs, the pincers of their jaws against the door in such great numbers that it sounded like we were deluged in a downpour of pea gravel.

My hands shook. I combed fingers through my hair, tried pulling my shirt away from the spots where my blood cemented it to my back.

And my hand kept bleeding.

"You still think this is home?"

Henry looked sick, gray.

He took another drag on his cigarette, then let the butt fall onto the rug. He stamped it out with his bare foot. Henry swallowed. I could tell he struggled with articulating words. "We need to get the fuck out of here."

The harvesters began pulling the rug through the crack beneath door.

They were going to get out.

Like everything, it was a matter only of time.

twenty-seven

Henry said, "Do something."

I didn't know what I could do.

All I knew was that from the moment I first opened my eyes, lying on my back in the doorway to Henry's toilet, I hunted for signs that this was not the place.

It would never be the place.

I was lost forever; we all were, skipping through layer after broken layer, hell after rearranged hell, not-worlds upon not-worlds, jumping men, every one of us.

It was the Marbury lens.

I was inside the broken lens, and it was inside me. I would never go home again. And maybe it was just one of those stupid and optimistic things that teenagers tell themselves—no matter how fucked up their lives are—but I could still imagine putting things right, waking up inside Ben and Griffin's sweaty garage, maybe in my own bed the morning of Conner's end-of-school party, or perhaps I'd be on top of a bare mattress again, inside an empty room at Freddie Horvath's house, my foot bound, aching, and I'd be scared, watching the light along the crack at the bottom of a doorway, telling myself *This is real, this is real* and living through the succession of days nervously watching everything so closely, observing it all with a microscope's unfailing attention to tiny details, each moment holding my breath, wondering when I'd detect the telltale clue that signified another broken string, as familiar as the sound of a doorbell that welcomes Jack home to another not-here.

But I had the lens.

It was inside my pocket.

The lens would set us free.

When I slipped my hand down inside the pocket of Ander's jeans, I watched the rug, pulling, jerking, as though it had come to life and was trying to crawl away from me and Henry. I could hear it ripping into shreds beneath the door, getting smaller, a cheap magic trick.

Look, no hands.

I felt it.

Something was wrong.

Something is always wrong.

I grabbed, pulled my hand up.

I was bleeding. Bad now.

Henry said, "You're bleeding."

No shit, Henry.

Drip.

Drip.

"What are you going to do?"

Like I could actually decide the outcome.

I opened my hand.

And I was holding on to a black knot, a tangled mass.

A thick nylon zip tie, the kind Freddie Horvath used to bind me down to a bed.

No lens.

It was a fucking zip tie in my pocket.

The rug twitched. It was nearly gone now.

This was it.

Jack was home for good.

"Fuck!" I dropped the black knot like it was burning a hole through my hand. I punched the door. The rug was nearly all the way inside the bedroom, disappearing beneath the crack at the bottom of the door.

"What's wrong?"

Henry was scared.

Something was wrong.

The lens had to be here.

I dug through my pockets again, frantic. All I had was my cell phone, a pair of yellow tickets for the Tube, and a ten-pound note.

"We need to get the fuck out of here."

The harvesters were coming for us.

I spun around. This was Marbury. Always something trying to kill you here.

In the tight corner of the main room, in Henry's kitchen, I began pulling out drawers, dumping them.

Henry caught on quick. He knew the game, too. After all, he'd been stuck in Marbury for most of my life. I grabbed a butcher knife. Henry picked up a stubby knife with a thick blade; it would be hard to break. But I didn't have time to shop for survival gear.

At least I had shoes.

Henry was barefoot.

Oh well, there would be corpses. There were always corpses, and shoes had half-lifes like goddamned uranium in Marbury.

The rug finally disappeared into the slit beneath the bedroom door. I found an ice pick on the kitchen floor, jammed it down into my back pocket, and we ran out to the hallway, slamming the front door to Henry's apartment shut behind us.

I don't know why, but as soon as we were out of Henry's flat, I thought, *This is Marbury with electricity.*

Lightbulbs burned in yellowed tulip sconces all the way down the hall, Henry's phone was ringing when I woke up, and the beers we drank had been cold.

Electricity.

And harvesters that eat people alive.

And no way out.

We ran toward the stairs. Henry's flat was three floors above the street, and although neither of us had any idea where we might be going, we both knew we had to move, to get out of there.

Henry followed, one step behind me as we made our way down to the first landing. And he nearly knocked me over when I stopped suddenly at the bottom step.

Standing directly in front of us, in the center of the worn carpet where the banister wrapped around and descended to the next floor, was Seth Mansfield.

And Seth was different now, too.

Again.

When I saw him in the desert, where the old man sat propped against his dead horse, I saw an older Seth, with rope burns that wrapped in red slashes around his neck. Now, here he was, this unmarked boy who just stood there watching me. He looked angry, too.

It was almost as if I could hear Seth telling me, *You fucked up, Jack. You need to put it back together before everything falls apart.*

His mouth was pressed tight, a straight line across his face. He was more clear to me now than I had ever seen him; almost solid, real.

This was real.

Seeing the ghost startled Henry. I felt him grab my shoulder, tightly, and I got the impression that he was using me as some sort of barrier between him and Seth.

Seth Mansfield wore shoes and a collared shirt, tucked in neatly beneath a pair of deep blue suspenders. His hair was combed. He looked like he could have been dressed for church, as clean as he was.

I thought about the harvesters in Henry's apartment, wondered if they were making their way through his front door, and what could possibly be waiting for us down on the street outside.

I asked Seth, "What do we do?"

Seth didn't answer me. He stood perfectly still, a color-washed portrait of the kid he used to be.

After a moment, I pleaded, "I don't have any way out of here, Seth. Can you help us get out?"

Seth spun around, his hand spread open, waving, as though clearing smoke from the air in front of him, and when he touched the plaster wall, the entire building started to shake and creak. It was almost like a bomb had gone off. Bits of dust, splinters from a ceiling somewhere above our heads, fell like noisy snow around my feet.

The wall crumbled. I watched as a hole tore open where Seth's hand passed inside the plaster. The masonry lay exposed, and when Seth pushed his body closer into the wall, I saw—counted—three, four, five bricks tumbling outward, away from him. They spun and scattered down onto the street below.

Everything was falling apart.

The stairwell rolled and shook.

Henry seemed to drain empty behind me. I felt him weaken, wavering as though he might fall down where he stood. He sat on the staircase.

Seth disappeared through the wall, out into the street and the gray fog of the London morning.

Not-London.

I looked back at Henry. "Get up. We need to get out of here."

Henry stood, weakly, his jaw slack as he stared at the opening Seth had left in the wall.

He'd been in Marbury for ten years. It wasn't like Henry had never seen a ghost before.

But this was different.

The building began to tilt, leaning out toward the street, following Seth, collapsing, as the entire world tipped, spilling, pouring its contents down into another empty hole.

And behind Henry, I could hear the clicking, grinding, chewing.

Harvesters were coming.

I took off, running down the stairs.

I didn't care if Henry followed or not. But he did.

At the bottom of the stairwell, a windowless door rattled on its hinges. It was the way out to the building's lobby.

And in the center of that door, pinned in place with a single black-shafted arrow, there was a small painted wooden horse, a spinning thread spool between its hind legs.

Spinning and spinning.

I couldn't help but stop on the landing and stare at the small thing.

Blood had been wiped all over the door behind the horse, smeared in clear and menacing handprints, like some frantic madman left a signature to mark a murder.

I was aware of throbbing pain in my hand. I held it up, saw that the tissue I'd wrapped around my palm had completely soaked through and was dissolving. I was bleeding everywhere.

Up the stairs behind us, thick, dark knots of blood marked the path we'd taken down.

And I knew the handprints on the door were mine.

I tried choking off my wrist with my left hand, but the flow of blood never lessened.

You're dying, Jack.

Henry nudged my arm as he pushed past me, stumbling into the lobby.

I looked away from the horse, its wheel still spinning, rolling. I followed Henry out of the creaking building and onto the cold and damp street.

What waits for us outside freezes us in our tracks.

Henry stands in front of me. I can't see his face.

He says, "What the fuck is this?"

Marbury.

What the fuck do you think it is?

The rolling and creaking goes on, endless and anguished, from every building. Even the lightposts along the street seem restless, itchy. They emit static snaps and pops. I can feel the individual fractures of the pavement stones beneath my feet grinding like nervous teeth.

I hold my hand up, arm bent at the elbow, and the bleeding paints a black pudding skin of blood in rounded streaks down my forearm.

Drip.

Drip.

I marvel at how white my body has become.

All down the street, infinite in every direction, the rows of buildings stack tightly one after another, each of them twisting, sighing as though inhaling, exhaling. Sleeping. And they are all decorated, adorned with spattered corpses: men, women, children, every one of them unclothed, bloodstained, pinned into the walls, the frame boards, gutters and eave joists, anywhere—some of them missing pieces, carefully restructured, headless or neutered, drawn, some of them remarkably unscarred like a frieze of angels, but all of them skewered through with the black arrows and the sharpened-bone pikes of Hunters. Some of them are still barely alive; they blink like random lightbulbs, faulty on burned-out strings, moving arms and hands slowly, gracefully, the way you'd wave in a parade.

And above it all, the hole in the sky tears and gapes open like a hungry mouth, Jack's mouth, Jack's hand, and it is the same hole that Seth had made through the wall of the apartment building, grinding and spitting fragments of stone, brick, the teeth of the universe, opening outward and exposing another gray street that is equally strewn with bodies, floating endlessly over our heads as far as I can see.

And Seth is running away from me down the street.

Henry repeats, "What the fuck—"

"What do you think? What do you think it is?" I ask, disgusted. I have no time for this.

363

A brick tumbles past my feet.

One droplet of blood splatters, a perfect circle, in the center of its upturned face.

Rolling dice.

The snake's eye.

I have to follow Seth.

I know this place.

And I know I will die here if I don't follow.

Henry knows this place.

It is all too fast. I cannot keep up with the boy, and Henry falls twice. His feet are cut, the skin on his hands, the knees of his trousers tear open like waking eyelids over the orbs of his pale and skeletal kneecaps. I help him up, turn my head to see where Seth has squeezed himself into a narrow walkway between two jittering brownstones.

"We have to follow him."

Henry wipes spit from his mouth and I continue after Seth.

There is something blocking the confined footpath between the buildings.

I know what it is.

Of course I know.

Perfect, flawless, a comforting shade of blue—it is the color of toys and swimming pools. A fifty-five-gallon plastic barrel.

Seth stops at the end of the alleyway, but he doesn't look back at me.

Everything is so loud: Henry's gasping pants, the crumbling stone, clicking. Harvesters coming, following us. And from where I am standing, I can see that there is no top on the barrel.

I know there are dark things inside it, crowded, folded together within the cramped space of the drum.

Seth turns down the street and I can't see him anymore.

I need to go.

Above me, a window explodes outward from its buckling frame, showering crystals of glass that stick in my hair.

Henry yells, "What are you doing?"

But I won't answer.

I walk toward the barrel.

Do not look inside, Jack.

How can you keep yourself from looking?

Fuck you, Jack.

I scream it, "Fuck you, Jack! Fuck you!"

I put my hands on the perfect rim of the drum and push my hips around it. I smear my blood across the raised lip of the barrel as it presses, cool and smooth, like naked skin against me. I can feel my balls tightening up inside me.

Don't look.

I can't stop it.

And inside the barrel, I see the boys.

Ben and Griffin.

They look so small and pale, naked, like unborn twins. Unconcerned by the confinement of their plastic womb, their arms fold, spiderlike, entwined. One of Ben's knees presses up between Griffin's shoulder blades, angular and rigid. Their heads lie so comfortably, slumbering, jaw to jaw, perfectly unmoving, brothers before and after everything.

I turn away.

I make it to the end of the alley.

Henry struggles past the barrel behind me, and as I emerge onto the next street, I see Seth just as he vanishes into the black square doorway to a Tube station.

Green Park.

This is it.

Of course this is it.

Seth waits for me inside.

The Green Park Underground was dark and empty, its floors strewn with trash: discarded papers, plastic bottles, wax-paper cups. It smelled like an old movie theatre, or maybe a library—musty and ancient in abandonment.

You never see Tube stations deserted like this.

But this was Marbury.

I felt as empty as the hall, lightheaded, floating unconnected like a fog above the rocking and undulating floor.

I dripped blood everywhere, and I was now too weak to hold my arm up. It ached.

On the other side of the turnstiles, I saw Seth vanish down the escalator. They were still moving, up one side, down the other; the place was lit up, but we were the only ones inside.

I had to follow him. I knew if he didn't get me out of here that I was going to die.

Tickets.

There were two tickets inside my pocket.

Drip.

Drip.

I handed one of the tickets to Henry.

"Come on." My voice was a garbled slur.

This is real.

I slipped my shirt over my head, and began winding it around my hand. Tight. Tighter. Dumbly, I thought about laundering it before giving the T-shirt back to Nickie's brother.

Henry followed me through the electric gates at the turnstile. They opened like mouths when we fed the tickets into the slots.

I staggered toward the top of the long escalator that went down into the belly of the Tube station. Henry shifted his weight from foot to foot, as though he felt like running, but I wasn't about to do that.

I leaned against the black rubber handrail and put my head down on the back of my forearm. Nothing I did slowed the flow of blood from the wound on my hand. The escalator shook, the hallway creaked and rumbled, and below us, I heard the whoosh of an arriving train.

Even the trains are running.

Everything was falling apart around us. A glass-framed advertisement shattered and dropped from the wall as the porcelain tiles behind it gave away and scattered like bones down onto the moving steps of the escalator.

Going down.

Then the phone inside my pocket buzzed.

My old Glenbrook ringtone, a song that I didn't think was especially cool, but had been too lazy to change. The escalator seemed to take forever to go all the way down to the dimness of the lower platform tunnels.

Victoria Line.

Piccadilly Line.

Not-lines.

I reached across my waist with my left hand. My phone vibrated like an insect trapped inside my pocket.

Someone is calling me.

I didn't look. My thumb smeared a swath of blood across the screen. I pushed a button and held the phone to my ear.

"Billy?"

"Huh?"

I felt sick; I nearly dropped the phone.

He said it again. "Billy?"

Quinn Cahill.

Of course.

"What?"

"It's me. Quinn."

"Where are you?"

"Turn around, Billy. I'm right behind you."

I looked back at Henry. He seemed to be watching the ceiling, as though the force of his stare was sufficient to keep everything from collapsing around us. And standing near the top of the escalator, following us down, all grins and red hair, was Quinn Cahill. He waved a cell phone in the air like we were long-lost cousins meeting for a reunion.

Quinn's laugh echoed off the tiles of the cavernous escalator flight. Then he shut his phone and tucked it into his back pocket.

My cell phone dropped from my hand. It slid the rest of the way down to the bottom, along the cool slide of stainless steel between the rubber handrail and the wall, smearing a trail of blood.

"Ha-ha! I got something for you, Billy!"

Quinn started down the stairs toward us.

Henry looked confused, scared.

We were nearly at the bottom.

Quinn said, "You maybe looking for these, Billy?"

And from his back pocket, he pulled out my green-and-blue glasses and let them dangle in front of his face. They were dead, lightless. The smaller green lens was flipped out, and Quinn held them between us, swinging back and forth, like a hypnotist's bauble, between my eyes and his stupid grin.

I nearly fell down trying to gauge my step at the landing of the escalator.

Once I had straightened myself from leaning on the rail, my knees buckled and I would have collapsed if Quinn didn't push past Henry and shove his hand up into my armpit to catch me.

Henry stood there. He watched us dumbly, his eyes darting from me to Quinn to the glasses. He looked hungry. He looked like he wanted out, too.

Quinn pushed me along toward the arched entryway of a platform. I was too dazed to read the signs, the direction.

"You don't look so good, Billy."

Drip.

Drip.

My head hung down. Quinn tugged and pinched at my armpit to keep me on my feet.

I felt him put his face up against my shoulder. I heard him sniff. "And you don't smell so good, neither." Then he whispered, "Who's the barefoot old man?"

"Heh—" I couldn't even say Henry's name.

"You can get us out of here," Henry said. "I've seen it work. Turn the lens down. Do it."

Quinn kept walking, push-dragging me along.

"We need to get on the train, Billy. Then we'll talk about getting out of here. If you make it that far. Heh-heh!"

"You're dead," I said.

"You're deader than me, Odd. Deader than me." Quinn wasn't smiling.

Odds.

I heard a train leave—*whoosh!*—the air sucked out into the platform with it.

Quinn pulled me over toward the opposite line.

"This way, Billy."

"There's Odds here in this world?" I said.

Quinn laughed. "Heh. This world? This world? Everything is everywhere, Billy. Always has been."

Then he grabbed at my bleeding hand, swiped his fingers in the oozing warmth of my blood and held them up in front of my face.

He pressed his bloody thumb and first finger together and said, "And it all fits here. In this tiny space, Odd. Ain't you figured that out yet? And you did it, Billy. It all opened up from that nasty cut on your palm. You know how I know? You know how I know?"

Quinn jerked me, like he was scolding me, trying to keep me awake. "Ask me how I know, Billy."

He tugged me toward the tracks, empty, black.

Seth was there, waiting at the edge of the platform.

Quinn nodded at the ghost and said, "He showed me that, Billy. That one there. I been following him ever since you sent me for a swim in the Under. Remember that? How you rolled me into the water? I fucking want to kill you right now, Billy."

A train was coming.

Everything shook.

I looked from Seth to Quinn.

"I saw you fucking go down the spill gate."

Quinn grabbed me harder, shook me. It hurt.

370

"You saw what you saw, I guess. You wouldn't know what I seen, where I been. Now I can't go back. Can't get my stuff. My house. 'Cause of you, is why. I can't go home 'cause of you."

Whoosh.

A train vomited in from the black mouth of the tunnel. It was so loud.

Henry was trying to say something. He'd grabbed Quinn's shoulder, obviously wanting to get the kid to listen to him, but I couldn't tell what he said.

The train stopped.

The doors hissed open.

I heard an accordion.

Everything is everywhere.

I said, "Seth."

But I couldn't see him on the platform. He had already gotten onto the train.

Henry tried to snatch the glasses out of Quinn's hand, but the kid was not an easy target. He never had been the kind for surprises. Quinn twisted away from Henry and shoved me through the open doors of the empty car.

I fell onto the dirty floor with my face landing against a chrome support pole.

Seth watched me from the end of the car, standing motionless near the doorway to the next compartment. Outside on the platform, Quinn and Henry fought over the glasses, but Henry was no match for the kid.

As the doors began closing, Henry collapsed to the concrete floor of the platform and Quinn spun around, just in time to jam an arm between the gaskets and squeeze his way into the train with me.

Good-bye, Henry.

371

The doors hissed shut.

The train shuddered and rocked. I couldn't tell if we were moving or if the whole world was simply falling apart on top of us.

Quinn stood over me, panting, holding the chrome rail that my forehead pressed against. "Get up, Billy. You ain't dead yet."

He raked his fingers into my hair and pulled my head from the floor.

The train picked up speed.

My eyes fixed on the glasses in Quinn's left hand.

I tried to steady myself on my knees in front of him; my bare chest leaned into the pole, and my face lolled with the motion of the accelerating train, coming to rest against the kid's thigh.

Quinn kept trying to pull me up by my hair.

"Stop it."

I turned my head to see Seth, but the ghost faded and slipped ahead of us into the forward compartment.

"Get up. You ain't dead."

I put my hands down onto the floor, attempted to scoot my feet under me so I could stand, so I could relieve the pulling on my fucking hair.

It felt like we were flying, and outside the windows there was nothing but thick velvet black.

"Get off me, Quinn."

I was dying.

I knew I was dying.

"You ready to take a jump again, Billy?"

I got one foot under me.

A light, just a solitary bulb, smeared past the windows, the length of the train, as fast as if we were falling, a burning eye. Like the flashlight in the Under.

"What the fuck are you trying to do?"

I didn't think I could stand, but the kid kept pulling on me. Another light.

"Look at me," he said. "This time, we're staying together. This time, you're taking me back home. Or I'll fucking kill you, Billy."

His words smeared like the trailing flashes of light.

Faster and faster.

"It doesn't work that way."

"Fuck you, Billy. Look at me."

And Quinn held the lenses in front of my face.

I made it up to my feet. And I looked at the kid, thinking, *I'm taller than you. I should fuck you up, you little prick.*

But I nearly fell down.

And Quinn said, "Give me your hand, Billy."

He swiped the glasses across my belly, flipping the green lens across the eyepiece as it dragged against my skin.

I saw things there.

Everything.

And Quinn said, "Give me your fucking hand."

Then he yanked the bloody shirt away from my hand and slid his fingers between mine.

I heard an accordion playing.

Wind in trees.

The sound of a small wooden toy horse; rolling, tapping.

twenty-eight

I was Seth Mansfield.

I remember so clearly being him, that sometimes, lying in my own bed at home in Glenbrook, I could recall the smell of the bedding in the house where Seth slept as a boy, the particular coldness of the plank floors beneath his bare feet in the morning; the feel, awkward and scratchy, of Davey's hand-me-down clothes against his skin.

The room at the end of the hallway, upstairs, where he and Davey's sister, Hannah, would meet, hidden in the absolute quiet of night.

I was Seth Mansfield.

I remember the small window in Davey's room where he slept alongside his adoptive brother, his curiosity about the great wooden hoops Ma used for stretching fabric; how they'd been stacked neatly against the wall opposite the stove in the downstairs of the house.

I thought about this when we were on the train.

Me and Quinn.

The thought was maybe a second, perhaps shorter.

A flash of light.

I remembered the wagon they rode in the day Russ and those other men took Seth and Pa out into the woods, away from Pope Valley. How the day seemed to crystallize in frozen brilliance as they tightened the rope around the boy's neck.

I was Seth.

And I remember one time, how he and Davey started a fire atop a hill of red ants. They'd used dry grass wound together in tight yellow broom whisks, bound with strings of willow bark. And when they set fire to the brooms, Seth watched, almost hypnotized by how the orange embers would come alive, brighten, breathe, migrate up and down along the strands of grass like they were living things, and they were alive, because they could jump across the fibrils of grass, from string to string, skipping from one to another every time Davey would turn the whisk in his hand and blow.

Quinn squeezed my hand.

I couldn't feel anything anymore, but I knew he was holding tight to my bloody hand.

And I thought, this is what it's like to be the fire, to skip across the strings.

The train was going so fast.

Jack slumped against Quinn's chest.

I said, "It doesn't work this way, Quinn."

And that was all.

Outside, in the tunnel, there is a light.

This is the arrow.

Jack is the arrow.

The light begins in the car ahead of me. It passes back like an electrified drape of blazing dust, or the train, the arrow, Jack, passes through it.

I can't tell, and it doesn't matter.

Sometimes, standing still is moving forward.

We are drifting through a membrane, and Seth vanishes. It's

Davey turning the wad of grass over in his hand, blowing to fan the flame.

Watch as it skips.

Instantly, through the first wall of light, Quinn disappears.

For a moment, I feel the lingering stickiness where his hand clasped the drying gum of blood. And the bleeding has stopped, but the train moves forward, silently, now, rocking, trembling.

Sunlight and color flood through the windows.

I can feel warmth.

On the other side of the glass there is a brilliant blue sky and endless undulations like the surface of a calm sea: the waving stalks of an infinite field, ablaze in green. Black stilt-poles pike up from the field, jabbing into the sky.

Crosses.

Scarecrow frames.

But these are no scarecrows.

The first is Conner.

Nickie, Ben, and Griffin follow.

Another wave of light.

Another wall.

The door ahead of me opens and a man stumbles awkwardly, drunk legs from the motion of the noiseless train, arms swimming through the air to counter the ricochet pulse of the swaying path he's on. He comes directly toward me, his eyes pinned with such intensity to some point beyond me that I want to turn and see, but I can't take my eyes from him.

Avery Scott.

The cop.

He stops directly in front of me.

He says, "You're dirty. You're a dirty fucking kid."

Light washes down the aisle, and it pushes him forward like he's been caught in an unexpected shorebreak.

He falls toward my feet and vanishes.

Everyone here is a ghost.

We are moving through trees. I can smell Pope Valley in the morning, in summer.

I hold my hand up. Open, close. The wound has healed, but there is still the pink gash, the jagged scar from the edge of the broken lens. I take a deep breath. I am alive again, and I am here, jumping somewhere between a burning strand and one about to catch fire with me.

When I turn back, Uncle Teddy is lying on the floor at my feet, exactly in the spot where Quinn had thrown down Ander's bloody shirt. The preacher's eyes are open; his chin hangs slack. But he is not breathing.

There is a hole in his side. His blood pools in the lined grooves of the rubber mat I'm standing on. Beside him, on the floor, are the glasses. They flash and wink.

Burning.

"Don't look, Jack."

Seth is standing at the front of the car.

"So, you're going to talk to me now?"

He's scared. It's a younger Seth. The boy, standing barefoot, scrawny in his worn dungarees, shirtless. He holds the wooden horse with both hands in front of his waist.

Seth shakes his head. "This may be our last chance, Jack."

Outside, the trees open up and I can see the sky.

It grows lighter in the train.

He pleads again, "Don't look, Jack."

But he's not talking about the glasses.

And I see the two figures hanging outside.

Then it's as if everything—the bar I'm holding on to, the seats, the train itself—all fold inside a grainy fog to vanish beneath a battering barrage of exploding lights.

Everything disappears.

And it is dark and silent, everything.

When I see, it is a line.

Somewhere away from me, a distance that could be immeasurable or a matter of inches, there is a line, frozen, exact.

I am lying on my back and I see a line of light, the color of an old man's teeth—not yellow, not white.

Not-here.

There is searing pain in my leg. I move my hands in the dark, track them across the surface beneath me, over my body, everywhere, staring at the line of light.

Where are your clothes?

I can't move my foot.

And I realize the light I see is the narrow space beneath a shut door.

The room is hot, dank, and smells of my own sweat, sterile plastic, and cigarette smoke.

I am tied down to a bed.

I know this place.

"Seth," I whisper. "Seth."

Click.

A television goes on in the other room.

I watch the light.

Everything is everywhere.

Freddie's house.

I see the shadow moving like a bead of oil trapped in the light of the gap beneath the door. But something is wrong. Not-Freddie's house. I am sick, cold, completely naked on this stinking mattress. I try sitting up, but it hurts. Everything hurts.

"Seth!" I whisper.

The bead of shadow stops. He stands just outside the door.

It cracks open, and I am blind in the flood of light behind the man standing there.

He has a cigarette in his hand.

And Freddie says, "I think we should go for a drive. Would you like to get some breakfast? You hungry, kid?"

I try to speak, but my throat is dry.

"Kid? You awake?"

"I . . . I'm awake."

I stay flat, motionless, make myself small, my eyes lower, fixing steady on the paleness of my chest beneath the invading light.

It is how we do things here. No looking at his face. He doesn't like it, and he has water.

I want water.

So I ask him, like he wants me to, "Will you please take me for a drive? Will you take me outside? Please?"

When he pushes open the door, it's like being unearthed after centuries. The light pours over my anemic skin and I pull my chest toward my knees, jam my hands over my crotch, an instinct to grab myself and cover, and the tightening of my muscles hurts, burns like the light that blinds me.

It's like being on the train again.

Like waking up in the Under.

Being born.

And all I can see is the burning yellow light; nothing else.

It is so hot.

When I open my eyes, I am staring along the ground, at the white Marbury ash, lying at the foot of a rock in the desert.

And someone is yelling, "A rider! Henry! There's a rider!"

part five

THE
ARROW

twenty-nine

The passenger arrives.

How long this time?

I stretched out, flat on my belly in the ash. My fingers were wedged beneath the pack, and I could feel the glasses in my sweaty grasp. Somehow, I'd gotten my hand covered in the cut-out pocket again. Of course, as always, I had no idea what I'd been doing or how I ended up where I was. I pressed onto my hands and knees, keeping my forehead down, resting it against the dirt.

My stomach knotted and retched.

It hurt bad.

Coming back never hurt like this.

I was afraid I'd missed something; that there were important things I needed to see, but had left behind.

It was sick—I knew it—but I honestly wanted to be back there in Freddie's room. I was certain there was an answer for Jack somewhere in that house; that I belonged there. Maybe I knew it anyway, and I wasn't ever going home again.

I coughed and spit, vaguely sensing the absence of the other boys, the Odds.

Sometimes you just know when you're all alone. It was a feeling Jack knew well.

When I finally raised my head so I could see where I was, I realized that Henry was gone, too.

"Do you need me to get help?"

A finger tapped my shoulder. I didn't know there was anyone else there, so I flinched, jerking around to see who stood behind me.

The English kid, Ethan, the bed wetter, hovered over me, straight and rail thin, like the topless trunk of a palm tree tufted in stringy amber hair.

I rubbed my head. "I'm sick or something."

Then I turned. I could see where all the other boys had gathered above us, crouching on the rim of the rocks. Henry was up there with them. I thought about the last time I saw him, when he was fighting with Quinn on the platform in the Underground. I couldn't help but wonder which Henry would show up here in Marbury with me. With the boys.

Ethan said, "Perhaps I can get you some of Frankie's water."

He looked honestly concerned. He shifted, and started to move back toward Frankie's distillery.

"No," I said. "Don't do that, Ethan. I'll be okay."

He stopped, and I glanced at the rim again and swallowed. My throat felt like sandpaper. "Maybe you shouldn't be talking to me, anyway."

Ethan shrugged dismissively, irritated. "All right, then. Suit yourself. I just thought you needed help or something. Henry Hewitt told me to stay here and look after you. Now I've seen you. You're alive. I guess there's nothing more to look after."

He started heading up to the ridgeline to join the other Odds.

Ethan said, "They've spotted a rider out there. Alone. Hewitt thinks it's a fucking Ranger. I believe some of the boys are debating if we should go kill it, whatever he is."

He kept walking away from me.

I knew the kid from somewhere.

Somewhere that wasn't here.

"Hey, wait a second. I . . ."

I tried to stand up, and nearly fell face-first into the boulder I'd been hiding under. It was like my head drained itself empty when I moved. I nearly blacked out.

And I dropped the glasses into the ash between my knees.

Ethan turned around and saw them.

"What's that?"

He saw something in them.

I tried not to look, tried brushing them away with my uncoordinated fingers. But Jack's brain hadn't connected yet, and I saw it, too. Couldn't help it.

"Don't look at that," I said. I finally managed to swipe the glasses back under the rock. But even then, Ethan stood there, hypnotized and staring slackjawed at the pulsing vibrations of light that came from inside the crevice.

"Let me see that again," he said.

I panicked. There was an excited energy coming from the kids on the ridge. I scanned above us, could see Ben and Griffin kneeling beside Henry.

The kid was frozen in place.

He said, "Jack."

It was the first time any of these Odds used my name.

And Ethan pleaded, "Let me see that once more."

"It's nothing."

I upended the pack, spilled everything out between my feet. As I twisted the ratty sock around in my hand, I said to him, "Ethan? Do you know where we are?"

He took two slow steps toward me, moving like he was hypnotized, falling, disconnected from his body.

"Ethan?"

The kid went down onto his knees. His face was blank, as though he'd fainted. Then he blinked, shook his head, and sat back in the ash across from me, bracing himself upright with his stick arms locked behind him.

I stuffed everything into the pack, zipping it shut, protecting the glasses again, even if it was too late for that shit. The kid spit and coughed. It sounded like he was throwing up, but I didn't want to look at him.

I threaded my arms through the pack's straps. A gray slick of puke spread out in the dirt next to where Ethan sat. He didn't blink. He just sat there, watching me like I was some kind of monster.

I was.

"Where is that place?"

"It's nothing. It isn't real. You weren't supposed to see that." I lied, scared. "It could kill you."

It made me sick to think what could happen if Ethan started talking about what he'd seen to the other Odds. He wouldn't do that. *He wasn't that kind of kid*, I thought.

I kneeled down beside him in the ash. Griffin was up on the ridge, scrambling down a craggy fissure like a crab on the rock face.

Ethan wiped a forearm across his wet mouth. He looked scared, confused. "But I know you."

"Please don't say anything." More boys started following Griffin down from the ridge. "It's something bad. And I have to make it stop."

"But we were there. You were there, too. You had to have seen it. We were there, together, all morning. Hours."

"No," I said. "It was a second, Ethan. That's why you have to understand. Please don't say anything to the others. Let me explain."

I needed to talk to the kid. He saw something that I didn't, and now he knew me. But it was too late. Griffin and the boys were already in earshot, coming through the pack of horses, watching us, curious about Jack and the other outcast.

But I had to know what Ethan saw; where we were.

"Please let me talk to you later, Ethan."

He looked straight at me.

I thought I could trust him.

There's a certain allegiance kids who aren't wanted naturally feel toward one another.

"I want to know about it, Jack."

And, whispering, I said, "I will tell you."

Griffin jogged across the flat of our encampment.

He was out of breath when he got to me.

Five other Odds followed him down to where Ethan and I sat in the crusty ash. Alex and his friends were in the group, naturally, always eager for an opportunity to pick on Ethan away from the majority of the others.

"I think you need to come up there and see before he gets too far away," Griffin said.

"Before who gets away?" I looked up at the ridge. Henry was there, standing beside Frankie and Ben.

Griffin put his hand out and pulled me up to my feet.

"The rider. Ben saw him, too. We think it's Conner."

Then I realized that for the whole time Henry and I sat there with the glasses, while we ducked into another not-world that was falling apart worse than anything I'd seen, the boys on the ridge had been shouting about a rider in the desert. And I was too selfishly involved in what I wanted, what I was doing, looking for home, and now worried about having to deal with what that skinny English kid saw, to even consider for a moment that this was it, what it was always supposed to be—that Conner would come this way, too, as he had promised.

It had to be him.

I took a deep breath, still feeling weak, wondering if I could make it up to the top of the ridge. I hurried toward the gap in the rocks the other boys had been using as their ladder.

And before I'd gotten ten feet away, Griffin grabbed my wrist and pulled me around.

He said, "They're fucking with that kid."

When I turned back, Fee was sitting on top of Ethan's chest, pinning the scrawny boy down, and giggling moronically while his tattooed brother worked at stealing the kid's shoes.

Stronger Odds always stole whatever they wanted from kids like Ethan.

Fee gurgled joyfully, "Sack his fucking face! Sack his fucking face!"

And the white-haired thug, Alex, squatted above Ethan's head, fumbling at unbuttoning his fly.

"Hey!"

When I screamed, the three assholes didn't even glance over at me.

That was enough. My hand went to my knife. I pulled it out and ran back to where the kids were fucking with Ethan.

He wasn't even trying to fight them, and that pissed me off even more. Rum had both the kid's shoes off and sat in the dirt, preparing to try them on. Fee laughed so hard it sounded like he was having a seizure, and Alex had just gotten his balls out of his pants when I grabbed him by the hair and jerked him back.

Before Alex knew what was happening, I laid him out flat on his back in the salty ash. Fee's expression turned serious when he saw the knife I held. I stepped the toe of my boot on Alex's hand that he had wrapped around his balls, and pressed the blade of my knife firmly beneath his nose.

Griffin knew there was a fight on. I caught a flashing view from the corner of my eye of him throwing a roundhouse kick directly into Fee's jaw.

I opened a small cut across the bottom of Alex's nose, still twisting his hair in my grasp. More Odds scrambled down from above to watch the fight. But it was over before much of anything else could happen.

Fee rolled around in the dirt, crying and squeezing his jaw. Rum dropped Ethan's shoes and put his hands in the air, backing away from me and Griffin like he was an arrestee held at gunpoint, and Alex just whimpered faintly, too scared to move.

I let go of his hair.

"You ever touch anyone again, I'll fucking kill you, kid. Anyone. Understand me?"

Alex nodded enough to let me know he got the message, so I pulled my knife away from his face.

389

Griffin had his hands in a fighting position, eyes shifting alternately between the brothers. I could tell he wanted to kick Fee again, but he wasn't about to fight back. Fee just rolled around and sobbed.

Ethan sat up.

I was disgusted with everything. "Get your shoes on and come with us."

I heard them following me, but I kept my eyes forward as we climbed the rocky chute that led up to the ridge where the lookouts perched.

I dug my fingers as forcefully as I could into the sharp rock face, trying to make it hurt so the anger might stop howling inside me. But it didn't work. It just made me madder. I wanted to run back down so I could feel the satisfaction of jamming my knife as far as it would go into Alex's belly, to marvel at the kid's warm blood as it spilled out on me, and watch the show of his eyes as they alternately flickered surprise and horror at what Jack was capable of doing.

I was sick of myself, of what I'd become.

I killed Quinn Cahill.

I climbed faster.

All the not-worlds left me numb. All the not-worlds trapped in the Marbury lens made Jack a monster no matter where he found himself.

Fun game.

I am the King of Marbury.

If I couldn't get home, back to Nickie, back to my friends and what was real, everything would be lost.

Everything except my kingdom.

———

Henry was different.

I could see it as soon as I looked at his face. He didn't need to say anything to me at all. He knew who I was.

Ben nodded to me and gave a wary glance past my shoulder at Ethan. "This is it, Jack."

Frankie hovered behind him, practically bumping into Ben with his chest. His voice sounded tense, ready for a fight. "This is *what*, Odd?"

When nobody answered him, he grabbed Henry's arm, made the man look at him. "This is *what*, Henry? What's going on?"

Henry shook his head and shrugged, as if to tell the boy he had no answers.

Then I saw the rider.

I squinted, cupped my hands around my eyes so I could screen out the endless wash of gray in the fading evening sky. Solitary, so far away that he nearly vanished, half in, half out of the Marbury haze, keeping his head down as he rode southeast; and I was certain beyond any doubt that it was Conner Kirk out there.

We'd been closer than brothers, and I could recognize Conner Kirk from the angle of his shoulders, the motion of his hand when he wiped across his eyes. Even as tired and worn as he must have been after being hunted by the Rangers since helping me to escape, I knew I was looking at my friend.

"That's him," I said.

"Fuck this," Frankie snapped. He started off down the path to the clearing. "I'll show you who he is. We'll fucking go kill him. I'll bring back his fucking head."

"You won't get anywhere near him," I said.

Frankie stopped. "I'm not afraid of guns. We've fucking killed Rangers before. There's more of us than him."

"Believe me, Frankie. You don't want to fuck with him."

Frankie's eyes darted from me to Henry, then to each of the other boys who stood there on the lookout with us, as though he were searching for any gesture of support.

He spit a long, stringy blob down on the rocks between us. Frankie put his hands up to Henry, like he was expecting something. "We're just going to let him go, then?"

Henry inhaled slowly and looked at the sky. "Nobody wants to go out there at night."

"I'm going to go after him," I said.

"Jack—" Ben started, but I cut him off.

"We'll talk about it later, Ben."

I already knew he was going to tell me I couldn't go out there looking for Conner without taking him and Griffin. I tried not to think about leaving, about not coming back. This was Marbury, after all. Or not-Marbury. Who knew where the four of us would be tomorrow, and the next day after that?

So I stared at Conner until I couldn't see him anymore. I tried to estimate the distance and direction where I might intercept his path, but calculations like those were meaningless in Marbury.

The dimness of the gray night fell over the silent Odds who stood on the ridge beside me.

We scanned the nothingness of the desert below until Frankie got tired of waiting for some affirmation from the other boys that he was right, that he was still in charge. When it never came, he started down the narrow path, half whispering that it was time to eat.

Frankie chose out the next shift of boys to keep guard on the watchposts. Nighttime meant Hunters would be out, and the Odds never slept. At least, they never all slept at the same time. It was perhaps the only reason they had survived to escape Glenbrook and attempt the crossing to the settlement in the first place.

So I half expected him to appoint me as a replacement for Ben or Griffin on the ridge, but the kid never asked me to do anything throughout the five days that I'd been with the Odds, and he continued to ignore me over the small rations of food that were distributed for our dinner.

We ate in segregated groups. The division was more than just the few feet of dirt that separated us from the other boys. The Odds were talking about me, about the three new kids and the bed wetter. No matter what happened to us tonight, I knew things would be different from now on.

Ben and Griffin sat with me while we ate. Henry stayed up on the ridge. *I knew he wanted to talk to me, but he was just waiting for the situation between the Odds and me to calm down,* I thought.

Ethan sat with us. There was nowhere else the kid could go. That was my fault, too. He never tried to fight back against the bullying of the other boys, and things would probably be calmer, easier, if I'd just let them get away with their shit.

But it was too late for that once Ethan had seen through the lens. He knew me. Another thread had been woven into this hopeless string, and I couldn't ignore it, no matter how much I wished I could.

In the other group, Frankie stayed where he could watch us. He always watched us. But the three assholes—Alex, Fee, and Rum— sat as far away from us as they could, wounded and angry, backs turned, never so much as glancing toward me.

Griffin broke our mournful silence with one word.

"When?"

I shook my head. "Henry needs to make it okay. I need to ask him to let us go, so he can help us."

Ben watched me, like he was waiting for me to say something more. Then he looked at Ethan.

"I'm not stupid, you know," Ethan said.

Ben spit in the dirt and turned away from the kid. "I guess putting up with all the shit those fuckers do to you makes you smart, then."

Something like that would have been the first act in a fistfight with any one of the other boys. Not the English kid, though.

Ethan shrugged. "I know you're not Odds. I know why you're not like them."

"Because you fit in so well, right?" Griffin said.

"Him, too," I said. I lowered my voice and scooted in closer to the other boys. "He went through the lens today."

I watched Ethan to see if what I said made any difference to him. But I just couldn't figure out that kid at all.

"He went through?" Griffin said.

He knew what it meant. Griffin and Ben couldn't see anything in the glasses. Because you don't see anything when you're dead and inside a fucking trash can in some twisted and rearranged goddamned not-world. And the first lens, the broken lens, the one that caused it all, could only destroy things now.

Nobody went through the broken lens. It only let things *out*. Ben and Griffin saw what it did at the market when we were attacked by Hunters, and again on the roof deck at Quinn's firehouse.

They knew what it meant.

"Where did you go?" Ben asked.

I watched the knobby Adam's apple in Ethan's neck twitch as he considered what he should say.

"Well?" I said. "You can tell us."

394

"You were there, Jack. You had to have seen it," Ethan said. "It was real."

He glanced around nervously. It was like he was trying to gauge our expressions to see if we thought he was crazy, or stupid. And he looked carefully, too, across the way at the other Odds.

Ethan's voice fell to a whisper. "It was morning. I think it was the most pleasant place I've ever seen. We were inside a room, our room. We lived there, and it was clean and felt cold beneath my feet, too. There was a window on a wall, between our two beds. Outside, it was raining, but I could see trees and the most fantastic colors I have ever seen."

I knew where it was.

Of course I knew.

Ethan looked directly at me. "You were still lying in bed." He looked down, embarrassed, and said, "I had just taken a piss. In a toilet. With water in it. And you asked me about some news. And I remembered we were leaving that morning, that we would be catching a train somewhere."

"London," I said.

"Yes. That was it. Do you remember, Jack?"

I shook my head.

Ben leaned in closer to us. "Fuck that. How come we couldn't get through, then? Fuck that, Jack."

"It's my fault," I said. "I messed it all up."

"That's why he talks like Henry," Griffin said. "He's English. That's why, isn't it?"

"He's from my school," I said. "St. Atticus."

Ethan's brow tightened. He was excited. "That's it! That's what it was called. St. Atticus Grammar School for Boys. You remember!"

"No. I just know it. But it's a good thing, Ben. Maybe he's right. Maybe we are all home, where we belong. We just need to—"

And Griffin said, "What? We need to *what*, Jack?"

I sighed. "I don't know. Change the fucking channel or something."

Ben stood up. "Fuck this place, Jack. So, where'd you leave the goddamned remote?"

Ben had every right to be as angry as he sounded.

Ethan cleared his throat, obviously confused. "How can I go back there?"

I kept my eyes on Ben. He started off, up the trail to the ridge.

I stood up. "You can't go back, Ethan."

Griffin got up, shaking his head. "Everything's fucked out of shape, Jack."

"Let's get Ben," I said. Then I figured there was nothing else I could do, and added, "Come on, Ethan."

The Odds watched us with untrusting eyes as we crossed the clearing and followed Ben up to the ridge where Henry was waiting for me.

thirty

"We need to leave before something else happens," I said.

When I saw Henry's eyes, the slate haze of the Marbury night made him seem so old and tired.

And for just an instant, he looked like the old preacher, and it scared me.

I believed in that moment that Jack had jumped across again, landed on another string; and I realized this was how my brain worked now—that from now on I would always wonder, or doubt, what not-world I'd quietly fallen into.

"Something else always happens," Henry said. "It's the only thing we know for certain, isn't it?"

The other boys stood away from us. They waited, shifting their feet impatiently at the top of the trail. I knew how bad Ben and Griffin wanted to leave, and Ethan, he was helplessly tied to us now.

Just another string in our knot.

"I'm afraid the Odds will fight us if we take horses. You can make it be okay."

Henry took a deep breath. He thought about it, but I already knew he wouldn't refuse. It had to happen.

He said, "One day soon, I expect to have another beer with you at The Prince of Wales."

"I'll buy."

"Will we be real friends, I wonder?"

"I don't know."

"I suppose we're always certain of that, too, aren't we? The not-knowing, I mean."

I nodded. "Will you come down with us?"

"You will be back. I'll tell them that."

"What if we don't?"

Henry smiled. "It has to be, doesn't it? You know what still has to happen, Jack."

Then Henry touched my side, just above my hip, with the point of his index finger. "You know. This. In. Out."

He raised his eyebrow as though asking if I remembered the arrow. The first time I'd set my feet down in Marbury.

I said, "It doesn't have to happen, Henry. This isn't the world. This is not the same place."

Henry waved his arm across the air between us, like he was painting the scenery with the sweep of his fingers. "Then what is it, Jack? Of course this is the world."

I shook my head. "This might be the only way for me and the boys to get back home."

"You know, Jack, everything we do, no matter how ordinary and insignificant the action, continually reinvents our future."

I thought about seeing Ben and Griffin in photographs, and inside a fucking barrel hidden in Freddie Horvath's garage.

"Maybe it's all my fault. Maybe I'll never go anywhere that's close to being home again. But I have to try. For them." I pointed to Ben and Griffin. "And everything's already been rearranged behind me, so it doesn't much matter what you do now, Henry. Scratch your head, don't scratch it, throw a rock off this wall, whatever. All things have been accomplished. That's what the preacher always says, so it doesn't matter. I saw . . . I saw . . ."

"What?" Henry said.

I shrugged. "I don't know."

Henry said, "I suppose I'll see you again."

"In a better place."

Henry patted my shoulder and walked around me toward the waiting boys. "What could possibly be better than this?"

Five of us rode out from the encampment that night.

Ben, Griffin, Ethan, me, and Frankie.

Frankie refused to let us go without him, despite Henry's assurance that we would come back before morning. Frankie considered the horses, like most of the things transported on the caravan, to be his property. He argued that it was he who'd orchestrated the theft

398

of the horses from the Rangers' holding pens, and he was the most capable rider of all the boys.

"I want to see for myself what that rider out there is trying to do," Frankie said. "If I have to, I'll kill him myself."

And I told him, "I think we're all going to die out there."

That was all we said about it.

With or without us, Henry decided, the Odds would all be leaving in the morning. They had rested long enough, and he was certain the Hunters were coming soon.

Stubbornly, Frankie led the way, as though he'd already calculated exactly the course we'd have to follow to intercept Conner's path. He'd chosen out the fittest horses and forced us to ride hard to keep up with him.

As we rode, I kept thinking about what Henry said to me before we left, how he seemed resigned to things that had already been determined, and from time to time I slipped my hand up inside my shirt so I could rub the spot near my belly where I'd been shot with a Hunter's arrow in some other world, at some other time.

This had to work.

Conner was waiting for me.

I had to believe we would get home, that I would see Nickie again, that everything would be put in its place, made whole. And Ben and Griffin would not be harmed.

Earlier, when we'd seen Conner passing across the desert, it was obvious that he was in no particular hurry to get to the settlement. He moved so slowly, and even at such distance I could see by the slump to Conner's shoulders and the angle of his downturned head that he was tired, possibly even asleep while his horse plodded forward.

Above us, the Marbury sky bled a constant shower of light. It looked like blazing powder that sprinkled like dusty embers in constant, undulating flows.

The hole had grown larger again.

Ben rode closest to me. "What are you going to do when we find him?"

I passed a hand over the one pocket I hadn't cut out of my jeans so I could feel the contour of the broken lens in there. And I wondered if, unnoticed, it may have turned into something else, black and knotted.

I exhaled. "I don't know, Ben."

"Make sure that asshole Frankie doesn't fuck things up."

"You mean worse than Jack already did?"

"Wasn't your fault. We all did it."

It was Ethan who saw him first.

Frankie overestimated. He rode past Conner by a good quarter-mile, so if the St. Atticus kid hadn't been paying attention, who knows how far off course Frankie might have taken us?

Ethan stopped his horse and turned to face the distant rider.

He pointed to the faint figure, hundreds of yards from us. "He's over there."

There was no way of knowing if Conner could see us or not. He rode with his head pillowed against the horse's neck.

I glanced back to get an idea of how far Frankie had gone, but I couldn't even see the kid at all. Still, I knew I needed to hurry.

"The three of you wait here for me."

Griffin argued, "You have to let us come, too."

"What if he doesn't remember you, Griff? What if it isn't really Conner out there?"

Griffin bit his lower lip, didn't say anything.

So I answered for him. "You'll know in a minute what needs to happen. Just watch me. And keep an eye out for Frankie, too."

Then I kicked my horse into a trot.

Of course it was him.

I knew it before I'd seen him. I knew Conner would be here before we ever left the camp that night; I could feel it.

And part of me knew, too, how when I found him, Conner would be sick.

It was supposed to happen, right?

All things accomplished.

So there I was, caught halfway between Ben and Griffin, the friends who I wished I might save, and Conner, the friend I hoped might save me.

And all I could do was worry, desperately, if this not-world was real, like Henry swore it was; if, maybe, there wouldn't be any way out for us this time. At least, not all of us together, whole again, going home.

I stopped a hundred feet away from him.

He didn't see me.

"Con?"

He moved his head, just a little, and the horse quivered.

"Con? I made it. Just like we said we would. You okay?"

I nudged my horse forward.

His horse spun around in a tight clockwise circle, and I saw that where Conner rested his face, all down the horse's side had been smeared wet with blood.

Conner coughed, his body rattling like he was broken inside, then he spit a black blob that elongated in a glistening cord from his mouth. He lifted a rifle in the air with one hand, but I could tell he wasn't nearly strong enough to hold it steady. He dropped it onto the ground beneath the horse.

Then he raised his eyes enough that he could see me.

"Jack?"

I jumped down and ran across the dusty ash to where my friend lay slumped on top of his horse.

"Jack?" he said again.

I grabbed the neck of Conner's shirt and slid him from the horse's back. He turned over in my arms, but I caught him. I couldn't believe how light he felt, how empty. I helped him down onto the ground so I could lay him flat.

He kept his eyes on me the whole time, unblinking, as though he weren't sure if it was all some kind of weird dream. His mouth hung open, crusted with dried blood.

One of his eyes was dark. It had turned almost entirely black, so I could barely see the circle of his pupil.

The bug.

I put the flat of my hand on his chest. "It's time we get the hell out of here, Conner."

This is how it was supposed to happen, right?

"How long we been here, Jack?"

I shook my head.

"Where is it?" I said.

"Huh?"

I pushed my hand into Conner's pocket.

"The lens. Where's the lens?"

The glove I had sacked around my palm snagged on his pocket and pulled Conner's pants down past his hips. And there it was, the little burning mark, the red blaze of the crossed loop, the exact shape and place where I'd seen it on my friend before, the first time we'd found each other in Marbury.

Conner raised his hands, attempted to push me away. "What the fuck are you doing?"

I tried to jam my hand down into his pocket again.

It had to be there.

"It's okay, Con." I patted his chest. "It's me. What did you do with the lens?"

Then there was shouting, curses, that came from across the empty desert where I'd left the boys.

I turned my head to look.

At the horizon, where the blank ground rose up and vanished seamlessly into the folding haze of the night, I made out the shapes of the boys and their horses. Frankie had returned, and behind them all hovered a flickering line of red embers.

Hunters were coming.

And at that moment I heard the *whish* from a volley of arrows as they cut through the sky, followed by the panicked cries of Ben and Griffin when they called my name.

"Fuck!"

I hesitated, tried to think of what to do.

"Hang on, Con," I said. "I'm coming back."

He coughed an answer.

I picked up Conner's rifle. It felt heavy. I braced the butt against my hip and pulled back the cocking slide so I could see if it was loaded.

An unspent cartridge ejected from the breech.

So I leapt onto my horse and rode to where the boys were coming under attack, toward the winking line of red brands. The Hunters were a small group, a patrol team; maybe ten of them, looking for food.

Us.

"Get on the ground!" I screamed. "Get down now! I have a gun!"

I was afraid I might shoot one of the boys, so I probably waited too long before I pulled off the first burst of fire.

My horse suddenly reared back. He'd been hit by an arrow above the right foreleg. I toppled down from the animal and hit my face hard into the ground as the horse snorted, terrified, and circled away from me.

The other four horses, riderless, thundered past.

One of them had an arrow in his head.

I spit. My mouth was full of ash and blood, and an open gash burned above my eye. I raised my head, stinging, then stood up and began shooting into the line.

More arrows came. They all fell short, dying impotently in the crust of salt ash.

One by one, the red brands of the Hunters collapsed and fell, too.

The rain of arrows stopped.

One of the attackers tried to run back to where he'd come from, but I could see him and kept firing until he finally collapsed, crumpling into the flat of the desert.

When I stopped shooting, I felt myself being swallowed up in an eternal silence.

My ears rang.

I breathed.

I whispered, "Ben? Griff? You guys okay?"

Nothing.

A black figure rose up, slowly, cautiously, from the flat of the ground.

Then others.

"Jack?" It was Griffin.

"Is anyone hurt?" I called back.

"Jack? Where are you?"

I could see the kid moving around, bent forward, as though he were scanning the ground around him.

"We're all okay," Ben said.

I shut my eyes and exhaled.

"Stay there," I said.

"Jack—" It was Frankie.

"Give me one minute," I said. "Ben. Griff. Just one fucking minute, okay?"

And Griffin said, "It better be good, Jack."

thirty-one

Conner was gone.

"Conner!"

I kicked the ground, sending a spray of salt and ash upward in a dusty gray cloud around my feet.

Maybe I'd gotten disoriented, I thought. Maybe he was still lying right where I'd left him. He had to be there.

I began moving back and forth, sweeping the ground with my eyes and feet.

"Con!"

"Jack!" Frankie shouted my name from the distant blank gray of the Marbury night.

I knew he'd be coming this way, too; I could feel it. There was no way to stop him. So I didn't answer him, hoping Frankie and the others might not see where I was standing.

I whispered for Conner, more frantic now as I began jogging around the empty area where I was certain I'd left him.

My foot twisted, caught up on something.

It was a shirt.

It had to be Conner's.

"Conner!" I whispered again, but there was no answer.

I jerked my head around, strained to see if I could detect the shapes of the four boys out there, looking for me. And I could hear them moving, the crunch of their boots on the crust of the ground as they came closer and closer.

I picked up the shirt. It was damp from sweat, it stunk, and the collar was slick with snotty blood. Holding the rifle with one hand, I fed the fabric of the shirt back and forth between my fingers, feeling, feeling, trying to find that goddamned lens.

Then I came upon a boot, thirty feet away from where I found Conner's shirt. It was lying on its side, laces wildly pulled out from eyes, the tongue lolling into the ash like the victim of a strangling.

I had to pick it up, had to look inside it, too.

Nothing.

Fuck this.

"Con. Please!"

Want to play a fucking game, Jack?

Getting warmer?

Colder?

Colder?

A trail of clothes led me out farther into the emptiness of the desert—another boot, empty, socks, wet with Conner's sweat. Jack liked keeping his lens inside his socks.

But not Conner.

There.

Pants.

And ten feet away from the twisted pants he'd flung away from his burning body, I saw Conner there, like an emaciated insect, naked, skeletal, squatting in the dust and watching me with a dark, empty stare.

"Con?"

I couldn't take my eyes off him, and slowly, cautiously, I lowered myself so I could scoop up his pants.

"Get away." Conner's voice was a garbled, raspy hiss.

"It's me, Con—"

"I fucking know who you are! You think I fucking don't know who you are? Get away from me!"

Slowly, steadily, I crept to where I could see him more clearly.

Conner jammed his fingers down into the crusty surface of the salt flat, digging. His hands gripped so tightly into the ground, like he was trying to hold himself down, or as though he were strong enough to keep the world from spinning away beneath our feet. It seemed that every muscle on his body was tensed to the point of bursting, exploding; his face contorted in anger, the tendons in his neck strained taut, like cables.

It was Conner, but it wasn't Conner.

I watched him as I squatted down and laid the rifle to rest across my knees. Then, cautious and deliberate, I began going through each of the pockets in his discarded pants.

"We're getting out of here, Con."

He spoke through bared, gritted teeth. "I . . . We waited too long. I can't stop this. . . ."

And behind me, Ethan's voice, not twenty feet away from us. "There he is."

Conner began whimpering. He covered his eyes with twisted, shaking hands. The mark above his groin blazed so fierce.

It could not be too late.

Then I found the lens.

He'd wrapped it up inside a scrap of torn cloth that looked like it had once been a sleeve on his T-shirt, wadded, just like Jack would do, tucked away in one of the buttoned outer pockets on the uniform fatigues of a Ranger.

He began to pant, grunting between breaths. I could hear him swallowing great gobs of drool.

"Get the fuck away from me, Jack Whitmore!" Conner growled. It sounded like it hurt him to free words from his constricted throat. He slammed his fist down into the ground.

Carefully, I placed the wrapped fragment of lens in my palm. Even then, as soon as I held it out beneath the hole that dripped fire from the sky, I could see how the thing burned within the stained cloth.

My hand felt heat, and through the sack in which I'd covered my scar, I saw the seep of blood that spread out across the dirty rag covering my palm.

"It's going to be okay, Con. I promise."

How the fuck could I promise that?

Blood ran, tickled the back of my wrist.

Drip.

Conner stood up.

He looked like a bug.

White eye.

Black eye.

The fire brand.

Hands, muscles, twitching like over-tight springs.

He wheezed and drooled.

"A fucking bug!" Ethan shouted.

"No!" I said. "He isn't! Stay back!"

I jammed my other hand into my pocket.

There it was, the Marbury lens. I could feel it tingle between my thumb and finger.

I pulled it out and placed it on my palm beside the piece wrapped in Conner's shirtsleeve.

Drip.

Jack is bleeding again.

The sky lights up, an instantaneous dawning of gray Marbury nothingness.

I flip Conner's lens around, try to unwind its cover.

He slurs, "Get the fuck out of here!"

Conner limps toward me, moving as though he's fighting himself, giving up.

As my fingers nervously grope the edges of the filthy cloth and begin to pull it free from the lens, I glance across and see the four boys standing, frozen, under the sudden blaze of the sky.

Only Frankie starts coming toward the place where I crouch in the ash.

And on my opposite side is Conner.

The lens tumbles from my bloody hand.

"Fuck!"

Frankie has a bow, captured from one of the dead Hunters. He notches an arrow, pulls it tight against the strain of the bowstring.

All arrows point to the center of the universe.

All arrows point to Jack.

I sweep my hand across the ground, let the other half of the lens fall there.

Conner growls like an animal. He is so close to me now I can feel the heat from his skin.

Frankie raises, aims.

He shouts, "Don't fucking move, Jack!"

Conner twists his fingers into my hair, grabbing, jerks my head so my chin notches upward. I look at him, but he can't see me anymore. He clenches his other hand into my throat.

"Con!"

And I can't breathe.

Blindly, my fingers find the pieces, lift the tattered rag away from the one I'd taken out of Conner's pocket.

Now I have them both.

Black dots begin to swallow everything I see, a closing aperture on a camera's lens. I can't say anything, and when I move my head I can feel Conner's fingers tear into the flesh on my neck.

But I see Frankie as he releases the arrow.

This is how it always is.

Drip.

I push myself up. It takes all my strength; and I can feel the aching, the blood as it runs down my chest.

The swimming shapes come back, rise up from the ground below us.

This is how it always is.

Drip.

I am standing in front of Conner as he slobbers and tears at my throat.

Everything is everywhere.

The arrow comes.

The aim is precise.

I cannot move.

Drip.

And in my hand, the lens is made whole again.

thirty-two

Every day begins the same.

I open my eyes and say to myself, *This is it.*

This is it.

And this is what I know.

I try to make myself stop thinking about what happened to us after that hot afternoon when we gathered, sick, sweating, scared, in the garage at Ben and Griffin's house.

But if I ever teach myself how to do that, I imagine there will be lots of other things Jack will cast off, abandon.

Remembered or not, everything happens, anyway.

They made Conner and me room with English kids at St. Atticus.

I supposed it was probably their way of immersing the transplanted California boys in their new culture, but that was only my guess.

Because I had no way of knowing what happened to any of us here in this world, from the moment I swung that hammer to when

I opened my eyes and stared up at a perfect, cream white ceiling I initially believed was the Marbury sky, and repeated those three words in my head.

This is it.

Isn't it?

Before that, the last thing I remembered seeing was Frankie's arrow flying directly toward my chest.

It was raining that morning.

I held my unsteady hand up between my eyes and the ceiling and examined my palm.

No blood.

No mark.

I lay in bed waiting for something—the first clue, a sign, maybe a sound. I couldn't guess how many minutes passed by. But then again, Jack was completely incapable of measuring such things as time. I listened to the rain, the deep and slow sleeping breaths that sounded like whispered secrets from the boy in the next bed.

Waiting, waiting.

Just listening to him, I knew it wasn't Conner. I recognized every sound Conner could ever make, no matter what world we were in. And I knew Conner's smell. I didn't have to see the kid to know it wasn't Conner asleep over there in a bed not three feet away from my face.

When I heard the stir of sheets and covers, the rodentlike squeak of old bedsprings, I turned my head and watched the boy who padded barefoot across the floor and faded like a ghost into the dark rectangle of an open doorway against the far wall.

No light came on in there.

And I listened while he took a loud, long piss. He didn't flush the toilet, either. He just reappeared through the open doorway, gangly, deathly pale, wearing nothing but tight red boxer briefs.

He yawned casually and rubbed his eyes.

And I knew his name. Not just his Odd name, his entire name, and everything that came with it.

Ethan Robson.

He saw I was awake, watching him.

"Morning, Jack."

Ethan turned on a television and, folding up his grasshopper-thin legs, climbed back into bed.

I cleared my throat and answered, "Good morning."

I felt sick.

Same as always.

A news program from London came on.

Ethan grabbed the remote control that was lying on a table between our beds, in the center of some kind of monument of stacked empty beer cans.

I couldn't help but think about Ben telling me, *Fuck this place, Jack. So, where'd you leave the goddamned remote?*

Click.

It seemed as though I'd heard those words only seconds ago, and I swear I still smelled the salt ash of Marbury in my hair, clinging to the sweat in my damp armpits.

My stomach tightened.

Click.

Ethan flipped through the channels until he found highlights from a Premier League match. Only then did I notice, remember all the soccer posters and banners, even a red jersey, that hung on the wall between me and what apparently was our bathroom.

"Can you put it back on the news for just a minute?"

Trying to speak made me feel awkward, drunk, even embarrassed, but I needed to see anything that might tell me more about where—or when—my world was now.

This is how it always was.

"It's raining, in case you hadn't noticed," Ethan said.

Black worms.

"Thank you for the weather update."

He switched the channel.

It was September 22.

Nearly an entire month had vanished at the swing of a hammer.

This is it.

Jack hit it out of the park.

"Okay. Never mind," I said. "You can turn it back to your game. Thanks, Ethan."

I needed to throw up.

Welcome here, Jack.

Wherever this is.

And, just maybe, this is it.

I tossed the covers off me, pasted my hand tightly across my lips, and staggered to the dark doorway, coughing and gagging. I found the open mouth of the toilet and dropped onto my knees—the familiar hugging position that Jack knew so well—just in time.

The toilet was dirty. It frothed with warm, thick urine; wet droplets of sticky piss flattened between the porcelain rim and the bloodless skin on my quaking forearms; and I could not stop the puking.

I sensed Ethan's shadow looming in the doorway behind me.

"You damn American lads never have been able to hold a proper drink."

414

And somehow, I remembered how we'd brought all that beer into the room the evening before—Friday night. Today, Ethan and I were supposed to be leaving St. Atticus for our weekends.

I vomited again.

The boys at St. Atticus drank all the time. I knew that, just like I remembered Ethan's favorite team was from Manchester.

Maybe this was it.

"Are you all right?"

I spit into the toilet. The back of my nose burned with acid.

"What the fuck happened to me?"

Ethan laughed.

He didn't know how bad I wished he might answer that question.

I sat there on the floor, watching, smelling the toilet, waiting for the nausea to recede.

Behind me, the shower came on. I immediately felt the humid breath of steam that exhaled through the lips of a moldy vinyl curtain.

Welcome home, Jack.

And Ethan helped me stand. He pulled me up from the cold floor by my hand and told me, "Come on, Jack. Get in. You'll feel better."

When I looked at him, I saw in his face so many things that all came rushing back to me: how Ethan the outcast, bed wetter, was the target of the stronger boys—the Odds—in Marbury. But here, I saw genuine friendship.

This is it.

It was almost as though I could hear Ethan Robson pleading with me in that piss-stained hell of a camp to let him look into the glasses one more time, just a peek; he was so desperate to get away from the other boys, to get out of Marbury.

"You don't remember it, do you?"

Ethan smirked. "What? You passing out last night? I think I recall it a bit more clearly than you do." He patted my shoulder lightly and said, "Don't worry, Jack. You behaved within the acceptable bounds of propriety. For an American, that is."

It was the same as Ben and Griffin.

They never knew anything. I could have left them there, unfucked, shooting hoops at Steckel Park. But I didn't. And just like Ethan, they'd begged me in Marbury, too. They wanted out.

So I took them.

And it made us all monsters.

I shook my head. I wouldn't do it again. I was going to leave this kid alone.

But I needed to know.

All the strings had come untied, and I had no idea what I'd see when I went looking for them—the frayed ends, my friends, my life.

The lens.

So I stood there, shivering in the stale darkness of our bathroom, watching the steam puke its way out from the gashes in the torn shower curtain, while Ethan went back to his soccer match.

I found a light switch beside the doorjamb, and as soon as I flicked it remembered how the bulb had burned out weeks ago, and we'd never bothered to replace it.

This is it.

I pulled the leathery curtain back, snaked my legs out of my briefs, and got inside the shower.

I shut my eyes and leaned my head on my hands against the tile wall, letting the hot water stream down my neck.

It was like waiting to be born.

In the dark, it felt like being in the Under.

I didn't know what I was waiting for. I only knew how much I didn't want to open my eyes again, how much I just wanted to stay there, naked and mute in the warm dark womb of a filthy shower stall and think about nothing.

September 22.

Eight in the morning.

This is it.

If I thought about things too much, I realized I got panicky about not knowing anything.

I didn't really know where I kept my clothes, or how this Jack got dressed, if he'd be uptight and nervous around other kids, just like the other Jack was.

Or if, maybe, this was not-Jack, confident and strong, funny and relaxed, and I didn't know the first thing about him, except that he got drunk last night, puked, and ended up with some other kid's piss all over his arms.

So what could I do?

I left my underwear soaking in the puddle of shower water that pooled on the dank floor of our toilet-cave, wrapped myself in the only towel that hung from the fake-chrome rail beside the tiled stall, and walked out into our room, aiming myself for the only piece of furniture that looked like it might contain clothing.

I tried not to think about which side of the wardrobe belonged to Jack, or what kind of clothes he'd brought along to school.

I just did it.

Ethan was still in bed, watching television when I came out of the shower.

"What time is the train in?" I said.

Everyone's dead on the train.

Quit it, Jack.

"I don't think I want to get out of bed."

Ethan's family lived outside Bath, a long trip for the kid to make and then have to come back to school tomorrow. From Orpington, where St. Atticus was, to London, took about forty minutes by train, including our walk from school to the station. Bath was another two hours beyond that.

And I remembered going to Ethan's house. My brain flashed images of his parents, his two small sisters. We'd all gone to Stonehenge together, just a week ago. I looked at the ring of empties on our nightstand.

I rubbed my temples, squeezed shut my eyes.

Ethan grunted as he sat up in bed.

"Head hurt?"

"Huh? Oh. No. I feel a lot better now."

There were school clothes scattered all over our floor: pants, socks, undershirts, shined dress shoes, shirts, and ties. The place was a complete mess, just like Jack's room always had been. I opened the wardrobe. Nothing looked like me.

I tried to think, *Where's my goddamned phone?*

Jack's always losing his shit.

This is how it always is.

Ethan got out of bed, turned on the shower.

"Throw me a clean towel, please?"

I found a towel neatly folded beneath a stack of them inside our wardrobe and tossed it to Ethan, who stood in the doorway to the bathroom. I was relieved to know I could look through the things in the dresser and pick out this Jack's clothes by size tags while the kid was under the shower. Ethan stood at least three inches taller than me, and was narrower around the waist.

It wouldn't be a difficult sorting process.

And after I'd managed to finish my clothes shopping and gotten myself dressed, I sat on the floor and pulled on a pair of clean gray socks. I'd searched through everything scattered around me; turned out each pocket on every article of clothing. I found some money in both pairs of pants, keys, and Ethan's wallet, too. But nothing of Jack's. No lens. No glasses. Nothing. I even looked under the beds and between the mattresses, where Ethan had stashed a porn magazine.

I put it back in its hiding place and sat on my bed with my head down in my hands.

I couldn't find anything.

"Are you sure you're all right, Jack?"

Ethan came out of the bathroom and started picking folded clothes out of the open dresser.

I sighed. "I can't find any of my shit. My phone, my wallet, nothing."

Ethan smiled and shook his head. He looked at me with an unbelieving expression, and then he slipped into a pair of jeans and began threading a belt around his hips.

"You've gone completely crazy." He pulled open the top drawer of our nightstand with his upturned bare foot and pointed a skeletal finger at it.

I stared down into the open drawer. It was like looking at an ancient tomb.

Jack's tomb.

Everything was there: my phone, wallet, my digital camera, a wad of American money, a stick of deodorant, a half-eaten candy bar, nail clippers, some balled-up white briefs, and socks.

I swallowed. "No more drinking for me."

Ethan Robson pulled a sweatshirt on over his head and shook out his long hair. He laughed at me.

"Right. That vow of abstinence will last for approximately ... oh ... three days, in my qualified opinion."

Almost as soon as he said it, there was an urgent pounding on our door, and from out in the hallway came the booming foghorn voice of another English boy: "Oh, come on, you fucking wankers. What's taking you? We were supposed to leave five fucking minutes ago."

I knew the voice. His name was Neal Genovese. He played soccer with Ethan, and roomed with Conner. I knew it.

The doorknob jiggled and shook impatiently.

We always locked it whenever we got drunk.

Neal said, "Open the fucking door."

Someone else down the hall shouted, "Shut the bloody hell up!"

When I stood, I tripped over my Vans, I was in such a rush to get to the door.

Ethan said, "You're going to kill yourself, Jack."

But I caught my balance and unlocked it without breaking anything.

When I opened the door, Neal was standing there in his Number-2 jersey and school warm-ups, square shouldered, hands on his hips, a little pissed off and red faced. He was broader and more angular than Ethan and wore a very unprofessional, uniform buzz cut that made his brown hair look like a shrunken bearskin cap.

And directly behind him, holding a small canvas bag for the

weekend, and leaning as though he were propping shut the door to the room across the hallway, was my best friend, Conner Kirk.

I don't think I've ever gasped in my life, but seeing Conner there, really looking into his eyes, gave me that rush, the fearful surge you get when you slip on ice. It was practically all I could do to resist shoving past Neal and throwing my arms around him.

He looked good.

It looked like home.

And this has to be it.

"Con!"

He just raised his chin toward me, and with that one nod, I knew it really was him; that we were back.

Conner dropped his bag in the hall and raised his hand to slap a stinging high five into mine. We grabbed on to each other so tightly it hurt, and I swear I could feel my eyes starting to well up.

Neal pushed his way past us and slung his duffel bag down on top of the mess of clothes that were strewn all over our floor, grumbling, "Bloody hell. There's so many fucking Americans here, you'd think there was a bloody war on." And, to Ethan, he snapped, "Are you not fucking ready to leave yet?"

Ethan, hopping, trying to get a sock over his bony foot, said, "Yeah."

But he wasn't ready. Ethan and I weren't known for being the most punctual kids at St. Atticus, so we were a good match as roommates. And Neal Genovese, as tightly wound as he was whenever we weren't drunk, was definitely not the ideal roomie for someone like Conner Kirk.

So Conner, still holding on to my hand, said, "There's a train every fucking few minutes. Chill the fuck out for once, Gino."

Gino. That's what Conner called him. Neal thought it was funny, but like a lot of things Conner Kirk said, it pissed him off sometimes, too.

Neal, mocking, shaking his head with impatient disapproval as he watched Ethan attempting to get dressed, in a sarcastic and fake California accent, said, "Oh. Right on, dude."

I pushed Conner out into the hall, away from the door, and whispered, "Is this it? Is this really it?"

He nodded, smirked. "Mind the gap, Jack."

I threw my arms around him and grabbed on to him, cursing myself that I was not going to cry.

"There is no fucking gap," I said.

Conner held me back at arm's length and slapped the top of my head, rubbing his fingers in my wet hair.

"When did you get back?"

"Just now. Half an hour ago. You?"

Conner laughed. "I was in here getting fucked up with you guys last night."

I heard Neal inside the room. He was chewing out Ethan for making him wait while Ethan stuffed random articles of clothing into an overnight bag.

"I better get my shit together before he blows up at me, too," I said.

Conner shook his head. "You? Shit together? You *are* Jack Whitmore, right?"

And just before we went inside my room, Conner grabbed my shoulder and whispered, "Where is it, Jack?"

I knew what he meant.

Of course I knew what he meant.

thirty-three

On the train to the city, Conner phoned our girlfriends, Nickie and Rachel.

He made lame excuses about Jack being sick, how we couldn't come to London for the weekend.

Ethan eyed me suspiciously. He listened to Conner's smooth and convincing sincerity about poor Jack sleeping in bed, laid up with chills and a fever.

"He looks terrible, Nickie."

Then he winked at me and said, "I'll tell him you said that, babe."

Conner was such a slick and practiced liar.

Ethan watched me, one eyebrow raised questioningly.

I shrugged and smiled crookedly. "Boys' night out, Ethan. I guess that vow of temperance I swore isn't going to last the day."

Ethan slapped my knee and gave me an I-told-you-so look.

And Neal said, "Lad's got to fucking play around sometimes, eh, Conner? One of these days, if you ever get a girlfriend, Ethan, you'll see. Ha! If. Aren't I right, Jackie?"

What could I say?

Neal Genovese and Ethan Robson went their own ways once the four of us arrived at Charing Cross.

Conner and I had other things to do now, and I didn't know where to start.

But I did read through the listings on my phone while we sat on the train.

I found Ben Miller's and Griffin Goodrich's numbers there.

At first, I was terrified to even look for them. I convinced myself that the only way I'd be brave enough to do it was if I was sitting there with three other boys. I kept imagining that goddamned barrel in some other Freddie's garage, in some other Glenbrook. If I closed my eyes, I saw images of the photographs of the boys, spread out on a tabletop in some fucking interrogation room, or I'd remember following Seth through an alleyway near Green Park, when I'd peered down into the mouth of the blue plastic drum and saw their bodies.

While London fell to pieces around me.

But this was it.

It had to be.

I even rechecked their names at least ten times before we'd gotten off the train and said good-bye to our roommates. I ignored the sympathetic text messages I received from Nickie and Rachel.

But there were changes, too.

I figured some things had to be different after an unobserved month slipped by.

Ander's cell number was saved on my phone, like it had been when Henry and I popped back into his crumbling flat that last time. And I'd even made a number of calls to Ander that I couldn't clearly remember.

My clothes were all different, too. They fit me strangely, and I couldn't remember having any of this stuff before the end of the summer. *Maybe I grew or my tastes changed*, I thought, *but when I woke up in bed that morning, I was wearing briefs.* Jack never owned or wore briefs one day in his life. The only way I could explain it was that I must have lost or run out of my regular clothes somehow, or maybe Nickie had taken me shopping.

It wasn't a big deal.

I wouldn't let myself make it a big deal.

Because this was it.

This was going to be it.

And, mostly, things seemed as normal as they probably should be. All my recent calls were between me and Conner, Nickie, her brother, Henry Hewitt, my grandmother, and at least a dozen calls in the last few days had come from Ben and Griffin in California.

So once Conner and I found a relatively quiet part of the station, I dropped the bag I'd been carrying and pulled the phone out of my pocket.

I hadn't been thinking about the lens, or the other glasses. I didn't care about them. And I knew I had them with me, somewhere.

Same old Jack, no matter how fucked up his universe gets.

Always keeping one foot in the door.

But I needed to hear Ben's and Griffin's voices, just so I could begin to feel more certain that we all really did make it back from Marbury.

Conner knew what I was doing.

"It's going to be after midnight," he said.

"They'll be up. If they're . . ."

I didn't need to say it; Conner knew what I meant.

If they're the same.

If they're alive.

If they're here.

I called.

Ben answered, in a whisper.

"Jack?"

I held my phone in front of my chin, so Conner could hear, and I watched his eyes to see if he gave a sign confirming that things were really okay.

"Hey. I'm here. With Conner."

425

Conner was staring at me, too, looking for the same thing.

"Glenbrook?"

"We're in London."

There was a rustling, the sound of motion, like Ben dropped the phone.

"Hang on. I'm in bed. I'm going in Griffin's room."

I took a long breath. I was so relieved. "Are you okay?"

I could hear a door opening, shutting. Then Griffin said, "It's Jack? Jack? Are you here?"

"We're back. When did you guys—"

"Three days ago. We been calling you and Conner for three days," Ben said. "You didn't know what the fuck I was talking about."

"Well, it's us now," Conner said. I could see the relief on his face, too.

"Is everything okay?" I asked.

Ben said, "Yeah. It was weird at first. We were scared. We were gone such a long time, Jack. We couldn't remember some shit. My stepdad thought we were smoking pot or something. They fucking piss-tested both of us this morning."

"Yeah. Screw that," Griffin said.

Conner smiled and nodded.

"But you're both okay?" I said.

"We don't fucking smoke pot, if that's what you mean," Ben answered.

"Do you remember what happened to us out in the desert?" I watched Conner. He shook his head.

Ben's voice lowered. "After the fight. The horses ran off. We came after you. Me, Griffin, that kid named Frankie, and Ethan."

"Ethan's a kid at school here."

426

"When we found you, there was a Hunter standing next to you, coming for you."

I watched Conner's eyes while Ben said it. He didn't show anything.

"Frankie took a bow from one of the dead bugs, and he was going to shoot the Hunter, but as soon as he did, it was like the sky opened up and you got to your feet, right in the way of the arrow."

"Frankie shot you," Griffin said. "He shot you with the arrow, Jack. It went completely through you and then it just fell down in the dirt like you weren't even there."

Ben continued, "And when it happened, both you and the Hunter disappeared. Then everything went blank, like it did when we were in the garage. That was all I knew. Next thing I knew, I was sitting on a bench in the locker room at Glenbrook, getting dressed for PE, and Griff was at his school sleeping through a test. I was so fucking scared. And then I forgot my fucking locker combination and had to spend the rest of the day in my gym clothes. I didn't see Griff till we got home from school. We both looked like shit. We've been trying to call you ever since. But whenever I did, you were, like, 'What are you talking about?'"

"And, Jack," Griffin said. "You know . . . What did you do with the lens?"

"I . . . I'm not sure yet," I lied. I was certain I'd find the lenses inside the bag I'd packed, hidden away inside the wadded socks and underwear I stashed in the nightstand beside my bed. Where else would Jack hide such things?

There was a long silence after that.

Conner watched me. He chewed the inside of his lip. To me, he already looked sick, like he needed to know the lens was still okay. It pissed me off. I almost wanted to punch him for it.

427

And he knew I was lying, too.

"Jack?" Ben said.

"Yeah?"

"I know it's fucked up of us. Um . . . we think we need to go back."

"We need to," Griffin added.

"Don't talk about it," I said.

Conner and I both stood there, staring at my silent phone like we were waiting for some kind of answer to just pop out and present itself to us.

But nothing came.

"Jack?" Griffin said. He sounded desperate and weak, not like the kid I knew, the kid I always thought was so strong and brave.

"What do you want me to do, Griff? What the fuck am I supposed to do? You were the one telling me to get you home. Remember that morning in the box? Now what the fuck do you want me to do?" I exhaled a long sigh. "Look. We're not going to do anything now. Me and Conner have to figure this out." Then I lied again, "I don't even know where the goddamned lens is. It might be gone for good this time, and that would be fine with me. I don't fucking care anymore."

Conner grabbed my arm, shook me slightly. "Hey. Easy."

I swallowed, cleared my throat. "I'm sorry, Griff. Ben. We'll figure it out. Call me back in the morning, your time. Promise you'll call me back. Look, it's not that long till Christmas. We're coming home for two weeks. We'll figure it out. Together. I promise."

And Conner said, "But we're not fucking breaking anything again."

I heard Ben try to laugh at that.

"Okay, Jack," he said. "Let's not talk about it."

428

"Good night, then," I said. "I'm glad we're all okay. It's going to be okay now. This is it, right?"

"Yeah. But, Jack? There's one thing I need to tell you. There was a cop looking up your cell number. He came here asking me and Griff a bunch of questions about you."

At that moment, it felt like my throat sank to my stomach.

Even Conner looked scared.

"Jack? Did you hear what I said?"

"I heard you." I shut my eyes tight, trying to think. "What did you say to him?"

"Nothing," Ben said. "What the fuck could I say? That we all know how to walk through some fucking piece of glass and into a different world called Marbury, or whatever the fuck place it is now? That we fucking kill shit there?"

"I bet he'd leave you alone if you did tell him that," Conner said.

"Or we'd be taken down and piss-tested again," Griffin answered.

I heard the knocking on the door, Ben's stepdad telling the boys to get off the phone.

"His name was Avery Scott, right?" I said.

"How'd you know that?"

More knocking.

"I gotta go, Jack."

"Okay. Call me in the morning, Ben."

"See ya."

"Promise?"

Click.

"Ben?"

I felt sick.

"Separate beds? Damn. I was hoping we'd get our same old room, Jack. What are we going to do in *separate beds*?"

He was trying to get me to lighten up.

But I was numb.

All I could think about was that fucking cop, what he knew, and what I didn't know.

It was Conner's idea for us to get a room at the White House—the same hotel we stayed in at the start of our summer.

The rain cleared up.

It was early afternoon, and it felt like autumn.

I stood in front of the window and looked out at Regent's Park.

From behind me, Conner said, "And the goddamned shower door works, too. This sucks. Everything's different."

He came up behind me, shoved me playfully.

"Let's go for a run, Jack. We're getting too lazy and fat hanging out with those fucking Brits."

"Yeah. Okay."

I sat on the bed and slipped my feet out of my shoes. I took off my shirt.

Conner watched me as I opened my bag, and it pissed me off. I knew why he was watching me. And I knew exactly what I could find in my bag if I wanted to.

"Are you going to change, or are you just going to stand there and look at me?"

Conner smiled and shrugged, gawking with his mouth and eyes wide, messing with me. He made it even more obvious that he was staring at me while I got undressed.

But I didn't look for the lens.

And just like I would expect him to, Conner naturally made a crack about me wearing briefs.

"Briefs? Since when do you wear *briefs?*"

I shook my head. "All my things . . . seem like they're different. I thought it was just maybe Nickie or something."

I sighed. "What about your stuff? Is any of your stuff . . . different?"

Conner unbuttoned his jeans and let them fall around his ankles. "Let's see."

I gave him a disappointed sigh.

Typical Conner Kirk.

"You still have that thing." I pointed to the little scar above Conner's groin—the faded mark, the brand, a souvenir from our first times in Marbury.

Conner pulled the waistband on his boxers down and looked. The thing used to scare him. Now, it seemed as though he'd completely shrugged it off as meaningless. Conner was so good at doing that, and I wished someday I could be that way, too.

But I couldn't.

He said, "Yeah. My tattoo from the happy place."

"But everything else seems the same, right? I mean, some things are bound to be different after being gone so long. Right?"

Conner kicked his feet out of his pants, walked over to the narrow closet across from the bathroom, and put them on a hanger.

"Don't think about that cop, Jack. He's not going to do anything to us. We didn't do anything wrong, okay?"

"Okay."

He pulled a pair of running shorts on over his boxers and sat down to lace his shoes.

"So, were you shitting Ben and Griff, or do you really not know where the lens is?"

431

If I stayed there much longer, I was certain we would get into a fistfight. And I never wanted to fight with Conner again.

So I turned around and made my way down the short hallway beside our bathroom. Conner left the closet door open. Inside, there was a folding ironing board, a safe, two thick terry-cloth bathrobes, and one of those webbed racks you put suitcases on. I saw Conner's pants and a dozen empty wooden hangers lined up like teeth on a chrome rod that spanned the width of the closet.

It looked strong enough to support my weight.

"Come on," I said. "Let's get out of here."

We ran around Regent's Park, just like we did together so many times in early summer.

The air felt cool and damp. Everything smelled like wet rotting leaves.

For the first few miles, we didn't say anything. I tried to stay in front of him, position myself so I wouldn't have to look at Conner; and he kept trying to slow us down, to block me with his shoulder, running me into hedges and the short fences that were set up in places to keep people off the grass.

When Conner and I ran together, we didn't have to say the words out loud. Sometimes just our pace or position told the other guy exactly what we were thinking.

I felt like shit, and Conner wanted to play.

I had missed him, missed this world, Nickie, so much. But now, all I could think about was getting away from it all—being left completely alone. Alone in a way that I would never bother, or be bothered by, anyone else.

And I could do it now, too.

I'd gotten them home.

Off the hook.

I needed to be left alone now.

Fuck you, Conner.

Fuck you, Jack.

Fuck this place.

As I ran, I pictured the strings, the burning clump of grass Davey fanned smoke from on a hot autumn afternoon in Pope Valley, the nesting dolls that Stella collected; and it dawned on me that every time I had skipped around—jumped onto another string, or deeper into another layer—that whether coming or going, there was always some little thing, here or there, that was almost unnoticeably different.

But things always changed.

When an echo comes back to you, the song is always different.

It was why the pictures disappeared from my camera back in June, and why Conner saw Henry sometimes, but other times it was like Henry didn't even exist.

So maybe I'd never gotten back home to begin with.

From the very first time I went to Marbury, things got moved, rearranged. And once those things shifted the slightest bit, they never went back to exactly the same spots they'd come from.

That's what I thought.

Conner elbowed me below the ribs.

That was it.

We stopped running.

I shoved him. Hard. I wanted to punch him so bad I was shaking. Both my hands tightened in fists. Of course he saw it.

"What the fuck, Con?"

He shook his head; his brow tightened up like I was speaking a different language.

"What's wrong with you, Jack?"

"Stop fucking with me! Leave me the fuck alone!"

Conner's tone was pleading. "What'd I do, Jack? Tell me what I did."

I spun around, away from Conner, and threw a wild hook punch at the air. Then I put my hands on top of my head, squeezing, pulling my hair.

"What is fucking wrong with me?"

I wasn't asking Conner. I was just sending the words out across the slate surface of the lake, skipping like stones, going nowhere but down. I didn't even want an answer, and Conner knew it.

So we stood there like that for the longest time, absolutely silent except for the panting breaths we gulped. And I think Conner was starting to get scared too.

"I'm sorry, Con."

He stepped toward me. I didn't see him, but I could feel his heat as he got close. Finally, he put his arm around my shoulder and squeezed me tight. He was sweating.

I said, "Dude. You fucking reek like BO."

He gripped my bicep and pulled me in to him.

"It's all okay, Jack. I'm not fucking with you. We're here. Safe. Together. Everything is good now. Finally, dude. We made it. I swear to God, everything's good now."

I swallowed a lump and nodded.

"What if—"

Conner cut me off. "There is no *what if*, Jack. This is fucking it. I promise."

434

He patted his hand on the back of my neck.

"This can be it, Jack."

"You think?"

"It's good enough for me, bud."

The sky began darkening again. It would rain soon.

And Conner said, "Don't you think this is far enough? Let's go get drunk out of our fucking minds."

This is it.

Conner didn't say anything else about the things that were eating us inside.

He just made small talk and teased me, picked on Jack like he always did, calling me gay, testing me.

And we didn't even clean up. Sweaty and stinking, we got dressed in the same jeans we'd worn on the train, slipped into our T-shirts and pullovers.

Conner put on his wool cap, and said, "There!" like we were racing each other out the door or something; and I just let my damp hair hang in darkened strings that went past my eyes.

It didn't matter.

Nothing mattered.

Because this was it.

And I knew what I needed to do.

I had a plan.

As soon as we shut the door behind us, I took out my phone.

Conner asked, "Nickie?"

"No. I owe someone a beer."

We walked to The Prince of Wales.

thirty-four

By the time Henry Hewitt showed up, Conner and I were drunk.

The place was noisy and alive.

I didn't even try to pace myself with the drinking. I wanted to poison every fear I held on to, work up the courage to finally let go of everything Jack kept balled up in the center of his fucked universe.

Conner laughed. "You know? You know what Gino fucking Genovese and Ethan call this? They say this is getting *piss maggot drunk*, Jack. We are *piss maggoted*."

He stood up, sat, and stood again, wavering unsteadily while he carried our empty pint glasses to the bar for refills.

And that's when Henry walked in.

Conner glanced at the door one time, but didn't pay any attention to Henry at all. He turned back to the bartender and noisily ordered another round for us.

I waved and held three fingers up, then pointed to the man at the door.

"Make it three."

It was almost funny to me, how after all this time when they'd both been so important in my life—in my worlds—Conner and Henry had never yet spoken to each other, sat face-to-face. And now that they were finally here together, it was almost like I could rest my case once and for all that this—whatever *this* was—was real.

I was the worm and I was the hole. We all were—me, Conner, Ben and Griffin, Henry, Seth, and Ethan, too. But I was the King of Marbury. Somehow I'd been chosen to go through, as Henry was chosen before me. And every time I did it, I fooled myself into thinking, *This is it*, but I never once got back to a place I'd been before.

I never fucking got us back home.

Maybe I was just drunk, but as I sat there in The Prince of Wales, I decided that the reason I never told anyone except Conner about what Freddie Horvath did to me was that I believed everyone else would think it was my fault.

Everything was Jack's fault.

But this could be it.

This was good enough, and I was tired. I wished I had the balls to hold Conner and tell him how sorry I was for everything I'd done.

This is it.

Henry stood at the door, eyeing me for a moment. Then he nodded and began snaking through the crowd.

I could say he looked older, but we'd both been through so much. As he made his way toward me, I wondered if he knew about the places I'd been, if maybe he'd had dreams, and in them, if he saw London falling to pieces, ghosts who came and went, Jack bleeding to death in front of him, and blue plastic drums with the tangled bodies of lost little boys sleeping endlessly inside them.

Maybe he had no stories except for the ones that trapped us together.

I wondered if he carried a small compass with him.

I was so sick of everything. I had called Henry here to say good-bye to him one last time.

When he got to our table, I stood politely and took his hand, but I didn't smile. Behind him, Conner balanced three pints of beer and worked at navigating a zigzagged return.

"The last time I saw you, I promised I'd buy you a beer," I said.

Henry cleared his throat and sat beside me. "And when, exactly, was that, Jack?"

"Funny. The *exactly* part. The day before yesterday, I guess. We stood together on a ridge of boulders and looked out at the desert in Marbury, the night before you left for Bass-Hove. Sound familiar?"

Henry shrugged one shoulder as if to say it didn't matter whether it sounded familiar or not. "Well, it's always nice to have a pint with a friend, I think."

Conner arrived, centering three nearly full glasses of beer on the table. He stood there for a while, gripping the back of his chair with both hands like he was having a hard time figuring out what changed about this picture while he was gone.

He leaned across the table and put his face so close to my ear that he almost fell on top of me. He whispered, "Hey, Jack. There's some creepy old guy sitting next to you. Just thought I'd let you know."

Then he laughed and sat down.

I raised my glass. "Conner Kirk, meet Henry Hewitt."

Our beers clinked together, and Henry said, "Cheers."

So we sat like drunken veterans trading war stories for two hours. We spoke with low voices, at times in whispers, like we were all escaped inmates from the same asylum.

Maybe we were crazy.

Each of us told of things the others hadn't seen, but the pieces all fit together in some rhythmic alcoholic order: the Odds, the battles in Glenbrook, the floods, Anamore Fent and the Rangers, the Under, the trip into the desert, the encampment, and, finally, Henry's loss at the settlement, which brought us all back here, to London, to The Prince of Wales.

And the glasses.

"So you knew, didn't you?" I said.

"I don't know nothing." Conner drained his beer. It was amazing to me how much he could drink.

"No. I mean Henry. You knew when you let us go out that night after the Ranger what was going to happen to you and the other boys, didn't you?"

"I thought I did. But there's always that chance, isn't there, that things will change?"

"Like Jack's briefs." Conner put his foot on top of mine. Always screwing with me. "Drink your beer, kid, you're lagging!"

My glass was still full. I couldn't take any more.

"I'm good, Con."

"Not me. I'm never good." Conner got up. "Never."

He pointed at Henry's empty. "How about you?"

"Thank you, yes," Henry said.

I held my glass to my lips, pretended to drink, but I had to hold my breath. The smell of the stuff was beginning to make me feel sick. Still, Conner and Henry hadn't noticed that I'd stopped drinking three rounds earlier.

When Conner came back and sat down, grinning sleepily, Henry steadied himself, square and upright, as though he had finally worked up the courage to say what he and Conner had been dancing around all evening.

"Tell me about breaking the lens. How you put it back together."

Conner leaned forward over the table, like it was story time and I was about to tell him something he didn't already know.

"There's nothing to tell, really. We . . . I used a hammer and vice, and when it broke, everything else sort of fell apart around us, and it all stayed that way, too—broken. That was why, everywhere we'd

439

go, we were followed around by this big oozing hole in the sky. And every time we'd take a piece of the lens out, things would change again, get worse, like stuff was coming out of the sky, or out of the hole in my hand, just coming up out of the middle of everything."

The center of the universe.

I turned my palm up and drew a line with my finger across the flesh where I'd been cut by the lens. "It was the other glasses that brought us—well, some of us—to different places, but everywhere I'd go, things just kept getting worse and worse."

Ben and Griffin dead inside a fucking trash can.

Like what happened to Nickie, what you did to those boys on the train.

Conner gulped at his drink and swiped a forearm across his wet mouth. "We went back to Glenbrook, but it was like the fucking end of the world there."

"Worse than that," I said. "We almost got trapped for good. So when we finally found each other in the desert, it was almost too late again. Things had gotten out of control. But we got the pieces back together."

Henry tipped his glass and looked from Conner to me, never blinking, like he was completely unfazed by the alcohol.

"What happened to it?" he said.

I shook my head. "I don't know. I only felt it turn whole inside my hand. It burned me. I never saw it again after that."

"And you don't know where it is now?"

Fuck you, Henry.

"What does it matter?" I said.

"I thought—" Henry said. "I just wanted to see it."

"That would be cool, Jack," Conner urged. "Let's see it."

He bumped his knee against mine.

I felt myself getting pissed off again.

"I don't know where the fuck it is," I said. "For all I know, you have it, Con."

Conner smirked. "I wish, dude."

"Why?" I said.

"'Cause I'm drunk and I feel like fucking with shit. That's why." He slapped the table eagerly, like a kid waiting for his allowance.

I could only stare at him and shake my head.

"And the other glasses?" Henry wouldn't let it go, either.

Conner was so drunk. "You know, the flip flip."

He made a little flapping windshield-wiper motion with his finger in front of his eyes and said, "How about those ones? Did you lose those, too? You fucking lose shit all the time, Jack."

"You don't get it, do you?"

Conner was definitely too drunk to hear the edge in my voice.

I looked squarely at Henry, then Conner. "It's done. I've had enough. And I don't fucking care about ever going back again. I wanted to tell both of you that tonight. I only asked Henry here to say it, and to tell him thank you for helping us get out for the last time. But that's it. The last time."

I scooted away from the table and stood.

When Conner got up, he knocked his chair over. It sounded like a gunshot. We didn't even notice how empty and quiet the place had become.

"Dude. Sit down. You're not leaving."

I sighed. "It's late. I'm really tired."

I stuck out my hand for Henry.

"Good-bye, Henry. And thank you."

He looked shocked, pale. He shook my hand, but didn't answer me.

And Conner nearly tripped over his upturned chair trying to

steer himself after me when I left The Prince of Wales and went out onto the street.

This is it.

It sounds like Conner is puking in the toilet. I wonder how he managed to get back here without stumbling into traffic. I don't think I've ever seen him this drunk.

The shower comes on.

Good.

Leave me alone, Conner.

There.

I pick up my bag and place it on top of the bed.

Zip.

I open it. The water runs loudly; Conner has left the bathroom door open.

There was never a question in my mind about what became of the lens, the glasses, too. I am so predictable, and this is my great disappointment. There is no wonder with me. I always know what Jack's done and where he's going, everything ordered.

Except now.

I imagine a time, ten minutes forward.

Measured motion.

The remarkable nothingness.

I swallow. The not knowing thrills me. I feel an excited tickle inside my chest, almost sexual, quietly churning.

One. My hand closes around a white cotton knot of underwear. The lens is inside, perfect, waiting.

Two. My socks. And here are the glasses. You know, the *flip flip*, Conner.

Here.

The water runs.

I place both gifts on Conner's pillow and I scratch a note for him on the hotel stationery pad.

These are for you.

I hear Conner cough and gargle in the shower and I remove all of my clothes so I am naked. I do not need anything.

A thick cloth belt from one of the robes in the closet knots and knots again around the shining crossbar. I'm watching Jack's hands tie it, like they aren't attached to me.

Strong.

Standing with my eyes against the cool chrome bar, I can judge the perfect height where I tie the loop.

I listen to the shower, the sounds of Conner moving around in there.

Then I hear another sound.

Roll.

Tap.

Tap.

Tap.

And when I turn around, I see Seth.

"Get the fuck away from me!"

"Jack."

My knees give and then catch. I cannot feel anything except the knot I hold between my fingers.

"Leave me the fuck alone. I did what I had to do."

"Jack."

It is tight. I feel the rope of the belt as I force it through my hair, down over my ears, and I fix my mouth straight because I will not say anything more. I watch the boy who stands beside the wall in front of me, the steam that rolls like the Pope Valley fog out from the open door of the bathroom as the water runs and runs.

"Jack."

Seth begins hitting his hands into the wall, pounding, but I can't hear anything over the rush of the water, the roar of the blood in my ears.

Tight.

There.

"Jack."

And I drop.

"Jack."

thirty-five

Nothing.

Just nothing.

It was the most beautifully complete thing Jack ever knew.

I floated in black, naked and warm.

Waiting, waiting.

Five seconds more and it would have been over.

Five fucking seconds.

Then I smelled a stale breath of alcohol, and from somewhere very far away, like it was slowly crawling out of a long dark tunnel, I heard Conner's voice calling, softly at first.

"Fuck! Fuck! What are you doing? What are you fucking doing?"

And he was crying. Conner never cries. He's never had a reason to.

He was scared, breathing hard.

I could feel his mouth on the side of my neck as he gasped and grunted. With one arm wrapped beneath my armpit, he squeezed me so tightly against his chest, and tried to hold me up off the floor so he could make enough slack to unknot the noose.

Leave me alone, Conner.

When the knots began to come off, the pain spread up and down from where the noose had been tied. It felt like my head was filled with needles, and now they were all rushing down through my neck. I tried to push him away from me, but my arms flopped heavily like soggy mop yarn. Once Conner pulled the noose over my head, he had to catch me as I collapsed, unbound, into him.

Then I was aware of the wetness on his face. Crying, struggling to pull me out of the closet, Conner carried me across the room, and I began to black out again.

Leave me alone.

"What are you thinking, man? What did you do this for? Why? Why?"

Conner shook me with every word, as though his punctuation would snap the life awake inside me.

Then I was down. He laid me on my bed and drunkenly tumbled on top of me. He was heavy and out of breath, dripping from the shower, and he pushed himself up. I felt him lift my feet, pulling the sheets out from the side of the bed so he could cover me. I knew my eyes were open, but everything looked purple and dark, out of focus, like Conner was just a big shadow hovering over me.

"You fucking asshole. Why are you doing this to me?"

He grasped my jaw and shook my face.

It started coming back then. The room began to grow lighter, as though the eye of some great pale sun were opening up above us.

Why couldn't he just leave me alone?

Five seconds.

445

Conner had one of his hands on top of my head; his fingers rubbed my hair, and he pressed the side of his face against my chest, listening. And I could feel how his breaths came short and spastic from the crying.

"You better fucking breathe, asshole."

I inhaled.

"I don't want to go back."

My voice was a dry croak.

"I'm sorry, Conner."

He straightened up, kneeling beside the bed where I lay naked like an unclaimed mortuary cadaver, drained and numb, twisted in the sheets and covers. Conner grabbed my face in his hands and wiped the wetness from my eyes with his thumbs.

I wasn't even aware that I'd been crying.

Maybe it was something else, because like Conner, Jack doesn't do that, either.

Then he kissed my forehead.

"You dumb fuck, Jack."

Conner stood, grunting. He didn't need to say anything else; I could feel how he seethed with anger, spinning around, looking for something that might give him a clue as to how we'd get out of this now.

This is it, after all.

We are home.

At that moment, I was so sorry for hurting him. I knew it was the worst thing I'd ever done, and I kept thinking about those five goddamned seconds.

It had to have been Seth.

He made Conner find me.

"I'm calling the fucking cops."

It was like an electric shock. Freddie's stun gun again. I felt every disconnected muscle in my body contract when he said it.

I tried to sit up. "No. Please don't do that, Con!"

He paced the floor like an animal in a cage. He stopped at his bed, looked down at the note I'd left. Of course he knew what was inside the two small bundles.

"Is that what it's about?" he said. He picked up the socks and underwear I'd used to hide the Marbury lenses from everyone. He cocked his arm back like he was going to throw them against the wall.

"Don't!"

He stopped himself.

Conner knew what would happen if he did it.

He dropped my little gifts to him on the bed.

And then I said it.

"I'd rather die than go back again, Con."

"I'm calling a fucking ambulance, Jack. I can't take this shit."

He went to the desk and picked up the handset for our room's phone.

"Conner, please don't do that."

I swung my feet around onto the floor. I thought I could stand up, try to stop him, but my head pounded so hard it felt like I was going to explode.

Conner inhaled deeply, closed his eyes, and hung up the phone. Then he wheeled a desk chair across the floor and sat down in front of me with his hands clasped between his knees, just watching me, waiting for me to fix things.

"What am I going to do with you?" he said.

"I don't know."

He smeared his forearm across his eyes.

"I would die without you, Jack."

447

"No, you wouldn't."

"You're full of shit!" Conner's voice shook. "You're not the only one who gets hurt in this world! You're not the only one who fucks things up and then has to fix them! Stop being so goddamned selfish for once!"

He was right.

"I . . . Shit, Conner."

He exhaled and loosened his shoulders, slumped back in the chair. "Dude, if you want to stay, I'll stay with you."

I lay on my back, shivering and staring up at the creamy blankness of the hotel room's ceiling.

"I'm afraid if one of us goes back to Marbury, we'll all end up getting sucked into it again, Con. And I . . ."

Conner rubbed his hands together and shook his head. He sniffled loudly. I could hear all the wet snot that bubbled in his nose.

"What about Ben and Griff?"

"I don't know. I don't know what to do anymore, Con."

And so he just sat there and watched me for several long and silent minutes until I rolled onto my side and pulled the sheets up around my shoulders.

It was so cold.

Conner got up and put the wadded-up lenses back inside my bag. He zipped it shut and placed it on top of his bed.

He turned out the lights, and then Conner lay down beside me.

He was still crying.

I felt so bad.

Conner got under the covers and slid his arm around me. He put his hand flat on the coldness of my naked belly, so his face was pressed tightly against the back of my neck.

He whispered, "I'm not ever going to let you leave, Jack."

I could lie and say that sleeping next to Conner wasn't sexual at all, even though we didn't actually do anything. But feeling him beside me was good, genuinely safe, and neither of us was ashamed of it.

For the first time in my life, it was like nothing could ever make me afraid again.

And I'm not scared to admit that it felt safer and closer than lying naked in bed with Nickie.

In the morning, we were awakened by an embarrassed housekeeper who walked into our room and quickly offered pleading apologies as she backed into the hallway.

I groaned. "That is totally fucked up."

Conner still had his arms around me. "Are you okay?"

"Yeah. I'll be all right. I'm sorry, Con."

"For what?"

"Nothing."

Conner pressed closer into me, like he was covering me against something poisonous. "Let's just stay here for, like, ten more minutes, okay?"

"Okay."

And more than an hour later, it was nearly noon when we got out of bed and put our clothes on, silent and awkward, nervously avoiding each other's eyes.

Outside, the air was so cold and heavy.

Feeling it was an amazing thing to me.

To feel.

I walked in a fog as thick and stubborn as the cover of leaden

clouds that pressed down on us from above. I couldn't stop myself
from wondering about everything.

Everything.

And how every day begins the same way.

This is it.

Maybe we were still drunk, I reasoned.

Maybe this was just another not-world.

I kept my eyes down and studied the backs of Conner's sneakers,
the faded upturn of the slight cuff on his Levi's as he walked in front
of me. He led me along the slate-gray sidewalk on Marylebone Road
in the direction of the Great Portland Street Underground.

Conner stopped, and it was the first time since we'd gotten out
of bed that we looked each other squarely in the face.

He said, "So. You want to get coffee?"

"Oh man, I am dying for some coffee."

Conner's mouth turned downward. He shook his head.

I said, "Um. Sorry. Bad choice of words."

Then he smiled cautiously and pointed me to the door of a coffee bar.

It made for a long stretch of silence, finishing two full cups of hot
coffee without saying a word. But nothing else needed to be said.
Sometimes Conner and I could sit together for hours and just know,
exactly, what we were thinking.

We didn't avoid each other's stare, though, because Conner and I
could never be embarrassed about anything around each other. In
fact, sitting there, having coffee with him, I understood Conner better
at that moment than I had in all the years we'd known each other.

He swallowed. I watched the knot in his throat bob down and up.

I reached across the table and bumped his hand with my
knuckles.

"You know, you've saved my life about a hundred times."

I watched Conner bite at the inside of his lip. He shifted in his seat.

I turned and looked at the traffic outside the window, and tried to change the subject. But every subject only ended up being about us, anyway.

"I really like it here. I mean, at St. Atticus. I can feel it."

Conner tipped his empty cup, like he was trying to read a message in the drying foam.

"This is it, right?"

"This is good enough for me, Con."

"I'm okay staying here if you are, Jack."

He sounded nervous, choked up.

I knew he was talking about much more than just England and St. Atticus Grammar School for Boys. We both knew it.

"Well, I'm okay staying here, Con. And, well . . . thanks."

"No prob." Then he squinted and smiled. "But don't ever try that shit again."

"Try what? The before thing, or . . . um . . . you know, after?"

Conner turned red and tried to clear his throat, pretended to look at the cars passing by outside, too.

"Hey," I said. "In case you're wondering, I'm not bugged about it at all. I thought it was totally cool. Really nice. Really. Okay?"

He looked at me and nodded.

"Oh fucking hell!" When I saw the station sign through the window, I shook my head. "We need to get off, Con. We're going the wrong fucking way."

We were on the Tube, at Finchley Road, heading in the entirely opposite direction, on the totally wrong line to get to the train station at Charing Cross.

We weren't paying attention to what was going on around us—outside our little universe—that morning, so in our daze we ended up boarding a wrong-way train at Baker Street. And we barely made it out of the car before the doors whooshed shut.

But after spending a few minutes decoding the colored lines on the Underground map, we switched tracks and headed south on the Jubilee Line, which unfortunately also took us out of our way.

I sighed, and slapped my head when we passed the Baker Street stop.

"Why the fuck didn't we get off there? What the fuck is wrong with me? I am so messed up today."

Conner sat beside me, our bags on the floor between our feet.

He laughed. It was a real laugh, and it sounded good.

Like home.

He pressed his foot against mine. "It's not like we have a plane to catch or something."

When the train slowed into the Bond Street station, I pulled a small folding map from my back pocket.

Like Henry's compass.

"We can switch at Westminster or Waterloo," I said. "Waterloo's probably better. Then we won't have to get off again till we're at Charing Cross."

I tucked the map away. "I'm sorry about getting us lost, Con."

Conner leaned forward and turned so he was looking straight into my eyes. He tapped his hand on my knee.

"I'm having a good time. Don't sweat it." He grinned. "It's kind of fun being together in a place where nobody cares about us, and nobody's trying to kill us."

"Yeah," I said. "Welcome home, huh?"

"Yeah. Home."

The train stopped.

The doors swished open.

We were at Green Park.

And this was it.

thirty-six

There is something about this particular place.

It is a magnet, and Jack cannot break free.

My head snaps around; Conner watches me. He senses something, too, and I am aware of a tightness that clamps down, invades the edges of my vision.

Like being in a vice.

Something is wrong.

Don't black out, Jack.

Conner's hand is on my back, between my shoulders, and he says, "Are you feeling all right?"

This is the arrow.

There are so many people waiting to board the train.

They begin pressing into the car, packing everywhere. Suddenly it is as though their collective mouths inhale every molecule of air around me. Suffocating, empty, I shake my head and hang my chin down to my chest.

"I don't know. I feel sick, Con. Like I'm going to pass out."

"Jack?"

He's rubbing my back, like he's trying to keep me awake, and I say, "Shhhhh . . ."

Everything is suddenly so noisy. I am trapped inside the howling engine of a jet.

Whiteness paints my drained skin; I feel the opening of each pore and I begin to bleed small tears of freezing sweat. I am shaking, and Conner has his arm around my shoulder.

"Let's get off for a second, Jack. Catch your breath."

Conner begins to lift me up, but it is too crowded and too late. The doors are closed. The air turns to chalk dust, and I drop back into my seat as the train sluggishly lurches, skips, accelerates.

Of course.

This is why we got onto the wrong train.

The train passes into a tunnel. Outside in the velvet black, a white light smears by; it burns a trail like a glowing worm across my eyes. And as it wriggles, I stare blankly at the glass, waiting for it to become real and swallow me.

I take a deep breath.

Breathe, Jack.

I know Conner is here, he's pressing his mouth up to my ear, saying something. I can feel the steam of the words that evaporate against my skin, but I can't tell what he's saying.

I feel along the seat beside me, find his hand, and grab on.

Tight.

I lean into him. "Conner, no matter what happens, I love you."

I feel him squeezing my hand.

"Jack?"

"Hey," he says, trying to shake me back. "Jack? Do you know that kid? What's he want?"

Someone is saying, "I have a score to settle with you."

The train begins to slow, it leans me forward, and I nearly fall into Conner.

Conner says again, "Do you know him?"

I shut my eyes tightly, reopen them.

Everything is everywhere.

Seated across the aisle on the bench directly facing us is a red-head kid.

The punk.

Quinn Cahill.

Slower.

Slower.

The kid is saying something.

"Billy? Billy? Isn't that you, Billy? Don't play games now. Hell . . . I knew I'd find you somewhere, as long as I only kept looking."

My words are slurred, drunk, and they disconnect, set loose from my mouth like crazy rabbits. "I don't know what the fuck you're talking about, kid."

The train stops.

Westminster.

Whoosh.

The doors.

The kid looks like he's been stung.

"Billy!"

I'm holding Conner's hand. I jerk it and lean forward, grab my bag.

I whisper, "Please get me out of here, Con."

I fall out of the train as the doors hiss shut behind us; end up flat on my face in a forest of legs on the crowded Westminster platform.

"He's okay. He's okay. He's just sick and couldn't breathe for a second."

455

Conner waved back the people standing around me, fanning the air above my face with his hand.

Someone said, "Do you need medical assistance?"

"No. Thank you. He gets like this sometimes."

Conner hovered over me, a serious look on his face. He combed my hair back from my eyes with his fingers. He was shaking, nervous. Something happened.

"You need to get up. Let's get the fuck out of here before we end up in trouble."

I knew what he was saying, but it took all my will just to move my legs.

The Underground.

This is it.

Conner pulled me to my feet, lifted my arm across the back of his neck. He held both our bags with one hand, and someone said, "Let me help."

But Conner dismissed the man. "We're okay. I just need to get him outside."

So he dragged me along. It seemed like we walked for miles in that station, through long subterranean tunnels that stunk like sweat and piss until we finally came up into the light of a gray afternoon. And the entire way, as we threaded like a weaver's string between the anonymous ghosts of people, knitting us and them all together into the fabric of my *this is it*, I kept searching for the redhead, expecting Quinn to be following along, always following, watching.

But he was gone.

In the cold outside, we sat on a low stone wall looking out at the churn of the Thames.

A bead of sweat crawled slowly along the front of Conner's ear and curled around the bend of his jaw.

I caught my breath, watched the river.

"What the fuck happened in there?" Conner tried to look into my eyes, to see if Jack was really here or not.

I swallowed.

He said, "Who was that kid? Why was he calling you that? Billy?"

This was it.

Right?

I shook my head. Conner knew about Quinn Cahill in Marbury. He told me how the Rangers made deals with the redhead who lived in the firehouse.

Not here.

What do I tell him?

This has to be it.

This is going to be it.

So I said, "I don't know, Con. I swear I never saw that kid before in my life."

Conner blew out a breath that fogged and then vanished in front of his face.

It was cold.

He said, "Are you okay?"

"Yeah."

"Well, if he didn't know you before, I don't think he's going to ever forget us now."

"What happened to him?"

Conner grinned. "I punched him in the fucking face when he tried to follow us off the train."

"Conner?"

"What?"

"You're amazing."

"I try, dude."

Farther down the bank, sheltered behind a row of square wooden stands that sold tickets for river cruises, an old man sat playing a concertina in the gray wind.

It would rain soon.

I could feel it coming.

"And, Con?"

"Yeah?"

"How about we just catch a taxi to Charing Cross?"

"Good call, Jack."

"I try."

a passenger's epilogue

In this winter, they sleep.

Nearly three months have passed, and I have never once taken them out, touched the Marbury lenses.

I know what would happen if I did.

I am done with that place, all those worlds and not-worlds.

And this is it.

It is okay for me and Conner to let this be it.

I have to keep telling myself that.

There was a time when I could almost hear it breathing, calling me, and each time the sound made such a convincing argument for how desperately Jack needed Marbury. But ever since I opened my eyes that rainy morning, safe inside the room Ethan Robson shares with me at St. Atticus, I have either been deaf, or Marbury has been silent, asleep.

I'm not fooling myself, though.

Jack's First Law of Marbury: Objects at rest are just waiting for some asshole to wake them up.

And Jack always knows where they are; where he keeps them.

What strikes me is the one thing I believe to be perfectly true: I caused it all to happen. Everything. Waking up drugged, stripped, bound to Freddie Horvath's bed, stumbling into Henry Hewitt, finding Ben and Griffin in Marbury, and all the terrible and destructive things that took place there—the choices I made—I caused it all.

Like Freddie said: He didn't do anything to me; I did it all to myself.

It's been six months since that happened. It seems like forever, but I still think about it every day.

And I'm still carrying around that garbage.

So fuck you, Jack.

But if nothing else, now that we've all made it back—even if this is just another not-world—I am determined to keep it this way. Forever. This will be it.

So there is no need for me to ever explain to Conner the truth about the redheaded kid who sat across from us on the train at Green Park, how Quinn Cahill is a part of our world in Marbury, too.

Everything is everywhere.

Conner knows it. He heard the old man playing the accordion on the bank of the Thames. The strings are always going to cross, weave, and burn; and I wonder if Conner wakes up every day saying those same three words to himself.

This is it.

None of it matters now, if I keep it this way.

Ben and Griffin started calling me again. For a while, it was almost like they'd vanished. They didn't call me for the longest stretch after we came back from Marbury the last time.

Sometimes, I'd start to take the phone out to see if they were okay, to be certain they hadn't ended up inside some fucking blue trash barrel, and every time I would stop myself, believing that never knowing is the same as not being. *Jack's Second Law.*

But all this past week, just minutes after the school day ends, my phone buzzes and it's the boys, asking when I'm coming back, and can they come over and see me when I do.

I know what they want.

And I haven't been able to tell them it's not going to happen.

Ben and Griffin want something else. Maybe they feel, as I once did, that all they need is one small peek at Marbury again. The boys aren't finished playing yet.

But I am the King of Marbury, and I say this is it.

Conner's been giving me shit for avoiding Ben and Griffin. He says it would be better if we all faced the truth, but I can't bring myself to tell Ben and Griffin that they can't go back to Marbury again.

I haven't seen Henry since the night I told him good-bye at The Prince of Wales. As far as I'm concerned, he's a sick sonofabitch who fucked me worse than Freddie ever did. And I knew two things for certain that night before I tried to hang myself, naked, inside our fucking closet: that I never wanted to see Henry Hewitt again; and that he would do anything to take another slide through the lenses, even if it meant winding up back in his crap-filled apartment in a crumbling city on a street plastered with fucking corpses and cruci-fied kids who were begging to die.

Fuck you back, Henry.

He called a few times. I deleted his number from my phone and erased whatever fucked-up pleading messages he left in his civilized and reasonable-sounding appeal to Jack's mercies.

We don't ever go to The Prince of Wales now, just because I'm afraid I'd see him there, stalking the place, waiting for Jack and his lenses to pop in.

Now, Conner and I hang out in the places the St. Atticus boys go.

I've decided I love being here at St. Atticus.

Conner does, too.

In some ways, I suppose it's almost like being in Marbury. There's a Jack who lives in the minds of the people back in Glenbrook, and a Jack that does the things they'll never find out about over here. We've talked about staying on through our senior year, too; and I think it's what Conner and I are going to end up doing.

So, good-bye, Glenbrook.

Fuck off.

And good-bye, Marbury, too.

Seth never came back after I told him to leave me alone, when his thrashing rousted Conner out of the shower so he could cut me free from my gallows. I know he's not gone forever, because I know more about Seth Mansfield than I know about myself.

So every time I hear some incidental tapping noise, my heart kind of tightens up and I look for him.

I do feel sorry for cursing him like I did that night, but there was nothing I could have done to stop myself.

He'll come back.

But Nickie won't.

That was my idea, too.

The day after Conner and I came home to St. Atticus from London, I took a crowded Monday-afternoon train to visit Nickie in Hampstead.

Nobody knew I went.

I didn't even let Conner know about it for a few days. When I finally worked up the nerve to tell him everything I said to Nickie about me and Conner, he just smiled and shook his head and said, *Holy shit.*

I do love Nickie. I always will love Nickie. But I'm not going to lie to her, and there is too much of my life—my universe—that she will never be part of.

Telling her about it was one of the toughest things I ever did, here or anywhere, but Nickie . . . well, she's just *Nickie,* and she's always been so strong when it comes to putting up with Jack's bullshit.

In the end, I guess she took the whole thing easier than I did. And she's coming with us to Heathrow today, too. Conner and I are going back to Glenbrook for our school's winter break. Our plane leaves this afternoon.

He had the "talk" with Rachel, too. Well, to be honest, there was nothing he could do about it after Nickie got involved. I didn't need to ask Conner about it. Afterward, I could see on his face how rough it must have been, and I felt bad about that.

My fault, too.

We fucked up and we hurt those girls.

When there's nothing we can do to make things better, at least Conner and I can stop letting them get worse.

Jack's Third Law.

I guess I should say a few things about my friend before we leave.

You know how you can go all your life knowing someone, everything about him, no secrets at all, and then you get just a peek—a moment's understanding—of one little thing that defines who he is, and then it's like a spotlight gets turned on at nighttime; and you can see stuff that was always there, now unhidden, so clearly?

But it's not a surprise, either.

That was what happened between Conner and me the night he

saved my life in London. I realized that all that time when I took his game playing so personally, he wasn't actually picking on me about being "gay" or whatever.

He was just trying to see if it might be okay.

Conner was testing himself more than he was testing me.

And, most of the times, acting like a dick about things is the only way Conner Kirk knows how to do stuff.

It's just how he is.

But he's always meant more to me than anyone in this world. Or any other world, I guess, for that matter. And one thing I do know for certain is that Conner has grown up so much since we've been here at St. Atticus.

Both of us have.

Anyway, I told him, it's not like we're talking about hyphenating our last names or anything.

He laughs about that still and, of course, makes fun of me just for having brought up the idea in the first place.

That's Conner.

Right now, Ethan is packing clothes for his trip home to Bath. We're riding into London together with Conner and Neal Genovese.

I watch Ethan for a moment. He's every bit as disorganized as I am.

I take a breath. There are a couple things making Jack a little nervous.

I haven't seen Nickie in weeks. I wonder if she'll still be as beautiful as always; if she'll act noticeably different toward Conner and Jack.

Maybe she'll have a new boyfriend tagging along, and he'll glare at me and Conner and mutter smartass British comments to her under his breath about American boys.

I pack just a few things in a small nylon bag. I don't need much. I have plenty of stuff at Wynn and Stella's house in Glenbrook. And I don't care if Jack's clothes are different than I remember or if they feel weird on me, because they're just clothes, after all, and I've changed, too. But who hasn't?

And this is it.

Conner's in the hall, knocking, rattling the doorknob, saying, *Hurry up, dipshits, let's go.*

Passengers again.

I zip the bag shut.

And never for one second do I think about bringing those two small bundles along with us on our trip.

Thank you for reading this FEIWEL AND FRIENDS book.

The Friends who made

PASSENGER

possible are:

jean feiwel, publisher

liz szabla, editor-in-chief

rich deas, creative director

elizabeth fithian, marketing director

holly west, assistant to the publisher

dave barrett, managing editor

lauren a. burniac, associate editor

nicole liebowitz moulaison, production manager

ksenia winnicki, publishing associate

anna roberto, assistant editor

ashley halsey, designer

Find out more about our authors and artists and our future publishing at Macteenbooks.Com.

our books are
friends for life

NOV 2 9 2012

DATE DUE

MAR 0 1 2013			
GAYLORD			PRINTED IN U.S.A.